Until I
found you

KURISTIEN ELIZABETH

Copyright
© 2020 Kuristien Elizabeth
All rights reserved.

It is not legal to reproduce, duplicate, or transmit any part of this document in either electronic means or printed format. Recording of this publication is strictly prohibited.

"The best thing about reading is the escape from your life, to be able to live hundreds or even thousands of different lives."

-Anna Todd

Prologue

Fate. The definition reads: the development of events beyond a person's control. Events destined to happen.

Up until recently, I thought the idea of fate was all bullshit. I believed that we ourselves determined what happens in our lives. That we have control over the outcome. Fate was merely a term to me that people used in wedding vows they had no intentions of keeping. A term you found in a shitty plot line of a movie or tv show. A romantic notion in a novella. Fate was just another meaningless word in the dictionary to me. That was…until I found you.

UNTIL I found you

One

They're at it again. Screaming, fighting. I hear our mother shouting at her newest boyfriend from inside our coat closet upstairs. Inside this tiny closet has been like a safe haven for me. A place I could hide, even if it was for a little while. I hear glass breaking down stairs and the screaming gets even louder. I cover my ears and wish it would all stop; the fighting. Her addiction. Her anger. When he leaves she'll take it out on us. She always does.

As I think this, I squint my eyes shut and hope she takes enough to pass out this time. Suddenly the closet door opens. My eyes flying open with it. My heart feels as if it'll beat out of my chest. I crawl backwards until my back hits the closet wall. The only thing shielding me is some old coats. I have nowhere else to go, nowhere else to run. Fear takes over and I close my eyes readying myself for whatever is about to happen. When I hear his voice calling my name sweetly.

"Leyna? It's okay. I'm here now."

My older brother Lyle closes the closet door behind him as he sits by me taking my small hand in his.

"It'll all be over soon," he reassures me.

I lay my head on Lyle's shoulder as we hear more chaos erupting downstairs. He's always been my biggest comfort, my best friend, my protector. He tries to distract me from the violence downstairs by telling me one of his elaborate stories. They always cheer me up. We begin to laugh when suddenly our laughter halts as we hear our mother coming up the stairs, yelling our names in a drunken stupor. It's only a matter of time before she looks here and finds us both. I look up at Lyle. Momentarily, I see the fear that flashes across his face before he meets my eyes. He squeezes my hand and tells me to keep quiet before leaving me in the closet. I hear her yelling at him before I hear a loud smack and see my brother fall to the ground.

"Helloooo? Earth to Leyna."

Maggie breaks me from my memories.

"Sorry, I was lost in thought," I say as I hang some clothes on the rack in our closet.

"You've been doing that a lot lately. Are you ok?"

I can see the worried look on my best friend's face.

"Yeah. Yeah I'm totally fine. Just thinking of exams and work and stuff."

I try to play it off like I just didn't have a flashback to a painful memory. But Maggie catches on.

UNTIL I found you

"Right," she drags out the word slowly and gives me a knowing look. "Well it's summer break, so no more exams. And you know what's good for overthinking? Getting out and having fun. Let off some steam, girl!" she says this as she spins to look at me. "YOU are coming out with us tonight! And, you're not ditching this time. No more excuses. No more staying in. Work and other trivial shit can wait. You are coming out and having a good time with your best friends. Now get dressed."

She says this with such authority as I roll my eyes at her.

"Fine. You win," I say with a little reluctance in my tone.

This makes her happy. She proceeds to pull clothes out of my side of our shared closet.

"We just have to find you something really cute and sexy to wear. Something that's different from your normal attire." she says.

"Gee thanks Maggie," I say with a sarcastic smile.

She really has no filter. Maggie was the type that was all about fashion. She kept up with the latest styles, the latest trends. The amount of shoes Maggie owned was borderline insane. Whereas I was happy to wear my favorite jeans and one of my two favorite pairs of shoes. My heeled ankle boots and my maroon slip on vans.

"What exactly are you looking for," I ask her.

"One of the outfits I got you that you never wear," she says annoyed, looking at me over her shoulder.

"I wish you wouldn't buy me stuff. You know it makes me feel bad," I say to her.

"For starters, I buy things for you because you're my best friend. And, I like to shop. And mostly because I'm trying to switch out your wardrobe. None of this really fits you, Leyna. It's all baggy and shapeless. You have killer curves. Flaunt them!"

I roll my eyes at her. Maggie was the one to talk. She had a body every girl dreamed of. She was tall and slender. Her warm, ivory complexion brought out the natural blush of her cheeks. She was a natural blonde even. Beautiful.

"I mean if you like to dress like a middle schooler by all means go for it. But tonight you're going out looking like the hot babe that you are. And who knows? Maybe you even met a guy and-" I interrupted her.

"Not likely. Plus, I don't have time for guys," I say.

"Don't have the time? Or just refuses to make the time?"

She challenges me. I look at her knowingly.

"You really need to start putting yourself out there, Leyna. You can't be alone forever," she says.

Before I can reply she whips out the short emerald green v-neck dress she got me for my birthday.

"Um, no." I shake my head. "What is wrong with this dress? We're going clubbing. It's perfect," she exclaims.

"It's too short," I replied.

Until I found you

"How would you know? You've never even tried it on," she says rolling her eyes before placing it back on the rack.

"Fine, how about this then?"

She holds up a dressy, royal blue romper. It's short and has a plunging neckline. Too revealing for my taste, but figure it's better than the gold dress.

"Fine," I said, taking it from her.

She gives me a victorious grin.

"Ok, now help me decide. Hair up or down," she asks me as she holds her long blonde hair up before dropping it back down.

Before I can answer, Jared chimes in.

"Up. But in a sexy sleek ponytail. It'll look dramatic with the red bodycon dress you have on."

"When did you get home," I asked him.

Jared, Maggie and I share a two bedroom apartment close to our college campus. Jared took the smaller of the rooms where Maggie and I share the master bedroom. It's a big room or was until we crowded our things into it. Maggie and I stayed at the dorms our freshman year of college, but found that living off campus was better suited for us. We became close to Jared that same year. We were like the three amigos, always together.

Jared had lived off campus with his boyfriend until they ended things. And by that point, it just made sense for the three of us to be roommates and split the rent. Plus, it's a bonus to be living with your best friends.

"Like ten minutes ago. I was in the kitchen eating. I ended my juice cleanse today and I'm starving," he says this as he rubs his stomach.

"So Leyna is going out with us tonight," Maggie tells Jared as she gives me a boastful smirk. Jared turns and looks at me, "It's about time! I hate leaving you here by yourself all the time. This will do you some good to get out."

Much to my chagrin, I let Maggie do my makeup and hair. I feel like one of her projects, but if this will make her happy then I'll go along with it.

"Please don't put too much crap on my face," I beg Maggie.

"What do I always say? Less is more. Now shut up. You're going to make me mess up your lips," she retorts.

"Ok, done," Maggie says as she lets me look in the mirror.

At first I don't recognize myself. I still look like me but better. She brought out all of my best features; my big, almond shaped eyes look even greener with the way she did my eyeshadow. My long lashes stand out thicker and darker from the mascara. My big lips look fuller, plumpier. All in all my makeup looks natural. Maggie curled the ends of my hair to give my already wavy hair more of a beach look.

"I love it Maggie! Thank you."

"You're welcome. Now let's get you dressed! Uber will be here in five! Chop, chop," Maggie says, clapping her hands in an orderly fashion.

Once I'm dressed and have my heeled ankle boots on, I take a glance in the mirror and I'm shocked at its reflection.

"Nope," I say, shaking my head back and forth as I look at myself in the mirror trying to pull the top of the romper up while attempting to pull the bottom of the romper down. Yeah, it's not going too well.

"You look hot!" Maggie and Jared both say in unison. The color of this outfit combined with my red hair and makeup makes me look way sexier than I normally dress. While girls try to show off their body, I try to hide mine. My breasts are large for someone of my petite stature.

And my bottom, well in the words of Jer, "rather a juicy peach for such a short little ginger." Where women want these features, I don't. I don't like the attention it brings me.

"You look hot, ok? Don't second guess it." Jared says, giving me a comforting smile.

He knows I'm out of my comfort zone. Just then we hear the Uber honking, signaling his arrival.

"Come on, we've got to go," Maggie says as she practically pulls me out of our front door.

Two

"So I was thinking dinner, then club," Jared asks.

"I mean, I guess it doesn't matter which order since you two are going to be barfing by the end of the night anyway," I say as I roll my eyes.

Maggie and Jared laugh as they remember that one night they both got stupid drunk. I'll never again agree to babysit the both of them when they're that drunk. Maggie may be slim but she's impossible to control or maneuver when she's drunk. Jared is even worse when he's wasted. My five-foot self is no match for Jared's six-foot drunken self. Both are impossible to handle. Memories of me chasing after both of them that night of the beach party makes us laugh.

Jared pays the Uber and we set off to eat first. We decide on a restaurant called Latitudes. I was sipping my virgin strawberry daiquiri waiting on our food to arrive when Maggie and Jared noticed two guys sitting across from us. Jared and Maggie banter back and forth on which one is hotter. Maggie settling on the tan, dark haired guy with a stocky build. He kinda resembles Ronnie from the jersey shore to me, definitely Maggie's type. Whereas, Jared sides with the taller, muscular, brown-haired guy with facial hair. I'll have to side with Jer on this one. The brown haired guy is hot.

He has a broad chest and wide shoulders with muscular arms. I notice he's got a tattoo on his left shoulder that runs almost down to his elbow, but his dark grey shirt is covering most of it so I can't tell what it is. As I'm taking in all his features, I move my eyes back up to his face to find he's doing the same to me. His eyes are scanning up my crossed legs. Studying my torso and chest as he licks his lips. Heat immediately finds its way to my cheeks. I should be weirded out; offended even. But, the way this man is observing my body. It leaves me feeling breathless. Our eyes meet and I instantly look away.

Against my better judgment, I allow myself a quick peek at him, only to find he's still staring at me, my lips this time. My cheeks must be blushing.

"Sweetie, you ok," Jared asked.

"Yeah, I'm good. It's the drink."

Jared gives me a look before saying, "But, you ordered a virgin though."

Shit. I'm bad at lying.

"It's just hot in here is all," I say as smoothly as possible.

Without thinking, I glance at the guy again. He's still looking at me, a seductive smile stretched across his face. I immediately look away. Well, this just got awkward.

"The temperature change in the room couldn't have anything to do with the hottie that's gawking at you right this second could it," Jared asks with amusement.

"Shut up Jer!"

I practically hiss at him as I kick him under the table.

"Ow," he says rubbing his leg.

Maggie laughs. Just then our food arrives. Maggie and Jared start picking off each other's plates like they're an actual couple. I'm about to dig into my yummy shrimp tacos when my cell phone rings.

Jean's name comes across the screen.

My face must say it all because Maggie speaks up, "Just let the bitch go to voicemail. Don't let her ruin another night of yours."

She's right. She's still my mother much to my own disappointment.

"Where's a falling house when you need one," Jared asks, popping a crouton in his mouth. "Don't forget the tornado," Maggie adds while sipping on her Cosmo.

This makes me laugh. The Wizard of Oz has always been our go to flick; that and any Nicholas Sparks movie adaptation. I don't answer it in time and a moment later I have a voicemail from her. I let out a deep breath and decided to see what she wants this time; probably money.

"I'll be right back guys," I announce as I get up to go somewhere a bit more private.

I can feel Maggie and Jer staring at me as I exit towards the lounge area of the restaurant. I'm coming down the short flight of stairs when I accidentally bump into a waiter. I quickly turn to

apologize and my foot misses a step. I'm about to fall when someone catches me snuggly around my waist.

"Woah, careful there."

I turn to look at who caught me and it's him.

"Oh, thanks. Those stairs and that guy just came out of nowhere," I say as I straighten up. *The stairs you used to enter the building came out of nowhere? Really Leyna?*

"I never understood why you girls wear those things," he says, pointing at my heels.

"Don't get me wrong. You look incredibly sexy in them, but you either wear them to impress us or you must enjoy falling on your face," he says, smirking, "And, obviously drinking doesn't help that. Might want to watch your consumption," he says this time with a more serious tone. "Excuse me," I ask incredulously. Who does this guy think he is? Was he seriously paying that much attention to me earlier that he noticed my drink? It was a virgin for God's sake. Not that there's any way for him to know that, but still. What a judgemental ass!

"Ok, first of all, I wear my shoes for myself because I happen to like them! I don't feel the need to impress the male population or anyone for that matter! Including a pompous ass, like yourself. Although, I'm sure I'm probably the only girl you've encountered that doesn't care to impress you. Second, my drink was a virgin! Not that it's any of your business!"

His jaw drops slightly. He's taken aback by my response. Good.

"And thirdly," I forget where in the hell I was going with this.

His eyes are so blue. So beautiful. He's so tall too. I'm getting distracted. Damn it.

"Well, one and two should be enough," I say placing my hands on my hips, ready for his rude remarks.

Except, I don't get a rude remark. I get a laugh. A genuine laugh. This makes me angrier than if he said something rude or vile. He's a stereotypical hot, arrogant, asshole that is clearly full of himself. I've been around these types before and I know no good comes out of being around them. With that thought I step around him and walk off. I hear him trying to say something through his laughter.

"Wait. Hold up," he says and steps in front of me while trying to stifle his laughter. "Look, I'm sorry. I didn't mean to upset you."

He's smiling at me now. He thinks he's so cute. "You're a little firecracker aren't you?" Amusement is clear in his voice, the nerve of this guy.

"A firecracker? Really? Oh just because I stand up for myself and tell you how it is, that makes me a firecracker? No. That makes me a woman. Something you clearly have never had."

With that, I turn on my heels and walk back towards our table. I can feel the jackass staring at me as I walk off.

"I'm Micah by the way. It was a pleasure talking to you."

I can practically hear the smirk in his tone.

"Don't care," I say over my shoulder.

Three

"I haven't seen you this mad since the season six finale of *The Walking Dead*," Jared says staring at me. "Between that guy and Jean calling, I just want to forget about it and have fun," I say, letting out a breath.

We head into the club, Levels. The place is nearly packed to full capacity.

"Be right back," Jared calls out as he goes to the nearest bar to get himself a drink.

Maggie follows to do the same. I stand there taking in all the people dancing. There's so much bumping and grinding going on. Just then, this guy wearing a preppy polo shirt and way too much cologne comes up to me wrapping his arm around my waist.

"Hey sexy. Want a drink," he asks, eyeing me up and down.

He tries to pull me closer to him.

"Um, no thanks," I say nicely as I pull his arm away from around my waist.

"Oh come on baby. Have one with me," he says as he snaked his arm around my waist again, this time with more grip.

His friends are smiling amongst themselves. I can feel myself blush from being so uncomfortable.

"I'm not your baby and I said no," I shout as I remove his arm from around my waist again.

I walk away from him and his snickering buddies, over to meet Maggie and Jared.

No one would mess with me as long as Jared was around. He was my and Maggie's bodyguard whenever we were out.

"What's wrong," Jared asks almost as soon as I join him and Maggie.

"Just some creeps," I say.

"Well, sweetie, that's just the club experience. People are thotting and plotting. Which is what I'm about to do," he says as he walks away.

Maggie rolls her eyes and says, "He's such a ho."

I shake my head as Maggie and I watch Jared flirt shamelessly with a guy. We walk onto the dance floor and I try not to laugh at Maggie. Her dance moves are terrible! She definitely dances like no one is watching. Unfortunately, a lot of people are. And some are even laughing at her which pisses me off.

Maggie catches on, "Screw them Leyna! I'm here to have fun, not to impress anyone."

She's right. I begin to have a "who's the worst dancer" dance-off with her. She starts by doing the wave and I finish it off by doing the Macarena. I'm sure we look ridiculous but neither of us care. We're laughing too hard to notice anyone staring.

UNTIL I found you

Just then Jared comes up, "Jesus, I'm gone two minutes and both of you bitches are already plastered. Listen, I'll catch up with you guys later."

We follow his gaze to that guy he was flirting with. We catch on.

Maggie rolls her eyes and says, "bye ho."

Jared laughs and flips his hand at us, "Don't hate the player, hate the game."

"Don't do anything I wouldn't do," I call out to him as he walks off.

"I wouldn't have a life or get ass then," he calls back.

I flip him off and with that he's gone.

"I hate when he leaves us," I say over the music.

Maggie shrugs her shoulders, "Imagine when it's just me and him going out. I'm always by myself."

This makes me annoyed and sad.

"Well, from now on I'll do my best to come out with you more."

This makes Maggie happy; and by her smug smile I'm beginning to wonder if she didn't make that part up just so I'd come out more. That didn't sound like something Jared would do anyway, leaving Maggie by herself.

"Good! You need to get out more," she says.

I knew it. I roll my eyes but appreciate her attempts to get me out more. You honestly couldn't be depressed around Maggie. She begins to do the sprinkler dance and I lose it laughing so hard that tears come out of my eyes. She begins to laugh just as hard.

"Oh my God. Ok, you win," I say through my laughter.

Maggie takes a dramatic bow. Just then that creep from earlier walks up behind Maggie and slaps her on the ass. Hard. Maggie let's out a painful yelp. I charge forward, pushing him back with all of my strength.

"Hey! Don't you dare touch her again you son of a bitch," I yell at the asshole over the music. Maggie grabs my arm trying to pull me back.

"Just back off and leave us alone," Maggie shouts at the creeps.

He and his two friends begin to chuckle at us in a menacing way as they eye our bodies up and down. We're prey in their eyes and they're on the hunt tonight. The leader steps forward. "Fuck you," I say through my teeth, glaring at him not backing down.

He looks at me for a second before answering, "I'd fuck you, but you seem like you're a mouthy little bitch and would be more of a hassle then you're worth."

He smiles at me sadistically. He and his friends begin to laugh at my and Maggie's expense. Before I realize what I'm doing, I slap him hard.

"Back the fuck off," I yell loudly with my teeth bared, my blood boiling.

He becomes enraged, "You little bitch!"

He raises his fist back to punch me.

"Leyna," I hear Maggie scream.

Before I can react, I see a tall, muscular figure punch the asshole to the ground. I realize it's the guy from the restaurant, Micah. He's hovered over the guy beating the living shit out of him, punching him over and over again. The creep's friends try to pull Micah off. He spins around and punches one of them in the nose while the stocky tan guy from the restaurant comes in and proceeds to punch the other one in the jaw.

"Micah!"

I hear the tan guy call out to his friend. Just then some bouncers yank Micah off of the guy. It takes two of them to do it. They escort them out then, more like throwing them out of the club. Maggie and I follow wanting to thank them. As we near them, we hear the two laughing as Micah wipes his bloody hand on his dark jeans.

"Oh my God, thank you so much," Maggie says once we reach them.

The tan stocky one replies, "Don't mention it. I'm Josiah by the way. But you can call me Jo." He offers his hand to Maggie. She takes it smiling at him.

"Nice to meet you. I'm Maggie."

The two smile at each other.

"Are you alright?"

I hear someone ask. I turn to see who spoke and realize Micah is looking at me as he asks this.

I take a second before answering, "Yes. Thank you. You didn't have to do that," I tell him.

He gives me this strange look, "What else was I supposed to do? Let that motherfucker hit you?"

Maggie interrupts, "That was very chivalrous of you gentlemen and we are in your debt," Maggie says with a small curtsy.

Jo laughs as he says, "Anytime," with a small bow.

I look at Micah who is staring at me.

"What," I ask defensively.

"You really are a little firecracker. You were seriously going to take on that guy weren't you," he asks this with an expression that was both equal parts amusement and horror at the idea. "So I should have done nothing and just let that asshole disrespect us and take it? It would be a cold day in hell," I say with annoyance.

Maggie and Jo are looking back and forth between Micah and I. I must look like I'm ready to put on boxing gloves whereas Micah is wearing an amused smile at our small banter.

Maggie catches on, "Oh right, you two met back at the restaurant."

Maggie says smiling, knowingly. I give her a glare.

Jo speaks up, "You girls wanna ditch the fight scene and maybe go do something that doesn't involve punching someone," he asks laughing lightly.

Maggie chimes in, "Sure. We were just talking about going to the boardwalk for some fun, weren't we?"

She quickly glances in my direction. I look over at the little liar rolling my eyes at her.

"It's only a few blocks away. We can walk there," she says wrapping her arm around Jo's as they began chatting away.

I look at them and then look at Micah. Who is standing there with his hands in his jacket pockets. I internally groan to myself but decide why the hell not? It's not like I'm going to ditch Maggie anyway.

So, I walk towards them. Micah is walking beside me.

After a few minutes, I glance over to him and ask simply, "How's your hand?"

He looks over at me smugly. "It's fine. Surprised you're concerned with you hating my guts and being angry with me apparently."

He says looking straight ahead.

I glance over to him, "I don't hate you. I'm not angry."

Without looking at me he asks, "Then what's with the attitude?"

"I suppose I'm still on edge from what happened. I'm sorr-," he cuts me off.

"I get it. It's fine."

"So were you two following us back there or was it merely a coincidence," I ask more as a snide comment or an ice breaker but I was curious.

He looks at me from the corner of his eye before replying, "Oh, I was totally following you. I had to come back for you to rip me a new one, since the first time didn't really work."

He looks over at me then, obviously amused.

"That wasn't me trying," I rebutted.

He stifles a laugh. Maggie and Jo are about ten feet ahead of us and I can already see they're hitting it off well.

After a minute or so of silence Micah speaks up, "So are you going to tell me your name?"

I look over to him to see he's giving me a small smile.

"My name is Leyna," I say smiling at him in return.

He offers his hand and says, "It's nice to meet you, Leyna."

I take his hand in mine. It's warm and large compared to mine.

"Maybe next time we see each other you won't be ripping me a new one," he says with humor in his voice.

I chuckle.

"What makes you think we'll be seeing each other again?"

We both look straight ahead and Micah says "Well, by the looks of it, my boy and your friend are hitting it off well."

Jo tells Maggie a dad joke and she begins to laugh.

"It would appear so," I say.

We make it to the boardwalk and see it's full of people on rides and playing carnival games. "So tell me about yourself. You know, besides the fact that you have a raging temper and that you rip grown men new ones for sport," Micah says after a moment.

I fight back a laugh.

"Not much to tell really," I reply not really wanting to go into details about myself.

In all honesty there really wasn't much to tell. I am a 21-year-old college student majoring in pediatric nursing, who works at an upscale restaurant to pay my bills and student loans. No way was I going to disclose to this guy, this stranger, how fucked up my mother was or about my brother; or my biggest dreams or aspirations. Not that I had any particular reason not to trust him with any of this information, but partly because I wasn't the type to bare my soul to someone; especially to someone I didn't know. Hell, only Maggie and Jared knew those parts about me because we're best friends and roommates.

"I don't believe that for a second," he replies, searching my face.

Obviously waiting for me to spill the secret beans.

He must see the hesitation on my face so he says, "Fine, I'll go first."

He clears his throat dramatically like he's preparing for a speech. I roll my eyes at him, but find myself curious.

"My name is Micah Eason. I'm 24. Born and raised in San Francisco. I'm an only child. My sign is Pisces. And my favorite color is green," he turns to look at me. "See how easy that was," he asks with a crooked smile.

"Why did that just sound like the corny beginning of an audition tape," I ask as I laugh.

He chuckles. "Hey, it's straight to the point. I feel like I am auditioning."

I look at him quizzically, "What do you mean?"

We approach a target gallery. I look to see Maggie and Jo a little ways away at a food vendor in conversation.

"You seem like you don't open up easily," he says looking at me as he searches my face.

"I don't," I reply matter of factly, and look away from his gaze.

I look over to the target gallery that we're standing next to and see a little girl who lost her game. I overhear her tell her grandmother how much she wanted to win that stuffed unicorn. I hate carnival games. Most of them are rigged. I look back at Micah who's apparently caught on to this as well. He looks over at the sad little girl and back at me.

"I'll make you a little wager. For every target I hit you have to answer a question."

I look at him confused.

"It's a win-win situation. I'll get answers out of you and the kid gets her toy," he explains. "So do we have a deal," he asks with a smirk.

This guy just doesn't quit. I have to admit I do like his persistence.

"Fine," I say begrudgingly.

He gives me a cocky smile.

"I'm an excellent shot by the way, so you're in for it," he says with assurance.

"For your and the kid's sake, I hope you are," I say.

He looks over at me and gives me a wink. Micah steadies himself and begins to shoot the targets with such fluidity I'm convinced he has to be in the service or something. Even the carnival guy looks bemused at Micah before handing him the prize. Micah turns to the little girl and hands it to her with a smile.

"Thank you," she says shyly as she hugs the unicorn to her chest.

Her grandmother thanks us both.

"No problem," Micah answers her with a small smile.

We begin to walk towards Maggie and Jo who are sharing a funnel cake. He turns to look at me and that small smile turns into a rather wicked grin. Oh no.

"So ten targets equals ten questions you have to answer," he says with satisfaction.

"Fine. Choose your questions wisely then."

"Why is that," he asks, raising his brow.

"Because I've only agreed to ten," I say to him.

He lets out a chuckle.

"The pressure is on," he exclaims as he rubs his hands together.

I can tell by the look in his eyes he's thinking hard on what to ask. This makes me let out a small laugh. He looks down at me and smiles.

"You've got a great smile, you know that," he says, grinning at me.

Micah's phone begins to ring then. Pulling it out of his jacket pocket, he looks at it for a moment before ignoring the call and putting it back in his jacket.

"Where to begin," he muses and then looks down at me. "What do you like to do for fun," he asks.

I think for a moment before answering, "Well, when I actually have the time, I love to read. Reading is a way of escaping, a way of going all over the world without leaving where you are. I love spending the day at the beach or outside just taking in the beauty around me-" I cut myself short because saying this out loud I realize how boring I sound. "Told you there wasn't much to tell," I say to him shyly. "

I pegged you for a reader; and outdoorsy girls are the best. I like the outdoors too," he says reassuringly.

He continues, "What's your favorite genre of music?"

"Well, I don't have a particular favorite genre. I love all kinds of music. My playlist consists of everything from Evanescence to Bob Marley, Aerosmith to Frank Sanatra. Eminem to Dolly Parton.Some of my favorite artists are Ed Sheeran, Judah and the Lion, Sleeping At Last and Harry Styles."

The last one makes him grimace.

"Oh God tell me you're not a 'One Directioner' fan girl," he says with mock disgust.

I playfully bump into him.

"I said Harry, not One Direction. And to be fair that boy band wasn't that bad. There's been far worse," I defend.

He chuckles.

"Yeah, like the Backstreet Boys."

"Hey, don't mess with my Nick or Brian ok? You can talk all the shit you want about *NSYNC or 98 Degrees but Brian and Nick are off limits," I say with mock finality.

This makes him laugh.

"Yes ma'am," he says with his hands up in defense.

Just then Maggie and Jo walk up to us.

"Wanna ride on the Ferris wheel," Jo asks us.

Before anyone can answer Micah interrupts, "We should go on that," as he points to a ride called *The Twister*.

Immediately we all look to see what ride he's suggesting and by the looks of it, it should've been named *The Barf Zone*. The ride picked you up while it

swung you back and forth high in the air as it spun you round and round. Yep definitely a barf attraction. No. Hell no!

"Yes," Maggie chimes in.

"Are you crazy," I hiss at her. "You literally just ate," I remind her.

"So? I have an iron stomach. Remember six flags freshman year," she rebuttals and walks towards the ride with a nervous looking Jo in hand. I look at Micah incredulously. "Come on firecracker, how bad can it be?"

I narrow my eyes at him and he laughs. He turns and begins to walk towards Maggie and Jo who are already standing in line waiting to get on. I stand there for a moment pondering what to do. Maggie begins to wave me over. I shake my head at her.

"Come on Leyna! Don't be such a scaredy cat," she shouts.

"It's fine let her be. She probably doesn't fit the height requirement for this anyway," Micah says staring at me smugly.

I glare at him and walk over to join them. We're nearing the front of the ride when my anxiety starts getting to me.

Micah must notice because he puts his arm around my waist as he says, "Ya know, I thought for a minute you weren't going to get on the ride with us."

I ignore the strange flutter in my stomach of him being so close to me and swallow the lump that's rising in my throat before I respond, "I'm not scared."

I hope I sound more confident than I feel. He smiles as he pulls me closer to him.

His nose skimmed my neck as he bends down and whispers in my ear, "I never mentioned you being scared, Leyna. You just admitted that one of your own."

His breath on my bare neck sends chills throughout me. He holds me against his chest for a moment longer before he releases me. My heart paces a little faster. I tell myself it's because of this stupid ride. Just then it's our turn to get on. I step up to the ride nervously and get seated. Micah on my right followed by Maggie and Jo on my left. The ride attendant begins to pull down our roller coaster like restraints over our heads. My anxiety heightens. My heart is already beating faster, panic setting in.

"Let's get it," Maggie screams out in excitement as the ride starts up.

"Shut up will you," I snap at her.

He looks over at me.

"Are you ok," he asks, stifling a laugh.

"I'm fucking fantastic," I say in a sarcastic tone.

The ride begins to move and I screw my eyes shut. It begins to turn slowly as it sways us back and forth gently. Picking up speed a little. Okay. Not so bad. Maybe this is just one of those rides that looks a lot faster than it actually is. Shit. I spoke too soon. I let out a scream as I grasped the handles for dear life. I can hear Maggie screaming with excitement. Why do people get on these things?!

"How are you doing," Micah shouts over screams and laughs.

"Do I have to answer," I yell back at him.

I can hear Micah laughing. I raise my middle finger to him and he laughs even harder. The sound

UNTIL I found you

might be lovely if I wasn't concentrating on not vomiting everywhere. Why did I get on this thing?

Four

"Do you need to find a trash can? You're seriously pale right now Leyna," Maggie says to me. "No, I'm fine."

I know I'm not. I never should have went on that stupid ride to begin with. Everything around me is spinning and I feel like I'm going to pass out from the queasiness.

"You don't look fine. You look like you're about to faint. You need to sit down," Micah says, as he wraps his arm around my waist guiding me towards a bench. I immediately place my head between my knees hoping it will help. "

She needs some water," he tells Maggie.

"I'll be right back," she says as she and Jo disappear. I close my eyes to make the spinning stop, but the feeling is still there. I fall over slightly before Micah catches me.

"Here, lay against me," he says gently pulling me to lay against his arm for support.

Until I found you

I have to admit it helps.

"This is embarrassing," I groan into his arm. He chuckles.

"It could be worse. You could have vomited all over yourself in front of everyone."

I grimace at the thought. It's taking everything in me not to puke right now. Micah begins rubbing my back to comfort me. His soft touches are soothing. I begin to take long deep inhales through my nose, letting them out slowly through my mouth. The combination helps drastically.

"Feeling better," Micah asks.

I look up to see he's staring down at me.

"Yeah. Just leave me here to die of embarrassment now."

He hides a smile. Maggie comes up to us, handing me bottled water. I drink it slowly. The cold water instantly makes me feel better.

"You ok now? You look better," Maggie says.

"Yeah I'm all good. You three go ahead. I'm just going to sit back for a bit."

"I'll stay here with her. You guys go ahead," Micah says to Jo and Maggie.

"If you need me, call me," Maggie says before she and Jo go off on their own.

"Now back to my questions," Micah says. "What is your favorite genre of films?"

He wastes no time.

I smile before replying, "Action and suspense movies are my favorite. I like comedies, but they actually have to be funny. Not that raunchy, or cringey kind with the bad, desperate skits. I like some romance films but the truly great kind are far and few in between."

"So not a chick flick kind of Girl, eh," he asks.

"Not really. I'm more of The Notebook or A Walk to Remember type versus the Legally Blonde or Clueless type."

"So you're a hopeless romantic," he asks, smiling.

I'm about to ask him what his favorite type of movies are when his phone rings. Like before, he ignores the call after looking at his screen and puts his phone back into his jacket. Before he can speak, it rings again and he ignores it. I can't help myself this time.

"Who was that," I ask nonchalantly.

He looks at me, a little taken aback by me asking him that. I should feel a bit sheepish being rude but I'm getting a funny feeling about this.

"No one. Just a friend. I'll call them back later," he says.

Just then his phone rings yet again.

This time he answers it, annoyed, "What? We had to leave. I'll explain later. No probably not." I look away from him.

"Look I'm in the middle of something. I'll call you later," and hangs up the phone. I look back over at him.

"Sorry about that," he replies coolly.

Before I can think too much into it he asks me, "Ok defining question... cheeseburger or celery stick?" I giggle.

"What kind of question is that?"

UNTIL I found you

"It's a serious question. I can't stand for a girl to eat like a bird around me. Eat a steak. Drink a milkshake."

I laugh a little non-laugh.

"Well clearly I don't have that issue," I say as I motion my hands up and down my body.

He looks at me, all humor gone.

"Don't. Don't do that," he says in a serious tone as he looks my body over before settling his eyes back on mine. "You're beautiful, Leyna. Never doubt that," he looks at me with those beautiful blue eyes of his.

He raises his hand slowly near my face as if he wants to stroke my cheek. My heart beats a little faster and I catch myself holding my breath. Is he about to kiss me? He searches my face for a moment before he decides against whatever he was about to do and drops his hand. I slowly let out the breath I was holding in.

He clears his throat and says, "Feel like getting on this thing?"

I look away from him to follow his gaze to the Ferris wheel.

"Sure."

He stands up; reaching for my hand. I take it as we make our way towards the short flight of stairs to get on.

"As I recall, you and stairs don't get along so well," he says, lacing his fingers through mine a little tighter.

I'd be lying to myself if I said I didn't enjoy the feeling of him holding my hand. The Ferris wheel begins to move slowly allowing everyone to get on. Micah and I just sit there awkwardly for a moment before he begins to ask me another question, but I have a few of my own.

I interrupt him by saying, "Ok enough interviewing me for now. Now it's my turn to ask the questions."

"Uh oh," he replies playfully.

"You have to give me your answers to every question you've asked me so far," I say.

He nods his head and begins telling me a little about himself. Like me, he likes all types of music but rock is his favorite. Some of his favorite bands include Sevendust, Queen and Linkin Park. He likes thriller and horror films. As a hobby, he likes to make sculptures from molten glass. He enjoys playing sports and working out. From the look of his body, I can tell he's very athletic, with his wide chest, and big muscular arms. Those arms...almost bursting through his jacket.

"Miss anything?"

He breaks me from my thoughts.

"W-What," I ask, confused.

He smirks.

"I asked, did I miss anything? Did I miss any questions?"

"No, I think you covered it," I say.

Just then a cool breeze blows through sending a chill throughout my body. I shiver slightly. "Are you cold," Micah asks me.

"No, I'm ok," I replied with a lie.

He doesn't look convinced. He begins to take his jacket off.

"No you don't have to. I'm fine really," I say as I try to decline, but he insists.

"Here. Take it, Leyna. You're shivering," he puts the jacket around me.

The warmth of him instantly heating me up. I get a whiff of his scent and it smells heavenly. I lean into the collar of his jacket slightly to get another whiff of it. He smells delicious. Without realizing it I let out a small humming sound. He hears it and looks at me smiling.

"Like the jacket," he asks with a smirk.

Shit! I've been caught.

"Yeah, it's warm; thanks," trying to recover from my slip up.

"No problem," he answers, looking out over the scenery.

I look at him without him noticing and find myself staring at his body. He had a natural sun-kissed tan to his skin. His shoulders and forearms were hard and muscular. His hands were large and had faint white scars on his knuckles. I study his neck and jaw and the way his Adam's apple moves when he swallows. I find myself wanting to reach over and kiss his neck as I wrap my hands into his thick, wavy hair. I'm surprised by my own thoughts.

Suddenly, the Ferris wheel comes to a complete stop as they begin to let people off. The force of it causes me to lean into him, his arm goes instinctively around my back steadying me. "Sorry," I say as I go to scoot away from him but he doesn't let go of me, instead he pulls me closer to him.

I look up at him and find that he's taking in my face in every detail as I do the same with him. His eyes were so beautiful. I've never seen eyes as blue as his. On the outer ring they were a dark blue like denim that turned lighter almost grey as it got closer to his pupils. His lashes were almost as long and dark as mine. His lips were deep pink, full and soft looking. His nose was even perfect. He had light freckles trailing over the bridge of his nose into his cheeks. His jawline was square, accentuating his attractive facial features. Even his facial hair looked sexy on him. He was a beautiful man. I want to reach over and touch him, glide my fingers softly over his cheek into his temple, to place my lips on his. He breaks me from my thoughts when he brushes my wind blown hair behind my ear, letting his fingers trail down my neck slowly. Goosebumps trail down my entire body.

  He doesn't take his eyes away from mine as he says, "Your eyes are so beautiful, so green and gold."

  He stares at them for a moment before he looks down at my lips. My breathing hitches slightly as he softly traces my lips with his fingers. Subtly licking his own lips as he does so. He glides his fingers up to my cheek. My lips part. My heart, beating fast. He looks down at my parted lips before looking back into my eyes. We both move our faces closer to the other. Our noses touch. He begins skimming his lips to mine. Barely grazing them before he pulls away slightly to look at me. He reaches his hand to the side of my face as he glides it down my neck, cupping it.

  He pulls me closer to him as he softly kisses my neck once. His lips are soft and warm on my flesh. My mouth instantly becomes dry. My heart feels as if it'll beat out of my chest. He skims his nose up my neck until he reaches the sensitive flesh just under my ear. I wrap my hand around his hard forearm. He looks at me before his eyes stare at my lips once more. Pulling me to him, I close my eyes as his lips brush mine. I feel the fire igniting within me. Before his lips are fully on mine, he pulls away. I let go of him and open my eyes. I let out a deep breath I didn't realize I was holding. Micah is looking past me at something. I turn to see what it could be. I see nothing but the crowd of people below.

"What's wrong," I ask him.

Why did he stop? He looks back at me.

"I thought I saw Jo waving us down," he says before giving me a smile.

It doesn't reach his eyes. I begin to feel embarrassed, self-conscious even.

Just then the Ferris wheel stops and it's our turn to get off. Micah tries to help me out but I decline. I text Maggie to meet me at the entrance. As I'm walking down the stairs I take off Micah's jacket and hand it to him.

"You don't need it," he asks.

"No. I'm all good. Thanks though."

I begin walking away from him when he asks, "Where are you going?"

"I'm going home," I call over my shoulder, not bothering to look at him.

He catches up to me. "

I'll walk with you to get a cab," he says.

"That's not necessary."

"Well, you still have to answer some questions. My next one being, what's your number," he asks seriously.

I huff, "My number?"

"Yes, your number. That's considered a question. And per our wager you have to answer it."

I'm hella confused. Just a second ago he was all over me, about to kiss me and then he suddenly changed his mind about it? He used his friend as an excuse. And now he wants my number?

"Why," I ask with a flat tone.

"You still owe me some answers. I'll leave those for another date."

Isn't he smug?

"Another date," I ask with my brow raised.

"Well, an official first date then. I don't think this one really counts," he says, smirking at me. "So what do you say?"

I'm about to reply something smart at him when I step down the wrong way and twist my ankle. I'm about to fall over when Micah catches me around my waist.

"Told you those things were dangerous," he says, fighting a smile as he looks at my high-heeled boots.

"Ha ha," I say sarcastically. I try to walk away when he stops me. "Don't. You're going to hurt yourself worse." He warns. "I'm fine," I say as I begin to limp away with what dignity I still have.

Each step hurts more than the last but I refuse to let him help me.

"You're going to hurt yourself. Stop," he says.

I ignore him, still limping away at the speed of a tortoise. My chin held high. I hear him mumble "stubborn ass" under his breath. Suddenly he scoops me up under my legs carrying me.

"Put me down," I say to him.

He ignores me and keeps walking.

UNTIL I found you

"I'll put you down in the cab when we reach it. Until then enjoy the ride," he says looking ahead.

I can tell he's resolved about carrying me so reluctantly I let it go.

"It doesn't even hurt that bad," I say under my breath.

He looks down at me and says, "You're a terrible liar."

Five

Our cab pulls up as Maggie hugs Jo goodbye. They exchange numbers and she tells him she'll text him tomorrow. Knowing Maggie she'll text him before we even get home. By the look on Jo's face he wouldn't mind.

"Bye Leyna. It was nice meeting you. I hope your ankle gets better," Jo says, giving me a wave.

I give him a smile and a wave back before replying, "It was nice meeting you too, Jo. I'm sure we'll see each other soon."

He looks back over at Maggie and they share a smile.

"So about our date," Micah starts, "How about Friday? I could pick you up around seven." Before I can reply, Maggie cuts in with "She'd love to. We'll make it a double date."

I give Maggie a glare. Micah catches on, fighting a smile.

"I never got your number by the way," he says.

UNTIL I found you

Before I can say a word, Maggie is already giving it to him.

Micah saves it into his phone and says smugly, "I'll be giving you a call later."

Before we even get on the interstate, I look at Maggie incredulously and say, "What the hell was that?"

"What," she asks in confusion.

"You butting in giving him my number and agreeing we'd go on a double date with them. You don't even know if I have to work Friday," I say as I cross my arms.

I love Maggie dearly, but she is so overbearing and pushy sometimes.

"Would you have said yes," she asks as she turns towards me with her arms crossed ready for a rebuttal.

"Yes, actually I was. Before you butted in that is," I say with a huff.

"Well, I had to make sure your ass was going on that date," she retorts.

"Why?"

"Because Leyna, you never go out. Even when a guy asks you out you always shut them down. I'm tired of always seeing you alone. Plus, Micah seems like a good guy for you." "What do you mean by that," I ask her. "I just mean that you aren't the easiest person to get to know. You're stubborn. You don't really open yourself up. And I get why but still... You can't live closed off forever Leyna. Sooner or later, you have to let someone in."

I don't bother with a response. I know she's right. It is hard for me to let people in. The more people you let in, the more you allow yourself to get hurt. I lay my head back on the head rest and look out at the city lights passing us by. Maggie and I are silent the rest of the way home.

I look over to her and see that like I had predicted, she's texting Jo. I smile to myself. Not only because I know Maggie like the back of my hand, but also because I think Jo is good for her too. He seemed to be a gentleman to her. He's not the usual douchebag she talks to. He was kind and sweet. Minutes later we pull up in our driveway and I'm exhausted. I can hear my bed calling my name. I take my boots off and limp barefoot to our front door. Just then Maggie and I get a text from Jared saying that we shouldn't wait up for him, that he'll be home by morning. I walk into our room and begin to undress into my comfy baggy t-shirt and sleep shorts.

I consider going to bed without washing the makeup off my face but decide against it. After my nightly ritual is completed, I fall onto my bed and begin to drift to sleep when my phone starts buzzing. I groan and roll over to grab it off my night stand. It's a text from an unknown number.

"Had a great time tonight. See you soon firecracker. Put ice on that ankle."

I don't have to guess who it is...Micah.

I send back, "You won't if you keep calling me that. Good night."

I save his number and smile to myself before rolling over. I'm almost asleep when Maggie comes up to me with a glass of water, some ibuprofen and a bag of frozen peas. A peace offering for her overbearing behavior I suppose. I take them smiling at her.

"Thank you," I say as I down the ibuprofen and water.

"How's the ankle," she asks as I place the frozen bag on it as I wince a little. "It's ok. I've had worse."

"Senior year field trip," we both say in unison.

We chuckle at the memory before both of us fall asleep. I'm sleeping peacefully for a while when I hear my phone going off again. I turn to silence the call when I see Jean's name come across the screen. It's 4:38 am. I answer it wondering if she's ok.

"Mom," I say into the receiver. "I called you earlier and you didn't answer. Where the hell were you," she slurs.

I pinch the bridge of my nose and internally groan. Not this again.

"Mom, it's almost five in the morning. You need to go to bed and sleep it off ok?"

"Don't talk to me like I'm a child. I'm a grown ass woman. I can do whatever I want," she says almost incoherently. "I don't even know why I call you. What for? You're useless," and with that she hangs up on me.

I throw my head back onto my pillow and just stare up at the ceiling trying not to let her words bother me too much. By tomorrow, she won't even remember what she said or that she even called me. So there's no use fighting with her about it. That's the thing about Jean. There's no point in arguing with her. It's a losing battle every time. She's always right and everyone else is always wrong. She's the victim even when she deals the blows.

Lyle had a theory on why she drank so much. If you drink until you're numb, you can't feel the guilt you have inside of you. I roll back over and try to fall back asleep. When I wake up hours later I hear Cardi B on the stereo and smell something cooking in the kitchen. A sign that Jared is home. Maggie is sprawled out on her bed fast asleep. I move my ankle a bit before climbing out of bed. It's barely sore, thank God. I walk into the kitchen finding Jared flipping an omelet while he's dancing along to Cardi's song. I stagger to our kitchen bar and take a seat on the bar stool.

"What time did you get in," I ask him as I pour myself some juice.

"Like 3 am," he says as he lays the omelet on a plate. "Want one," he asks.

I nod my head yes, "Cheese and tomatoes please."

"So how was your and Maggie's night? Did I miss anything exciting," he says as he begins preparing my omelet.

"Well," I begin before Maggie interrupts with, "Actually yes! I have all the tea."

"Oooh," Jared coos dramatically.

Maggie sits beside me and steals my glass of juice before filling Jared in on everything that happened last night, from those creeps messing with us in the club, to Micah saving me from getting punched in the face, to us agreeing to see them again Friday. Jared looks astonished as he learns I agreed to go on a date.

"You must see something you like to agree to a date," he teases me.

I give him a scowl. Maggie chuckles.

"Okay, yes obviously he's attractive but that's not why I agreed to it. I lost a wager," I try to explain.

"What," Maggie and Jared ask in unison.

I fill them in on Micah basically tricking me into it knowing he'd win. That reminds me, I need to ask him where he learned his skillful marksmanship from.

"Oh, that was smooth," Jared remarks.

"Yeah too smooth. He's probably such a player," I add with skepticism in my voice. "Don't do that. Don't start playing the what-if game in that pretty little head of yours. Give the guy a chance. Not all men are dogs." Jared says, sitting my omelet in front of me.

"He does seem like a great guy, Leyna," Maggie adds.

"Well, only time will tell won't it," I ask as I stick a fork into my omelet.

"Mmm. That looks good," Maggie says as she sticks a fork into my omelet and takes a bite.

"I can't even pray to Jesus before you steal food off my plate," I tease her.

"Now Leyna, be a good little Christian and share," she says as she takes my plate completely with a wicked grin.

Jared laughs.

I look at him as I say, "I really don't like her sometimes."

Six

I'm getting ready for my work shift at the restaurant when the text tone on my phone goes off. I grab it from my nightstand and find that I have two text messages from Micah.

The first text reads, "Good morning beautiful. How's your ankle?"

This makes me smile and causes that weird feeling in my stomach.

I shake it off and read the second text, "So what would you like to do tomorrow?"

Well he doesn't waste any time.

I replied, "Good morning. I'm down for almost anything. As long as it doesn't involve twisty rides," I smile to myself as I send it.

I slip my shoes on and grab my keys before heading out. I try calling Jean to check on her, but she doesn't answer. She's more than likely passed out from her late night binge. I'm almost at the restaurant when my phone goes off. I look to see it's not my mother, it's Micah calling me. "Well hello," I say into the receiver.

"Told you I would be giving you a call," he replies.

I smile, "Yes you did. Called to ask me those questions?"

I hear him chuckle lightly "No. I'm saving those for our dates. Speaking of which, you had mentioned you liked the outdoors. If your ankle is up to it, want to make it a day and go? It'll be fun."

The way he said "dates," takes me by surprise.

"Dates? Well aren't you cocky."

"Not cocky, confident," he replies smugly.

I roll my eyes but smile.

"So what do you say," he asks. "My ankle is fine. So I'm up to it. But Maggie isn't exactly the outdoorsy kind like I am."

"Ah come on. We will all make it fun for her. She'll love it by the time we're through. We may even convert her," he says.

I start to say I'll ask Maggie before giving him an answer but then again why not give Maggie a taste of her own medicine.

"Fine. Count us in," I say instead.

"Awesome. We'll pick you girls up around 10 am. Just text me the address," he says.

"10 am," I exclaim. "Told you we were making a day of it. It'll be fun trust me."

"Maggie is going to love this," I say sarcastically.

He chuckles, "Can't wait. So what are your plans today?"

I pull up at the restaurant and see that I'm 15 minutes early for my shift as usual.

"Working. Going home. I told you there wasn't much about me," I say.

God, I sound so boring.

"That's not true. Otherwise I wouldn't be trying to get to know you or figure you out," he says. We're both silent for a moment when he clears his throat, "I've gotta go. I'm late for a business meeting. I'll talk to you later, firecracker."

I groan, "Stop calling me that!"

He chuckles before hanging up.

I head into work to see that Chelsea and Tony are already into another one of their arguments; sibling rivalry at its finest. Chelsea and Tony run their parents' restaurant. Chelsea being the manager, while Tony is the head cook. How this place hasn't burned up in flames already is beyond me.

"So what have I missed so far," I ask Rachel, my favorite coworker.

She rolls her eyes and replies, "Well, this time Chelsea is wanting to change the menu up again and Tony over there wants to keep it the same. Personally, I don't give two shits. I'm just here for my check."

My shift is going by pretty quickly when my cell phone begins to vibrate in my pocket. Knowing it must be important since Maggie and Jared wouldn't call unless it was urgent. I sneak to the back to answer it and see it's an unknown number.

"Hello?"

A robotic voice greets me.

"This is an incoming call from the Lamar County Jail. An inmate"-

I hear my Mother's voice "Jean Blake."

Until I found you

Fuck.

The robotic voice continues, "Is trying to reach you. To accept the call press 1. Charges will be incurred."

What in the fuck did she do this time? I press 1 readying myself.

"Mom?"

"Leyna? Leyna, I need you to come bail me out. I'm booked in Lamar."

"Mom. What did you do now," I ask, already exasperated.

"I didn't do anything. It was all just a big misunderstanding. I was at the wrong place at the wrong time. I was with John. And, he had a warrant."

"For what? And I told you that guy was a loser," I say almost hissing into the phone.

"Look I don't have time to talk about all this. Come bail me out already. They won't even give me a cup of coffee here. They're dicks."

I take in a deep breath and let it out.

"Mom. I can't just stop what I'm doing. I'm in the middle of a work shift. I can't just leave and come bail you out. I'll come get you when my shift is over."

"Are you fucking kidding me right now? Get over here and get me out of this shit hole," she yells into the receiver.

My face must say it all because Rachel walks over to me and says, "Go. I'll cover your section."

I mouth "Thank you" to her and give her a hug before heading out.

"I'm on the way. This needs to be the last time mom. I'm serious."

"It will be. I'm done with John."

I roll my eyes.

"I'm not talking about John. I'm talking about you getting yourself in trouble mom. You can't keep doing this."

She replies nothing other than, "Call Barry the bond guy," and hangs up.

I get in my car and lay my head against the steering wheel. Allowing myself a moment of silence before starting my car and heading to bail my delinquent mother out of jail.

Seven

"I'm serious Mom, I'm not doing this again. You can't keep doing shit like this or you'll end up going to jail for real. I can't keep bailing you out. I have my own bills and student loans I'm trying to pay. And I can't afford any lawyer fees on top of everything else."

"How dare you talk down to me. I'm your mother! I gave you life. You can't even help me in my time of need! I don't have anyone but you. And you are just going to talk down to me like that? I wasn't even the one that did anything wrong! I'm innocent in this. He was the one that was driving a stolen car. My only crime was being the unknowing passenger and trusting the wrong man. Giving him my trust when he didn't deserve it. And for that you are just going to turn your back on me?"

The thing about my mother is she's always the victim. She could set the world on fire and it would be the lighters fault.

"Mom, I'm not turning my back on you. All I'm saying is quit getting yourself in these predicaments, before you end up in serious trouble."

She gives me a look of disgust before saying, "Just go ahead and judge me, Leyna. You're good at that. Some daughter you are to me," and proceeds to pull her cell phone out of the plastic bag of her belongings.

"Mom what are you doing," I ask exasperated.

Crying, she answers, "calling someone to come pick me up."

I fight the urge to facepalm myself.

"Mom, don't. I'll take you back home."

"No," she practically shouts at me. "Mom please don't do this. Just, just get in the car. Ok?" She looks at me; considering her options before finally ending the call and getting into my car. If I had to guess whoever she was calling wasn't going to pick up in the first place.

My mother was the best in burning bridges with people. She didn't keep around what wasn't useful to her. Friendships were an ever changing occurrence with her, so were her boyfriends. People joke about the flavor of the month, but that was almost the literal case with my mother. She was charming, conniving, beautiful, and was always looking for someone to use; someone to charm.

She was the ultimate con artist. Memories of her when Lyle and I were little come flooding in. Memories of us taking car rides on beautiful sunny days with the windows down jamming out to Bon Jovi, or when the weather would get bad and she would concoct "storm parties" to keep us distracted from all the thunder and lightning outside. There were times she was sober. Healthy. Really trying to make a go of it.

Those were the best times. She was funny and playful, even kind. With our mother, when it was good, it was great, but when it was bad, it was horrific. I look over to the woman sitting next to me and I begin to feel pity for her. She had it in her to be a good person, a good mom. Those few precious memories of my mother when she did try, prove that to me. I wonder if she had, had a better mother herself, a childhood not filled with violence and addiction, would she have been better?

"What are you staring at," she asked defensively, pulling me from my thoughts.

"Um, nothing. I just thought you had something in your hair, but you don't."

My mother instinctively rubs her hands through her wavy blonde hair trying to shake out the imaginary debris from it. I almost smile at this.

"Don't take me home. Take me to Jackie's," she says. I look at her confused but comply.

A few minutes later, we pulled into her friend, Jackie's driveway. She's about to get out when I notice just how thin she is. She's losing weight. Rapidly.

"Hey, have you eaten recently," I ask my mother, stopping her from getting out.

She's thinner since I've seen her last.

"Yeah yesterday. Why," she asks annoyed.

"You just look like you've lost weight," I reply as I shrug. My mother was already thin to begin with. Now she looks… sickly. Like she's not taking care of herself.

"So?"

She's becoming agitated by my questions.

"Mom, you've got to start taking better care of yourself. Make sure you're eating regularly. You don't need to lose any more weight. It's not healthy for you."

"Well since you're giving me advice here's some for you. It wouldn't hurt for you to skip a few meals yourself, Leyna. Your ass is almost busting out of those pants," she snickers before continuing, "Beauty is the only thing that gets a woman where she needs to be in life. It isn't brains and it sure as hell isn't a good heart. This is a man's world. It's your looks and what's in between your legs and how you use it, is what gets you things in life. You want men to see you, to desire you, so they give you things. Fat girls don't get gifts or second glances. The sooner you realize that and utilize it, the better."

I swallow the lump rising in my throat and ignore the stinging in my eyes.

My mother looks at me up and down with pursed lips before getting out of my car and saying, "thanks for the ride," as she slams the door.

I pull off and let the tears flow. I wasn't obese by any means. But I did have hips and a bottom on me. I was thick, curvy. I wouldn't consider myself fat. Apparently, Jean disagrees. Once I'm on the road I call Rachel to tell her I'm coming back to finish my shift; thanking her again for helping me out. Once I get back to the restaurant there's only two hours left of my shift. I hurry through the back entryway and begin to resume my shift when Chelsea stops me in my tracks.

Until I found you

"Where in the hell have you been? You were gone for over an hour," she begins to yell.

"I'm sorry Chelsea. I had a family emergency. Rachel took over my section until I could get back."

"This is a business. Not a charity. I hired you to work shifts. Not give me excuses about your mommy. Now get back to work," she says before stomping away in her heels.

"What a bitch. Don't worry about it. I'd be mad too if I looked like I was constipated constantly," Rachel says rolling her eyes.

I force a smile before heading out on the floor and finishing my shift.

Eight

Once I get home, Jared's famous spaghetti fills my senses. I can literally feel my mouth watering. Jared and I are the cooks of the house since Maggie can't seem to boil rice without burning it.

"That smells so good, Jer."

"You know it," Jared replies, stirring the skillet.

I find Maggie laying on the couch FaceTiming Jo.

"They've been talking for almost two hours. Like, good grief, enough already. I have been dying to tell her what happened to me today and miss chatty cathy over there won't shut up long enough for me to tell her," Jared says, venting.

"I heard that," Maggie shouts from the living room.

"Well now I'm here, so spill," I reply.

Jared begins telling me how he saw his ex at the market place and the not so subtle way he called him out in front of his now new boyfriend when he

UNTIL I found you

saw them together. I laugh lightly throughout the story listening to Jared causing an embarrassing scene for his ex. Usually Jared wasn't the scene causing type. But when he was, he was Broadway baby. Jared wasn't your stereotypical flamboyant gay. In fact, unless you got to know him, you wouldn't really know.

I think back to when Maggie first saw Jared freshman year. She immediately called "dibs" on him. She had her eye on him for nearly half of the semester until he had mercy on her and came clean about his preferences. I can hear Maggie ending her conversation with Jo.

"Yeah can't wait. See you tomorrow. Bye babe."

I look over to see Maggie blowing Jo a kiss through the phone only for him to pretend to grab it and put it in his pocket for later.

"Fucking dorks," Jared says under his breath.

I smack his arm playfully.

"Goodnight pretty girl," Jo tells Maggie before ending the call.

Jared rolls his eyes and asks sarcastically, "When's the wedding?"

"Mid June at the Plaza. I'm registered at Macy's," Maggie retorts.

I shake my head at them and help myself to the spaghetti Jared made. I never realize how hungry I am until I start eating.

"Mmmm. Food-gasm Jer," I coo, shoving a forkful in my mouth.

"Yummy," Maggie says while chewing and giving Jared a thumbs up. "It's so good," she attempts to say through chewing her food.

"Geez, Mags chew and swallow before talking. You resemble a farm animal chewing that big bite right now," Jared says jokingly.

Maggie replies by mooing like a cow. Making us all laugh. I almost choke in the process. Suddenly Jean's words come to mind. "You could skip a few meals." I put my fork down. Looking at my thighs for a moment. I get up and scrape the remains of my bowl into the trash before loading it into the dishwasher. After taking a shower, I'm putting my phone on charge when I see I have multiple texts from Micah.

"Hey shorty, how's work going?"

"I've been wondering. Do they supply a ladder for you to reach things? Or do you just threaten someone into getting it for you?"

I roll my eyes and mutter "Jackass" at his text messages. Just then my phone goes off. It's Micah FaceTiming me. I fluff my hair and check myself in the mirror before answering it.

"Hi beautiful," Micah greets me with a smile.

He's laying back on his bed shirtless. Propping himself up with his arm resting behind his head. His hard muscles are on perfect display. God, he's hot.

"Hello," I say as I sit on my bed.

I was trying my hardest not to blush.

"So how was your day," he asks.

Oh you know, just had to bail my terrible decision-making alcoholic mother out of jail. Almost got fired today because of it. The usual.

"It was good. Just busy," I say instead. "How was your day? Punch anyone new in the face yet," I ask.

He smiles, "Na. Maybe tomorrow. My day was good overall. You never sent me your address. I ended up getting it from Jo who got it from-"

"Maggie," we both say in unison.

"Of course you did. Well for your information I'm just now checking my phone and haven't had the time to send it to you yet," I say.

"Excited for our date," he asks.

Actually I am but I can't let him know that.

"It's whatever," I say in mock boredom.

"Look at you already falling asleep over there. I'm not used to that."

"Used to what," I ask.

"Girls being bored around me. That never happens," He replies as my face falls.

He starts, "Hey, I'm joking."

I interrupt, "Wasn't funny."

He gives me a wicked grin and says, "Are you jealous, Leyna?"

"What," I ask in disbelief.

"No! I am not jealous. I just don't like little boys that play with girls for sport."

In a more serious tone he replies, "Is that what you think of me? That I'm some playboy?" Before I can respond he adds, "oh and baby, nothing about me is little" as he licks his lips.

I'm taken aback for a moment. I can feel the heat pull to my cheeks, and a strange feeling in my stomach.

I quickly recover and give him an 'oh please' look and say, "That'll do pig. That'll do."

He begins to laugh. Before I can stop myself, I'm joining in.

"What's so funny in here, woman," Jared asks as he flops onto my bed.

Laying his head beside me.

"Nothing," I replied biting my lip as I smiled, trying to halt my laughter.

Jared then notices me on the phone with Micah and mouths "sorry" as he walks off.

"Who was that," Micah asks.

All humor is gone. "Oh, that's Jared."

"Jared who," he asks with an annoyance clear on his face.

Is he seriously jealous?

"Well look who's jealous now," I tease.

Only there's no trace of humor anywhere on his face. Oh my God, he's actually jealous right now, of Jared, my gay best friend. This makes me laugh.

"What's so funny," Micah asks.

"He's my roommate."

"Your roommate," he asks with an edge to his tone.

"Yes, my roommate."

"Is there something going on with you two," he asks bluntly.

"With Jared? No! No way. He's my best friend."

"So the poor bastard has been friend zoned," he says curtly.

"For your information, we're in each other's friend zones indefinitely. He's- well, I'm not his type" I retort back.

"Not his type? Is he blind? Look at you. You would be any man's type, Leyna. Your full lips alone make me hard."

Until I found you

His eyes darken a bit on that last part. My breath hitches. The sensation returns to my stomach when I hear his words. I begin to blush at the way he's staring at me and tuck my hair behind my ear before looking away from his gaze.

"Look at you. You're beautiful," he says softly.

I look at him again, "well thank you," I reply shyly.

This makes him smile. Thankfully he changes the subject and we begin talking about other things we have in common. Before I know it, I look up to see it's already past midnight. I find Maggie is in her bed with her earphones on watching Hulu. This is her way of giving me privacy.

"It's almost 1am," I say to Micah.

"Already? Seems like we've only been talking a few minutes. Get some rest, firecracker. I'll see you in the morning," he says smirking.

I roll my eyes, "Stop calling me that! It really gets on my nerves."

He grins, "I know. That's why I call you that. I like seeing the fire that sparks in you."

Nine

My alarm goes off waking me from a deep sleep. I'm about to get up when my phone rings. It's Micah FaceTiming me. I don't answer it at first because I always look hideous in the morning. I rush up and begin my morning beauty ritual. By the time I'm done my phone rings again. It's Micah FaceTiming.

"Good morning firecracker! Thought you were dipping out on me today."

I can see he's already in his car, presumably on the way here.

"Call me firecracker one more time and I will," I threaten.

He chuckles.

"Well I've got to figure out a new nickname for you then," he teases.

"I have a name you know."

He's replying when I notice he's alone in the car. Jo must be bringing his car separately.

"So are we going in separate cars or all riding together," I ask him.

He looks a bit confused by my question.

"You're riding with me of course," he states.

"No, I mean, are all four of us going in your car," I rephrase my question. His look of confusion doesn't pass.

"What do you mean 'all four of us'? Blondie didn't tell you?"

Now I'm the confused one.

"Didn't blondie tell me what," I ask him.

This makes him chuckle, "I suppose not."

What in the world is going on? I turn to see Maggie isn't in her bed. I assumed she was up getting ready like me. Maggie!

"One sec," I say to him as I put myself on mute. "Maggie!" I shout, obvious annoyance laced in my tone.

"What," Maggie asks, entering our room.

"What's this about our 'double date' becoming just me and him now?"

Maggie gives me a shit eating grin and says, "I'm not the canoeing type, Leyna. So me and Jo are going into the city for the day."

"What do you mean you're going into the cit- I'm sorry did you say canoeing," I ask in horror.

"Kayaking. Actually," Micah corrects us.

I'm startled at his response.

"It helps if you actually put me on mute."

Shit.

"Kayaking? You said we were doing outdoorsy stuff," I exclaim.

"The river is outdoors." he says.

"Well, I assumed we were going hiking or something."

"I'll let you two kids go. Have fun," Maggie says as she walks out of our room waving behind her.

"Maggie, you brat," I yell.

I hear Micah laughing, "I'm pulling up funny girl. Let me in."

I hang up on him and walk to the front door.

"Well hello," he replies trying to hold back a laugh.

Even with that smug look on his face, he looks incredible.

"It's not funny," I say.

"It kind of is. So are you ready to get this thing started or what," he says rubbing his hands together.

"Not really."

"Sorry shortcake. We're kayaking this venture."

"Don't call me that," I say with a serious tone.

That was Lyle's nickname for me. I don't allow anyone to call me that joking or not.

I clear my throat and add, "Well that's not going to work for me. Because I can't swim," I say matter of factly.

I'm waiting for him to laugh at this information about myself but he doesn't.

He just takes my hand and gives it a light squeeze before saying, "Interesting fact, I'm a great swimmer. And, an even greater swimming instructor. What do you say? Wanna give it a try?"

I'm hesitant but give in.

"It'll be fun," he reassures me.

Until I found you

"Fine. Let me go get dressed," I say and walk to my dresser when I realize I don't own a swimsuit.

Maggie must be on the same brain wave as me for she says, "Here, borrow one of mine," while rummaging through her drawer.

"Maggie I can't. I'm- well I'm built differently than you."

"Just say it, Leyna. You have big tits and an ass for a short girl," and throws me her bikini. "No." I shake my head, "no mm mmm."

"Shut up and put the bikini on already," she demands.

I begrudgingly do as I'm told. Once I have it on, I look in our full length mirror and my mouth becomes floored when I see my reflection.

This is Maggie's most conservative swimsuit she owns and half of my ass cheeks still hangout. It compliments my hourglass figure wonderfully but my sideboobs have their own show.

"I don't know Maggie," I say slowly.

"Um, yes! I'm even slightly turned on," she teases. "Just put a tank top and shorts over it if you want," she adds.

"You better," Jared exclaims walking over. "I can see your liver in that."

Maggie hits Jared on the shoulder.

"Sorry. No, she's right. Yes, you look hot. Just be careful and bring that pepper spray I got you," he corrects himself.

I give Jared a hug. He's become like a big brother of sorts to me, and I love him for it. I put on my white tank top and shorts over the bikini and head out with Micah.

We're driving for a bit when he asks, "So how do you live in an area near beaches and rivers and grow up not knowing how to swim?"

I look over at him before saying, "Well, my mom never brought us growing up. It wasn't until Lyle got his license that we started going on the weekends. By that point, I was a teenager. I suppose I just never had a teacher."

"Who's Lyle? Your brother," he asks.

Hearing Lyle's name come out of Micah's mouth so casually sends a wave of unexpected emotion over me that I wasn't expecting. I clear my throat and fight the unfamiliar feeling away.

"Yes," I reply simply.

Hoping he leaves it at that, but he doesn't.

"How old is he?"

I stare ahead, "He was 18."

I see Micah looking at me from the corner of my eye before I look out onto the trees passing us by. He doesn't ask anything else of him. Instead he changes the subject. He begins talking about something else when I see a turtle crossing the road.

"Stop," I tell Micah.

"What's wrong? Are you ok," he asks, placing his hand on my knee as he pulls over.

"Yeah I'm fine, it's just that poor turtle is going to get crushed trying to cross the road," I say as I get out of the car.

"Leyna, are you serious? You're a turtle saver too," he asks jokingly as he gets out to assist me with my mission.

"Yes, I'm a turtle saver. But I also save any other poor little creatures that need my help."

Until I found you

I pick the turtle up and carry it across to the other side. Laying it gently down in the grass. I walk back towards Micah when I see he's smiling at me, but it's not his usual cocky smile. This smile is different somehow.

"What," I ask.

"You're a sweetheart. Most people don't care enough to do stuff like that," he replies.

"Well, I couldn't let the poor thing get crushed," I replied.

"And yet that was the turtle's name on finding Nemo, Crush. Sort of ironic when you think of it," he says humor across his beautiful face.

"Oh you're so fucking twisted for that," he begins to laugh. "So twisted. I don't even know you, if anyone asks," I say as I get back in the Jeep.

Micah laughs so hard I think he may cry. We pull onto a long gravel road leading us into the woods. I can't help but think, yep this guy was too good to be true. You can't be that hot and interested in me without being a serial killer or some shit.

He interrupts my thoughts by saying jokingly, "I swear I didn't bring you out here to murder you. We have private access to the river from here."

"Private access," I repeat. "Yeah. This is my house."

I look around at the thick, lush green forest surrounding us. The branches create almost a canopy of sorts. A grey stone gravel driveway is leading us to a grand riverside home. The large two-story house is elevated; built on elegant stilts. In the center of the circle driveway is a large water fountain surrounded by roses. The front porch is spacious and welcoming. Four white columns line the front of it, giving it a luxurious look. Micah comes around and opens the car door for me. He offers me a tour of the property.

The view of the backyard must be beautiful. We walk up the wide brick steps and into the house. I assumed it was going to be a bachelor pad of sorts, but it's not. The house looks like a home. Everything is so light and open. A big portion of the back wall is made of glass, giving a gorgeous view of the river and scenery. The kitchen is big and open. Connecting to a large dining room that has access to a back patio. The living room is wide and spacious with a fireplace that looks like it came out of a hallmark Christmas movie. Where Bing Crosby or Nat King Cole's Christmas album would be playing in the background while the perfect s'mores would be made. We walk out onto the back patio.

The view is lovely. I look down at the back yard and see that the green grass is thick. Almost as lush as the surrounding trees. On one side of the yard, he has a flower garden of beautiful lilies with wind chimes hanging above them from a tree. The backyard has its own dock to the river. Even a hammock swings from two trees. I can only imagine how beautiful the sunsets must be here. "Micah, this is beautiful."

"Thank You. My mother designed it. This was her dream home. She loved it here," he says. The way he says it and the look in his eyes I already know. I know that look. "I'm so sorry." "For what," He asks with his brow raised.

"For losing your mother," I reply softly.
He looks a bit taken aback.
"How did you know," he asks.

Until I found you

"I've seen that look. I've heard that tone of admiration and sadness of a person, or a memory before."

A few moments go by before he says, "I'm sorry also."

"For?"

"You lost your brother didn't you," he asks softly.

I nod my head. I expect him to pry and ask questions but he doesn't.

"Ready to have some fun," he asks, offering his hand. I nod my head and smile, taking it. I'm grateful that he didn't ask questions. I don't think I'm ready for that yet.

Ten

He unloads the kayaks and carries one above his head walking to the dock with it.

"Let me help you. I've got this one," I say.

"No, I've got it," he replies, setting down the first kayak.

I go to pick it up but it's not working out too well. Damn this thing is heavy.

"Leyna," he calls out to me. "Stop you're going to hurt yourself."

I can do this. I tried dragging it this time. Nope. Nope. Definitely not. He walks over and takes it out of my hands.

"Drop the kayak, shortcake."

I look up to face him.

"Quit calling me shortcake," I say seriously, already getting annoyed.

"Well if you'd stop trying to carry something 5 times your height-" he begins to laugh.

Oh he thinks he's so cute.

UNTIL I found you

He continues, "then maybe you wouldn't be getting so frustrated now would you?"

I roll my eyes at him and drop the kayak dramatically. The two inches that it fell was a lot more dramatic in my head. He chuckles.

"Look at you listening to me now," he says. Amusement clear in his voice.

"Listening to you?"

I repeat his words, bemused. I playfully hit him on the arm "well, now I'm definitely dragging this."

Before I can reach for it, he bends down and lifts me over his shoulder. Grabbing the remaining kayak and dragging it with his other hand.

"Put me down," I yell trying to fight my laughter as I playfully kick at him.

He responds by putting me in the kayak and begins dragging me in it like I'm on a sled. He begins to laugh when I yell "mush!" like he's an Alaskan sled dog. He pulls me fast and hard making me squeal. "Alright, are you ready to kayak on the water or are you enjoying land too much," he asks.

I respond by patting the grass. He chuckles and then flips me out of it.

"So you can't swim, at all," he asks.

"Well, I can doggy paddle. But, if you were to just fling me into water that's above my head, no."

He looks serious for a moment before saying, "So four feet right," and begins to laugh.

How did I know that was coming?

"Ha. Ha. Like I haven't heard that one before. You know, if we're going to start being around each other more you're really going to have to come up with some new material."

He smiles a genuine smile.

"So we're going to be around each other often?"

I go to retort a remark but his smile stops me.

"So are you ready to be an Olympic swimmer today," he asks.

"It's been a mission in my life," I reply.

He smiles and shakes his head. He puts the kayaks onto the dock and hands me a life vest. I go to put it on and I'm stopped in my tracks when I see him take his shirt off; his hard abs, his toned stomach, his big muscular, tanned arms with his tattoos. Even his tattoos looked sexy on him. His big hands that look so hard but have touched me those few times with nothing but tenderness. And suddenly, I want him touching me everywhere with those hands. He turns to lower the kayaks in the water when I see his back. His muscles look hard and taut under his skin. His ass is even hot. I'm biting my lip when he turns to tell me something. "

Enjoying your view," he asks.

I clear my throat.

"Yes. Told you I was the outdoorsy girl."

He smiles and asks, "Are you really wearing that tank top and shorts?"

I look down, "Um yeah."

"What are you going to wear after we get out?"

Shit! I had forgotten to pack a spare change of clothes.

He shrugs his shoulders and says, "just wear your swimsuit."

Until I found you

Before turning back around, he fiddles with the other life vest pretending to do something to it. And I realize that's his way of giving me some privacy. This makes me smile and appreciate his act of respect. He is such a gentleman. After removing my shorts and top, I look down at my body and instantly become self conscious about my appearance. My thick thighs and large hips, I dislike them so much. Micah has probably seen so many girls. So many prettier, skinnier girls. I can't think about that now. I take in a deep breath. Calming myself before saying "ok."

He turns and his eyes rake over my body, up and down; down and back up. As if he were trying to remember every detail of me this way.

"Holy fuck," he says lowly.

Almost inaudible, it was so low, but I heard it. He doesn't even bother to be subtle about his staring. He licks his lips, walking towards me cautiously. I halt my breathing and suddenly I become excited.

"What are you doing," I ask quietly.

"I'm walking towards you, slowly," he replies.

"Why," I ask; swallowing a lump in my throat. My stomach is doing cartwheels.

"Because if I ran towards you I'd probably scare you. I have to be next to you," he says as he approaches me.

We're standing not even an inch apart from each other. I can feel the heat from his body. We hold each other's gaze for a few moments before he trails his fingers across my face slowly. Taking in every feature of me. He licks his lips as he studies my own. He gently lifts my chin up as he looks into my eyes before settling on my lips again. I think he's about to kiss me. My breathing hitches slightly. Involuntarily, I part my lips ready for his mouth to be on mine. His fingers leave under my chin and gently caress up towards my cheeks before trailing back down to my jawline. A gust of wind blows gently between us, causing some of my hair to blow in the wind. He stares at me for a moment before trailing his fingers lightly up to my temple and tucking my wind blown hair behind my ear like he did at the boardwalk.

"You are so utterly beautiful," he says softly.

Goosebumps begin to form from his touch and the way he's staring at me so intensely.

Eleven

After Micah spends what seems like five minutes laughing at me because of that damn life vest we get on our kayaks.

"It's not funny Micah," I say splashing him with water.

Through his laughter he says, "you know when a little kid tries to wear their parents shoes? And the shoes look 5 sizes too big on their feet? That was you just now."

"Well you can't expect a life vest that fits a 6'3 grown man, to fit the same way on a 5 foot-" he interrupts me.

"Midget?" He begins to laugh.

"This midget is about to smack you with this damn paddle. Keep on."

I threaten him by waving it in his direction. Which only makes him laugh harder. We begin to play with each other by using our paddles as tools to splash each other with. I almost flip my kayak trying to out splash him. He laughs but steadies me. Almost flipping himself over too in the process. I can't help but break into laughter myself.

"I love that sound," he says with a wide grin.

"I haven't laughed like this in a while," I admit.

"I'm glad you're having fun," he says.

"Me too. I was a tad nervous to be on the water honestly. But, I have to admit this is fun so far. It would have been funnier to see Maggie do this."

I begin to giggle at the thought. Maggie was not an outdoorsy girl at all. She would have hated this. I would have loved seeing every minute of it.

"Yeah, I can't imagine Blondie out here. Most girls aren't into doing stuff like this anyway. They're too afraid to mess their hair up or some shit. It's refreshing to meet someone that's different. That is willing to try new things. Especially, considering the fact that you can't swim and you're still doing this. You're a little badass."

I smile at his compliment.

He continues, "Speaking of swimming, there's a perfect spot not too far ahead that we can stop at. The river is low and so is the current so it'll be perfect for you."

A few minutes later, we come to a spot with a large sandbar. After pulling our kayaks up to it, we lay out on it like it's our own little personal beach.

"I'll take this over crowded beaches any day," I say with my eyes closed and soaking up the warm sun.

"Why do you think I moved away from the city," Micah asks.

After a while of us talking about various subjects and laughing at each other as we built sand castles, Micah says, "ok let's get this thing started."

He says and begins walking into the water. Once he's up to his navel in it, he motions for me to join him.

"I'm fine, thanks," I say as I pat the sand.

"Oh come on, babe. Live a little," he says.

Butterflies swarm my stomach. I can't help but smile at him calling me babe. I get up and walk towards him. Once I meet him, he takes my hand and leads us to deeper water.

"I thought you said the water was low," I replied.

"I said low. Not barren. The water depth can still be over 15 feet in some spots," he replies. "Just hold onto me. I got you," he says, gripping my waist protectively with his large hands.

He holds me like this for a moment before pulling me to his warm chest. The feeling of his skin on mine is exquisite. This should feel foreign, but it doesn't, it feels natural. His arms are holding me tight but so gentle at the same time. All the while, our eyes never leave each other as I become lost in those beautiful ocean eyes of his. I can feel my heart quicken as I wrap my arms around his shoulders and place my hands on the back of his neck. I begin rubbing him lightly in soft circles. He closes his eyes and lays his head back slightly enjoying the feeling of my soft caresses.

"That feels amazing," he says opening his eyes and staring at me once more.

I bite down on my lip, taking in this beautiful man before me. He brings his hand to the side of my face. Tracing my bottom lip with his thumb before pushing my hair back behind my shoulders, letting his fingers trail lightly down my neck. My breath hitches as goosebumps form under his touch. He pulls me closer to him and I instinctively wrap my legs around his torso. He sucks in a sharp breath through his teeth. The sound of it makes me let out a soft moan. His eyes become darker, hungry. He parts his lips and we both connect like magnets.

Our mouths feverishly consume the other. His tongue invades my mouth, wrapping around mine. The feeling of his hard flesh pressed against me through his trunks makes me let out a whimper. He wraps one of his hands into my hair and uses it to guide my head back. Giving him full access to my neck. He plants feverish kisses across my neck, onto my throat and trails them up to my jawline. He sucks across my jaw trailing back down to my neck where he begins to tenderly nip and suck my sensitive flesh. All the while he's tugging my hair with slightly more force sending chills throughout me. The sensation is amazing. I let out a moan, this time pulling his hair.

He thrusts his hard cock against me slightly and returns back to my mouth. Claiming it. Devouring it. He lets go of my hair and with both hands grabs handfuls of my ass, lifting me higher onto him. He begins to walk us out of the water. He pulls his tongue from my mouth and begins licking my breasts. Kissing, biting, sucking them. I feel as though I'm about to explode from his kissing alone. He gets us on the sand bar and lays me on the beach towel. He peppers kisses all the way down from my neck to my stomach, kissing his way down to my thighs before kissing my most sensitive area. My hips buck off the ground causing his face to press into me.

He looks my body over. Taking in every part of me as he glides his hands down my breasts, to my stomach and stops at the bikini bottoms.

He meets my eyes and says, "Please Leyna, let me taste you," licking his lips as he does so.

I moan and shake my head yes vigorously. I've never had this done to me before. All of my nervousness is replaced with want and need as he unties the strings of my bikini bottoms slowly, teasing me. I can't take it anymore.

"Micah," I practically beg.

He licks his lips and begins kissing my thighs as he removes the bikini bottoms.

"I know baby," he says as he kisses closer and closer to my sex.

He rubs his finger down my slit collecting the moisture from my spot. With dark eyes he puts his fingers in his mouth tasting me.

"Fucking delicious," he says before pressing his tongue flat against me.

My hips buck off the ground pressing myself even deeper into his mouth. His strong hands grip my hips keeping me from moving. I place my hand in his hair. Pulling, tugging, as he brings me closer and closer to the edge. With my other hand I cup my mouth. Biting down on my palm to quiet myself.

"Let go baby, no one can hear you," Micah says before returning his tongue to me.

His tongue is so hot, so incredibly skilled. The feeling is euphoric and before I know it, my orgasm rips through me so powerfully. I begin to feel light-headed. As I'm riding out my ecstasy he begins planting small kisses up my body until he reaches my neck. He takes the side of my face with one of his hands. Willing me to look at him.

"You are so beautiful."

He breathes, looking me over. He parts my mouth with his and begins kissing me again. I taste sweetness on his tongue.

He pulls back, looking at me as he says, "I told you you were delicious," before lowering his head and kissing me again.

I wrap my legs around his torso, my hands around his neck and maneuver him to let me on top. He lies on his back pulling me on top of him, never breaking our kiss. Straddling him like this feels amazing. His cock is hard pressed against me, making me eager for him. I'm not like this. I don't sleep with guys I've just met. Hell, I don't sleep around at all. I've only had sex one other time. But there's something between us, a connection drawing us to each other, like magnets.

I begin to swirl my hips rubbing my bare sex against his hardened cock through his trunks. He growls as he grabs two fistfuls of my ass encouraging me to rock faster. I break our kiss and look into his eyes. Am I really about to do this? Am I just another conquest of his? Wait, what am I doing? Why am I freaking out right now? I'm ruining this.

"Are you ok," he asks panting, searching my face as he does.

I decide to shut all rational thought out of my head; to hell with consequences right now. I want him and he wants me. I reconnect our kiss as I begin rocking against his hard flesh. He deepens our kiss before he sits up in a quick motion. Flipping us to where he is on top now hovering over me. He grabs the back of my thigh halting our movements as he breaks our kiss. I give him a confused look as I'm panting.

He starts, "I want you so bad, but I don't want to go too fast. I saw that look on your face just a second ago. I don't want you waking up tomorrow regretting this. And, you will if we keep going," he says, pressing his forehead to mine.

The amount of respect this man has for me already is incredible. I answer him by giving him a gentle kiss on his lips and brushing his hair back from his forehead. He plants a kiss on my temple and lays on his back. Pulling me to lie on his side. He wraps his arms around me but freezes when his hands touch my bare ass.

"Um, do me a favor, cover that beautiful ass of yours or I won't be able to control myself with you," he says before kissing me on my lips.

He hands me my bikini bottoms. I laugh lightly into his chest as I grab the bottoms from him, putting them on as he watches me.

Twelve

This feels so good. So right. We're laying in each other's arms talking and laughing. Such a simple act but so profound. I'm tracing random patterns on his chest next to the cross tattooed there, the number 33 inked under it. I observe the tattoo on his shoulder, a lily. I think of those beautiful lilies planted in his backyard with the collection of wind chimes. He notices me staring at his tattoos and says, "My mother's name was Lillian."

I look into his eyes, full of admiration and sadness for his mother.

"I'm so sorry," I say as I lay my chin on his chest and begin running my hand through his hair, comforting him.

"It was a long time ago," he replies simply, looking up at the sky.

"What happened," I asked sheepishly, almost regretting that question.

He looks at me, "Cancer. I was nine when she passed. They didn't find out about it until she was in the final stage of it. And by then-" He trails off.

"It was too late," I say.

He nods his head; "She came home, spent the remainder of her time with me. She wanted to make it as normal as possible. As precious as possible. Three months later she was gone."

I can see he was another world away as he recalls it all. "I suppose my father couldn't handle it. So, he stayed gone. Always working. Always taking business trips. He was absent those last weeks of her. He flew in for the funeral, returning back to work the next day. He's been absent ever since really. In a way I lost both of my parents".

"That's why you have these," I say as I touch his tattoos.

"Yes. They're meant to remind me of the ones I've lost. They're a part of me now."

He looks down at me and smiles but it doesn't reach his eyes. I don't like seeing the sadness he carries behind them. So to get his mind off of it I decide to humor him. I lifted off of him then.

He looks a bit confused by my abrupt move before I say, "Ok, Eason, it's time you teach me how to swim. So get up," I say offering my hand.

He gives me a smile and stands to his feet. Taking my hand in his as we walk into the water. After a while, I slowly get the hang of it. I must say, he really is a good teacher.

"See you've got it now," he commends me as I tread the water steadily.

Suddenly the wind picks up and the sky darkens. We both look up.

"We should head back," Micah says, taking my hand and pulling me back to shore. Once we get back in our kayaks it begins to thunder. "Just a little bit down river and we dock. I have a four wheeler we'll ride to get back home," he calls over his shoulder.

A few minutes go by and we pull our kayaks up to the bank. He helps me up and drags the kayaks up on the grass. I have the paddles since we both know it's futile for me to help with the kayaks. He takes them from my hands and places them down. Suddenly lightning strikes. "Yeah we should go," he remarks as we walk to the four wheeler.

I climb on wrapping my arms around his waist.

"Do you like to go fast," he asks as he turns to look at me with a wicked grin.

Before I can respond, he takes off as I tighten my grip on him. We're approaching a mud hole then.

"Don't you dare," I threaten him.

He laughs but does slow down. We're nearly through it when we become bogged down. "Shit," Micah mutters under his breath.

Now it's my turn to laugh at him.

"You steer, I'll push," he commands. He begins to push as I give it gas. All we're accomplishing is getting mud everywhere and bogging ourselves down even more.

"Turn it," he yells.

I turn the steering and it causes mud to sling all over Micah. I cut the engine off and began to laugh at him. Hard; almost snorting in the process.

Until I found you

"You think it's funny huh," he says, wiping mud from his face.

"Hilarious", I say through my laughter.

"Oh yeah," he says charging towards me.

"No," I yell between bellows of laughter as he grabs me off the four wheeler and proceeds to lather his body to mine, getting mud all over me.

I shriek. "Ooooh you are so dead," I say through my laughter.

Grabbing a handful of mud, I threw it at him. Before I know it we're in a full blown mud war. I'm doing pretty well at hitting my target, but then so is Micah. We're both running around chasing each other with mud.

"Ok I surrender," he yells out through his laughter.

We're both laughing so hard we're crying. Just then it begins to rain. He takes my hand and we make a mad dash for his house. Once we reach his back yard we rinse ourselves off with the water hose before going in. At this point I'm so cold I'm shaking. He notices and turns the heater on.

"You can take a shower if you want. I've got some clothes you can wear."

He leads me towards the master bathroom upstairs. We walk in his room and I immediately fall in love with the layout. A large king-sized bed is centered on a raised platform. The whole front wall is glass panes making the wall a panoramic view of the river and lush trees. I look at the back wall and find shelves full of beautiful glass sculptures and vases of all different colors and sizes. I'm looking each of them over, mesmerized by the beauty of them. A few catch my eye. One of them being a sculpture that looks like a rose on raging fire with burning embers at the bottom. Another being one that looks like an angel's wings, one wing being broken; and a beautiful blue colored vase that was sculpted to look like a waterfall. They all have so much detail to them.

"You like," Micah asks.

"Very much. They're beautiful! Where did you get these?"

"I made them."

I turn to look at him, "You made these," I ask in awe.

"Is that so hard to believe," he asks with a small smile.

"No, not at all. It's just you're so talented. In every sense of the way."

I trail off slowly thinking of when we were on the sand bar. A smile creeps on my face. I turn to him and see he has a smug grin on his face. Realizing what I just said out loud, my cheeks begin to blush. He closes the gap between us slowly. A lump begins to rise in my throat.

He's only an inch away from my face when he says quietly, "Baby, you haven't seen anything yet."

He then planted a small, teasing kiss on my lips. I want more. I stand on my tippy toes beckoning him to me, I cup his neck with my hands and begin deepening our kiss. He wraps one of his arms around my waist, with the other he cups my ass and squeezes lightly. This causes me to whimper. He pushes his tongue further into my mouth claiming it as his own. I can feel him hardening against me.

He pulls away from me and says, "let's get in the shower. Get ourselves cleaned up."

I nod agreeing before thinking. Taking my hand, he leads us in the bathroom and turns the shower on. I begin to feel nervous. I've never showered with another guy before. He turns to look at me, giving me a comforting smile.

He says, "We don't have to shower together if you don't want to."

I think for a moment. I want to. But, it's my fear. I want to. But I'm a chicken. He walks up to me slowly, placing his finger under my chin so I'm looking at him.

"Towels are hanging on the rack. I'll place some clothes on the bed for you." Giving me a soft kiss on my forehead, he walks out. I stand there for a moment battling my thoughts. I really did want to shower with him. I was so nervous about it and still am. I look in the mirror and see a coward. A girl that knows what she wants but is too scared to go for it.

"Don't be a coward," I say to the girl in the mirror and walk out of the bathroom to find Micah. I walk into the kitchen to find him on the phone.

"Yeah I was busy. Still am. What do you want? No, it's not a good time. Because, it's not. I'll call you later," he hangs up and turns around to get himself some water when he sees me standing there.

He looks a bit taken aback.

"Hey. Do you need anything," he offers.

"Um no. Actually, I was coming to find you," I say sheepishly.

He gives me a smile, "You found me."

"Yep," I say, dragging the word out.

He chuckles and walks towards me.

"What do you want, Leyna," he asks me seductively.

I looked into his eyes, memorized at how beautiful they are. After a moment of silence goes by, he traces my lips with his thumb before taking my hand and leading us to the shower.

Thirteen

Micah turns the shower on, setting the temperature.

"How hot do you like your water?"

"Hot," I reply.

I'm shivering at this point. Although I'm not sure if it's because I'm cold, or nervous.

"Me too," he replies.

He turns to grab an extra towel. I almost ask him to turn around while I undress but realize how dumb that sounds. *Don't be a coward,* I tell myself. I take a breath in and begin to untie the bikini top. Micah stills, watching my every move. I untie the top and let it fall to the ground. Micah's eyes trail over my half naked body. He licks his lips slowly at the sight of my exposed breasts, which instantly makes me feel pressure in between my legs. I untie the sides of the bikini bottoms, letting them fall to the ground. Micah's eyes rake over my body. Taking in every curve of me. He reaches to untie his swim trunks and my breath hitches. Butterflies swarm my stomach.

He pulls his trunks down slowly and his manhood comes into full view. I swallow hard. He's so big. I take in his naked body and he's divine. The perfect man. He walks over to me slowly. Once he reaches me, he wraps one arm around my waist pulling me closer to him. With his other hand, he raises my chin to look up at him.

"You are so beautiful," he coos.

I give him a small smile before he kisses my jawline and works his way to my mouth. He kisses me sweetly. Once the water is the right temperature, we step into the enormous shower. The hot water feels amazing and instantly warms me up. Micah grabs a washcloth and fills it with shower gel before walking over and rubbing it on my back. I let out a humming sound.

"Feel good," he asks before planting kisses on my shoulder.

"Mm hmm."

He chuckles. He moves to my chest. Moving the cloth over my breasts as he gently massages them. I close my eyes, enjoying the feeling. He moves lower and begins washing my belly as he lowers his face into my neck kissing it sensually. Goosebumps begin to rise on my skin as he moves his way back up to my breasts. He drops the wash cloth and begins gently pinching my nipples as he scrapes his teeth on my earlobe. I push into him instinctively and he lets out a low growl as he moves his hand around my throat. Fire instantly ignites me. He spins me around to face him. His eyes lustfully piercing mine. With his hand still on my throat, he takes the other one and begins kneading my breast in his palm before reaching down and sucking on it.

Pressure is building between my legs. He removes his mouth and hand from my breast as he glides his hand down my belly and towards my sex.

My mouth becomes dry. My heart is racing. He slides his finger down my clit before rubbing it with his thumb and forefinger. I let out a moan as he does. Micah swallows the sound as his lips melt into mine. He's rubbing me at a torturously slow pace. I have to have more. I buck my hips at him. Begging him to speed up.

He breaks our kiss and asks, "want more?"

I nod, panting. Never breaking eye contact with me he removes his hand from my clit and places his fingers near my mouth.

"Open and suck," he says.

I gulp but open my mouth as he places two fingers inside. I begin to suck on them. He furrows his brows as I do so.

"Fuck," he mouths.

He then pulls his fingers from my mouth and guides them down as he begins to rub my clit with more friction and speed as he adds his finger inside of me. The combination is divine. I begin panting as he pumps into me at a deep, calculated pace.

"Fuck baby. You're tight," he says in a low voice.

I place my hands around his hard forearm where his hand is still wrapped around my throat. If someone would have told me this morning that Micah would be choking me out as he finger fucked me against his shower wall, I would have called them a liar. But, here I am. The pure erotica of this sends me over the edge, and I come undone. I let out a moan as I rode Micah's hand. Our stare, never breaking from each other. Micah's lips are parted as he watches me orgasm.

He looks as if he could cum himself. He removes his hand from my throat and takes a fistful of my hair in his hand as he guides my head back so he can kiss me. His kiss is passionate. I pull away. He gives me a look of confusion as he pants. I bend down and grab the washcloth from the shower floor, adding soap to it.

I look up at him batting my lashes in full effect as I say, "it's your turn."

I begin running the cloth across his tight chest, slowly down his torso. I can feel his eyes on Me. I'm by his V line when I look up to gage his reaction. His jaw is clenched as his chest is heaving. He's a statue of hard muscle beneath my hands. I find the courage and lower the washcloth to his cock. He draws a sharp breath in through his teeth, staring at me with almost black hungry eyes. I stroke him slowly as he lays his head back against the shower wall. "Fuck."

I increase my pace as I begin kissing his chest. I run my free hand along his body, feeling his hot, hard muscles. I begin kissing down his chest, gently nipping as I do.

He looks down at me bewildered as I work my lips down his torso. He starts breathing heavily. He's looking down at me with furrowed brows when he rubs my lips with his thumb before slowly inserting it into my mouth. I swirl my tongue around it teasingly.

"Fuck baby," he practically hisses as he removes his thumb from my mouth.

UNTIL I found you

    His cock twitches in my hand. I'm nervous about what I'm about to do. I've never done this before, but I want to. I want to, with him. His length in my hand, I begin to stroke him, giving him a few pumps as I go. He grabs a fistful of my wet hair in his hand. I look up at him and see that his jaw is clenched as he's looking down at me. Hunger and anticipation in his eyes.

    The sight of him like this is so sexy. The way he's towering over me. The way he's looking at me. I lick the tip of him then. He takes in a sharp breath through his teeth. I take him into my mouth half way at first and begin dragging my tongue up and down his length while stroking him.

    "Fuck," he drags the word out.

    He gently guides my head up and down him, using my hair in his fist.

    "Fuck baby. Yeah like that," he says biting his lip.

    I squeeze my legs together to relieve the pressure building there already. I take more of him in my mouth, batting my lashes up at him. He furrows his brows, biting his bottom lip even harder. He pulls my hair and a moan escapes me.

    "Your mouth is heaven."

    My eyes are watering and I'm nearly gagging on him. I wrap my free hand around the back of his leg to steady myself. He rocks into me, pushing himself down my throat even farther. "Fuck baby I'm about to cum already. Stop if you don't want it in your mouth."

    I answer him by picking up my pace and hollowing my cheeks, gagging as I do.

"Oh fuck," he says throwing his head back and releasing himself down my throat.

The warm liquid didn't taste as bad as Maggie says it does. He helps me to my feet. Wrapping his arms around my waist, he plants a soft kiss to my forehead. We hold each other like this for a few minutes. He's rubbing soft circles on my shoulder blade as the hot water sprays over us.

Once we've caught our breaths and finished showering, we get out and dry off. We walk in his room to get changed when I hear my phone going off in the kitchen. I hurry up and throw his shirt on. It goes to my mid thigh clinging to my hips. I hurry up and answer it before it goes to voicemail. I should have checked the number.

"Leyna."

My mother. Oh no. Not right now. I speak quietly into the phone.

"Mom?"

"I need to borrow some money," she slurs. "This damn place doesn't take my card."

"Mom, where are you?"

I can't make out her next words. All I can hear is loud music in the background. A bar.

"Mom?" "Well hey there," she says to someone else and hangs up. I
let out a frustrated breath and rub my temples. I turn around to find Micah standing behind me. I jump back a little in surprise.

"Everything ok," he asks.

"Yeah it's fine," I say and walk past him.

"Who was that," he asks following me.

"It was my mom," I say without making eye contact with him.

UNTIL I found you

What am I supposed to tell him? Oh, that's just my alcoholic mother calling me for more money so she can pay up her bar tab. Oh and, I had to go bail her out of jail yesterday too. I look up to find him already staring at me.

"What," I ask.

"Your cheeks are turning red and you won't look at me," he states matter-of-factly.

"I did just do a lot of things that were first for me," I say walking into the kitchen.

He gently grabs my elbow, turning me to face him. He looks confused.

"What do you mean first for you? You've never done that before?"

Suddenly, I feel like I'm being put on the spot.

"No. Any of it," I say looking down.

I can feel myself blushing. He takes ahold of my chin, forcing me to look up at him. He looks my face over and something clicks within him after a moment.

"You're telling the truth," he says astonished.

"You think I'd lie," I say almost hurt.

"No no. I didn't mean it like that. It's just- well I can't believe it," he says, looking me over. "For someone so beautiful, so sexy, it's just hard to believe no one has touched you."

"I've been touched, only once before. But, I've never done those things we just did," I stammered, turning my face away from him.

Is it possible to die of embarrassment? He places his fingers under my chin forcing me to look at him.

"Don't do that," he says looking into my eyes.

"Do what?"

"Hide away from me. Feeling ashamed. Don't. You have nothing to be ashamed or embarrassed of Leyna."

He steps closer to me wrapping his arms around my waist.

"I do have to ask though, why did you choose to do it with me?"

Without letting myself think too much into it I say truthfully, "I don't know really. I just felt this pull towards you." Micah places his hand to the side of my face as he says, "like a magnet."

Fourteen

"What are you doing?" I ask Micah. "Ordering take out. What are you in the mood for? I know you're hungry. You haven't eaten anything other than that bag of popcorn since you've been here," he says.

I shrug and pop a piece of it in my mouth, "it's fine I'll just eat this."

He walks over and takes the bag of popcorn. "You're not eating popcorn for dinner. What do you want to eat," he asks.

I shrug my shoulders, "I don't care. I'm not picky."

He gives me a look, "Sure that's what every girl says until you go to order something and then that's when they don't want that place."

Annoyed at his assumption of me I say, "Your typical girl? Yes. Me? No. I'm not your typical girl thank you very much." I say putting my hands on my hips.

"I'm starting to learn that," he says with a smile.

"Why don't I just cook us something," I offer.

He looks a tad sheepish and says, "I don't think you'll find anything to cook in there except frozen dinners."

I walk towards the fridge and freezer, "I can make something out of nothing. Watch," and pull the doors open to see indeed there's only frozen dinners in the freezer and your typical bachelor pad ensemble of foods in the fridge.

"When was the last time you had a home cooked meal," I ask him as I close the doors.

"Hmm. Does a restaurant count," he asks.

I giggle, "no."

"Well then it's been years," he replies. "Ok, we've got to change that. You're coming over and I'm cooking for you. Name your favorite dish and I'll make it for you."

He smiles and says, "Anything you cook should be delicious."

He starts walking towards me, "as long as I get you for dessert," he says, grabbing my hips and giving them a light squeeze while licking his lips.

I love when he does that. He lets go of me and walks over to his phone ordering pizza.

After we're done eating, we're laying on his couch cuddled up watching a movie when Jared texts me. "I come home and both of you bitches are gone. Maggie I expect this from. But you missy? Now I'm bored. Help." I smile and reply. "We have the golden girls recorded on the DVR to keep you occupied and if that doesn't do it we also have the first season of

YOU. You is good but Sophia Petrillo is the best. She never disappoints." Jared replies back, "ooh I forgot about that. Yeah I'm not picking Sophia tonight. I'm picking you. It turns me on anyway lol it's been awhile I need some."

Imaging Jared laying on the couch with a bowl of popcorn fueling his obsession of Penn Badgley causes me to let out a small chuckle.

I'm about to reply to Jer when Micah interrupts, "what the fuck" He practically shouts.

I turn to look up at him. He looks pissed. "Wha-?"

Before I can speak he says, "I knew it! So you're going to leave here and go fuck that guy? Fucking really? 'Indefinite friendzone' my ass."

He lifts me off of him and stands to his feet. Fists clenched at his sides. "I didn't peg you for a liar or a whore."

My jaw drops. The wind feels like it's been kicked out of me. I know he just didn't. I stand up and shove him.

"How fucking dare you! You don't even know what the fuck you're talking about!"

I'm pissed.

"Oh no?" He steps closer to me. "'I'm not picking Sophie, I'm picking you. You really turn me on'. I saw what I fucking saw! Don't try to deny it" he says through his teeth.

The realization that we're about to kill each other over a misunderstanding stagers me. "What?! He wasn't talking about me!" I yell back at him. He comes forward slightly.

"You think I'm stupid? I saw the text! If he wants you that bad he can fucking have you!" he yells louder.

Before I can stop myself, I push Micah hard and yell, "He's gay you asshole!"

Micah's shocked expression takes over his previous look of anger.

"We were talking about tv shows you fucking idiot! The Golden Girls, as in Sophia. And the show called YOU! That's what the show is called! Jer has an attraction to the guy that stars in the show "You" because Jared is Gay! Don't believe me since I'm a fucking 'liar'?"

I throw my phone at him. He catches it and reads Mine and Jared's conversation. Realization of just how stupid he's been hits him like a ton of bricks. He's floored. Guilt clear on his face. Good.

"Fuck. I'm sorry."

He begins to walk towards me when I snatch my phone from him and hold my arm out stopping his movements.

"I'm sorry, ok? To be fair that was worded really badly and it looked even worse. And then last night when he laid on you in your bed. What else was I supposed to think? Besides why didn't you just tell me your friend was gay?"

Now I'm livid.

"Because it was none of your business! What? Am I supposed to lay out everyone's sexual preferences when they are around me so you don't feel threatened?"

He tries to walk towards me. I give him a look that I'm sure makes me resemble a rabid dog. "Fuck no. I'm not threatened by anyone! Look I'm sorry. I jumped to conclusions. I should have never assumed any of that."

"Assumed I was a whore you mean?"

My voice breaks at the end and I can feel the tears beginning to pull in my eyes. Seeing me like this, he furrows his brows in a painful look of guilt that covers his features. I won't let him see me cry. Fuck that. I walk towards his bathroom.

"Wait, where are you going?"

I can hear him following me up the stairs.

"Leyna."

I walked into his bathroom and shut the door, locking it.

"Leyna. I'm- I'm sorry. I'm a fucking asshole sometimes. I never should have said that. I was just angry I didn't mean any of it," he says through the door.

I've already stripped his clothes off and put my tank top and shorts on. The realization that I have no kind of bra on under this tank top or panties on under these shorts hits me. I pick up Maggie's still soaked bikini and place it in my bag. I wipe under my eyes before unlocking the door and walking past him. I nearly make it out of his room when he grabs my wrist gently stopping me.

"Don't," I shout at him, pulling my wrist away.

"Don't go. I'm sorry, Leyna," he says.

I can see the regret in his eyes, but I can't let him weaken my resolve. I pull my wrist away from him and walk towards the front door. I'm calling an Uber when I hear his footsteps behind me.

"Just leave me alone," I call over my shoulder.

I hear him unlocking his car, but I walk right past it.

"Leyna, where are you going?"

"Home," I yell.

"You're going to walk home in the dark? This is ridiculous. Just get in my car. It's too dangerous."

I ignore him and keep walking.

"Get in the car. Get in the car, Leyna," he commands with a loud, authoritative tone.

I halt my steps and turn to face him giving him a death stare. He softens his features.

"I'm asking you to please get in the car and let me take you home."

Fifteen

We've been silent the entire car ride back to my house. I would have been happy walking until my Uber caught up to me, but it started raining and lightning. Refusing to make eye contact with him, I stare out of the passenger window of his Jeep. Watching the rain move across the glass.

We're pulling onto my street when he says, "can I walk you in?"

I look at him. "Why?"

"I know I've said it ten times over now but I am truly sorry."

I say nothing as we pull up and we get out of his car. I'm walking to the front door when Jo opens it stepping out.

"Hey Leyna," he says as he greets me.

I give him a small "Hello," in return.

Maggie steps out behind Jo.

"Hey you two love birds," she greets Micah and I.

Neither of us responds.

"So Jo and I felt bad about ditching our double date with you guys today so we've rescheduled it for tomorrow night. Sounds good?"

Micah and I both mumble "yeah". Jo turns to Maggie giving her a peck on the lips before waving at me and getting into his car and driving off. Maggie stands there a moment before excusing herself back in. Leaving Micah and I alone outside together.

We stand in awkward silence for a moment before I say, "Thanks for the ride home."

"You're welcome."

Neither of us looked at the other. Without another word, I head inside and shut the door. I walk into the living room and find Jer sprawled out on the long sofa. I walk over to him and say "scootch over."

He looks at me and says knowingly "tell me what happened" as he makes room for me to lay next to him. I take the opportunity of Maggie being in the shower to tell him everything that happened. Jared remained silent throughout my rant. Only giving me looks of surprise when hearing of my giving and receiving of pleasure.

He's silent for a moment before saying, "In his defense, I am a sexy mother fucker."

"Jer," I smack him on the arm. "Well it's true. How was he supposed to know I don't roll that way? For all he knew you had a straight heterosexual male living amongst you and Maggie. He probably thought we were a kinky three some," he starts chuckling. "Give the guy a break. It was an honest mistake. And from what you're telling me, you two really have something. Don't ruin that over a misunderstanding, an epic misunderstanding. But, a misunderstanding all the same. Sounds to me like both of you have a temper," Jared says with amusement.

"So what should I do," I ask my best friend.

"Talk to him. Fix it," he says simply.

I nod my head, "fine I will."

I grab my phone and I'm about to text Micah when Maggie comes walking in, "Ok, so give me all the details," she says.

Instead of going into everything I tell Maggie, "it was fun. We went kayaking."

"And," Maggie draws out the word.

Jared comes to my rescue, "And this was their first date. Not everyone falls madly in love on the first date like you," he teases her.

"Why don't you give us all the details of your and Jo's day then?"

I give Jared a "thank you for saving me" smile. He gives me a subtle wink as Maggie goes into her day. Apparently the two have some things in common, they both were adopted. Both being the only child in their families. They even share the same birthday coincidentally. Jo being 3 years her senior. All in all, they hit it off great and already have tomorrow's date planned out, dinner and a movie.

"You and Micah are coming with us," she says more than asks.

"Maybe. I'll have to wait and see," I tell her.

"Why," she asks.

Before I can figure out how to explain what happened, Maggie's cuts in.

"Oh no. Leyna what happened," she asks, almost exasperated. Like she already assumed something was going to happen.

"We got into a misunderstanding," I say simply. I was hoping she'd leave it at that, but she doesn't.

"A misunderstanding? Like what," she asks. "I was texting Jer and Micah assumed I was talking to another guy. Anyway it blew up. He blew up, I blew up, words were thrown and that's that," I say.

Hoping she doesn't pry more. But Maggie being Maggie says, "well did either of you try to fix it? If it's only a misunderstanding resolve it. You two were hitting it off so well, Leyna. Don't let your pride ruin this."

Now I'm annoyed, "Wow, Maggie, I'd ask how you feel about the situation but something tells me you already have. If me not taking any shit off of him or anyone else makes me prideful, then so be it!"

Maggie presses her lips into a line before saying, "You can be mad at me. I'm only speaking the truth. You are prideful. Overly guarded, and temperamental. And if you don't start letting people in, you'll spend your life alone," she says in a calm tone.

"Well thanks for the advice," I say walking off to our room.

Once I plop myself on my bed I lay there for a while staring up at the ceiling. I am processing the events that took place today. I did have to admit that for the first time in a long time, I was genuinely happy. Spending time with Micah made me happy. I was even beginning to feel something for him. That part scared me the most. I tell myself it was all just a physical attraction. Nothing more, but there was something there. I tell myself it's only because we

UNTIL I found you

share the pain of losing someone close to us. I felt his pain when he told me about losing his mom. The sting of it, familiar. We connected through our shared loss. The more I think about it, the more I have to admit to myself that we did have something, an unexplainable pull to each other. It wasn't just an attraction. It was a connection. Something I didn't think I'd be able to feel again. Not after Chase, he was my first.

I was in my sophomore year of high school when I met him. I thought he was the most beautiful boy I'd ever seen. With his jet black hair and green eyes. I couldn't believe a boy like that would like a girl like me. Lyle didn't like him from the beginning. He even told me to stay away from him, but I wouldn't hear of his warnings. That was the first time I felt that kind of love, well what I thought was love. I believed I was in love with him. And what does a girl do when the boy she thinks she's in love with wants intimacy from her? Deep down I knew I wasn't ready, but he wanted me. He said he loved me, and so I gave myself to him.

It wasn't too long after when I found out he was only with me for that one purpose. He had the audacity to act like he didn't know me around his friends at school. They would laugh and snicker at me. I was nothing but a game he had won. I was crushed. Heartbroken. Utterly mortified. I remember Lyle walking into my room finding me sobbing into my pillow. He knew then what had happened. He let me cry into his lap while I told him how his friends all laughed at me as I was walking away from Chase after confronting him. I must have cried myself to sleep on Lyle's lap.

When I woke up, I was laying on the end of my bed with a blanket draped over me. The next morning Lyle had a bandage over his knuckles. As we walked into school he told me, "keep your head high, and don't look ashamed. If anyone gives you any shit let me know about it." When I walked into 2nd period, Chase and two of his buddies' faces were busted up. Chase having the worst of it. They claimed they were in a car wreck. I knew then that my brother had brought vengeance to them. Before Maggie and Jared came into my life, all I had was my brother Lyle; Lyle and his girlfriend Claire. Claire had become a big sister to me. She was always so sweet. So kind. But Lyle, he was my best friend, my protector, my confidant. Losing him, I lost a part of myself.

Words fall flat when trying to describe the pain I felt, the pain I still feel of losing my brother. I miss him every single day. Claire and I kept in touch the first year after his death, but it just became too painful for her I suppose, to see me, to be reminded of him every single time. I understood. I understood why she had to leave it all behind. People grieve differently. Even now, every year when I visit Lyle at the cemetery I always find a bouquet of flowers on his grave from her.

Every year I see it and I know that my brother meant a great deal to a lot of people. Knowing that brings a smile to my face. That smile is quickly overtaken by the loss of him. Ever since his death I feel as if I'll never smile again. That if I do, it's a jinx of sorts. I feel if the universe notices my happiness, it has to bring something crashing down on top of it. Happiness and I aren't that compatible

Until I found you

it seems. There have been some men that have tried coming into my life, to tear this wall of titanium down brick by brick inside me. I never budge. The more people you allow into your life, the more you allow yourself to get hurt.

The truth is I'm broken, only put back together again with the pieces left of me, no longer whole. Now I'm just shattered pieces of glass glued into an object. They'll never be able to fix me. Not completely. You can't go through that much trauma and come out untouched. Unbroken. I felt that in Micah. Part of him is broken too. Unless you've felt that type of resilience yourself, you'd never know it. He was a mask of witt and cockiness; a charming, muscular, sexual prowess. He wants people to think he's on top of the world without a care or heartache. He doesn't want people to see his vulnerable side. I saw differently.

I saw the admiration and pain behind his eyes when mentioning his mother's memory; how he planted Lilies in his backyard to remind him of her, the tattoos he wears in her memory, the passion he possessed when touching me, kissing me, this was a man of feeling. Micah is a man of passion. I couldn't deny the fact that I was beginning to feel things for him. It was terrifying. It still is to allow myself to feel something for someone, to become connected or attached to someone in this way? It was a genuine fear. That meant I was allowing myself the possibility of getting hurt. I couldn't handle that, not again. The thought of not seeing Micah again hurt even more. Jer's words telling me I should talk it out with Micah, play through my head as I drift to sleep.

Sixteen

He didn't show up to pick me up. This isn't like him. I've called him 4 times now. He's always in Mrs. Lenoir's driveway early, ready to pick me up after tutoring her son. I grab my bag and begin to walk down the street calling Claire. A few minutes later, she pulls up.

"Leyna, I'm worried. This isn't like him. Have you tried calling him again," she asks me. Worry clear in her voice.

"Yeah. Over and over. It just keeps ringing and ringing."

"Have you tried calling Jean? Maybe she knows where he is," she asks of my mother.

We both give each other a look.

,"That was a dumb question" she states quietly after a moment.

I keep calling Lyle but he's still not answering. We're driving down the road when there's a police car blocking our path. The officer is directing us to turn around when I see something up

UNTIL I found you

ahead that makes my heart stop dead in its tracks. My brother's mangled car flipped over on its top. Before I know what I'm doing I dodge out of the car and run towards the wreckage. I can hear Claire screaming. She realizes it's Lyle. I run across the yellow tape. Approaching paramedics working on a pale, lifeless Lyle. His chest thrusting violently from the defibrillator. I hear nothing other than the sound of my heart pounding and the sirens of the ambulance.

    I fling my eyes open from my sleep as I hear a police siren going past our house. I look around me disoriented for a moment before I realize the passing siren triggered one of the worst memories I have. I take long deep breaths steadying my breathing as I stare up at my ceiling for a while, telling myself I'm ok. This kind of pain is not ok. They say time heals all wounds. Five years later and the pain hasn't healed, but fuck if I wasn't cut open. I get up and take a shower to relax myself. I close my eyes and let the water spray over my head encasing me in its warmth. I take in a deep breath through my nose when I smell Jared's body wash. The scent instantly reminds me of Micah, the way he washed my back, the way he held me. The way I held him; the way his hands were on my body. I open my eyes forcing myself away from my thoughts. A few moments later Jer is knocking on the bathroom door, "Hey Leyna, there's a delivery for you."

    " What? A delivery for me," I ask dumbfounded.

    I haven't ordered anything off of Amazon lately.

"Yep. Why don't you come take a look-sees" he says and walks away.

I cut my shower short to see what in the world it is. Only wrapping myself in a towel, I walk into the kitchen when I see a bouquet of three dozen long stem white roses. I'm in awe.

"I don't know what's prettier, the roses or the vase it came in," Jared says admiring them just as much as I am.

"They're for me," I ask in disbelief.

"Read the card," Jared says, handing me the small envelope.

My name is written in an elegant font on the front of it. When I open the card it reads, "For a girl that deserves the entire garden. I'm truly sorry. Micah-" I look at the vase and instantly recognize it. It's the one from his room that I admired so much. The one that resembles a waterfall. I'm taking in the beautiful design of it with my fingers, while I look over the gorgeous bouquet of roses. No one has ever gotten me flowers before. I feel tears pulling in my eyes. My heart swells. This is the most beautiful gift I've ever gotten. I feel the tears fall over my cheeks as I wipe them away.

Jared reads the card and says, "Wow. That's a real man right there."

I smile.

"Yes it is."

Jared rubs my back up and down.

"Ok you need to call him. Like now. But don't sound too impressed otherwise he'll think three dozen gorgeous roses will fix every argument."

He chuckles.

Maggie walks in, "Oh my God! Those are so beautiful!" She says walking past me admiring the roses.

"Leyna got her first bouquet of flowers today," Jared says.

"They're beautiful, girl. Now forgive him already," she says.

"Ok I'm about to call him," I say, turning to go to my bedroom to call Micah.

"Oh no you don't! I've got a better idea," Jared says, stopping me. "

What," Maggie and I both ask in unison.

"I just had an idea. Let him sweat it out for a bit. Don't you two have a date again tonight? Just talk to him then. Let him know you're hard to get. Make him suffer a bit. Let his mind be blown when he sees you. Get all dressed up. Look like pure sex," Jared says.

I'm about to interject when Maggie speaks up, "Oh my God that's brilliant! Yeah, let him think about whatever he said. By the way, what exactly did he say? We never got to that," Jared saves me by playfully smacking her butt and saying "enough of that hair salon gossip talk, go get your nails done. You're late."

Reminding her of her nail appointment she was supposed to be at 5 minutes ago.

Maggie looks at the clock, "Shit! I've got to go. Bye!"

"Bye," Jared and I yell in unison as she rushes out the front door. "

Think I should let him sweat it out a bit," I ask Jared after a minute.

He rolls his eyes, "Yes I'm sure. Play hard to get. Guys love that shit trust me."

I get busy in the kitchen cooking me and Jer some lunch. Cooking always gets my mind off things. I've decided on fried chicken and waffles. Jared is walking in the kitchen as I'm fixing our plates.

"Mmmm lawd this smells good," he says, eyeing his favorite dish.

We're half way through our plate when my phone rings. Thinking it's Micah I run to my room to answer it in time.

"Pushover," I hear Jer calling to me as I enter my room.

I notice it isn't Micah calling me. It's my mother. Much to my own annoyance I answer it. "Mom?"

"Hey lovey. What are you doing?"

Two things are alerting me already. The first is her calling me "lovey". She only calls me that when she's feeling like being a mother to me for whatever reason. Usually it's when she wants something, and the second is her sounding sober.

"Um hey. Nothing just got done eating. You?"

I'm trying not to sound cut off or clipped but this is never good when she calls me like this.
"Listen, I've been doing a lot of thinking lately and I think it's time I go to one of those rehabs. I think it'll do me some good Leyna-"

And here we go...her annual pay for my rehab pitch.

"Mom, I can't afford that. Not the place you want to go."

UNTIL I *found you*

The thing about my mother wanting to go to rehab is, it's just a way for her to distract herself. The Palms was her main place. It was a beach vacation with psychiatrists. The patients had money. Connections. Even some A-list celebrities have been known to seek treatment there before. This wasn't about seeking treatment. This was about her seeking a new source, a new boyfriend. One with money and resources. Plus, her court date was coming up and admitting yourself into rehab looked really good in the eyes of a judge. My mother was the greatest actress to ever walk the streets of this town.

"Yet you can afford whatever you want in life," she snaps at me.

"Mom, I literally share an apartment with 2 other people just to make rent cheaper. I'm paying for myself to go through college. And, paying other bills without any help. So no, I can't afford whatever I want in life."

Jared walks in. I cover the end of my phone and mouth "Jean." He rolls his eyes. And holds his finger up while mouthing "one second." He goes into mine and Maggie's closet looking for something. I turn my attention back to my mother.

"-You don't even care do you," she says, only catching the end of her rant.

I kinda tuned her out when Jared entered the room being nosey. I look back over to Jared who is rummaging through the pockets of my jacket.

"Yes mom I do care. Otherwise I wouldn't have bailed you out."

"Don't even patronize me!-" she's going off now.

I mouth "what are you doing," to Jared.

He walks over with a peppermint. I mouth "da fuck," when he removes the mint from the wrapper and starts rubbing it near the mouth piece of my phone creating a static sound. I instantly cover my mouth keeping me from laughing.

He takes my phone from me and continues rattling the plastic into the phone and says in a mock girly voice, "krrrr I can't hear you krrrrr you're breaking up krrrrr. Poor connection krrrrr." rattling the plastic wrapper a couple of seconds before finally hanging up.

We both burst out laughing so hard I began to snort. Tears falling down my eyes, I fall onto my bed holding my stomach.

"Oh my God Jer that was amazing! You're so mean," I say through my bellows of laughter and tears, only laughing even harder because of Jared's wheezing laugh. His laugh was often funnier than his jokes; making you laugh at them anyway. Ten minutes passsed and we're both chuckling. That's the thing about Jared anytime you were around him, sadness really couldn't follow. I look at my best friend and become very thankful that he is in my life. Sure he made it a point to put things higher up on the shelf just to see me struggle to reach them. Sure he would cry laughing at me as I was forced to use the step ladder. But he was my best friend. He and Maggie were my family, the family I chose. I couldn't be more grateful for them. He notices me staring at him, "what?"

I smile at him and say, "I just love you, Jer."

He gives me a genuine smile before rolling his eyes and says, "I love you, too, red" and tugs on my hair playfully before getting up and walking to my closet.

"What are you doing? Looking for more mints?" I ask sarcastically. "Nope. Finding you a hot outfit to make this guy drool over you tonight."

Seventeen

I'm putting the finishing touches on my hair and makeup when Maggie walks in.

"Whoa! You look hot," she says walking towards me.

"Is it too much," I ask, looking at myself in the mirror.

My eyes look a brighter shade of green in contrast with the black eye liner. My hair was in a half up, half down braid. Wavy curls falling down my shoulders. My makeup looks natural apart from the subtle smokey eyes I did.

"No. You look beautiful babes. Now feel it," Jared says as he kisses the top of my head.

I smile as Maggie walks over and says, "Gorgeous."

I hug my best friends.

"Jo will be here in 30 minutes to pick us up so we need to hurry," she says as she walks to the bathroom.

"Us," I ask her, confused.

Was Micah not picking me up? Maybe he was going to ride with jo?

Until I found you

Maggie answers my thoughts by calling from the bathroom, "Jo said he's going to meet us at the restaurant."

I'm changing my outfit for the fifth time when I finally settle on the black off shoulder top that Maggie got me. It accentuates my large breasts without showing too much, along with my dark skinny jeans, and my high heeled ankle boots. I'm putting on my earrings when I hear Maggie greeting Jo at the door.

"Leyna you coming," she calls.

"Yeah," I say back, as I spray myself with my favorite scent from bath and bodyworks. Grabbing my purse we head out. We're driving for a few minutes when it dawns on me, I don't even know where we're going to eat or what we're watching after dinner. Maggie must be on the same brain wave as me because she turns to me from the front seat.

"We're going to Mario's Italian Restaurant and then we're catching the new Keanu Reeves movie."

"Nice," I replied.

I loved Mario's. It was my favorite restaurant. And who doesn't like Keanu Reeves? Overall it sounded like a good evening. As long as it wouldn't be awkward between Micah and myself. I had planned to thank him for the beautiful roses and the vase he sent me. I wondered if he'd be happy to see me? I wondered if he'd act strange over it all. I was letting my mind wander with all these questions that I didn't even notice we pulled into the restaurant. Jo opens Maggie's door for her, lending his hand to help her out. I think that's very chivalrous of him. It makes me admire him more.

I haven't told Maggie yet, but I believe Jo may be a keeper. I don't get any creepy or asshole vibes from this one like I do every other guy she goes out with. I look around the parking lot for Micah's Jeep. I don't see it. Maybe he's running late. The waiter has seated us and has taken our drink orders when I see Jo texting on his phone. Maggie starts conversating. I tune her out mostly. Giving a nod here and there. I notice Jo has a look on his face as he's texting someone.

I'm about to ask him if everything is ok when he clears his throat and says almost nervously, "Um, so it appears Micah isn't coming tonight."

Maggie and I both share the same angered expression on our faces. Jo looking back and forth between us adds, "I'm not sure why. He just said he isn't coming," and holds his hands up slightly as if he was surrendering himself.

"Um wow ok," Maggie says. Annoyance in her tone.

"Yeah I- I'm sorry. I'm not sure-" Jo begins when I cut him off.

"It's ok Jo. Really."

He looks a bit relieved.

"Honestly it's totally fine. I'm sure he had his reasons," I say.

Jo opens his mouth to say something.

"Reasons that include being a dick. Like who ditches people like that? Huh? Dicks do! Who stands people up? That's so- so- you know what? He's a dick. Not a little one either. A big one."

Until I found you

Poor Jo is looking at me, mouth still open when my rant continues.

"You'd think after the guy sent me roses he'd at least show up for our date but oh no. No, he has to be an asshole and ditch our date? What, because I didn't immediately run into his arms and thank him repeatedly for sending me flowers? Oh, he probably expected me to run in his arms and suck his-" the realization of what I was about to say and how loudly I was saying it, dawns on me.

I shut my mouth and looked at Maggie and then back to Jo. Jo looks like he just witnessed a bear attack and Maggie is covering her mouth with her napkin. More than likely concealing her smile and resisting a laugh. I can feel my cheeks flushing.

"Wow ok. This has been fun but ya know I think I'm going to go, so," I say standing up from our booth.

"Leyna you don't have to go. Plus, we drove you here. Come on sit down. Join us, we can still have a fun night. The three of us. Right?"

She turns to look at Jo who is already nodding his head yes. Poor guy would probably say yes to anything Maggie wanted.

"No, it's fine guys really. You two enjoy your night. I'm calling a cab." I say laying a $5 down for the coke I ordered.

"You're really going home," Maggie asks, disappointed.

Before heading out the door I turn and reply, "Nope!"

Eighteen

I can hardly believe myself what I'm doing. I'm not like this. I'm not that clingy girl that demands answers. But, fuck if I'm not angry! The audacity of this asshole! Sends me beautiful flowers and a vase that he made himself, only to stand me up and embarrass me like that in front of people? He's probably had himself a good laugh at my expense. I'm going to give this asshole a piece of my mind! I pay the cab driver and remind myself to thank Jo later for texting me Micah's address.

I would have never remembered how to get back here on my own. I'm walking up his stairs when I hear music coming from the house. I hadn't thought about other people being here. An eye for an eye. He embarrassed me in front of my friends, well Maggie. I guess Jo now too. So it's only right that I do it to him in front of his friends. I take a deep breath and knock on his door. More like pounding. I hear the music being paused from the other room. Moments later Micah answers the door sweaty and shirtless in grey workout pants that's hanging dangerously low on his hips. Showing that perfect v

UNTIL I found you

line that I love so much. God, he's beautiful. I'm getting distracted. He looks shocked seeing me here but quickly recovers.

"Hey firecracker," he says with a smug smile.

"You," I say, pushing him back with my finger on his chest. "You want a firecracker? Well, you're about to get a fucking Fourth of July star spangled banner."

"Well come on in," he says smiling at me as he shuts the door behind me.

"What the hell was that? You stood me up! What the hell is wrong with you? You think you can just humiliate me like that and think I wouldn't have anything to say about it? You send me beautiful flowers and include that vase you made which shows me you put a lot of thought into it, only to ditch me later on? What the fuck was that? You think it's funny to play with my emotions? You get a real kick out of that shit?"

I'm out of breath at this point. I could literally slap him, I'm so mad. He's just staring at me. Looking me up and down. His eyes trail down from my neck to my hips before landing on my heeled boots. Making him smile slightly.

"Well," I ask exasperatedly, with my hands on my hips.

He catches me off guard by snaking his arm around my waist, pulling me closer to him. I resist him at first, pushing myself away from him. He tightens his arm around my waist not allowing me to budge. He lowers his head down closer to my face. Using his other hand to gently stroke my cheek.

"I'm sorry," he says.

I look into those beautiful eyes of his before looking away from them.

"That was a real asshole thing to do," I say quietly.

He places his fingers under my chin forcing me to look at him.

"I know. I didn't mean to embarrass you. I just honestly thought you weren't going to show. I didn't hear from you so I thought I blew it. I have a temper, a bad one. Sometimes I act before I think and it gets the best of me."

I look at him in a sarcastic shocked expression as I say, "You don't say?"

He chuckles.

"I am sorry," he says, placing his forehead on mine. "You look incredible," he says, looking me up and down. "Incredibly sexy," he adds, before slowly bringing his face closer to mine. My breathing hitches as he barely brushes his lips over mine before pulling back some. I move my face closer to his and he pulls back further in a cat and mouse game.

"Stop teasing me," I say to him.

He moves his face closer to mine as he skims my lips with his just barely before pulling away again.

"What are you doing," I ask, angry.

He smiles, "Now you get a taste of what it's like waiting eagerly for something. I waited for a call or text from you all day. Every time my phone would go off I thought it was you, only to realize it wasn't. Do you know how much torture that was for me?"

"You're such an asshole," I say as I attempt to push away from him again.

Until I found you

I'm angry. Angry and wanting him badly. The two emotions are battling each other. I want to slap him and kiss him all at the same time. He smiles seductively as his fingers glide down my neck slowly causing goosebumps to spread over my body.

"It's true I am."

He replies as he cups one of my breasts in his large palm before gently massaging it.

"I'm mad at you," I say with less conviction than I intended.

He's weakening my resolve and he knows it.

"And I'm mad at you," he replies as he slides his hand down my waist. "But, none of that matters right now because of the way you look, so beautiful even when you're so angry."

He moves his hand to my face.

"Did you dress like this for me," he asks.

I look away from his piercing blue eyes and look down at his soft, full lips.

"Yes," I admit.

He takes me by surprise when he pulls me closer into him and molds his lips to mine. I can't ignore the relief I feel from his touch. It's incredible. Our kiss becomes more passionate when I wrap my fingers through his hair, tugging gently. He parts my mouth with his tongue, caressing mine with his. He pulls me closer to him as I place my hand on his bare chest trailing down slowly to his lower abdomen. I slip my fingers under the waistband of his pants when he breaks our kiss then.

His hand still cupping my face he says almost panting, "I wouldn't do that if I were you. I won't be able to control myself with you. Especially you looking like this."

His eyes are focused on mine with such intensity I look down at his muscular chest and say softly, "Maybe I don't want you to control yourself."

He rubs my lips with his thumb before placing his fingers under my chin forcing me to look at him once more.

"What do you want, Leyna?"

His eyes are still searching mine. My heart quickens.

"I want you," I admit. "Do you want me?" I ask, almost a whisper.

My heart is pounding. He answers me by dropping his hands from my face and grabs me by my ass, lifting me onto his torso. My legs instinctively wrap around him as he carries me. Us like this instantly reminds me of our first kiss and when he brought me to ecstasy before. How much I wanted him then. How much I desperately want him now. I place one hand on the back of his neck while the other tugs his hair as I kiss his neck. He moans slightly in response as I trail my tongue up his neck, licking the salt from him. He squeezes my ass harder making me let out a whimper of excitement.

I can feel his large, hard cock brush against me. The anticipation of having him inside of me is building. I want him, need him. He collapses us on top of his bed as he begins kissing my neck, sucking and biting as he pulls my hair. He rocks his hips into me in a teasing motion. My hips buck off the bed involuntarily into his hard cock. He growls, moving his mouth back to my lips before grabbing the bottom of my top and pulling it over my head. He unhooked my bra then and began kneading my full breasts with his large hands. Palming the undersides

UNTIL I found you

of my breasts, I let out a small moan as his hot mouth found my nipples.

He begins sucking and flicking his tongue across me. I roll my head back at the incredible feeling. He connects his mouth to mine once more as he moves his hands from my breasts to my stomach as he begins unbuttoning my jeans. I raise my hips off the bed to assist him in taking them off. Once I'm completely naked, he trails slow kisses up my leg. He is nibbling as he reaches my inner thigh. My hips buck off the mattress involuntarily as he gets closer to my clit. I bite down on my lip as he swirls his tongue across my hip bone and just under my navel.

He begins teasingly kissing me down towards my sex. I can't take much more.

"Micah" I say, pleading with him.

Suddenly he presses his tongue to my clit. I arch my back and my head as my toes dig into the mattress. I cover my mouth but his hand pulls mine away as he looks up at me.

"I want to hear you baby. I want to hear what I do to you," he whispers before pressing his tongue to me again.

His tongue is hot, so wet as he swirls it around and around me. Flicking. Sucking. I can feel myself coming to the edge when he pulls away. I look down at him between my legs, as he grabs my hand and places it on his large, hard cock.

"This is what you do to me," he says, before connecting our mouths.

I pull his pants down as he grabs a foil packet out of his night stand. He rips the packet open with his teeth before sliding the condom on. The way his hand is holding his large, hard cock makes me tremble slightly in anticipation. Our eyes meet and I'm breathing heavily. He gently inserts a finger into me as I moan from the pleasure.

"You're so wet for me baby," he coos as he spreads my legs further apart.

He grabs the side of my hip as he begins sliding his tip into me before pulling out and pushing back in only half way several times. Slowly stretching me around him. The feeling is exquisite. I want more. I need more.

"Micah, please," I beg.

He answers me by pressing into me all at once, filling me completely. I gasp and we both let out a moan.

"Fuck, baby. You're so damn tight. So warm," he says, breathing into my neck.

He rolls his hips into me at a steady pace. The feeling is incredible. Painful but heavenly all the same. I claw down his back slightly and he growls into my neck. I press my hands to his lower back beckoning him to increase his pace, he obliges me by doing so. I bite down on my lip and screw my eyes shut. It's a good kind of pain. After a few moments of this, I've begun to fit around him. The feeling is euphoric. He places one of his arms up under my back holding me by the back of my neck with his hand while pushing into me. Deeper. Slower; more intimate than before. He begins kissing me passionately.

"Open your eyes baby. Look at me," he says in a low, raspy voice.

I look into his beautiful piercing blue eyes and the way he's furrowing his brows as he fills me completely. The feeling of him holding me this way as he makes love to me it's all it takes. I feel myself coming over the edge.

"Cum for me baby. Cum," he says, thrusting into me at a faster pace.

The feeling is like an explosion, the pleasure ripping all throughout me. I come around him as I press my nails into his back, surely to leave marks. I lean my head up towards him, riding out my euphoric high. He supports my head up with his hand still cupping me behind my neck. He brings his mouth to mine, as he swallows my moans of ecstasy.

"Fuck," he mouths into me fiercely. "Baby, I'm going to cum."

I nod my head vigorously as he stiffens spilling himself into the condom. I go limp beneath him. Still supporting my head with his hand, he brings our faces closer. Kissing me softly, tenderly. He lays my head gently down onto the bed. Caressing the side of my face with his thumb. Our chests are heaving, our breathing in perfect sync with each other. After a few moments, he slowly pulls out of me. I wince slightly from the emptiness. He pulls the condom off and sits it on the floor as he pulls me to lay on his chest, rubbing softly on my back.

"Are you ok," he asks me.

I smile at his being concerned for me. I answer him by kissing his lips and nuzzling my face into his chest. He pulls me closer to him as he kisses my forehead. We're both hot, sweaty and out of breath. We lay there for a while enjoying the feeling of being in each other's arms like this. Micah is playing in my hair, gently stroking it. The feeling is so relaxing. I catch myself drifting off and try to sit up.

"What's wrong," he asks.

"I was falling asleep."

He smiles and gently grabs my wrist, pulling me to lay back down on him. We're quiet for a few minutes when Micah clears his throat.

"If you want, you could sleep here."

I feel him tense a little when I turn my head up at him. He looks down at me with those beautiful blue eyes waiting for my reply.

"Ok," I say.

He smiles, "So you're staying?"

I lay my head back onto his chest and smile to myself.

"It appears that way," I say.

He starts playing in my hair again.

"Good. I thought you were going to say no," he says after a moment. "I probably would have. But you caught me at a moment." After a minute I add, "to be honest, I've never stayed the night with a guy before. Well besides Jared but that's different for obvious reasons."

I can feel him chuckle beneath me, "ya know I heard about that."

I playfully smack his chest. He laughs. I'm about to doze off.

"I guess if we're being honest, I've never let a girl stay overnight with me before either."

"Why is that," I ask.

He takes a few moments before answering, "I'm not really sure. But I like how it feels so far. With you."

Butterflies swarm my stomach at his words. The thought that I'm the only girl he's ever let spend the night with him before, warms my heart.

Until I found you

After a moment he adds, "You're special to Me, Leyna," before planting a kiss on the top of my head as he pulls me closer to him intertwining our legs.

Nineteen

I'm sleeping peacefully in Micah's arms when a cell phone ringing wakes me up. At first I think it's my own when I realize the tone is different. Plus it's still in my purse in the living room. I go to wake Micah who's laying on his side with his arms wrapped securely around me, cuddling me like I'm his favorite teddy bear. Seeing him holding me like this in his sleep instantly makes me smile. I softly rub up and down his large arm trying to wake him.

"Micah," I call softly.

He stirs in his sleep pulling me closer to him.

"Micah" I say softly again, rubbing his arm.

He wakes, "are you ok?"

He asks, confused and disoriented.

"Yeah I'm ok. But, someone is calling you."

He let's go of me with only one of his arms to reach for his phone. By the time he does, the call goes to voicemail. I look at the time, it's 2:38am. Who would be calling him this late at night? My mind immediately goes to Jo. Jo and Maggie. My paranoid mind starts to run. Is everything ok? Did they make it home safe? Did they get in a wreck? I get up from the bed. "Where are you going? Is something wrong," Micah asks.

"Nothing's wrong. Just checking in with Maggie. Letting her know I won't be home tonight."

I walk downstairs into the living room and find my purse lying on the floor where I dropped it. Visions of our first time just a few hours ago replay in my head. The way he touched me. The way I touched him. The passion. The fire. My phone vibrating breaks me from my thoughts. Almost causing me to drop it. I look to see both Maggie and Jared have messaged me multiple times. I reply to our group chat letting them both know that I'm fine and with Micah tonight and that I wouldn't be back home until tomorrow. Adding that I'd give them all the details when I got home. Just then I receive a text from Jean.

"Call me."

I go to dial her number when I become startled.

"Is everything ok," Micah asks from behind me.

I jump slightly. We both begin to chuckle from him scaring me.

"Yeah it's just dark in here and I didn't hear you coming. Maggie and Jer have been blowing up my phone wondering if I'm ok. I guess it's a good thing that call woke me up otherwise I wouldn't have woken up long enough to tell them I was staying over. By the way, who calls this late at night? Whoever it was better have had a hell of an excuse," I joke.

Micah is about to reply when suddenly my phone begins to ring. I look down to see it's Jean calling me. I don't want Micah knowing about my mother. At least, not yet. I decline it nervously.

"Who was that," He asks, suspiciously.

"Um..."

Before I can reply, it rings again. Jean is giving me no other option at this point, I answer it. "Mom?"

"Leyna," she says through her tears. I instantly become alarmed. "Mom? What happened? What's going on," I step away from Micah's gaze. My heart begins to race. Jean never cries. Not like this.

"I need you to come pick me up. It's John. We got into a fight and-." She begins to sob. "I tried leaving and he won't let me. I can't do this anymore-" Her sobs become heavier. She's unable to finish speaking.

"Did he touch you?"

She sniffles. My blood begins to boil.

"I'm calling the police-" my mother cuts me off.

"No! No! Don't! Do not involve the cops. Trust me. Just come get me Leyna. Please."

She sobs into the phone. "Go into a room and lock the door. I'm coming to get you! Text me where you are."

I hear yelling and glass breaking in the background before the call ends. I quickly head into Micah's bedroom to get dressed. He's hot on my trail.

"What's going on," he asks.

"Everything's fine. I've just got to go," I say, already throwing on my bra and shirt.

"That didn't sound like it was fine. What's going on, Leyna?"

UNTIL I
found you

I ignore his question, throwing my jeans and heels on. I go to walk out of his room when he stops me in the doorway. I look up at him. My temper flaring.

"Move," I say, giving him a warning glare.

"Tell me what's going on," he demands.

I shove past him. Just then the realization hits that I took a cab here. Fuck! I'm already calling for an Uber when he grabs my elbow turning me towards him.

"You're not leaving until you tell me what's going on. Whatever the situation is, it sounds dangerous," he says, furrowing his brows at me.

I pull my elbow away from him.

"This has nothing to do with you and I suggest you stay out of it."

I go to walk away but he stops me again.

"If it involves you getting hurt then it has everything to do with me. You're not walking into something dangerous," he says, containing his anger.

I push past him.

"This is none of your fucking business," I say as I walk out the door.

My Uber driver won't be here for another 20 minutes. I'm about to go into panic mode when suddenly Micah's Jeep blinks. The car doors unlocking. I look behind me to see he's dressed and coming down the flight of stairs in a hurry.

"Whatever is going on, you won't make it to your mom in time," he says flatly, before getting in and starting the engine.

I hurry around and get in. I give Micah the address where my mom is and pray whatever happened that she's ok. I've never liked John. I've never liked any of her boyfriends. But John gave me the worst vibes of them all. I swear if that son of a bitch hurt my mom… Tears begin to pull at my eyes at the thought.

"Hey," Micah says, placing a calming hand on my thigh. "It's going to be ok."

He says looking over to me. His act of kindness and understanding, even after I was so cold to him causes tears to overflow. I quickly look away from him and wipe the tears so he doesn't see them. I refuse to cry in front of him. I rein my tears back in as we spend the rest of the drive in silence. Micah's hand on my leg the whole time, comforting me. When we pull up to John's house I see his truck is gone. Then I notice the tire marks in the yard and the front door wide open, symbolizing he left in a hurry. Panic sets in.

"Mom?!"

I jump out of the car. I run into the house and see it's a mess of scattered debris. It looks like a hurricane came through. Broken glass is scattered across the floor. A coffee table is flipped over on its side. There are obvious signs of a struggle. I see droplets of blood on the floor. Micah notices it too. Suddenly, I hear a clicking sound. I look down to see that Micah has loaded a bullet into the chamber of a handgun. "Leyna, get behind me" he says, wrapping his strong arm around my waist as he pulls me behind him. He's pointing the gun straight out in front of him. By the way he's holding the gun so precisely and with such confidence, I can tell he's well trained. Just then I hear a whimper coming from the bathroom. I run around Micah; his hand grabbing my wrist to stop me but I pull away from his grip. I walk in to see Jean laying on the bathroom floor, her face busted up and bleeding.

"Mom!"

I rush to her side. Her lip and cheek is busted. Her eyes swollen. Bruises are already forming on her face and arms. I notice blood on the floor coming from her head. She has a cut that's bleeding at an alarming rate.

"Oh my God," I exclaim.

I try lifting her, but can't. Micah gently pushes me back. Taking Jean in his arms, cradling her to his chest as he lifts her off the floor.

"We're taking her to the hospital," he says, already running towards the car with her. "Start the car,' he orders, placing her in his back seat. I start the car and jump in the back with her. Trying to keep her awake.

"Mom," I say through my tears. "Mom, can you hear me? Hey wake up. Please wake up," I say, pleading.

Memories of my mother being passed out on our kitchen floor from her binge of pills the night before, come flooding in. Lyle hovered over her, shaking her shoulders relentlessly as he cried, begging for her to wake up.

"Mom, wake up! Get up! Don't do this to us! Get up mom! Leyna, call 911!"

I've never seen Lyle so scared. He thought she was already gone. She almost was. As I look at my mother's current state, I can't help but wonder how long until she's really gone this time? How many close calls will she have before I'm all alone? I look up to see Micah's expression through the mirror. He's looking at me as though I'm wounded. He's seen it now. He's seen what I wish he never would. Now it's only a matter of time before he walks out of my life. People tend to not want messes in their life. I was the biggest mess I've ever seen. Who could blame him? Minutes later we make it to the ER.

"We need help," Micah shouts, carrying Jean.

A few nurses come running over with a gurnee. Micah gently lays her down onto it. The nurses start asking me questions. I give them all the answers I know. I watched them work on my mom before they shut me out of the room. Medically, I know she'll be okay. But I can't help but feel that my mother's terrible decisions will one day leave me an orphan.

Twenty

We're sitting in the waiting room. Micah is rubbing my back to comfort me. He's already tried getting me to eat and drink something, but I can't. I can't wrap my mind around why he is even here. Why is he still here? If he were with any other girl, any normal girl, he wouldn't be dealing with this. This isn't fair to him. I took my anger out on him earlier and he's still here for me. He was there for a complete stranger he never knew, just because he knew she was my mom. I look up at him, finding he is already looking at me. Gauging my state of mind I suppose. He then reaches over and gently kisses my temple before saying,

"You are so strong, you know that," In a tone that resembles admiration.

I look at him. I see it in his eyes. A mixture of deeper understanding, sympathy and realization of why I am the way I am. I blink back tears and stand up. Walking away from him. He follows. I turn to face him, "I'm not strong. I'm far from it. I'm a mess, Micah. My life is a mess. And you don't need that kind of chaos in your life. You don't need me in your-" I'm cut off when he cups both sides of my face with his hands.

"Don't," he says sternly.

I look away from his piercing gaze.

"Look at me," he commands.

I can't.

"Leyna, look at me," he says softer.

I blink back my tears and look at him.

"Don't pull away from me. Don't do that. Don't take it upon yourself to say what I can and can not handle. I'm a man. I can handle this."

Suddenly I'm terrified. He wants to be here with me? Through this? Why on earth would he want to deal with this? I shake my head. He'll leave. He'll be the one to leave, to break my heart. He won't want to deal with this. He doesn't know how broken I am. No.

"I can't do this. I can't let you-" I say cutting myself off.

I'm attempting to walk away from him but he has my face in his hands still not allowing me to leave his side.

"Stop this. Don't walk away from me," he says, sternly.

"You think I can't handle this?"

I push away from him.

"Why would you," I exclaim to him. "Why would you want that? Is your life that boring that you need all of this chaos from mine? You already got what you wanted from me. So enough with the charades-" He cuts me off.

"Really? Fucking Really? You assume sex is all I wanted from you? All I'm looking for from you?

Tell me, if that's all I wanted then why am I standing here with you?"

I look away from him trying to regain my composure. I will not cry in front of him.

"Hmm? Answer me that since you apparently know everything. I'm standing here with you because I care about you. And because I want to be here for you."

"Why," I ask, incredulously.

"I can't explain it really. And you'll probably think I'm full of shit, but I feel drawn to you. You're unlike any other girl I've ever met. You're so incredibly stubborn. You have this fire in you that I admire so much. Even though you haven't told me, I can tell you've been through a lot. You're used to going through all of it by yourself. That's why you're so guarded. You don't think someone is capable of being there for you without taking something from you in return or leaving you out to dry. But you're wrong, I want to be here for you. I feel this pull towards you. A connection I've never felt before. You feel it too. That's why you're scared."

He's right. "I'm not scared," I say defensively.

"Prove it then," he says, extending his hand.

I look up at him confused.

"Take a leap of faith. Let me be here for you. Have faith that I can handle it. Have faith that someone can genuinely care about you for all the right reasons."

I look at him for a moment before looking down at his large open hand in front of me. I take a deep breath. Here's to falling into oblivion. I take his hand in mine before he brings me in for a close hug.

His big arms wrap around me. The comfort of his embrace is something I can hardly describe in words. It's like him holding me like this, feels like somehow everything will be ok. Like some of the weight has been lifted. Like some of the void is being filled. I begin to tear up with emotions. Just then the nurse walks up. Giving us an update on Jean's condition. She'll make a full recovery. Besides a fractured rib, the laceration on her head was the worst of her injuries. The nurse asked if I wanted to involve the police in it since clearly this was a domestic violence case. With my mother not yet conscious, it was my call to make. The decision wasn't hard. An officer came to take my statement. Collecting information for the case. I wasn't surprised to learn that John had a long history of domestic violence charges, among other things. A little while later Jean wakes up. I stop in front of her door before walking in.

I turn to Micah, "Let me go first," I say.

He gives me a small smile, "I'll be here if you need me" he says, before kissing the top of my head.

I take a deep breath and walk in to see my mother fully up and alert. She looks at me, rage takes over her face. "Are you fucking stupid? Why did you involve the fucking cops," she shouts at me.

I step back, surprised by her outburst at me.

"I told you not to involve the police, you idiot! Why would you do that," she shouts.

I look at her bewildered before saying, "Why did I involve the cops? Really? Look at you! Look where you're at! You're in the emergency room because your piece of shit boyfriend beat you! And you're mad at me? That son of a bitch deserves to be in jail for what he did to you! What is wrong with me? What is wrong with you?" I say, almost out of breath.

"All of this could have been smoothed over. But no, you had to go and involve the fucking cops. You always go and fuck everything up for me! Just like you're fucking father. Not good for a thing."

I blink back my tears. She looks at me and starts laughing. "Oh what? You're going to cry now? Poor little Leyna," she says sneering.

I compose myself before saying, "You know, I'm honestly relieved my brother is in a better place right now. He doesn't have to see how far you've fallen. He'd be sick to see you like this" I say through my teeth.

She's taken aback. Good.

She composes herself before saying, "Clearly I lost the better of my children. Perhaps the universe chose the wrong one to take."

A sharp pain goes through my chest nearly knocking me backward. I turn around to leave the room when Micah appears in the door taking my hand.

Pointing a finger at Jean he says with venom laced in his words, "I don't know what you're fucking problem is, you miserable bitch, but you don't deserve this woman."

Twenty-one

We're pulling up in my driveway when the sun is coming up. At least a new day is beginning. "Can I come in," he asks, giving me a small smile.

"Sure. I'll cook us some breakfast before you leave."

I offer. He tries to decline but I insist. The least I can do is feed the poor guy after the night we've had. I turn the coffee pot on, eagerly awaiting the smell of it's aroma.

"Thank God you're a coffee drinker. I think I'll need half the pot just to drive back home."

He teases.

"You could crash here if you want. You could sleep with me in my bed. But Maggie is in there sleeping too. So if you'd rather, the couch," I offer shyly.

He gives me a sleepy smile, "Just might take you up on that offer as long as you sleep next to me."

Until I found you

I smile back at him. Suddenly I become chilly.

"I'll be right back. I'm going to grab my hoodie," I say to Micah who sits on the couch looking like he's fighting sleep already.

Poor guy. I quietly open the bedroom door so as not to wake Maggie when I'm greeted with a sight I'll never get out of my head. A naked Maggie on top of Jo swirling her hips around him. "Oh my God!"

I yell covering my eyes. Maggie begins to screech.

"Leyna! Get out," she screams.

With my eyes still covered I try to turn to leave out the door when I trip over some shoes and fall onto the floor. I hurriedly crawl out of our room. Reaching up, I slam the door behind me. I look up to see Micah standing over me. Amusement all over his face. He's trying his hardest not to laugh at me.

"Um. I wouldn't go in there," I say, nonchalantly, shaking my head back and forth.

"They're having sex in there," Micah guesses.

"Yep," I draw the word out.

"Today just isn't your day is it," he asks, fighting a laugh.

"Nope," I saw slowly drawing that word out too.

Micah laughs. Hard.

Suddenly I hear Jo yell, "Sorry Leyna!"

"She was supposed to be at Micah's house," I hear Maggie say annoyingly.

Micah bends down helping me off the floor.

"How about we ditch this place and go to my house," he asks.

"Sounds like a plan," I replied, heading to the dryer to get a change of clothes instead of getting some from my room.

Lord knows I don't want to relive that horrifying moment again. I place the clothes into my bag before we head out. We stop at McDonalds on the way to Micah's to order coffee and breakfast. Since my plans of cooking breakfast was- um, interrupted.

By the time we pull into his driveway, we've both eaten. After opening the door he takes my hand in his, leading us towards his bathroom.

"Where are we going," I ask him.

"Shower," he says, simply. "It'll relax you baby" he adds.

He turns the hot water on and steam quickly begins to rise. He takes his shirt off in a quick motion before walking over to me and grabbing the hem of my top before slowly pulling it over my head. I keep my eyes fixed on him as he removes my bra and unzips my pants. Tugging them slowly down my legs before removing my shoes. Once I'm fully naked he looks me over and places a soft kiss to my lips. I run my small hands down his chest until my fingers reach the waistband of his pants. I tug them down his legs and stare at the beautiful man before me. He takes my hand as we step into the shower. Micah pulls me into his chest.

He was right; this is relaxing. My head is on his chest. His arms are wrapped tightly around me, while the hot water falls onto my tense shoulders, easing them. I let out a breath I didn't realize I was holding. I begin to relax feeling at peace.

After a few minutes of him holding me I say, "Hand me the shampoo, please."

He turns to the caddy and grabs it. After removing my braid from my hair, I hold my hand out for him to give it to me but he shakes his head. I tilt my head to the side giving him a puzzled look.

"Wet your hair," he commands, smiling.

I roll my eyes but lay my head back letting the water drench my hair. His fingers trail down my neck. Sending goosebumps up my legs and arms. Once my hair is wet, he takes a quarter size amount in his hand and starts running it through my hair. Massaging my scalp as he does it. I close my eyes.

"Mmmmm" is all I can say.

It feels heavenly. He chuckles.

"Feels good?"

"Like you have to ask" I replied.

I open my eyes to see he's smiling at me sweetly.

He's still massaging my scalp when I say, "ok hand me some," with my hand held out.

He looks confused.

"Just hand me it, Eason."

"Yes, Ma'am," he responds, smirking.

Once I have some in my hand I begin washing his hair. Well, I try to wash his hair. This is a bit difficult for me. I'm having to stand on my tippy toes to get to the top of his head. He chuckles and bends his knees making it easier for me to reach him.

"Shorty," he says, biting back a smile.

I smack him on the butt and say, "watch it Mister."

He responds by biting his lip playfully and grabbing handfuls of my ass, giving them a light squeeze.

I'm putting Micah's hair into a soap Mohawk when He begins to chuckle, "having fun?"

I giggle, "actually I am."

He tries doing the same with my hair, but it ends up falling. We both start laughing as he decides to go with a soap mustache on my lips.

I wiggle my eyebrows at him and say in a deep voice, "Hey baby! What's shakin?"

He throws his head back in laughter, "I'd still do you. You'd just have to be silent during sex." Now it's my turn to laugh. He chuckles along with me, putting his hands on either side of my face wiping away the soap from my lips with his thumbs.

"I do have to admit I prefer you like this though. So beautiful," he coos, planting a sweet kiss to my lips.

After we rinse our hair, he grabs the body wash and loofah before spinning me around, placing my long hair over my shoulder so he can wash my back. He begins at the back of my neck working into my shoulders and down my spine. Once he reaches the small of my back he bends down. I look down at him as he washes my calves, bringing the loofah slowly up the back of my legs. He rubs across my ass and back up to my shoulders when he plants kisses on my neck. I tremble slightly from his touch. I can feel him smile against my neck.

"I love how your body responds to me," he coos in my ear.

I turn around and grab the loofah from him. Slowly moving it across his chest, while I begin backing him up against the shower tile. Micah's eyes never leave mine. I lower the loofah down his chest and begin slowly dragging it across his V line. He tenses under me. Becoming a statue of stone. His chest begins to rise and fall at a quicker pace. He takes the hand I had placed on his shoulder and brings it to his length.

"That's what you do to me," he says in a husky voice.

He's staring down at me, as I place my hand around his hard flesh, pumping him lightly. "Fuck," he whispers as he rolls his head back onto the shower tile before looking back down at me with hungry eyes.

Pressure builds in between my legs.

I look up at him, batting my lashes as I say to him, "I want you now."

He replies by cupping both sides of my face with his hands, before invading my mouth with his delicious tongue. He lifts me onto his torso as my legs wrap around him. He is what I need. I need this distraction. I need him, and he knows it. He twirls us around where I'm against the shower tile now. My arms wrap around his shoulders and cup the back of his neck as he begins licking and sucking my neck. Pressing me further into the shower wall. I moan as the tip of his cock teases my opening.

"Micah," I plead.

Grabbing a fistful of my hair, he hisses in my ear, "I'm going to fuck you so hard that you forget everything else," before slamming into me.

Thrusting deep. I screw my eyes shut and let out a pleasurable scream.

"That's it baby. I want to hear you scream my name," he says darkly as he thrusts into me, filling all of me.

I tighten my grip around his shoulders and neck. He quickened his pace. Thrusting faster, deeper. He wraps his forearm across my chest grabbing one of my breasts with his hand, kneading it roughly. He begins kissing me with a feverish fury. He pulls away from our kiss. Staring at me with His piercing blue eyes, He says through clenched jaws, "You're mine."

I roll my head back onto the tile wall moaning.

"Do you understand me? You're all mine, Leyna" he says staring at me with furrowed brows as he bites his lower lip.

Fuck, he's so hot.

"Say it," he commands, still thrusting into me.

"I'm yours, Micah," I say through euphoric cries.

The way he's claiming me against the shower wall is the hottest thing I've ever seen. I graze my nails up his back. Our tongues hot and wet, lathering each other in a deep passionate kiss.

He pulls away saying, "Fuck baby. You're so fucking tight around my cock."

His dirty words elicited a whimper from me. I close my eyes and revel in the feeling of him thrusting into me.

"Look at me baby," he says in a low husky voice.

Until I
found you

I open my eyes and stare into him.

"Cum for me baby. Let me see what I do to you. What only I can do to you."

He grabs the side of my neck and adds just enough pressure that it sends me over the edge. I begin to orgasm all around him. My own sounds of pleasure, amplifying my orgasm. I call out his name like a prayer through it. We never break eye contact.

He furrows his brows and bites down on his lower lip before tugging a fistful of my hair and yelling, "oh fuck baby!" as he hurriedly pulls out of me and releases onto the shower floor.

He buries his face into my neck. Our chests are heaving up and down at a dangerously fast pace. I begin rubbing his head in soothing motions. His hot breath is blowing on my neck. We stay like this for a few moments, steadying our breathing. After a minute of this, he removes his face out of my neck before planting soft, sweet kisses to my lips and gently sets my feet down on the floor. I wobble a bit and he catches my elbow steadying me.

"Are you ok," he asks.

"Yeah," I say breathlessly, "I'm just exhausted now," I say, placing my forehead onto his chest. He kisses the top of my head and says out of breath, "that makes both of us."

Once we've cleaned ourselves, Micah helps me out of the shower and hands me a towel to dry off.

"You wouldn't happen to have a spare toothbrush would you," I ask him.

He gives me a half smile before saying, "actually I think I do."

He reaches in one of the cabinets and pulls out a travel toothbrush still in its package.

"Thank you" I say, taking it from him.

Once we've brushed our teeth we walk into the bedroom to get dressed. I go to grab the clothes out of my bag when he stops me.

"I've already got you something to sleep in," and hands me a white t-shirt of his and a pair of his boxers.

"Thank you," I say as I take them from him.

I place his shirt up to my face. They smell heavenly, just like Micah. I can hardly describe the scent of him, it's almost a dark amber smell with a mixture of a delicious musk, a scent I could never get tired of. I go to put them on when I notice he's staring at me. Embarrassed he may have caught me enjoying the scent of him.

I ask sheepishly, "what?"

He responds, "I want to see you put them on."

I smile as I start with his t-shirt first draping it over my head and letting it fall down past my breasts and hips. He licks his lips at me. He always makes me feel so desirable, so beautiful. I go to put his boxers on but they cling to my hips and ass. Tightly. Way too tightly. I give him a look and say, "not working" before removing them.

He chuckles and says mischievously, "I was kind of hoping you wouldn't wear underwear anyway baby."

Until I Found You

Twenty-two

After last night, and this morning's events we decided to take a nap. Micah looks like pure sex in nothing but his boxers. The way the material clings to his thighs and hips is very seductive. The way the band of his boxers hang just below his sinful V line makes me stare, not caring if I'm being subtle or not. He peels the comforter back, climbing into bed, he reaches his hand out to me. I take it and he pulls me into his warm chest, encasing us in the comforter. I entangle my legs in his. He pulls me closer to him.

Wrapping his arms around me, "This feels amazing. You feel amazing," he says playing in my hair.

"Mmmm hmmm," I agree with him.

He chuckles.

"Tired," he asks.

I look up at him, "aren't you?"

"Exhausted," he admits.

He places his hand on my back rubbing in soft caresses. I begin to drift off to sleep when he kisses my lips softly.

"Sweet dreams, beautiful."

With my eyes still closed, I kiss him back and say, "goodnight baby."

Realizing I just called him baby. I fling my eyes open and look at him. He's already staring down at me smiling.

My cheeks must be blushing some because he rubs them and says, "ya know, I've never been into the pet names before. But with you? I love it. Baby." he puts emphasis on the last word.

I shake my head and hide my face into his chest. He chuckles and kisses the top of my head before we both drift off to sleep. I wake up to my hair being played with. I'm still in a groggy sleep when I open one eye to look up at Micah who's already smiling down at me and twirling the ends of my red hair in his fingers.

"Good morning," he says in a sexy sleepy voice.

I look at the clock. It reads 1:38pm. I gruff and place my face back into Micah's chest.

"We've barely had 4 hours of sleep. You better have coffee."

I can feel Micah's chest move with his laughter.

"Yeah babe, I've got coffee."

I look up at him and smile.

"This is when it would have been great for your fridge to have groceries in it. I would have cooked you lunch".

He raises his eyebrow playfully, "is that so?"

"It 'tis so," I say jokingly.

"What would you have cooked me," he asks intrigued.

"Anything," I say with confidence.

"Anything, eh," he asks, challenging me.

"Yes. I'm a hell of a cook," I answer.

He chuckles into my hair, "Not many girls cook anymore. I'll definitely have to keep you around now," he says teasingly.

I playfully smack him on his chest in response. After a few moments, I look up at him to find his face has turned serious, "are you ok? How are you feeling?"

Memories of our act or rather acts of passion last night and in the shower earlier, flood my mind.

I smile and say, "I'm fine. Better than fine actually," as I trace his face with my finger.

In all honesty I was fine. I was great. A little sore, but great all the same. Still looking serious, he takes my hand from his face and starts tracing random patterns on my palm.

"I was afraid I hurt you."

I pulled my brows together, "why would you think that?"

He puts his hand in mine before saying, "because I know you've never done that so intensely before."

He's looking down at me gauging my response. I can feel my cheeks heating. I pull my hand out of his.

"Was it bad for you or something," I ask, turning away from him.

Already embarrassed. He gently grabs a hold of me so I can't move away from him.

"What? No, baby that's not what I meant. Look at me," he says, placing his fingers under my chin, forcing me to look at him. "Earlier and last night was amazing. Beyond amazing. I've never experienced something like that before."

I roll my eyes at him and look away.

He chuckles, "No, I'm serious, look at me," he makes me look at him again. "What I mean is, I can tell you're pure, Leyna. You're not like all these other girls I've ever met. You're unlike anyone I've ever met before. You're so genuinely caring. And, stubborn" he fights a chuckle, "you don't throw yourself at me or fall at my feet like all these other girls do. You know who you are and what you want in life. You're ambitious. You're determined." He starts trailing his fingers at the bottom hem of the t-shirt I'm wearing, "You're pure. You're sexy without being immodest to your character. You're incredible. And, you're mine" he says looking into my eyes at that last part.

He truly wants me. But for how long? Would he leave in the end? He could find a girl that had her life in order. He could find a girl that didn't have an alcoholic addict as a mother. He could find a girl that didn't struggle with her childhood; that never fully recovered from it. Deep down I'm broken. Only glued back together just enough. He deserves more. More than me. "Leyna?"

Micah breaks me from my thoughts.

"You're perfect. You know that," I say stroking his beautiful face before sitting up and saying, "that's why I can't have you."

My voice breaks at the end. He sits up. Anger and worry are on his face.

"Woah, not this again," he says, trying to touch my face.

Until I found you

I turn away, about to get up from the bed when he gently grabs me around my waist pulling me to straddle his lap. I'm holding my tears back at this point.

"Hey. Baby, look at me. Why are we talking about this again," he asks, holding my face gently forcing me to look at him.

"My life is a mess, Micah. It's too messy. My mother is an alcoholic who struggles with addiction. I don't know who my father is and the only person I ever truly had in my life before Maggie and Jared was my brother. He was the only real family I ever had, and he's gone now. The only actual family member I have left is my crazy ass mother. Who I literally had to bail out of jail just the other day. No one in their right mind would want that. No one in their right mind would want me-"

I'm cut off by Micah's mouth on mine. He kisses me with so much meaning I begin to cry. He pulls away from me slightly to look at me. His hands still on either side of my face.

"ANYONE would want you Leyna. Anyone. Everyone has a past ok? Everyone. Including me. But our past doesn't define us. Scars remind us where we've been but they do not get to dictate where we are going. They're just scars, baby. They're just scars," he says gently wiping tears from my cheeks with his thumbs.

He pulls me to his chest and just holds me for a while.

"You could have anyone, Micah," I say, trying to pull away.

"Don't," he says sternly. "I want you. Don't ruin your happiness because you feel like you don't deserve it or that the sky is going to fall."

I look up at him knowingly. He nods. "I know more about self destruction than you think. There was a time in my life that I ruined things for myself. I ruined things before they even began because somehow in my mind, I felt I either didn't deserve it or I could handle the pain better if I were the one to set matches to it myself instead of someone else. I never allowed anyone to get close to me. Until you," he says looking into my eyes.

"Why me," I ask, sniffling.

He smiles, "I'm drawn to you. I can't explain it. Whether it's your fiery temper and this red hair to match," he begins playing with the ends of my hair. "I feel this connection to you. Like somehow I've known you all my life."

Searching his eyes, I see the sincerity behind them.

He continues, "You feel it too and it scares you. That's why you're already trying to run for the hills. I won't allow it," he says with finality.

"Is that so," I ask, slightly amused at his final say so on the matter.

"It is so. This is new territory for both of us. I've never had feelings for someone before. I've never wanted to with anyone before. What you're warning me about is a small price to pay to be able to call you mine, Leyna."

UNTIL I found you

Twenty-three

After drinking our coffee, I convinced Micah to take us grocery shopping for him. Stating if I'm coming over more I'll need stuff to cook since it's something I enjoy doing anyway. He chuckles and finally agrees. I'm getting dressed, when Micah walks in still shirtless. I instinctively go to cover my breasts until I realize how dumb that is. Instead I stand there. Letting him take in every curve of me. He stares at my naked body up and down before licking his lips. Heat instantly ignites my core.

"You could have knocked," I say teasingly.

"And miss this beautiful sight? I don't think so," he says, wrapping his arms around my waist. Pulling me closer to him. We're skin to skin. Our chests, bare. He starts rubbing small circles with his thumbs on my back while trailing sweet kisses across my shoulder. His kisses become more sensual as he reaches down my breasts. I wrap my arms around him, looking adoringly at him as he kisses across my chest before he moves up towards my neck. Licking as he trails upward. I lean my head back to give him better access. I can feel him hardening already.

Instinctively I move my hand to his large, growing bulge. He growls into my neck. "Don't do that or I won't be taking you anywhere but back to my bed," he says nibbling my collarbone.

A small whimper escapes my lips at his words. He pulls away from my neck at the sound, staring at me for a fraction of a second before he collides his mouth to mine. His tongue dancing with mine. He pulls away after a moment, leaving me panting.

"Later," he smiles before squeezing my ass. "Now get dressed before I lose my self control with you," he calls over his shoulder as he exits the bathroom.

I stand there for a few moments collecting myself. This man does things to me and I love it. I glance in the mirror and find small red patches across my chest going up my neck. They're already fading as I trace them with my hands, admiring them and the sexy man that left them on me. I look at my reflection and barely recognize myself. My eyes are wild, a bright shade of green, almost jade. My cheeks are a rosey pink. My coral lips swollen from Micah kissing me. My hair is in waves cascading down my back. I have a glow to myself. I feel beautiful. Micah makes me feel that way. I smile before getting myself dressed and heading into the living room where Micah is. I hear him in the kitchen on the phone with someone before I turn the corner.

"You don't stop do you? No, today isn't good. Or tomorrow," he pauses. "Because things have changed." The other person must be speaking. He replies, "Yeah. I've met someone."

UNTIL I found you

The person talks. Their voice raises in volume. That's when I notice it's a female voice. My blood instantly boils. "It's none of your business really. The point of this conversation is that I'm done with the texts and calls from you. I'm done with the late night visits from you too. I'm with her now." She speaks. "Don't fucking call her that Nadia," he growls into the phone. Nadia. The bitch I'm going to kill. Her name is Nadia. I make the note in my head.

"I'm hanging up now," he ends the call and runs his hand through his hair. I turn the corner as he turns around, his expression unreadable. "How much did you hear," He asks, already walking towards me.

I back away, "enough," I say, through my teeth.

"It's not what you think," he says, still walking towards me.

"Oh it's not? My God. She's your girlfriend isn't she," I accuse.

"No! She's not my girlfriend," he spits.

"Then who is she Micah?"

I all but shout at him.

He takes a deep breath before saying, "She's a past hookup of mine. Ok? She's nothing to me. We were never anything other than-"

I raise my hand, stopping him from finishing. I can't hear the words. I can't have that revolting image playing in my head.

"She's the one that called you last night wasn't she? She's the one that's called you this whole time," I state.

His expression hardens, "Yes, but I didn't answer last night did I?"

I huff, "Yeah because you already had a toy in front of you. I'm sure you'll call her over for a slumber party once I'm gone," I say, stalking off in a hurry.

He hurriedly walks over to me in seconds, pulling my wrist to stop me. He stands in front of me towering over me.

"Move," I say, blinking back my tears.

I know I shouldn't be this upset. I heard him say for her to not text or call him again, that he was with me. But, I also heard "no more late night visits" and that she was "a past hookup of his." The thought of him touching her makes my heart sink, causing me to feel sick to my stomach. The thought of her touching him makes me want to draw blood from her. Was he lying when he said I was the only girl he ever let spend the night with him before? Am I just a toy to him? Was he lying when he said he had feelings for me? Is this all too good to be true? He lowers his head to where our eyes meet.

"No. I'm not moving and you aren't going anywhere! You aren't my toy, Leyna. Jesus, did you not hear me those times when I made that perfectly fucking clear?"

He's angry now.

I straighten my shoulders, raising my chin in defiance before saying, "Well let me make this perfectly clear to you, I am not a toy for you to amuse yourself with. My feelings are not your personal playground."

His eyes are bewildered.

"You're fucked up you know that? You're not a fucking toy to me! How bad has someone hurt

Until I found you

you for you to fucking think like this," he spits, venom laced in his words.

"A lot," I yell, throwing my hands up in the air. "Ok? Not just from my fucked up mom either but from a guy before. He took my innocence for sport and left me. I was nothing but a game to him," I say fighting back tears.

His face softens before morphing into a look of anger as my words sink in.

He places his hands on either side of my face and says with clenched jaws, "He deserves every circle of hell for putting you through that."

I close my eyes as tears fall down my face.

"Look at me baby," he says softly.

I love when he calls me Baby. It's like him saying that makes my whole world okay for once. I look up at him. His eyes are so beautiful.

"You are not some toy or game to me. I'm not some guy that's just trying to get into your pants. Well, only get into your pants. I'm not blind. Leyna, look at you. You're so incredibly sexy. So beautiful. You turn me on more than any woman ever has. You aren't just a physical attraction to me. You mean more to me than that. The very moment you ripped me a new one over your shoes and drink at the restaurant I knew there was more to you than your sexy bodice and beautiful face. I had hoped we'd meet again. Even planned on breaking away from Jo that night to try to find you again, to convince you to let me take you out. Get your number. Anything. Then fate casted it's stone when I saw you and Maggie dancing terribly at the club." he laughs at the memory.

As do I.

He continues, "I was walking over to you when I saw those mother fuckers harassing you and Maggie. Jo saw it too and followed. I was coming to your rescue when I saw you slap him." He wipes my tears away. "My strong, temperamental girl," he says in awe. His expression and tone takes a primal change when he recounts that guy about to punch me. "I wanted to kill him for even thinking of laying a hand on you. I would have if I hadn't got to you in time."

I place my hand to the side of his face, staring up adoringly at this man.

He continues, "That night I knew it even then. You sparked something in me I've never felt before. I had to have you. And to be honest it scared me too. And, that is something hard to do. That's the reason I bailed that night. I thought I had already lost you over that stupid misunderstanding. I thought you wouldn't come. But, when you barged in ready to tear me a new asshole, that's when I knew it was certain. You cared for me just as much as I cared for you." his voice softens on the last part. "So no Leyna Blake, you aren't some toy to me," he says putting his forehead on mine.

"I'm sorry," I say, feeling immensely guilty for accusing him of that.

He's never done anything to me for me to even think that of him. I blink back tears from my guilt.

"Baby, It's ok. Don't apologize," he says as he kisses my nose.

I laugh light heartedly at his sweet gesture.

"I love to see your jealous side though. It's cute," he says grinning smugly.

"I'm not jealous of her," I huff.

He chuckles planting a small kiss to my temple, "you shouldn't be. Ever."

Twenty-four

I'm walking towards his Jeep when he says, "We're not going in that one."

I look at him puzzled.

"Then what are we going in," I ask, confused.

His garage door opens revealing a shiny new model red Chevrolet Corvette.

"This is your car," I say in awe.

He's smiling, "beautiful isn't she," he says, opening the passenger door for me.

I get in and admire the all black leather interior. This is definitely a chick magnet car. He gets in and buckles my seatbelt for me.

"Oh thanks. I was about to put it on and got caught up in this beauty," I say looking around. He chuckles before saying, "You like cars?"

I nod. He smiles and takes my hand in his as we pull out.

"Do you work for the mafia or something," I ask teasingly. "This car is easily $70,000 with all the upgrades and customs you have on it."

UNTIL I found you

He looks over to me impressed, "sexy, smart, AND knows cars?"

I chuckle.

"My brother was all into it. I learned from him really," I smile mentioning him.

He squeezes my hand before saying, "you'll have to tell me about him sometime. When you're ready I mean."

I smile at him before lifting his hand to my lips, placing a gentle kiss.

"My sweetheart," he says sweetly.

We pull up at the grocery store and Micah grabs a buggy following me to the dry goods first. He notices my organization and preparedness for all of this. I look at him knowingly.

"I get the cold stuff last."

He chuckles, "Smart girl."

"Okay, any allergies or dislikes I should know about?"

He smiles at me, "I don't like Brussels sprouts or pickles. Other than that I'm good to go."

"Noted," I say as I step on my tippy toes to grab a box of linguine pasta from the shelf.

He goes to grab it when I say, "no I've got this."

He throws his hands up and steps back watching me struggle. I jump up and grab it. Looking pleased with myself. He throws his head back in laughter.

"Shut up," I say giggling.

We make our way to the spices when Tony comes around the corner, "Hey shorty."

"Hi Tony," I say rolling my eyes.

"Heads up we're changing the menu next week."

He says, giving quick glances in Micah's direction.

"Already? Chelsea keeps me and Hanna busy remembering the constant menu changes."

He laughs, "that's Chelsea for you. Always making things difficult. You might want to come in early to review the menu changes. I'll see you tomorrow," he waves as he leaves.

"Bye Tony," I say as he walks off.

I'm picking up a box of salt when Micah asks, "Who was that? Why are you seeing him tomorrow?"

His eyes narrow slightly. Look who's jealous now. I chuckle at the thought of him being jealous over Tony.

"Why are you laughing," he asks, getting annoyed.

"That was Tony. He's my boss. Well, one of my bosses. I work at his restaurant."

His face calms, "Which restaurant?"

"Amoroso's" I answer. "

That overrated, overly priced restaurant downtown," he asks.

"Yep that's the one. Where the food is mediocre and the co-owner is a bitch."

He chuckles, "He looked like a bitch," he says more to himself than me.

"No Tony's cool, it's his sister that I'm referring to. She can get nasty with her employees."

His jaw clenches slightly, "Why work there then?"

I shrug, "Because the pay is pretty decent for it to be a waitressing job. The tips are good," I say placing fresh rosemary into a produce bag.

"I could help you find a better job," he offers.

I look up at him.

"With me actually," he adds.

I giggle. "Work with you?"

He smiles widely, "work for me, actually. A secretary."

I raise my brow at him.

"I work as an investor at a firm," he says.

"Where," I ask, intrigued.

"Eason Enterprises," he says gauging my reaction.

"Eason," I ask, connecting the name of the business to his own.

"It's my father's company. But I'll be taking it over eventually," he states.

"That's amazing. That's a great accomplishment for yourself," I say praising him.

He smiles, "so will you think about it?"

I shrug my shoulders, "maybe."

I see out of the corner of my eye he's staring down at me smiling. I look over and notice a woman gawking at Micah. She's got way too much makeup on and her clothes are two sizes too small. She's looking him over when she notices me. She gives me a once over with pursed lips before reverting her eyes back on him. Not even being subtle of her eyeing him. Time to show Felicia what's up. Stepping closer to him, I reach up on my tippy toes and pull his face to mine. He smiles, his lips instantly part for me. I slip my tongue in and he begins caressing it with his own. He pulls me closer to him, grabbing my ass as he squeezes lightly. I glance my eyes to her and see she's pissed. Good. I pull away and subtly slide my hand over his ass in front of her.

He smiles at me, "Well, if that doesn't give her the hint, I don't know what will," he says smugly.

"Wha-what?" I ask, a bit embarrassed he's caught on.

"Babe, that chick has been staring me down since aisle four."

I look over to her, giving her a death glare as she walks off.

He chuckles, "Easy tiger."

"Why didn't you say anything," I snapped.

"Because, I was too busy shopping with my girl to notice anyone else," he says, pulling me in his arms and planting a kiss on my forehead.

After we load the groceries into his car we head back to his house. He almost has all of the grocery bags on either of his wrists. Leaving me to only carry a few.

"Put some of those down or give some of them to me. Your wrists are already turning red," I warn.

He scoffs before saying, "I'd rather break my arms than make multiple trips. I've got this babe."

I roll my eyes but follow him up the stairs. Once we unload and put away all of the groceries I start on dinner. I've decided to make him my Blackened Chicken Fettuccine Alfredo. I begin by washing my hands and getting out the pots and pans I'll need to cook. I skip over to the fridge and grab the ingredients. Micah watching my every move. I look up to see him smiling big at me.

"What," I ask.

"I love seeing you parade around my kitchen."

I point a wooden spoon at him teasingly, "I'm not the only one that will be cooking either mister. You'll have to show your hand in cooking too," I say as I twirl on my tippy toes to grab the mixing bowl from the top shelf.

I jump to try to grab it but it's too far up. Before I know it, Micah is behind me lifting me up by my waist to grab the bowl. I grab it but he takes it away from me sitting it on the counter beside us. He turns me around to face him, sitting me on the counter. I wrap my arms and legs around him instinctively.

"Delicious," he says with hooded eyes.

I giggle, "I haven't even started cooking yet babe."

"Oh I wasn't talking about food, baby," he says, licking his lips.

I gulp. My chest rising and falling at a quickening pace. He takes handfuls of my ass and squeezes, eliciting a whimper from me. He takes my bottom lip in between his teeth pulling gently. I rock myself against him. Already feeling his hard cock through his jeans. He lifts me higher onto his torso walking us to his bedroom.

"What are you doing," I ask through ragged breaths.

"I've always liked my dessert first." he says, pushing his hot, wet tongue into my mouth.

Twenty-five

Micah's fist is in my hair tugging as he works his mouth around mine. He moans into me as I slide myself up and down his torso as he walks us to his bed.

"Are you a sex addict or something," I tease.

"Only when it's with you. I can't get enough of you," he says in between kisses.

We collapse on top of the bed, laughing as we kiss each other. I arch my back, assisting him in pulling my jeans and panties down my legs. His mouth moves to my neck as he does so. I pull the bottom of his shirt up and over his head. His muscles flex as he throws it onto the floor. I lift up undoing his jeans. He wraps his hands in my hair as I pull his jeans down along with his boxers. Gripping his large length in my hand I give him a few pumps.

He bites his bottom lip as he traces my lips with his thumb before sliding it into my mouth, "I fucking love your mouth," he says in a husky voice as his cock twitches in my hand.

I already know what my man wants from me, and I'm eager to give it to him. I swirl my tongue

UNTIL I
found you

around his thumb, instantly making him moan my name. I love seeing him react to me knowing I can pleasure him the way he pleasures me. I gently bite down on the pad of his thumb.

He furrows his brows and hisses, "fuck, baby."

His large, hard length is throbbing for me. He removes his thumb from my mouth trailing it down my jawline and neck. I lick my lips wetting them. He grabs a fistful of my hair and pulls my head closer to his length. I lick the tip of him and he growls. The sound resonates through my core making me squeeze my legs together to relieve the pressure forming there. I take him in halfway before looking up at him batting my lashes in full effect.

"I could fuck your mouth forever," he says before gripping my hair with slightly more force and shoving himself down my throat. I begin to gag on him. My eyes instantly water. I rake my tongue up and down him. Hollowing my cheeks.

"Fuck, baby," he says through clenched jaws.

He bobs my head up and down him at a faster pace. I moan, sending vibrations through him. He's looking down at me with furrowed brows as he bites his bottom lip. His chest rising and falling from the pleasure I'm giving him. God he's so fucking hot. I can already taste his precum on my tongue. He pulls out of my mouth suddenly.

"If you want me to fuck you, you better stop sucking my dick."

I pull back and lay on top of the bed as I prop myself up with my elbows. He's looking at me like he wants to ravish me as I spread my legs eager for him.

"Fucking hell," he breathes in a husky voice.

He kneels down and pulls me by my thighs to the edge of the bed to meet him. He begins skimming his lips up my thighs, teasing me as he does so. I arch my back as he sucks the sensitive skin on my hip bone. There's a stinging sensation before he licks at it with his hot, wet tongue. I look down to see a hickey forming there. Him marking me this way only makes me want him more. He works his way down. Kissing, licking, sucking. He's so close to my clit. I can't take the teasing anymore, it's too much.

I buck my hips skimming his face to my pussy. He looks at me with wild, hungry eyes before pressing his hot tongue flat to my center and begins sucking my clit. I cry out. Euphoria completely taking me over. I look down at Micah between my legs, the sight is incredibly sexy. I'm so close already when he pulls away suddenly. His lips glistening from my wetness.

"Why did you stop," I whine.

He begins kissing up my stomach as he inserts a finger inside of me. Pumping at a torturously slow pace. I arch my back begging him for more. He withdrawals his finger from me.

"Because, I'm about to fuck you senseless," and slams into me.

I let out a cry of pleasure. He wraps one of his arms around my back holding me in place while his other hand is wrapped gently around my throat giving light squeezes as he thrusts into me at a dangerously fast pace. I scream out. The pleasure intensifies as he rocks into me.

"That's right baby. Let me hear you scream my name as I ram into your tight wet pussy," he said so sexy.

My eyes roll into the back of my head as I moan. His filthy, seductive words in combination with how he's fucking me, I'm already so close to my orgasm. Micah is filling every inch of me, and the feeling is complete euphoria. I claw his back. Signaling how much I'm loving this. He growls in response. The sound causes me to moan.

"Look at me baby," he commands through clenched jaws.

I look up at him batting my lashes in full effect and he's done for.

"Oh fuck. Cum for me baby! Cum for me," he says barely keeping himself contained.

I do just that. I throw my head back into the mattress as I cum around him. My body going limp beneath him from the euphoric state he's just brought me to. He pulls out hastily and marks me with his warm cum on my stomach. I'm taken aback by him doing so, but I have to admit that I'm seriously turned on by it. There's something about Micah's dirty words and the way he's so completely confident when it comes to sex that it makes this seem so natural between us.

A month ago I wouldn't have believed someone if they told me this man would bring out my inner sexual goddess. Or hell, that I would even have a guy like Micah in my life. I tried so hard to push any guy that dared to get close to me away. He persistently crept his way in. I stare at the beautiful man before me as he falls onto the bed by my side in ragged, heavy breaths. After a moment of calming his breathing he looks over to me and the mess he created on my stomach. He looks at me, taking his bottom lip between his teeth before rubbing the sticky matter up towards my chest.

    He palms my breast as he says, "all mine."

Until I found you

Twenty-six

After we've taken a quick shower, I'm back in the kitchen cooking Blackened Chicken Fettuccine Alfredo for dinner. Micah is on his laptop typing away notes for his meeting in the morning. I'm cleaning up my mess as I'm cooking. Already loading the dirty utensils into the dishwasher and wiping the counters down. Dinner is about done. The homemade Alfredo sauce is delicious! The chicken smells amazing. It's all done. All that's needed is for the pasta to be drained and it'll be ready to serve.

    I cut the burners off and I rinse the sink before putting the colander in to strain the pasta. I look up at Micah who's laid across the couch in only his grey sweatpants with a pen in between his teeth. Deep in concentration as he's going over some paperwork. I'm allowing myself to become distracted looking at Micah when some of the boiling water spills over onto my wrist. I let out a painful yelp as I set the pot down. Micah instantly jumps up and comes around to me.

"Leyna what happened? Let me look," he says taking my wrist, carefully inspecting it.

"It's nothing," I say, trying to hide my discomfort.

"The hell it's not, you're hurt," he says, already placing my wrist under the cold water.

He leaves me for a moment before going into the spare bathroom, retrieving bandages and some aloe vera gel. He cuts the water off and pat drys my burn.

"This should help," he says, gently putting the gel on me before placing a bandage on top. "Are you a nurse too," I tease.

He chuckles.

"Does that feel better," he asks, inspecting it before looking at me.

I nod my head and smile at him. I thanked him. He makes me sit down as he fixes our plates. He takes his first bite.

"Holy shit," he mumbles.

Which causes me to giggle, "good?"

"Better than good. It's delicious, baby. My girl is one hell of a cook," he praises, smiling at me as he chews. "Why aren't you in culinary school," he asks.

"Because I need to choose a career that has a shelf life. Plus cooking is more of a passion of mine than it is a career choice."

He ponders this for a moment before asking, "what is your major?"

I smile before answering, "I'm majoring in Pediatric nursing."

He gives me a smile, a bit of a smirk seeping through it.

Until I found you

"What," I raise my brow at him.

"I thought you would say something like that. It fits you," he says, taking my hand and giving it a gentle squeeze.

"Another semester and I'll finally have my degree. Of course I still have to take the NCLEX-RN exam. Which I'm nervous for because finals were hell. I'm glad summer break is here."

He nods, "I don't miss those days."

We're almost done eating when my phone starts ringing. I stand to get it when Micah beats me to it. I roll my eyes when I see him peeking at the screen to see who's calling before handing it to me.

"It's Jared," he states.

I answered, "hey Jer."

"Well at least I know you're alive and well. I was beginning to worry about you. I haven't heard from you all day. How's it going? I mean it must be going good since you've been gone all day." He chuckles lightly before continuing, "I'll let you get back to it, miss thang. Will you be home tonight?"

I roll my eyes, "Yes dad," I say sarcastically.

He laughs and says, "Don't forget to use protection. I'm too young to be an uncle. Bye," drawing out the last word before hanging up.

I shake my head at him. I add the mental note in my head to get on birth control since there's a need for it now.

"What was all that about," Micah asks.

"Nothing. Jared being Jared. He was calling to make sure I was ok and checking if I was coming home tonight."

"Why is that," he asks, indifferently.

"Jared is just protective over me is all. Maggie too. Jared and I have a lot in common as far as parental absence in our life goes."

Micah's facial expression softens.

"I know all too well what you mean," he says. "I'm sorry babe," I say, placing my hand over his.

Comforting him.

"It's okay. It was a long time ago," he says, trying to shake it off.

I know the loss of his mom is felt everyday. After Micah helps me clean up from dinner, I go into his bedroom to grab my purse. Without my noticing, he's standing in the doorway when I turn around. I collide into his chest. He wraps his arms around me kissing my forehead. "Maybe I'll just keep you here. Keep you all to myself," he says, with humor in his eyes.

"You'd get tired of me eventually," I say tapping his chin with my index finger playfully.

"Quite the opposite really. I can't get enough of you it seems," he says, lowering his head into my neck before planting a small kiss just below my ear.

I tremble slightly at his touch. He gives me a wicked grin.

"Let's get out of here before I hold you captive."

He takes my hand in his as we walk to his car. We're driving for a few minutes when Ed Sheeran's song "Thinking Out Loud" starts playing on the radio. It's one of my favorites from him. I turn it up slightly and start humming along to it. Micah looks over at me out of the corner of his eye and I see him smiling at me. His hand tightens around mine ever so slightly when the part of the song says "I'm thinking 'bout how people fall in love in mysterious ways. Maybe by just the touch of a hand. For me I fall in love with you every single day."

My breath hitches slightly. I know he cares about me but, could he be falling in love with me? Butterflies swell in my stomach at the thought. I push that thought to the back of my mind for now. Micah goes to pull into my driveway when I see a car I don't recognize.

"Who is that," he asks.

"It must be someone for Jared," I say.

Before Micah can come around to open my car door for me I'm already out and heading up the porch. He's right behind me. His hand on the small of my back. Before I can grab the door knob it's already twisting open from the inside. I see Maggie hugging a guy that isn't Jo. When the guy turns around I instantly recognize him.

It's Maggie's older cousin, Connor. His brown eyes scan my face. Focusing on my eyes and lips, eyeing my body up and down before settling back on my face, giving me a killer smile. A few years ago I would have welcomed that smile. Truth be told I had a bit of a crush on him back then. But, being Maggie's cousin, and the fact that he was way out of my league, I grew out of it pretty quickly.

"Hey Leyna," Maggie greets me.

"Leyna," he asks, unsure.

"Hey," I say, giving him a small wave.

He looks me up and down. Shocked. He doesn't even notice Micah standing behind me. "Wow. How long has it been, two years? You look incredible," he says, still eyeing me before giving me a hug.

I blush uncomfortably. In the two years since I've seen Connor last, I've lost some weight. And by some I mean a lot.

"Um, thanks. Yeah it's been a while," I say uncomfortably.

I point to Micah, "This is my- uh" not exactly knowing what to call our relationship, I turn to introduce Micah to Connor when I see Micah is staring at him, almost primal. Connor is staring back at him with the same amount of tension. I'm beginning to wonder if I'm missing something when Micah speaks up.

"I'm the boyfriend," he states simply, wrapping his arm around my waist, pulling me closer to him.

Micah is still eyeing Connor. Well at least I know where our relationship stands. I fight back a smile at this revelation.

"I'm Maggie's cousin. How've you been Eason," Connor nods towards Micah.

Then it clicks. These two know each other and from the awkward tension I would say not on good terms.

"You two know each other," Maggie smirks.

I glare at her.

"Yeah we go way back. We're old pals isn't that right," Connor asks Micah with a smug expression.

I can feel Micah tense. I look up to see he's holding back his anger. His fist is clenched at his side and his nostrils are slightly flared.

UNTIL I found you

Before Micah can respond Connor interrupts, "Well, I should be going. I'll be seeing you around Maggie. It was great seeing you again Leyna. I suppose since you're roomies with Maggie I'll be seeing you soon too," he smiles at me before looking at Micah. "Eason."

He nods at him before walking to his car. I catch him looking over his shoulder at me before smiling to himself. Maggie, Micah and myself just stand there awkwardly for a moment before she breaks the silence.

"So Connor moved back. He's gotten a job with Daddy at his law firm in the city," she says more to me than Micah.

I nod my head, "that's good," I say.

I hear Micah mumble lowly under his breath, "fucking fantastic."

I nudge him with my elbow. He tightens his grip around my waist slightly.

Maggie looks around before saying with no subtlety, "I'm going to go do stuff."

She shuts the front door giving Micah and I some privacy. I roll my eyes at her.

I look up at Micah, "explain."

He looks at me incredulously, "No, you explain. What was that," he asks, already annoyed. "What was what? That was Maggie's cousin Connor." I say shortly. "But you already knew him apparently. How do you know him anyway," I ask.

"Yeah I caught that. Why were you two flirting?"

I don't miss the way he's ignoring my question.

"Flirting? I wasn't flirting with him," I say shaking my head.

"Well he was certainly flirting with you, Leyna. He had his eyes all over you," he says, becoming angry.

"I don't think he was flirting. Just surprised is all," I say trying to calm Micah.

"What do you mean," Micah cocks his head slightly.

I begin to blush.

"Well I've lost some weight since he's seen me last. Over 50 pounds to be exact."

My words trailing towards the end. I veered my eyes away from Micah in embarrassment. I'm still not at my ideal weight. I'm sure other girls he's been with seem like supermodels compared to me. The thought makes me sad.

He cups my face, "baby, stop it."

I look up at him.

"Stop being ashamed or embarrassed about your past weight. Don't you fucking dare question your beauty. Do you understand me? You are beautiful and so incredibly sexy Leyna."

I give him a small smile. "Fuck that guy for not looking at you the way he just did, two years ago. He missed out. And I'm sure fucking glad for it," he says and steps closer to me, cupping his hand on the back of my neck. "Because now you're mine" he says, taking my bottom lip between his teeth. Gently tugging before he lets go to plant a soft kiss to my lips.

I break away from his kiss long enough for me to reply, "I'm yours."

Twenty-seven

If it wasn't for Jared flashing the porch lights at us in a mock dad move, I don't think Micah and I would have stopped kissing. I pull away from Micah as I begin laughing at Jared. Seconds later, he opens the front door.

"Micah, Jared. Jer, Micah." I wave my hands between them, introducing them to each other.

"Nice to meet you man," Micah extends his hand to Jared.

"How formal," Jared teases as he shakes Micah's hand.

"Leyna has spoken highly of you," Micah says.

"Don't believe a word of it. I'm simply awful. Come on in. I'll invite you in since Miss thang won't. Forgive her, we haven't quite got her manners down pat."

I smack Jared on the chest.

"Jerk."

Micah chuckles.

"Maybe it's because I didn't want a certain someone embarrassing me," I say crossing my arms.

"Why? He's met Maggie before," Jared retorts, causing Micah to stifle a laugh.

After a while of conversating, Micah says his goodbyes to Jared and Maggie.

I'm walking him out when I look up at him and say, "You know you still owe me an explanation to how you two know each other right?"

He nods. "I know. But it's a story for another day. Rain check?"

I roll my eyes; "Fine."

He tells me he'll text me later before kissing me goodbye. I watch as he drives off already knowing I'm going to get my answers from Maggie tonight.

I'm not even through the bedroom door yet when Maggie says, "Ok spill! What the hell was that? How do they know each other?"

I shrug my shoulders, "I was kind of hoping you'd know."

"He didn't tell you," Maggie asks.

I shake my head.

"Hmm very interesting," Maggie's muses. "I'll get to the bottom of this shortly," she says as she pulls out her phone.

Assumingly texting Connor to get his side of the story. I roll my eyes at her but find myself grateful this one time for Maggie's intrusive curiosity. An hour later I hear my phone ding and eagerly read the text.

"My bed is lonely without you. It's missing a certain sexy redhead of mine."

I hold back a giggle and smile to myself before replying, "Is that so? I miss you too. Sweet dreams babe."

UNTIL I found you

He replies, "I'll call you tomorrow. Tell your friends you're booked this coming weekend. Goodnight baby."

I smile knowing he misses me. I miss him too. It's crazy how we're becoming almost inseparable. It's an amazing feeling but a terrifying feeling all the same. I just hope that we don't crash and burn.

Jared walks in, "ok, missy, tomorrow you're giving me all the details. Every dirty one."

"Me too," I hear Maggie calling from the kitchen.

"In fact, I also have some news in that department myself," he says smiling. "Tell me all about him," I say happily for my best friend.

I hear Maggie jogging into our room, "You slut! spill it!" she says to Jared, hopping on her bed.

He sits at the edge of my bed and goes into this adorably romantic story of how he saved this guy's dog from running out in the street. They instantly connected and had their first coffee date right after. He starts going into all of their mutual likes and hobbies they share. I can see how happy Jared is just talking about it.

"Aww shut your face! You're living in a hallmark movie," Maggie says, throwing a pillow at Jared playfully.

"His name is Jamie. He's dreamy! Look," Jared gushes as he shows off a picture of him to us. I'm so happy for Jared. He deserves every bit of happiness.

"He's almost as cute as mine," Maggie says, referring to Jo.

"How's that going by the way," I ask sarcastically.

From the looks of this morning, I'd say it's going great for them.

"Ha. Ha," she says and rolls her eyes at me before going into their relationship. "He's so carrying. So sweet. He's not like all the other douchebags I've dated. Ya know that just wants me for sex. He actually wants to know how my day is going. He wants to see me happy. It's a wonderful feeling."

I'm happy for Maggie. She deserves a guy like Jo. She deserves a guy that aims to please her. To treat her the way she should be treated. I couldn't be happier for my best friends, my family. They are the family that I chose. We're always cheering each other on. We are always that shoulder to cry on, always giving each other pep talks when we need them the most. We have each other's back. This is the family we three created. To think that both of my best friends may be bringing two more into that family, causes me so much happiness for them. Maggie and Jared both look at me. Waiting for me to tell them all the "juicy details" between Micah and I.

"It's going good," I say simply.

Maggie and Jared look at each other before rolling their eyes at me.

"You were gone all night and all day. It had to have been going better than 'good' for you to stay with him that long," Maggie says, crossing her arms.

"What she said," Jared chimes in.

I chuckle but say, "I just don't want to jinx it guys."

UNTIL I found you

Jared snorts, "well with that attitude you will. Have a little faith in it. In him."

Maggie nods her head in agreement, "Jo told me Micah must really like you. That ever since he's known Micah he's never seen him like this before. Hanging around and talking to only one girl. Jo said that Micah has never been the dating type. So he must care about you a lot, Leyna."

Twenty-eight

I'm on my way to work when I check my phone and see that I have a few texts from Micah. I really need to get in the habit of checking my phone in the mornings, now that I have someone. I pull into work and read his texts.

"Good morning, beautiful. Busy day ahead. I'll text as often as I can. Have a good day baby."

I smile at his texts. He's so sweet to me.

I reply back, "Good morning, babe. I'll have a busy day as well. Hope yours goes great."

I'm walking into work when my phone buzzes.

"It'll be great when I get to see you later."

I smile to myself and go to put my phone into my apron when I get another text. Thinking it's Micah, I open it. It's not Micah. It's Jean.

"We need to talk. Call me when u can."

My smile instantly fades. The nerve of her. Why would I want to talk to her after what she said? After how she acted towards me? That was the last straw. I'm never speaking to her again. I put my phone in my apron when Lyle's words play in my head.

Until I found you

"Leyna she's sick. Her words and actions are a part of her disease. Just ignore her."

"Ignore her?! How are we supposed to ignore something like that? She's fucked up Lyle," I shouted.

"You're right. But we're all she's got Leyna."

We're all she's got. Those words keep playing in my head as I walk into the restaurant. I'm all she has. Whether she's fucked up or not she's my mother. And we're all that's left. Me and her. I internally groan as I text her back "working. I'll call you when my shift ends". Chelsea is already yelling at the new waitress she hired over the weekend. Poor girl.

"Leyna, I need you to cover Angelica's section since she doesn't remember the menu correctly," she torts to the girl.

"It's Angelina," she corrects Chelsea shyly.

"Well whatever it is, read the menu, memorize it or find yourself another job." she says before stomping away in her heels.

The girl looks like she already wants to cry. "Don't worry about her. Just keep your head down around her. Tony is nice. Nothing like his sister. If the customer asks what the daily special is and you don't remember, just state something off the top of your head. Odds are they won't even pick it anyway. You'll have a few drunken assholes in here from time to time. Especially during cocktail specials. Just hold your ground," I say to her, giving her the advice Rachel gave me when I first started here.

Angelina smiles at me, thanking me over and over again. She seems so sweet. I hope she can handle hurricane Chelsea. We need more sweetness around here.

My shift goes by pretty quick. People are coming and going in a blur. Table eight in my section is being a little loud. Multiple shots of Grey Goose will do that to you. I'm passing by them when I ask if there is anything I could do for them.

One of the guys says drunkenly, "you could come sit on my lap. That would be most helpful," before laughing and slapping his palm on the table loudly.

It makes me jump slightly. His friends laugh along with him. I fake a laugh before walking away. You learn after a while not to get so offended by stuff. I'm loading a tray of food to serve when Angelina comes over.

"Um, there's a guy out there that wants to be seated in your section. He named you specifically."

I nod at her already knowing who it is. A smile plastered on my face. I serve table 11 their food and look over to see Micah in a business suit his hair combed over in a professional manner. The watch on his wrist accentuating his overall business attire. He looks like pure sex. So perfect. I nearly dropped my tray looking at him. His eyes meet mine and he gives me the most beautiful smile I've ever seen.

I smile at him just as big as I walk over to him and ask in mock professionalism, "what can I get you today, sir?"

He looks me over as he licks his lips.

"Can I get an order of you with a side of whipped cream?"

Until I found you

My jaw drops slightly before I close it and start blushing. He starts laughing lightly. Giving me a huge grin.

"What's delicious here baby," he asks after a moment. Before I can answer, he adds, "besides you," flashing me his dimpled smile.

"Micah," I say softly, drawing out his name as I blush.

He chuckles, "Glad to see me?"

"Always," I answer.

"Miss I need some assistance," the guy from table eight slurs.

Already laughing with his friends. I roll my eyes.

"Be right back," I tell Micah.

Who already has his eyes on me as I walk over to them.

"Yes sir, what can I do for you," I ask the bald one.

"Our table needs cleaning," he replies while looking at my breasts without any subtlety.

I have on a camisole under this shirt, but my breasts are just there for the world to see.

I ignore his staring, "yes sir, let me get those out of your way," I say clearing their plates.

I walk them into the kitchen placing them in the big sink. Washing my hands, I fix Micah a glass of Dr. Pepper. I know that is his favorite from us grocery shopping together. I walk over to him sitting the glass down. His facial expression hardened. I look at him confused before following his gaze to the drunken idiots.

I wave them off, "they're just drunk babe. Don't worry about them," I say trying to calm him.

"If they put one fucking finger on you-" I cut him off.

"I'm fine. I'll be okay."

He doesn't look convinced.

"Do you know what you want?" I ask, trying to distract him from baldy and his drunken friends over there. "Yeah, I want you to come work with me. I don't like you being here. I've seen enough. That's what I want. Get your stuff, we're leaving." he says trying to stand.

I place my hand on his shoulder making him sit back down.

"Micah you're being ridiculous. I've dealt with much worse than them before. I can handle my own," he nods his head like he is contemplating something, "that may be. But, that was before you were mine. I won't have you work in an environment like this. Your boss is a complete bitch. I overheard her yelling and talking down to that other girl when I walked in. There's no security provided for you or any other of the employees when they serve alcohol at this rate. This is obviously going against the law by them overserving customers. And what's worse there's drunken mother fuckers staring at your ass and tits all day harassing you. No. Absolutely not. If you don't want to work for me fine, I'll find you something else. But this is unacceptable," he says with finality.

"Miss," the guy from table eight slurs.

I turn to see them waving me down.

"Leyna," Chelsea stomps over, pointing her finger in my face, she says, "Are you blind? Are you deaf? Those customers have been trying to get your

Until I found you

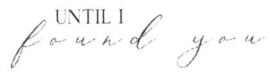

attention. Your job is being a waitress so go wait on them," she barks.

Micah slams his hand on the table loudly before he stands towering over her. She instantly shuts up, looking intimidated by an angry Micah. This is probably the first time someone has ever rendered her speechless.

"Miss," they call out.

I turn to see Angelina walking over to them. I decide to walk over to them instead of her dealing with it. She's so new and so timid if they try something with her it'd scare her. As for me, I know a mean drunk when I see one. I know the difference between a violent drunk and a harmless drunk. These men wouldn't cause real harm to me. I walk over to them, waving Angelina off.

"Yes sir, what can I do for you?"

They begin to chuckle, "well, it seems I've dropped my spoon," just then he bumps it off of the table with his elbow.

I shake my head, "you guys really have to get more clever with your antics. I saw this coming from a mile away you know," they start laughing and clapping. "How about I get you all a cup of coffee to sober you up," I say as I go to walk towards the kitchen.

One of them grabs my wrist too tightly. I let out a painful yelp. He grabbed the wrist that was burned. He immediately let's go and begins to apologize when he's silenced by Micah's large fist clashing against his jaw.

Twenty-nine

"Micah," I yell. Micah is hovered over the guy punching him again and again.

"Micah stop," I yell, grabbing his arm for him to stop.

He spins around, his eyes wild until he sees it's me. His eyes instantly calm. His chest is heaving up and down. He finally lets go of the guy and he falls the rest of the way on the floor. Everyone in the restaurant is looking at us as they whisper to themselves. Still breathing heavily, he looks over at Chelsea before declaring, "She quits," as he grabs my hand and leads us out of the restaurant.

With my hand still in his, he paces over to his corvette instructing me to get in.

"Are you crazy? You just beat the hell out of that guy," I shout at him.

"Get in, Leyna" he instructs.

"No. My car is here and I didn't get the chance to grab my bag before you dragged me out there," I state.

"Screw the bag! I'll replace whatever is in it. Get in the car Leyna," he demands.

UNTIL I
found you

I roll my eyes at him as I turn to walk back in to grab my things.

"Don't you go back in there," he says, still pissed.

Before I can walk in to go get my things, I see Angelina jogging over with my bag. I thank her before she runs back inside where chaos awaits her. Poor girl. I turn around to see Micah looking angry.

"Follow me home," he instructs before getting in his car and starting the engine.

I think about ignoring his request and just driving back to my house, but decide against it. Once we pull up at his house, I get out of my Altima still processing what happened back there.

He comes over to me.

"Are you ok," he asks, examining my wrist.

"Yeah. My wrist is fine. I don't think that guy's face was so lucky though," I say annoyed.

He tilts his head slightly at me, "What would you have me do to him? Nothing? First, he disrespected you. Secondly, he hurt you, Leyna. Thirdly? I hurt him. It's that simple."

I huff before saying, "He was drunk! They wouldn't have actually hurt me. Besides he was apologizing when-" he cuts me off.

"You're seriously defending their behavior? Really? How do you know they wouldn't have hurt you? They did," he says almost shouting.

"I've been around mean, aggressive drunks before. Trust me I know one when I see one and they weren't that. He didn't know my wrist was already injured. It was an honest mistake. You shouldn't have gone that far with it. He'll wake up tomorrow not even remembering what happened."

He looks at me as if I were a math equation impossible to solve.

"You need to stop defending people that don't deserve it. They don't deserve you."

I look at my brooding man as I admire the way he's so protective of me. He's staring at me with those beautiful blue eyes of his, anger peeking behind them. His chest is rising and falling as I place my hands on either side of his face. Keeping eye contact with him, I begin trailing his lips with my fingers before gliding up his cheeks into his temples. I can see the storm that was brewing behind his eyes are now subsiding as my skin touches his. The fact that my bare touch can calm him, bring him comfort this way, it warms my heart. I stand on my tippy toes and move my hands into his hair. Still holding his gaze as I smile at him.

His hands cup either side of my face as he places his forehead against mine; closing his eyes as he does. We stay like this for a moment before he skims the bridge of his nose ever so slightly up and down my cheek. He gives me sweet, soft kisses along the way. I close my eyes, reveling in the sweetness of him. This is My Micah. My angry, brooding man has shifted back into my sweet, tender Micah.

The one that holds me as if I'll float away should he let go. The one that makes me feel as though I'm being mended back together somehow. The one that makes me feel beautiful. Wanted. Like I'm the only girl that's ever truly mattered to him. He is surely stealing my heart little by little, claiming it as his own. I only pray that he doesn't crush it beneath

Until I found you

his hands. I look into his eyes and see no maliciousness behind them, only want and need; only devotion and admiration.

I look down and see the blood on his busted hand. I take his injured hand in mine.

"Let's get this cleaned up," I say as I lead him up the front stairs.

Once he unlocks the door, I walk him into the bathroom. Grabbing the first aid kit that's still sitting on the sink from where I burned myself here. I grab a washcloth and turn the hot water on wetting the cloth. He surprises me by lifting me onto the counter.

I smile at him before saying, "this might sting a little."

I gently wipe the blood from his knuckles, being extra attentive to his busted flesh. He looks down at me adoringly as I clean his wounds.

"A cook and a nurse? I'm a lucky man," he muses.

I smile at his words. I pour rubbing alcohol onto a pad and begin blotting his knuckles. He doesn't flinch, even though I know it has to sting. I pull his hand up to my face and blow on it. Easing the stinging before applying ointment and wrapping his hand in a bandage.

"Better," I ask once I'm done.

He looks at me sweetly before planting a tender kiss to my lips.

"I'm always better when my sweetheart is near me," he says as he touches my cheek lightly. Butterflies instantly swell in my stomach. He helps me down off the counter and we walk back downstairs.

"Hungry," he asks, heading to the fridge.

"Yes, actually I am," I say holding my tummy.

I didn't get the chance to eat breakfast before I left for work this morning. He pulls out raw steaks from the fridge along with some fresh vegetables, placing them on the counter. He grabs two skillets and reaches for the spice cabinet. I raise my eyebrow at him. He notices and chuckles.

"I hope you like steak and grilled vegetables. It's one of the few things I know how to cook," he says smiling.

I nod and smile back at him.

"Want me to help," I offer.

"No babe. I've got it. Just relax," he says, motioning for me to sit on the couch.

I take my vans and top shirt off. Stacking them neatly beside the couch. Feeling more relaxed in my pants and white camisole top. I pull my hair out of its side braid letting my long wavy curls fall down my shoulders. I see Micah out of the corner of my eye staring at me. I smile at him. He smiles back sweetly before resuming his cooking. I curl into a ball on the couch, relaxing my body and before I know it, I'm asleep. I get woken up by Micah peppering sweet, soft kisses to my cheek.

"Come eat baby," he says sweetly, taking my hand.

He walks me to the kitchen table, opening a chair for me.

"Awe thank you," I reply, giving him a shy smile.

"I wasn't sure how you liked your steak so I cooked it medium well," he says.

Until I found you

"Perfect" I reply, smiling at him. "This looks delicious", I add.

"I hope it tastes as good as it looks," he replies and chuckles. "I'm not much of a cook," he admits.

We begin to eat and it tastes great overall. After we've finished eating and cleaned the kitchen, we're cuddled up on the couch together watching Kevin Hart on Comedy Central. It's one of his older skits, the one where his teacher left a note for his mom to read. Later Kevin's mom tells him to give his teacher a message of her own back involving two cuss words. It's still one of my favorites from him. Kevin's voice comes through the tv.

"Oh he said she ain't got no nipple," dragging out the last word.

I begin to laugh so hard I snort slightly. Micah throws his head back in laughter. I instantly cover my face still laughing.

He's pulling my hands away, laughing as he says, "Wait, did you just snort?" fighting his laughter he adds, "I didn't realize we had a little piggy in the house."

I playfully hit his shoulder and hid my face in his chest, embarrassed.

"Let me hear it again," he asks through his laughter.

"No," I say pouty.

"Come on babe," he pleads, containing his laughter.

I shake my head. He surprises me by flipping us over to where he's hovering above me, he starts tickling me. I instantly start laughing and kicking at him.

"Do it," he says through his laughter, still tickling me.

I'm trying so hard not to laugh but he starts tickling me in my most ticklish spot, the sides of my hips. No longer being able to contain myself, I start laughing so hard I begin to snort. Micah laughs harder than I've ever seen him laugh before as he falls backwards on the couch grabbing his stomach as he does.

"You think that's funny do you," I ask, laughing.

Enjoying the sound of his laughter and the way his dimples pop when he's smiling big. He looks so youthful, so care free right now.

"I really do," he's crying from laughter now.

I smack him on the shoulder playfully. He grabs my elbows pulling me onto his chest as he wraps his arms around me.

He kisses my nose before saying, "My funny girl."

His smile is so beautiful. I kiss him on the cheek, wiping his tears of laughter away before lifting off of him. He pulls me closer to him, stopping my movements.

"Where do you think you're going baby," he asks, smiling.

"To watch the sunset with you," I say, lifting off of him as I take his hand in mine as I lead us to his balcony then. "I would be out here every evening if this were my house. The view is beautiful," I say in awe as I look out over the scenery.

"Yes it is," he says looking at me.

I smile.

"It's so romantic out here. All you need now is stringed lights and music to slow dance to," I say, teasingly.

Smiling, he then grabs his phone out of his pocket. I begin to giggle when I hear music start playing.

"May I have this dance," he asks me as he steps closer to me, offering his hand.

I bite my lip and smile, placing my hand in his. He wraps his arm around my waist, pulling me closer to him, holding my hand in his other. I look up at him and smile. Ed Sheeran's song "Kiss Me" begins to play.

"I love this song," I muse quietly.

He's staring into my eyes admiringly.

"I thought you would," as he began swaying us.

He never takes his eyes off of me as he spins me slowly before pulling me close to him again. I can't help but feel he's played this song intentionally for me, for us. He swallows and his breathing hitches slightly when the lyrics say, "Kiss me like you wanna be loved. For this feels like falling in love. I was made to keep your body warm but I'm cold as the wind blows so hold me in your arms. My heart's against your chest, I'm falling for your eyes. This feels like falling in love. We're falling in love."

He's staring into my eyes as though he's found something he's been searching for. He pulls me closer to him placing his forehead to mine. Gently swaying us as the song plays.

Thirty

We're wrapped in each other's arms on the balcony watching the sunset. I close my eyes and enjoy the sound of the river and the birds singing. A light breeze rolls through creating a serene moment. Micah is playing with the ends of my hair as I nuzzle my face into his chest breathing him in. His scent and his warm embrace becoming home to me. He kisses the top of my head when suddenly we hear a heavy knock on the door.

"Who is that," I ask looking up at him.

"I'm not sure," Micah says, looking guarded as he lets go of me to walk to the door.

I follow but stop at the staircase.

Micah looks through the peephole and says, "My father."

I hurriedly straighten my clothes and hair. I had hoped I'd meet him looking better than I currently do. Micah opens the door only half way. I can't see his father, but I can hear him. "You forgot

UNTIL I
found you

these at the office. I need those completed by Thursday morning. No later," I hear his father say.

"They'll be done." Micah says, flatly. "While I'm here I also need the paperwork from the Allen-Morgan accounts. Can I come in? It's been a while since I've seen the old place."

Micah looks over at me before he lets out a deep frustrated breath through his nose, reluctantly opening the door for his father. His father steps into full view looking around the space. He's tall like Micah, but not the same build as him. He's tall and slender whereas Micah is tall and muscular. He turns around meeting my eyes then.

His are almost a grayish blue color. Dull compared to Micah's brighter ocean shade of blue. "Hello," I say, nicely.

I'm waiting for Micah to introduce me but he doesn't. Instead he just stands there awkwardly.

I walk over to him, extending my hand as I say, "It's nice to meet You Mr. Eason. I'm Leyna."

He looks a bit stunned by my friendliness but takes my hand shaking it.

"Likewise. I must say, it's hard to find such friendly help these days."

My mouth gapes open at his response.

"Um," I say.

Before I can reply, Micah is beside me.

"She's not a maid," he says, annoyed with his father.

"Oh. I apologize. Your attire looked like a uniform of sorts."

I looked down at my appearance and could see why he was confused. I'm still in my waitressing clothes.

"Let me get this so you can go," Micah huffs at his father before walking upstairs to his office.

I stand there awkwardly.

His father speaks up then, "So you're a friend of my son?"

Has Micah not mentioned me to his dad yet? Apparently not. Should I even tell him? He's looking at me, waiting for my response.

"Actually I'm his girlfriend."

I decided to go with the truth. He looks a bit taken aback by my response.

Looking me up and down before saying, "Must be a new development."

I shift uncomfortably, "Yes sir, it is" I say back.

"Who are your parents," he asks.

Why is He asking who my parents are?

"I belong to several clubs. I'm sure I know of them," he adds.

So He's a country club kind of guy.

"Oh. My mother doesn't belong to anything like that."

"Your father," he asks.

I shake my head, "My father isn't in the picture."

He looks at me, sizing me up before saying, "I see. Well that's unfortunate. Are you attending any universities?"

Before I can reply that I attend Stanford, he says, "Probably not. Silly of Me to ask really."

I'm floored. This man doesn't even know me. Doesn't know that I've worked my ass off, that I still work my ass off to put myself through college. Instead of living a normal teenage life of partying,

UNTIL I
found you

hanging out with friends and playing xbox, I locked myself up in my room everyday studying for hours on end. Taking every prep course I could. In the end it paid off because in my junior year of high school, my ACT scores were already 32, and I was offered academic scholarships to Stanford, Berkeley, UCLA and other different colleges of my choosing before my senior year even began.

He doesn't know this. All he sees is a waitress in his son's grand big house. Tears brim my eyes.

"Excuse me," I say, blinking back tears as I collect my shoes and keys.

"Nice meeting you," I hear him call as I run down the stairs.

I get into my car and drive off as tears pour down my face. A few minutes later, my phone begins to ring. It's Micah. I begin to cry harder. I was so worried that he would hurt me or that he would leave. I never stopped to consider just how out of my league he is. I knew I didn't deserve him. He's too good for me. He comes from a well-to-do family. I come from an addict mother. He knows who his father is. I don't. Lyle and I had different fathers. His father wasn't a teenage waste of space like mine was, according to Jean. I don't even know what my father looks like. From memories Micah told me about his mother, she would not have gone off and left her two kids in a hotel room alone for days at a time.

Only supplying them with pop tarts and stale cereal to eat while she was gone with countless men. Micah had a great and loving mother. I don't. He has opportunities at his feet. I have to break my back just to get my foot in the door. The way Micah held his door so as for his father not to see me makes me wonder, is Micah embarrassed of me? He didn't tell his father about me. That must be it. My phone rings and rings. Micah has called me over and over now.

I pull up to my house to see both Maggie and Jared's cars are gone. There's another car in its place. I look down at my phone and find a text from Maggie. "Got someone coming by to fix the sink. It busted again this morning."

I look to see multiple texts from Micah. "What happened? What did he say? Baby please answer me. Answer the phone Leyna!"

I begin to cry harder, sobbing into my hands. I'm thankful Maggie and Jared aren't home. At least, I won't have to explain to them why I'm crying as I walk through the house. Just then there's a tap on my car window. I jump at the sound. I expect it to be Micah, but it's not. It's Connor.

Thirty-one

"What are you doing here?" I ask, wiping my tears away as I walk towards the front door. Connor follows me.

"Maggie called and said your sink was busted. I offered to fix it- what's wrong? Why are you crying?"

I ignore him and keep walking. He grabs my wrist to turn me to face him. A small cry escapes my lips. It's my damned burned wrist. He immediately let's go.

"I'm sorry. Are you ok," he asks looking at my bandaged wrist.

"What happened? And why are you crying?"

Wiping tears from my eyes, I say "It's nothing Connor."

"It's definitely something. Talk to me Leyna. Please," he says, placing his hand around my arm gently.

He searches my face before looking down at my injured wrist.

"Wait. Did he hurt you," he asks, becoming angry.

"Micah" I ask, shocked.

"Yes. Did he hurt you," Connor asks, becoming more agitated by the second.

Micah, hurting me? Never.

"No. It's just his-" before I can finish Micah's Corvette comes to a screeching halt in front of my house.

Oh no. He gets out of his car in a hurry, striding over to me when he notices Connor standing closely in front of me with his hand wrapped around my arm. Micah's eyes turn dark. Primal. He instantly clinches his hands into fists at his sides. I pull away from Connor then. I'm about to walk over to Micah to calm him, when Connor grabs my arm stopping me. He pulls me behind him protectively and throws his arm back around me, wrapping it around my back shielding me. I'm not the one that needs shielding. I remove his arm from around me.

"Did you fucking touch her," Connor accuses, walking towards Micah.

His finger pointed at him.

"What the fuck did you just say," Micah growls, as he pushes Connor back with all his strength.

He nearly knocked Connor to the ground. I run to Micah begging him to stop before the two of them end up fighting.

"Micah stop," I say, trying to push him away from Connor.

It's futile, he's too strong.

"I said, did you fucking touch her," Connor is shouting now.

Until I found you

Micah's chest is heaving up and down at an alarming rate. Rage radiating throughout him. He charges forward.

"I would NEVER hurt her, you mother fucker," he spits through clenched jaws.

Fists of fury at his sides.

"Micah, no," I shout, trying to rein him back.

Connor stalks forward. His fists in a ball.

I turn around and shout, "Connor stop!"

"Get out of the way, Leyna," he barks.

"Dont fucking tell her what to do," Micah points, shouting at him.

Connor tries stepping around me but I press my hands against his chest stopping him.

"He didn't do anything! He didn't hurt me! He wouldn't do that!"

Connor stops in his tracks as my words sink in. Micah is still stalking towards him ready to fight. I spin around quickly stopping him.

I step on my tippy toes, grabbing Micah's face between my hands, "Look at me. Micah, look at Me. Look at me," I plead with him, shouting towards the end.

He takes his savage glare away from Connor long enough to look down at me. His nostrils are flared. His eyes a vibrant blue from his rage. His chest is heaving. His fists are clenched at his sides. He's a ticking bomb.

"Calm down. Baby, please. Please don't fight," I beg him, softly.

Rubbing his face lightly, willing him to turn back into my sweet Micah. He places one of his hands on the side of my face. Looking into my eyes as he steadies his breathing.

"That's it. Calm baby. Calm," I say to him softly.

He takes a deep concentrated breath before looking back at Connor and shouting, "Leave! Now!"

Connor laughs at Micah, which only pushes Micah further.

"I'm not leaving. I was asked to come here," Connor says.

"By who," Micah demands.

Connor looks at me for a moment, eyeing me up and down slowly. I can feel Micah tensing under my touch.

He then gives Micah a devious smile before saying, "How pissed would you be if I said it was your girlfriend that wanted me here?"

My jaw drops at his audacity. Is he fucking insane?!

"That's it," Micah shouts, charging forward.

"No," I plead.

Grabbing Micah's arm trying to stop him, but he's dragging me at this point. He's an unstoppable force. Just then I see Jo and Maggie running towards us from Maggie's car. Thankful that I now have help. Unfortunately for Connor, Jo doesn't reach Micah in time. Micah swings his fist and it connects with Connor's jaw. Hard. The force of Micah swinging causes me to fall back onto the pavement driveway. The back of my head hits it, hard. Connor recovers and punches Micah in the jaw as well. Micah doesn't even stagger back as he reconnects his fist to the side of Connor's head. Connor falls to the ground as

Micah hovers over him, dealing another blow to his face.

"Micah, stop," I yell.

"Walk away Mike," Jo shouts at Micah as he grabs him up under the arms, stopping Micah from dealing another vicious blow to Connor.

Jo slings Micah and himself around towards his car, separating him from Connor.

"Leyna," Maggie exclaims, running over to me on the ground.

"Are you ok," she asks horrified, checking my head over for any sign of injury.

"I'm fine."

Micah then meets my eyes and panic takes over his face as he realizes I'm on the ground. He shrugs Jo off of him and runs over to me.

"Leyna! My God. I'm so sorry," he says, lifting me off the ground, remorse clear on his face. Maggie then looks over at a bleeding Connor as Jo helps him off the ground. Maggie's face instantly turns red.

"Baby, I'm so sorry. I didn't mean to-" Micah is cut off by a furious Maggie.

"Leave Micah! You've done enough," she shouts, shoving him back away from me.

Micah's expression becomes hardened, "I'm not leaving without her," he says to Maggie.

"Well she's not going with you," Maggie shouts at him.

Both of them in a staring contest with the other. Jo begins to walk towards them. I can't have all of them fighting because of me. "It wasn't his fault," I say, defending Micah.

Maggie looks astonished. So does everyone else.

"Connor accused me of inviting him over in front of Micah. Which for the record, isn't true!" Maggie looks over to her cousin, "No wonder he fucking hit you. What did you think was going to happen," she responds to him.

He stands up, wiping his bloody jaw.

"It was a joke. Apparently I had forgotten the guy was a total fucking psychopath. What are you even doing with this guy, Leyna? He's no good for you," he retorts.

Anger rises in me.

"Leave," I demand.

Connor shakes his head at me before getting in his car and peeling out of our driveway.

After a moment Jo says, "Everyone just take a deep breath. Micah, you good?"

"Only if she is," Micah says, looking at me.

I open my mouth to speak when Maggie cuts in, "Dude, Your hand is bleeding. Like really bad," she says pointing to Micah's already busted knuckles.

They're dripping blood at this point. I take his hand in mine and see it's worse now than it was just hours ago.

"Let's get this cleaned up. You may need stitches," I say trying to walk inside.

Micah stops me, "Fuck the bloody hand. I could care less about my hand right now. We need to talk."

Maggie and Jo look at each other before they turn to walk inside giving us some privacy. "Why did you leave? What did that asshole say to you for you

UNTIL I found you

to just leave like that," Micah asks, his eyes searching mine. "What did he say baby," he asks softer.

"Nothing I didn't already realize," I say.

He becomes angry, "What the fuck is that supposed to mean?"

I begin to walk away from him. When he steps in front of me holding my arms stopping me. "Hey. Talk to me. Now," he says, containing his anger.

"I'm not good enough for you," I say simply. "I'm not some high society debutante. I don't come from a rich family. I'm not like you. I'm not good for you."

I say, every word hurts more than the last. I blink back my tears.

"Not good enough for me" he repeats quietly.

Nodding his head up and down as he does so, becoming angrier.

"Stop saying that," he shouts angrily.

His outburst causes me to take a step back.

"You think I give a shit about any of that? You think just because my father is wealthy now that means I came from generations of wealth? My grandparents weren't rich. They were poor as hell. They pushed my father to do better in life; to have a better life then they did. They instilled that in him so much to the point that's all he cared about in life was money. All he focused on was building himself an empire. He cared about nothing else other than that. Not my mom. Not even me. His family came second to his wealth and career. The only thing that even made us a family was my mom. When she died it all went to hell. We weren't a family after that. We still aren't. My father and I may share the same blood. But we're strangers. So fuck him. Fuck what he thinks! He lost the right to give his input into my life a long time ago. I don't care what he fucking thinks, Leyna. And neither should you! He didn't care what I thought when he left my mom and I alone those last three months of her life. Left her while she was dying! He didn't care what I thought when he took all those business trips. Leaving me alone with an unfamiliar nanny, a stranger, for months at a time while I was grieving my mom. Night after night I would cry myself to sleep. Alone in an empty house surrounded by strangers. So no, I don't care what he thinks. To hell with him!" He spits.

I'm floored. I assumed Micah came from generations of wealth and prominence. I assumed he was wanting someone of that same class. I misjudged him. I thought he was embarrassed of me, of where I came from.

He notices I'm in deep thought, "What is it," he asks, searching my face.

I look at him and ask, "are you embarrassed of me?"

"What," he asks, incredulously. "Of course not! Look at you! Why would you think that," he asks, shouting again.

"Why would I think that," I repeat, my volume increasing. "Because you didn't tell your father about me."

He huffs, "The reason I didn't tell my father about you is because I was trying to protect you from his crudeness, Leyna. Nothing, and I do mean nothing I do is good enough for him. I went to the university he wanted. I was at the top of my class. I

UNTIL I
found you

began creating my own client list right after graduation. It may be my father's company, but I've brought in more revenue and clientele since I've been there than he has in the past decade. I bought my mom's house from him within six months of working. That's how much I have brought into that company. And still, nothing is good enough for him. So to hell what he thinks! I don't care about his opinions concerning my life. Or the people in it. We don't talk. Work is the only thing we communicate about. We haven't spent a holiday together in almost 12 years. He may be my father, and I his son, but *we* are not a family. We're nowhere even close."

His last statement resonates through my heart. I may have a mom, but we're not a family either. I know the pain of those words and the factual truth behind them. It breaks my heart for him. I know the loneliness it carries. The want and need for a family that doesn't exist. Tears begin to pull at my eyes. His expression of anger turns into an expression of sadness.

"Baby, don't. Please don't cry. I can't take it," he says taking my face in his hands. Wiping my tears away with his thumbs, "I'm sorry. I'm sorry for whatever he said to you. None of it is remotely the truth. Don't listen to him. Listen to me. Believe what I tell you. You are important to me, Leyna. I'm sorry I ever made you feel like I was embarrassed of you. But baby, I could never be embarrassed of you. You are seriously the only great thing in my life. I've never felt happiness like this. I've never had feelings like this before. I've never wanted to. Until you," he pauses. "And honestly it's scary to admit that. But it's the truth. You mean more to me than you realize," he says.

My breath hitches.

"I don't want to hear one more fucking word come out of your mouth about you not being good enough for me. I want you. You're mine. Do you understand me?"

UNTIL I
found you

Thirty-two

I'm in the bathroom cleaning Micah's hand when Maggie taps on the door.

"Hey Leyna, I'm grabbing an overnight bag and heading out. I'm staying with Jo tonight. Jared is with his boy toy for the night too. So it'll just be you," she says through the door.

"Okay. Be careful," I reply not even looking up from cleaning Micah's hand.

"Enough babe. I'm fine. It doesn't even hurt, " he lies, giving me a small smile as I look down at his busted knuckles.

I look at the small white scars across his fist as I place a second bandage over his knuckles. I hear Maggie leave as she shuts the front door behind her.

"I really think you need stitches or something. It's even worse than before," I say to him.

"I've had worse busted knuckles than this. I'm fine. Trust me."

I furrow my brows at him.

"What," he asks.

"Do you fight a lot," I ask, crossing my arms.

All the scars across his knuckles are giving me my answer already but I want to hear it from him.

He pauses, "I used to. I have a bad temper in case you haven't noticed. I've had one for as long as I can remember really. My teenage and college years were the worst. But I've managed to get a rein on it over time....Mostly," he adds after a moment.

He gives me his most charming smile.

"Well, I don't like you fighting," I say looking down. "You could get hurt," I added.

He chuckles, "You shouldn't worry about that."

"Well Rocky, I do. Plus violence doesn't solve anything."

"Well, if that didn't teach that fucker to stay away from you nothing will," he smiles darkly.

I roll my eyes, "You're such a caveman. There's no need to be so jealous." I huff, attempting to walk away.

He places his hands on either side of my waist pulling me to him. "There's a few things you need to know baby," he says as he runs his hands down my waist slowly. "First, I'm not jealous. I'm territorial of what's mine. Jealous would imply that he has something I want. You're mine. Not his. If anyone is jealous it's him. Secondly, I'm not a caveman. But I can sling you over my shoulder and take you to bed, fuck your brains out if that's what you'd like," he says seductively as he glides his large hands down my hips and across my ass.

He licks his lips as he trails his hands over my curves slowly. Suddenly my mouth has become dry. My breathing hitches slightly. I swallow a lump in my throat at his words and the way he's touching me. He must notice what he's doing to me. He grins knowingly before he kisses the top of my head.

"Pack your things," he says simply.

I look at him confused.

"What? Why," I ask.

"Because, you're staying with me tonight," he replies, taking my hand and leading us into my bedroom.

This is the first time he's ever been in here. He looks around the room and chuckles lightly to himself seeing the difference between my side of the room and Maggie's. Maggie's side of the wall is filled with an array of fashion design sketches and posters of Adam Levine and Heath Ledger. Her bedspread is a ballerina pink, made of Chiffon material. Whereas, my side of the wall is filled with shelves containing worn books I no longer have the time to read. One of the shelves is filled with vinyl records I've been collecting over the years. He studies my collection of books and records, smiling as he does.

"Bookworm, eh," Micah asks with a bit of a smirk looking over my book collection.

"Figured that out all by yourself did you," I ask teasingly.

He chuckles. Noticing all of my books he asks, "So which is your favorite? Ernest Hemingway or Jane Austen?"

I smile at him.

"It's a tie. Ernest Hemingway for his truth. Jane Austen for her powerhouse writing. Her work is mixed with humor and romance."

He smiles.

"I don't know much about Austen other than her Pride and Prejudice but I do know some Hemingway," he says, before clearing his throat dramatically and recites, "The world breaks everyone, and afterward, some are strong at the broken places".

I clap playfully at him, "I'm impressed".

He takes a playful bow; "My mom was a Hemingway fan also. She used to quote him a lot. Him and Maya Angelou. She was one of her favorites," he smiles at the memory before looking over my record collection.

He smiles to himself, "I don't know anyone who collects these anymore."

"Apparently style and class are dying," I say.

He chuckles at my response as he glances over to the other shelf and sees the framed pictures sitting on it. He walks over to examine them. He laughs lightly at the picture of Maggie, Jared and myself. It was Halloween and we decided to dress up as a group. Jared being Batman, Maggie being Catwoman and I was Poison Ivy.

"Damn baby," he says, eyeing me.

I grab the picture from him and set it back down.

"You'll have to put that costume on for me sometime," he says wiggling his brows.

I playfully hit his arm. He grabs the picture of me and Lyle from when we were little.

"That's My brother Lyle and me," I say softly. "It was taken on the first day of school. Lyle was going into the 2nd grade whereas I was just starting kindergarten. I remember being so nervous. Lyle held my hand all the way to my classroom."

UNTIL I found you

I smile at the memory. Micah pulls me closer to him, laying his cheek on top of my head. Just then my phone begins to ring. Suddenly, I remember the text from Jean earlier. I internally groan knowing I'd eventually have to call my mother back. I pull my phone out of my back pocket and see that it's Tony calling me. Oh, this can't be good. Micah eyes me curiously.

I answer nervously, "hello?"

"Hey Leyna, sorry I'm calling late but I wanted to discuss what happened earlier today," he says flatly.

Is he calling to officially fire me? I assumed Chelsea would jump at that opportunity herself. Plus, I'm sure the whole restaurant heard Micah's declaration that I quit.

"I know Tony. I'm sorry. It's just that those guys were belligerently intoxicated and were giving me a hard time and-"

Tony cuts me off, "No Leyna, don't apologize. I didn't call you for that. I called you to see if you would consider coming back actually. After everything that happened today, my parents finally decided to remove Chelsea from being in charge. She'll be working in the kitchen with me," he snickers at this. "They wanted me to manage it. But I don't know anything about managing. So I was hoping you'd do me the favor and come back, to take the manager position. You'd get a pay raise of course, with the benefit of bossing Chelsea around now. And, honestly, there would be people that take this job for that reason alone," he laughs.

I laugh light heartedly along with him. The idea was pretty funny. I look up to see Micah staring at me. His expression is unreadable.

"Anyway, would you at least think about coming back," Tony asks after a moment.

Micah shakes his head no the same time I reply, "yeah. I'll think about it," to Tony before hanging up.

Micah lets out a deep frustrated breath.

He looks at me sternly before saying, "No, absolutely not. You're not going back. End of discussion."

I place my hands on my hips, "excuse me," I ask sternly.

"You heard me. You're not going back there. Either you work with me or I'll help you find something else. You're not going back there. And, that's the end of it," he says with finality.

I'm becoming pissed.

"Ok first off, you don't own me. Secondly, it's my decision not yours. I'll do what I want."

He looks at me with narrowed eyes.

"Why must you be so damn difficult? You're not going back," he says with an authoritative tone of voice. "And since you're too busy arguing with me to pack your bag, I'll do it for you," he adds, walking over to my dresser.

"I'm not going," I say, crossing my arms.

He looks mad for a moment before it fades into a look of amusement.

"You're a stubborn, defiant little thing aren't you? Quit acting like a brat and pack your bag. Or I'll do it for you," he says standing over me.

until I found you

I stare into his eyes as I slowly rise higher on my tippy toes to face him when I say flatly, "Make me."

He smiles to himself before saying, "you really shouldn't have said that."

Thirty-three

He takes me by surprise when he dips down and picks me up slinging me over his shoulder. I begin to kick at him. Trying to still be mad at him but I can't, I'm fighting laughter.

"Put me down you asshole," I shout, swatting at him.

He walks over to my bed and throws me on it before flipping me on my stomach and slaps me on my ass. Hard.

"Ow!" I yell.

He does it again, this time softer.

"That's what you get for acting a brat and defying me at every turn," he says trying to hide the humor in his tone.

We're both still trying to be mad at the other but it's not working for either of us. I'm the one that breaks. I let out a laugh, flipping on my back so I can whip his ass. Except I whip him harder and faster. He growls playfully before grabbing my hands, pinning me on the bed beneath him. He's hovered over me. His eyes are wild and playful.

"What was that for," he asks, trying not to laugh.

Until I found you

"If you get to spank me for being a brat, then I get to spank you for being such a bossy asshole," I say fighting a giggle.

He shakes his head back and forth, smiling at me. "Leyna Blake, what am I going to do with you?"

He dipped his head down and kissed me. It begins as a teasing kiss. It soon turns into a sweet one. He still has my hands pinned down when his lips leave my mouth, kissing me tenderly on my cheeks, my temple, my nose. He touches his nose to mine in the sweetest gesture. The way he's looking at me has my heart soaring. His smile is so soft, pure. It reaches his beautiful eyes as I see the admiration he holds for me behind them. He lets go of my hands and begins stroking my cheek lightly. Never breaking his eyes from mine.

"My beautiful, feisty girl," he says quietly, before brushing his lips to mine.

"You're too sweet to me. You know that," I say, smiling while running my hand through his hair. He frowns slightly, "No I'm not. This is how a woman like you is supposed to be treated. I've never met anyone like you before. You have it all. The beauty, the intelligents, the compassion. Such a pure heart," he says admiringly as he traces circles over my heart with his finger.

Never taking his eyes from mine. I begin to blush.

"Stop it," I say covering my face.

I'm not good at receiving compliments. He chuckles, gently removing my hands from my face.

"I'm serious. You are a beautiful person, baby."

I can feel myself blushing more from his words and the way he's looking at me. Because I'm awkward, I squint my nose and cross my eyes.

I ask him, "how about now?"

He throws his head back in laughter.

"Yes, even with that ridiculous face you're making, you're still beautiful to me," he smiles. "And, even when you snort like a little piggy," he begins laughing again.

I mock a pout at him, "That's not funny."

"It's not? How about now," he asks, tickling me.

"No," I yell.

He begins tickling my sides as I kick at him, fighting my laughter. He goes in for the kill when he places his lips on my neck blowing hard raspberries into it. His facial hair tickling my neck further. Sending me over the edge into a fit of snorts and giggles. He falls on his back from his bellowing laughter. Holding his sides as he does. He looks like he's about to cry, he's laughing so hard. I can't help but laugh with him.

I playfully hit him on the shoulder, "you jerk," I say through my giggles.

He gently pulls me onto his chest, wrapping his arms snuggly around me, anchoring me to him as his chest bounces from his laughter.

"I'm glad I amuse you," I say smiling.

"I haven't laughed like this in years," he says.

"Really? You're always laughing around me. You seem like a jolly person. You know when you're not beating people up I mean," I say.

He chuckles at my snide comment, "I'm jolly only because I'm around you. You should see me when you're not around. You probably wouldn't think me jolly then."

I cock my brow at him.

"Why is that," I ask.

"Because I'm typically not like this at all. Far from it really. I don't like people. I only put on the persona for business meetings and dealings when needed. In truth, people annoy me with their predictability."

I chuckle at him, "You're so brooding," I say.

He shrugs, "I get that part from my father I suppose. People are predictable. They only think of themselves. What they can do to benefit themselves. How many people they can step on to get to the top. How what they say or do will make them look in the eyes of the masses instead of what they truly think. Everyone wants the same things in life. To be liked. To be at the top. There's no mystery. They lack in originality or character. It's all the same generic people. No one strives to be good or fair anymore. The world is full of assholes waiting to use you for their benefit. People only want you for something you can give them," he says.

I ponder this for a moment. He's mostly right. That's why I'm not a big people person either. Don't get me wrong, I'd give someone my last dollar if they needed it. But trust them? Or expect the same treatment in return? No.

"And then, there's you," he says after a moment.

I look up at him.

"You are the most selfless person I know. You care for people when they don't deserve your affection or loyalty. You genuinely care about others. You're passionate in your beliefs. And you're not afraid to let anyone know what you're thinking. You're not scared to go head to head with someone," he chuckles. "I knew the second you tore into me that night at the restaurant I had to know you. I've never met another girl so spirited in my life, so sure of herself. My charms didn't work on you. You weren't afraid to stand up to me at all. You're so brave. So certain of yourself. So strong," he trails off. Pausing to look at me with thoughtful eyes before continuing. "I can tell you've been through a lot. You've been used, hurt. Neglected even. I can tell this even though you haven't told me in words yourself yet. I know life hasn't been kind to you. And yet, through all the hell you've been through, you haven't allowed that to deteriorate your character, to negatively change who you are as a person. Most people would crumble. Most people would become cold hearted and uncaring. But you? You're so incredibly loving. And, strong," he says, touching my cheek. "Leyna, I admire you. I'm in awe of you, of your bravery, your ability to forgive those that don't deserve it, and your kindness. You're unlike any woman I've ever met. I had to have you. I had to make you mine."

    I'm floored. No one has ever said things to me like this before. My eyes sting as tears threaten to come. I swallow the lump rising in my throat. I don't have the words to express how he's made me feel, so instead I show him. I place my hands on either side of his face and pull his lips to mine, kissing him sensually. Our lips move in perfect rhythm. He pulls me closer, deepening our kiss. Parting his lips with mine, I slip my tongue into his mouth. The taste of him is delicious. He swirled his tongue with mine as he drew back some before pushing back into my mouth in a slow tease. This is the first time we've ever kissed like this.

Usually we're lost in each other's passionate fire for one another. But in this moment, we're wrapped in each other's arms silently expressing our feelings for each other. The way we're holding each other, the way we're kissing each other, there are no words needed. As terrifying to me as the truth is, I believe this man is falling in love with me. And what terrifies me the most, is that I am without a shadow of doubt falling in love with this man.

Thirty-four

After a while of us cuddling on my bed and laughing like kids as we conversed, he gets up and walks towards my door.

"I'm going to the kitchen to get some water. Do you want anything babe," he asks.

I shake my head and he leaves. I'm rummaging through my drawers trying to find my sexiest bra and panties to pack. I came up with my black and white silk set. The cups are made of white silk with black lace decorating the sides and top of the bra, same as the panties. Cute, but I wouldn't consider them sexy. I need to invest in some sexier sets now that I have Micah. I've never worn sexy lingerie before.

I smile to myself thinking about what Micah's reaction would be seeing me in it. He makes me feel so beautiful, so sexy. I grab the bra and panties and throw them in my bag along with my sleeping shorts and baggy t-shirt. Yep I'm definitely going shopping soon. I go to my and Maggie's closet and begin to rummage through my clothes. I grab my most flattering pair of jeans along with my yoga pants and a few tops.

UNTIL I
found you

I grab my hair brush, my makeup bag and my favorite perfume from Bath and Body Works off my dresser. I'm about to walk over to my bed to put them in my bag when I hear Micah in the kitchen talking to someone on the phone. His tone is harsh. Cold.

"What do you want? I told you to stop calling me."

I toss my stuff onto the bed and tip toe into the hallway to eavesdrop.

"I don't answer your countless texts or calls anymore for a reason, Nadia. Get that fact through your head."

Nadia. My blood instantly boils.

"If you feel like you're being thrown to the side that's your problem. We were never anything to begin with and you know it." He pauses. "It was never going to be a relationship with us. It was a mutual benefit only and that's all it was ever going to be. I suggest you accept that and move on. Don't call me anymore."

He hangs up on her. His jaw is clenched when he turns around and sees me already staring at him.

"Why in the fuck is she calling you," I ask, already pissed off.

"Why do you think Leyna? She's a needy little whore," he responds coldly.

I'm not sure if it's because I'm mad or because of the way he said that to me just now but I begin to cry. He walks over to me, pulling me into his arms.

"Baby, I'm sorry," he says as I'm already wiping my tears away.

"It's been a long day ok? My emotions are running high. I'm pissed. I cry when I get like that," I explain.

He tucks a strand of hair behind my ear before planting a gentle kiss to my forehead.

"You have nothing to worry about. She's nothing to me. Never was," he says, before taking my hand in his and leading us back to my room to finish packing.

I'm locking the front door behind me when my neighbor from across the street, Mr. Edgar waves me over.

"Hello, Leyna. I know it's late and I hate to bug you but can I have a word with you before you go please?"

His dog Charlie is already barking excitedly at me.

"Sure thing, Mr Edgar," I say to him.

"Who's that," Micah asks.

"That's my neighbor. I dogsit Charlie for him from time to time. He's a sweet old man."

"Which one," Micah asks jokingly.

I elbow his arm in response. We walk over to Mr. Edgar where Charlie sits patiently at his feet waiting for his ear scratches.

"Hey Charlie! Come here boy," I say in a praising voice.

He runs over to me, jumping up on me. Standing on his hind legs, he starts licking my chin. "Charlie down! You know better than that, you old rascal you," Mr. Edgar says, shaking his head.

I begin to giggle at Charlie's expression. He looks as though he's smiling at me.

"He's fine. Aren't you fine boy?"

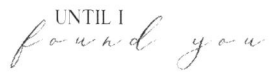

I give him ear scratches.

"Oh, I'd like You to meet my boyfriend. This is Micah," I say gesturing to him.

Micah extends his hand, "It's nice to meet you, sir," Micah says, giving Mr. Edgar a firm shake. They shake hands and Mr Edgar says, "A firm shake. I like that. That's how a man is supposed to shake hands. You kids these days shake hands like a sissy. It's embarrassing." Micah and I stifle a laugh.

"In my day, if you didn't take a man's hand firmly in yours and look him in the eye, you weren't a man."

"Yes sir. You're right," Micah says.

Mr. Edgar looks over to me, "I like him."

I giggle.

"Anyway, the reason I called you over here is because I'll be needing you to dog sit Charlie for me next Friday and Saturday. We have a bowling tournament in Las Vegas."

"Oh that's awesome! See I told you you'd beat that other team," I say.

"Well the Asians might make everything we own and beat us at math. But they can't out bowl this old coot," he says winking at me.

Micah and I both let out a laugh. Mr Edgar joins in.

"Well, I'll let you kids get back at it. Leyna, I'll see you Friday?"

I give Charlie one last ear scratch, "Sure thing Mr. Edgar. Good luck!"

"When you're this good, you don't need luck," he says winking.

Micah shakes his head stifling another laugh.

"It was a pleasure meeting you sir," he says, extending his hand once more.

Mr. Edgar takes it, "Likewise young man. You take care of this one. She's a jewel. I may be old but I can still wrestle with the best of them. You best be good to her."

I smile at him.

"Yes sir, I will. You have my word on that," Micah says.

We wave at Mr. Edgar and Charlie as we drive off. Micah starts laughing a few minutes later. "What," I ask, already laughing myself.

"I like him. He's something else," Micah says. "And, obviously he knows a jewel when he sees one," he adds, smiling at me.

Suddenly I remember Micah mentioning that he had something planned for us this coming weekend. "Shit. I forgot you already planned something for us this weekend. I can tell Mr. Edgar He needs to find someone else to watch Charlie."

Micah shakes his head.

"No, it's fine baby. Honestly I hadn't planned anything in particular yet. I just wanted you with me is all," he says grinning at me.

I smile at him. How lucky am I to have found someone like him? I take a moment to thank whoever is listening for bringing him into my life.

Thirty-five

I feel at peace when I'm in his arms; so strong and protective, so warm and comforting. They're wrapped around me as I straddle him on the couch. My head laying on his chest. His hands playing in my hair. I smile to myself at his touch.

"Are you falling asleep on me," he asks.

I look up to see he's already smiling at me. I smile back and shake my head.

"No. I'm just enjoying you holding me like this," I muse.

"Me too, baby," he says, before he plants a soft, gentle kiss to my head.

He pulls me closer to him, tightening his grip on me ever so slightly as he does. I love when he does that. It's like if he doesn't hold me close I'll somehow float away from him.

After a moment of him holding me like this he asks, "what would you like to do tomorrow?"

I look up at him, "After you get home from work?"

He smiles, "I'm not going in tomorrow. I'm spending the day with you," he says.

"Won't you get in trouble for ditching work," I ask.

He chuckles, "get in trouble? Babe, not only am I part owner of the company, I'm also a shareholder. Relax. It'll be fine. They can go a day without me. So what would you like to do tomorrow?"

I ponder for a moment before saying, "We could go to the city. I haven't been to San Francisco in a while. Unless you have something else you'd like to do."

"Is that what you want to do," he asks.

I nod, "We have to stop by sticky lips while we're out. It's an ice cream shop. They have the most delicious ice cream you'll ever eat. You'll never want Ben and Jerry's again."

"I like sweet treats," he says, eyeing me up and down.

I blush, "Micah," I say bashfully.

He chuckles while kissing the top of my head.

"Ready to go to bed," he asks.

I nod. He takes my hand leading us up the stairs. Micah insisted that I wear one of his shirts to sleep in. I rolled my eyes playfully as I took his shirt from him, putting it on as he watched. His eyes greedily taking my body in. I couldn't help the smile that crept on my face knowing he wanted to see me in his shirt. I spray my favorite bath and body works scent onto my wrists and neck before climbing in bed with him. He wraps his arms around me, bringing me closer to him. He inhales deeply into my neck. Smelling me.

"Heaven," he says before planting gentle kisses to my neck.

I giggle, "You like my perfume?"

He smiles into my neck taking in another deep scent of me, before humming into my ear. "Mmm hmmm," he said.

We both chuckle.

"Delicious" he says, nibbling my ear.

I playfully swat at him and he dramatically falls onto his pillow. I laugh. I love seeing the playful side of him. He pulls me into his chest, cuddling me as we watch TV in bed. He's flipping through channels when he reaches the TCM channel.

"Ooh wait go back! I love old movies."

He rolls his eyes but flips it back. It's a Bing Crosby film.

"There's something so beautiful about films in black and white," I muse.

He looks down at me and smiles.

"I love how you find beauty in everything," he says, planting a kiss on the top of my head.

I snuggle in closer to him as we watch. A while later an old jazz song begins to play through the TV. Micah stiffens and I turn my head to look at him. His face in deep thought, his jaw clenched. I place my hand gently to his face, breaking him from his thoughts.

"Hey," I say softly, "You are a whole other world away. Where'd you go babe," I ask sweetly.

He takes my hand from his face, kissing my palm before interlocking our fingers.

"This song just brings back memories. My mother was an old soul and she loved listening to old jazz music. Billie Holiday was her favorite. This song was my mother's song to me right before she-" he trails off.

Listening to the lyrics of this song combined with His mother's meaning behind it, my heart brakes for him.

I grab the remote and turn it off.

"Baby, I'm so sorry," I say.

"She used to dance with me all the time when I was a boy. But once she got sick, she couldn't. Right before she passed away though, she would dance with me on the balcony to that song. It took every ounce of strength for her to do it. I remember her being so frail towards the end. She still held that spark behind her eyes all the way to the end. Despite the fact my fucking father abandoned her those last few months of her life. She had me and that was enough for her. She deserved more, so much more," he says, becoming angry at the thought of his father.

All I can do is wrap my arms around his neck comforting him.

"It's ok. It was a long time ago," he says, trying to brush it off like it doesn't still hurt him.

"What was she like," I ask, trying to get his mind off of his father.

"She was kind. Had a voice like an angel. I remember hearing her sing as she'd tend to her flower garden outside. She was so caring to everyone she met. She was genuinely such a good person. Beautiful. A lot like you in that way."

I smile at him. He shows me a picture of her from his phone and he's right. She was beautiful. She had dark blonde hair with olive complexion. Her eyes were a beautiful golden brown, like honey. Micah inherited her full lips, nose and eye shape. More importantly he inherited his mother's kindness and nobility. We begin to laugh lightly at the memories Micah tells me about his mom; how she couldn't bake to save her life, that she almost set the stove on fire attempting to bake a cake once. She would spend hours outside playing with him as a child or how she would act silly just to make him laugh and smile.

"I would've loved to have met her," I muse.

"She would have loved you," he says smiling.

"Tell me about your brother," he says after a few moments.

My smile fades at the mention of Lyle. I miss him so much.

"I'm sorry. I shouldn't have mentioned-" I cut him off.

"No it's fine. Where to begin? Okay so we were two years apart. We were the exact opposite of each other in almost every way. He had brown hair, I have red. He was tall. I'm not. Except for our eyes, we didn't look alike much," I chuckle. "But having different dads will do that I suppose. He didn't act like me. Where I was temperamental, he was reserved. He was also a force to be reckoned with. Especially when it came to me or Claire."

"Who's Claire? Is that your sister?" Micah asks.

"Claire is- was my brother's girlfriend. She was also like a sister to me. I really think they would have ended up married eventually. If he hadn't," I cut myself off. I clear my throat. "Anyway, they were the cutest couple. Like nauseously cute. He was a football player. She was a cheerleader. They were so in love with each other. She still puts flowers on his grave to this day," I say, giving him a small smile.

"I'd like to meet her one day," he says, giving me an encouraging smile back.

"I haven't seen her in almost four years. We stayed in contact the first year after his death but after that it just became too hard for her I think."

I miss her.

"How do you know she leaves flowers then," He asks curiously.

"Because every year when I visit my brother's headstone there's always flowers there."

A few moments pass before he asks hesitantly, "how did it happen?"

"Car accident," I say simply.

He looks away and frowns. I take his hand in mine. We both know the pain of losing someone precious to us. A moment later he pulls me closer to him.

"There should be a limit to how much suffering one person can endure in a lifetime. I'm so sorry baby," he says as he nuzzles his face into my neck, comforting me as he does.

"I think he would have liked you," I say.

He removes his face from my neck then, looking at me as he asks, "why do you say that?"
"You and he are similar in some ways. Both of you have things in common. You both love cars for instance. Lyle would race though. He loved street racing. I guess there was something about the adrenaline of it he loved so much. You both love the outdoors. Lyle was always outside either tuning his car or running. You both played sports in high school. Both love the same types of music and

movies. You both love me-" I say jokingly but then I realize what I just said.

My cheeks begin to blush. "I- I mean," I stammer. "Well what I meant was..." Micah cuts me off by placing his lips to mine.

He pulls away and smiles at me, "Ready to get some sleep? We have a big day ahead of us tomorrow," he says pulling me closer into his chest as he wraps his arms around me.

I can feel my cheeks heat from the embarrassment. I just insensated that he was in love with me. What if this makes him distant or put off towards me somehow? I don't think he'd be the type to react weirdly towards this. It's not like I actually said the three words to him. My heart is steadily beating at a fast pace. Before I can beat myself up over it anymore he begins playing in my hair, calming me.

As I'm dozing off I hear him whisper, "Goodnight Love."

Thirty-six

I end up waking up 30 minutes before our alarm is set to go off. Micah's long legs are snaked through mine. His head is laying on my chest while his big arms are wrapped around my waist. I look down and admire the beautiful man before me. He looks so young, so peaceful when he's sleeping. I begin to stroke his cheek when he stirs a bit. I retract my hand immediately, not wanting to wake him. He nuzzles his face into my chest before falling back into a deep sleep once more. I brush his hair back from his forehead and kiss the top of his head, admiring him as he sleeps.

After a few moments, I really have to pee and Micah is entangled in me. I wiggle beneath him slowly so as not to wake him. It's going good until he tightens his grip around my waist in his sleep, making me need to pee even more. I hurry up and wiggle out of his grip. After I peed for what seemed like five minutes, I brushed my teeth and decided to go into the kitchen and cook us some breakfast. I pull my hair up in a messy bun and wash my hands before gathering the ingredients to make eggs, bacon and blueberry pancakes.

Until I found you

I decide to play some music on my phone as I cook. I'm bopping along to the song, twirling as I mix the pancake batter. I'm flipping the bacon as I hum along with the lyrics. I spin around on my tippy toes, grabbing a plate for the bacon when I see Micah leaned up against the wall with only his grey sweatpants on. They hang sinfully low on his hips. Showing off His sexy V shape that I love so much. His hair is a disheveled mess, a bright smile is plastered on his face as I begin to blush.

I place the plate over my face, lowering it down some so my eyes are peeking over it.

"How long have you been standing there," I ask sheepishly.

He bites his lip to keep from laughing, "I came down once you started mixing that stuff in the bowl," he says.

Fucking hell.

"Why didn't you say anything," I ask, whining.

"I was enjoying the show too much," he says smiling.

He must see the embarrassment on my face. He walks over to me then, chuckling. I place the plate over my face and he takes it from me, sitting it on the counter.

"That was the best way to wake up. To come down here and find you dancing in my kitchen while you're cooking," he says laughing as he cups my face with his hands.

"I'm embarrassed," I admit.

"Don't be embraced. You're adorable," he says, playfully smushing my cheeks together, causing my lips to pucker out.

I give him a playful pouty face. He kisses me, chuckling.

"My funny girl," he says, releasing my face as he smacks me playfully on the butt.

After we've eaten breakfast and cleaned up the kitchen, we head upstairs to get dressed. I decided on my favorite pair of jeans, my cute white ruffle spaghetti strap top and my other favorite pair of shoes, my maroon slip-on Vans. After I'm dressed, I apply two layers of mascara to my lashes and some blush to my cheeks. I look in the mirror to check my appearance. I feel pretty. My hair is in a half up half down braid, long wavy curls falling down my shoulders. My eyes look brighter today for some reason.

I smile knowing Micah will love seeing these jeans on me. They hug the curves of my hips and show off my ass in the best way. My breasts look prominent in this top. It's sexy without being immodest. I spray myself with my perfume for the finishing touch. As I leave the bathroom, I see Micah pulling his shirt over his head. He looks incredibly sexy in his casual dark jeans and black boots. The dark grey shirt he's wearing accentuates his big arms and wide chest in a delicious way.

I'm walking past him when he catches me off guard by taking my elbow and turning me back towards him before he scoops me up by the back of my legs. I instinctively wrap my legs around his waist.

"Where do you think you're going, pretty girl," he asks, smiling as he traces kisses on my jaw. "Looking for my hot boyfriend. Have you seen him?" I ask teasingly as I peck him with kisses. He

Until I found you

laughs carrying us down the stairs. Once we reach the bottom of the stairway I slide off of him to grab my phone and bag as we head out to the city. I convinced Micah to take the Jeep instead of his Corvette. After all, it's not a fun road trip unless you have the windows down and the wind blowing through your hair.

I instantly smile as memories of Lyle and me jamming out to Linkin Park in his car come flooding in. On the weekends he wasn't working, he'd take Claire and me to the city for fun. We'd walk the streets enjoying the sights, stop at different food vendors, and watch the beautiful sunset on the beach by the Golden Gate Bridge. I typically wandered off from them at that point giving the couple some privacy. Even though I was almost always with them, they never made me feel like a third wheel. I remember sitting in the backseat, watching them holding hands and hoping that someday I'd be lucky enough to find someone to share moments like that with. I look down at Micah's large hand wrapped in mine.

He's absentmindedly tracing patterns on my wrist with his thumb. I look over at him as he drives. I take in the amazing man before me, my man. I thank whoever is listening for bringing him into my life. He catches me staring at him.

"Enjoying your view," he asks with a smirk.
"Yes, actually I am," I say.

He smiles, bringing the top of my hand to his soft lips before planting a kiss to it. I love when he does that. It's the sweet little things that mean the most to me. Most of the hour long commute to San Francisco consists of Micah and I talking and laughing. 'Bennie and The Jets,' began playing on the radio as Micah sang along to it horribly, purposely bad just to make me laugh. We were both singing along as the beautiful Golden Gate Bridge came into view. After parking His Jeep, we hopped onto a cable car. This was always one of my favorite things to do when I would come here.

We're riding it for a while, when I ask excitedly, "So where to first?"

"Wherever you want babe," he says smiling down at me.

I wrap my arms around his waist as I lay my head on his chest taking in the steeping hills surrounding us until I see something that catches my eye up ahead.

"There," I say, pointing to an indoor paintball arena.

"No. Absolutely not," he says looking at me.

"Come on! Please?"

"No way."

Thirty-seven

"These suits are ridiculous," he says.

I knew once I poked my bottom lip out it was settled. He tried so hard not to smile as he gave into me.

"The suits protect your clothes from getting ruined," I say, as I'm pulling my hair into a low bun.

"Just so you know, You're going to get pummeled," he says.

"Oh, and how do you figure that?"

"Because you lack height and athleticism. I outrank you in both. Not to mention I'm a hell of a shot. Remember," he says cockily.

I slowly grab a paintball out of my ammo bag without his noticing.

"Is that so? Well indeed you may have height and athleticism on me but there's one thing you are lacking sir."

He's smirking now.

"Oh yeah, and what's that shorty," he asks, looking down at me.

"Spunk," I reply, as I bust a paintball on his chin.

I'm already laughing when he says, "You're so going to pay for that."

I turn around and run into the arena. He's already shooting towards me. Laughing as he does. I turn a sharp corner, but not before he gets me on my back. Thank God these paintball guns aren't powerful otherwise this would hurt. I hide behind a barrel as he rounds the corner. The sight of him dressed in a painter's suit with booties on and overly large goggles makes me stifle a laugh. I wait until he's a safe distance away before I start unloading paintballs at him. He quickly turns around and starts shooting back at me. I run and dodge as fast as I can. He's gaining on me. I turn a corner and find it's a dead end.

With nowhere left to run, I turn around and say, "Truce," with a wide smile.

He shakes his head and goes to shoot when he's out of paintballs. I smile devilishly at him as I raise my paintball gun.

"Babe, let's talk about this" he starts, but I silence him when I turn him into a colorful looking cheetah.

I'm laughing so hard as he wipes some paint off of his goggles.

"Think you're pretty cute don't you," he asks, stalking towards me slowly.

"Actually I am," I say through my laughter, a snort escaping.

"Oh yeah Miss Piggy," he says, charging at me.

He grabs me around by my waist and starts tickling me.

"Ok! Ok! I give," I say laughing.

He releases me, cupping both sides of my face with his large hands.

Until I found you

"You are pretty cute," he says, laughing along.

After our game is finished, we clean ourselves up and head out on another adventure.

"You know, you never told me how you became such an excellent marksman," I ask, cocking my brow at him.

He smiles, "Jo competed in our school's archery team, and his dad would take him skeet shooting all the time to help him with hitting his targets. We always hung out so I was always around. One day his dad placed a rifle in my hand and told me to shoot. I had never even held a gun before that day. Call it beginners luck or a natural talent but I hit my target on the first shot. Jo convinced me to join the team. Soon we were winning our tournaments. I remember coming home after winning my first one and was so excited to tell my father about it. Thought it would make him proud of me. When I tried showing him my medal and trophy, he waved me off. To my father it wasn't a big accomplishment. If it didn't make a profit or lead you down a road of great success, it wasn't worth doing," he says, looking ahead absentmindedly as he recalls the memory.

This makes me so sad to imagine Micah as a young teenager showing his father something he was so happy and excited about just to get shut down every time. My sadness turns into anger when I think just how much of a self absorbed, narcissistic asshole Keith Eason truly is towards his son. I snake my arm around his waist as we walk bringing him closer to me.

"I'm so sorry babe," I say as I lay my head against his side.

He wraps his arm around me, as he changes the subject.

"We have to get an Irish coffee while we're here. Have you ever had one," Micah asks.

I shake my head no. His eyes grow wide with humor and suddenly he hails us in a cab.

"What are you doing?"

"I can't let you miss out on this mind blowing experience one more second," he says as the taxi comes to a halt.

We pull up to a corner cafe called the Buenavista. Apparently, it's famous for this Irish coffee Micah kept going on about during the cab ride here.

"Seriously have you been living under a rock," he teasingly asked me.

We sit down at the bar and Micah orders us two.

"Watching them make it is half the fun," he says.

"What do you mean? It's just coffee isn't it," I ask.

"Watch," Micah says simply.

I look over at the bartender as he lays out ten stemmed glasses in a perfect row, dropping sugar cubes in each one as he does. He grabs the pot of hot coffee and begins pouring down the line in fast movements. He grabs a bottle of Whiskey and flips it in the air before catching it. He begins to do a few more stunts with the bottle before adding whiskey to the coffee. He begins to tell Irish inspired jokes as he adds the final ingredients to the drink. I laugh along

UNTIL I found you

with the onlooking patrons. Everyone whistles and claps as the bartender finishes. Micah hands me mine. I take my first sip.

"Well," Micah asks intrigued by my response.

"It's delicious," I say. "My God it's good. "Mmm," is all I manage to say as I enjoy my first Irish Coffee.

I really was missing out. Micah smiles.

"I told you it was good," he says before taking a sip Himself.

"It's so delicious," I say as I lick the sweetness from my lips.

He watches me, giving me a crooked smile before leaning in.

"I can think of something else that's even more delicious," he says as he subtly rubs over my clit through my jeans.

I gasp, between him touching me, his words and the way he's looking at me, my lips part automatically. He wastes no time placing his lips on mine; kissing me slowly, before pressing his tongue in my mouth. Teasingly swirling his against mine before pulling away. Leaving me almost panting.

"What was that for," I ask.

"That was me getting back at you for all the paintballs," he says, fighting a laugh.

I playfully hit him on the arm.

"Leyna," A familiar voice says from behind me as I turn around.

"Claire?"

Before I know it, we're in each other's embrace.

"Oh my God! It's been so long! Look at you! You're so beautiful," she says through her tears. "How have you been?"

She asks as we finally pull away from our embrace.

"Great actually! I've missed you. How are you," I ask, looking her over.

That's when I noticed a bump on her stomach. I look at her. Tears of joy welling in my eyes. She rubs her tummy knowingly.

"I'm 6 months along. It's a boy. We're naming Him Carson," she says smiling as she wipes her tears.

I give her another hug.

"I'm so happy for you," I say, giving her a light squeeze before I release her.

"Thank you. That means the world to me. I'm sorry I haven't kept in touch. It- it's just that it was too—"

I cut her off, "I know," I say, giving her a small encouraging smile.

She takes my hands in hers.

"I think about you all the time, Leyna," she says.

"Me too," I reply, before turning behind me and saying with a smile,

"Micah, this is Claire. Claire, this is My boyfriend Micah."

The two shake hands.

"It's a pleasure to meet you. Leyna has spoken highly of you," Micah says, giving her a small smile. "Baby, I'm going to let you two catch up while I go pay the bill," he says before kissing my forehead; his way of giving the two of us privacy.

UNTIL I
found you

I adore him for that. She looks over to me and smiles.

"I'm so happy you found someone. He seems so nice. You look so happy."

I smile at her, "For the first time in a long time, I am happy. And I'm so glad you're happy, Claire. You deserve it. He would want you to be happy too."

Tears begin to pull in her eyes at me mentioning Lyle.

"I still love him, you know," she says looking down.

"I know you do," I reply quietly.

"Well I should be going, my mother and sister in law are waiting on me. It was so good seeing you Leyna. I've missed you," she says, taking me into a hug once more.

"I've missed you too. We need to catch up when you come home in a few weeks."

She looks at me quizzingly.

"What do you mean?" "You know for Lyle's— when you come home to visit him I mean".

"Oh," she looks a bit sheepish.

"I know you must think I'm terrible," she says looking away.

"What? Not at all! After five years you still love him enough to put flowers on his grave."

She looks at me confused, like I've grown another head.

"Leyna, I don't know what you're talking about. I haven't been to that cemetery in years."

Now I'm the one looking at her weird. If it's not her, then who? My heart sinks. Jean.

"I'm sorry. I have to go," Claire says as she leaves the cafe.

As I'm standing there, I realize maybe my mother does have a heart after all. I have spent the last almost five years begging her to come with me to visit Lyle's resting place. That's the one time we should both put aside our differences and be there as a family for each other. To grieve, to heal. She never would. To Jean, if she didn't talk about it, and didn't think about it, it would go away. When that didn't work, she tried drinking his memory away.

After my brother died, she spun out of control. She lost her son. I lost my brother, my best friend. He took a huge part of us both when he left. Each of us were left with a giant sized hole. Each of us is trying to fill that hole in our own way. Jean with her constant drinking, and me? I knew nothing would fill it. So instead I built an impenetrable wall never allowing myself the possibility of getting attached to someone. I couldn't allow my heart to be broken. I had spent years building that wall. I reject anyone that tried to break through it. The only ones even close to breaking through were Jared and Maggie. That was different though. They were my best friends. My adoptive siblings as I like to call them.

But Micah? He is tearing my wall down brick by brick. It hasn't been easy for him. I've fought him every step of the way. And yet, he still keeps at it. He's claiming my heart as his own. I suppose that's what love does. That revelation terrifies me.

Thirty-eight

"Are you ok? Ever since you saw Claire back at the cafe you've seemed off. Sad even." Micah asks.

We walk down the street hand in hand.

"Yeah, I'm totally fine. I just wasn't expecting to see her. You know?"

He stops us.

"I can't imagine what that was like for you, baby. I'm sorry."

He's looking at me sadly.

"Ok, enough with the heavy. Hail a cab and let's go have some fun, Eason," I say, changing the subject.

"Yes ma'am," he says smiling.

He walks to the curb to flag a taxi down when my phone starts buzzing. I pull my phone from my bag and see I have a text from Jean. I click on the message.

"Leyna we need to talk. Call me when you can."

Oh no. I forgot yet again to call her back. I wonder what she wants? This can't be good. I internally groan at the thought of having a "we need to talk" conversation with Jean. I put my phone back into my bag. I refuse to ruin my day with Micah because of her. Her toxicity and antics can wait until tomorrow. I'm making the mental note in my head to call her in the morning when I'm greeted by a brute force, knocking me down, causing the wind to be knocked out of me momentarily. I let out a gasp.

"Shit. I'm so sorry! I couldn't stop in time," a guy on skates says.

He attempts to help me up.

"It's fine," I say, standing up on my own.

"What the fuck," Micah shouts angrily, as he grabs the guy up by his shirt.

"Hey man, relax! It was an accident," the guy pleads.

"Micah stop! What are you doing," I say, grabbing him by his forearm; "Let him go!" I plead. Micah's lips tighten in a line before he shoves the guy back with excessive force as he releases him. The guy falls onto the ground and struggles to stand up right.

"Get the fuck out of here," He yells at him.

The guy does what he's told and hurriedly skates away. Micah turns to me.

"Are you ok? Where are you hurt," he asks, looking me over.

"I'm not hurt. You shouldn't have done that! It was an accident," I say.

He looks confused before it morphs into a look of anger.

"I actually heard it when that asshole slammed into you. I turn around to find you on the ground. He hurt you. I know he did! What else did you think I was going to do Leyna," he asks with his brows pulled together.

I stare at my brooding man for a moment. I know this is his way of protecting me. His instinct. I just wish he wouldn't resort to violence every time. Instead of scolding him or getting into an argument with him, I gently place my hand to the side of his face. He looks caught off guard at me doing this, like he was expecting me to argue back with him.

"I had the wind knocked out of me momentarily. He didn't hurt me. I appreciate your need to protect me. But please, don't fight. I can't stand the thought of you getting hurt," I say.

He laughs cockily.

"Do you know how many fights I've been in? Out of all those times, I may have gotten my ass kicked once or twice, but no one could ever hurt me."

I huff; "You're so cocky," I remark.

"Not cocky, confident," he says, smirking at me.

I roll my eyes at him; "Let's go Rocky," I say as I pull him by the hand.

After a while we finally reached my favorite Ice cream shop.

"What's good here? Besides you," Micah asks.

I playfully nudge him with my elbow.

"Everything here is delicious. So you can't go wrong."

He looks at me with a devilish grin before saying, "Well I've only had one delicious flavor in this place. It's by far my most favorite."

His grin widens as he licks his lips.

"Micah," I say blushing.

He chuckles into my neck before placing a small kiss just below my ear.

"You are rather delicious, baby," he whispers in my ear seductively, causing goosebumps to rise on my arms.

Once we've ordered our ice cream cones to go, we're walking down by the pier. "Ok this really is the best ice cream I've ever had."

"Told you," I gloat. "Want to try some of mine?"

I offer holding my cone up to him. He goes to take a bite when I playfully smash it against his lips and nose. I begin to laugh. He stands there still as stone trying his best not to laugh. I go to kiss him but he refuses to bend down. I step on my tippy toes and pucker my lips to him through my laughter.

"Nope," he says looking down at me.

Still fighting the urge to laugh, "Give me a kiss you jerk," I say jumping up a few times before I jump high, wrapping my legs tightly around his waist. "God, it's like climbing Mount Everest," I say as I cup the back of his neck with my hands.

He's smiling at me now. I'm still laughing as I pucker my lips out to him.

"Just one," I ask.

"Fine," he says and acts like he's going to kiss me but instead takes his ice cream cone and smashes it onto my nose.

My eyes widened in surprise. He bursts out into a hard laughter seeing my reaction. I begin to giggle as he licks the ice cream from my nose and lips. Suddenly he looks at me with a look I can barely describe. Smiling at me the entire time. His eyes hold a deeper meaning than just joy or amusement behind them.

"What," I ask him.

He widens his smile.

"You're mine," he says simply.

"I'm yours," I say cupping his face with my hands before placing soft, tender kisses to his lips. Suddenly I hear a click. I look up to see Micah has taken a picture of us with his phone. I try to hide my face as he takes another.

"Oh come on baby, take one."

"Fine," I grumble.

I hate taking pictures. I hate the way I look in them. I stick my tongue out first. Micah follows suit before licking my cheek, causing me to laugh. He snaps the picture. Followed by another picture of us cheek to cheek smiling, my hand holding the side of his face. And lastly he captures a picture of me kissing his cheek and another of him kissing mine.

"I'm not usually a picture taking person by the way. But I think I'm going to become one now" he says moments later as he's giving me a piggyback ride.

"Oh. And why is that," I ask, kissing the side of his jaw.

He sets me down before wrapping his large arms around my waist.

"Because pictures are a permanent fixture. They capture memories and moments with someone you want to keep forever. I didn't care about any of that before. I didn't want to keep anything for forever. Until I found you."

Thirty-nine

"Awww babe look how cute," I say cooing at the sea lions across the way. I talked Micah into taking us to the zoo after he told me he'd only gone once before as a child. "Look at the little baby one," I say in a mock baby voice.

He begins to chuckle and shake his head.

"What," I ask, giggling.

"You're too adorable," he says smiling.

"No, you were adorable on that merry go round," I say, fighting yet another fit of laughter.

"Oh God, after today we're never bringing that up again," he says covering his face with his hands in exasperation.

I begin to laugh again. For as long as I live I will never forget the sight of Micah on the merry go round with me. His long legs draped over the brass pony awkwardly. He looked like a giant compared to it. All of the little kids laughed at him the entire time. I even was guilty of it. I tried holding my composure

UNTIL I
found you

but as soon as he looked over to me with a sullen expression I was done for. A fit of laughter and snorts ensued.

"Remind me to never bet against you again," he said rolling his eyes.

As we walked through the zoo, a zoo keeper had a python she was letting people hold around their shoulders. Micah bet I couldn't last two minutes with that snake wrapped around me, knowing I'm afraid of snakes. I suppose my need to prove someone wrong about me is greater than my fear, so the bet was made. I won. I giggle at his expense once more.

He distracts me by whispering in my ear, "If you want to hold a snake wait until we get home," and squeezes my ass.

"Micah," I whisper hiss at him while smacking him on the arm.

He's the one laughing now. After a while of watching the sea lions play, We made our way to the gorilla exhibit. They were one of my favorite animals besides elephants. We stood in front of the exhibit and watched as two baby gorillas fought playfully with each other. Micah began laughing at them when they started throwing palm branches at each other. Soon the mother gorilla had enough of their antics and separated them, taking the smallest of the two with her. The other one found his way to the father gorilla. He began playing roughly with him.

The father gorilla actually played along with the baby acting as if the baby was striking blows to him. It was so cute to watch. I look over to Micah and see that he's in deep thought about something.

"What's wrong," I ask him as I hold his hand.

Still looking at the family of gorillas as he says, "It just astounds me that these animals treat their kids better than either of our parents ever did to us. It's pathetic really when you think about it."

His words surprise me. As true as they are, I wasn't expecting them. Not at this moment at least. Watching the nurturing way these mammals interacted with their babies must have sparked something.

"I'm sorry," is all I know to say as I lean my head against his shoulder, comforting him.

"They should be the sorry ones," he says.

His voice took on an edge to his tone.

"All we can do is move on. Move forward. Be better than they were," I say to him.

Trying to comfort him the best I can. He nods his head.

"And I will be. I will be a better father to my son than he could have ever been to me. I will be better than him."

I can tell from the suppressed pain behind his eyes that he's never fully recovered from his childhood. Same way I haven't.

"Have you tried confronting him? Talking to him about all this," I ask in a quiet, soothing voice.

He huffs, "He was never around long enough to talk about the fucking weather let alone my feelings."

"Well maybe one day the two of you could-"

He cuts me off.

"Let's just move on ok? I shouldn't have brought it up," he says.

Until I found you

      I feel helpless. I know more than anyone the kind of pain he's enduring, still, even into his adult years. It's not natural for a parent to disregard their own child, to wreak havoc and emotional turmoil on their children and not even attempt to fix it. It's not natural to have a childhood that you have to recover from. This is the reason he's so angry all the time. The neglect and abandonment he felt towards his father as a child, it's still there. That feeling was never resolved. We both were left on our own at a young age. Defenseless. Helpless. Each of us having a comfort the other didn't. He had a loving mother for the first nine years of his life. Micah has memories of his mom tucking him into bed at night, kissing him on his cheek as he drifted to sleep. I have memories of being woken up by the sound of shattering glass and my mother yelling profanities. I have memories of crying while Lyle was beside me, comforting me the entire time. Micah has memories of laying in his bed alone, crying himself to sleep after his mom died, wishing his dad was there to comfort him. Instead waking up to an empty house, being greeted by strangers instead of his father. He had a loving mom. I had a protective brother. In the end we both lost them. We lost our comfort. We lost the only family we truly had and known. Now all we have left are the parents that caused us all that pain.

      "I'm sorry. I know you're just trying to help," he says after a moment.

      Guilt taking over his features. I take his hand in mine.

      "I understand you more than you think. You're not alone in this you know. I'm here, for you." He looks at me, pain and relief flicker simultaneously in his eyes.

"I know baby. I'm sorry," he says, pulling me into a hug.

He nuzzles his face into my neck, taking a few deep breaths before taking my hand and leading us away.

"Are you getting hungry," he asks after a few minutes of us walking in silence.

His hand never left mine all the while.

"Actually I am," I say to him and begin to turn us around.

Looking confused he asks, "where are going?"

Raising my brow I say, "the cafeteria."

He shakes his head, "We're not eating at the zoo. I have somewhere else I want to take you." I raise my brow. "And where's that," I ask curiously.

"Chapeau. Ever ate there?"

"Um, no. It sounds fancy."

He chuckles, "It is a nice restaurant. I think you'll like it. The food is delicious. I know the owner so we can get in without a reservation."

I mean, this girl loves to eat, "I'm sold."

Forty

Micah is handing his keys to the valet boy as I compare appearances between how we're dressed and how patrons exiting the restaurant are dressed. The comparison is vast. Suddenly I feel extremely underdressed. Micah doesn't seem to pay much attention to the difference in how we're dressed, that or he just doesn't care.

Micah walks beside me, his hand pressed against the small of my back as we enter the restaurant. I look around at the magnificent decor. The large walls were eggshell white, adorned with golden molding and light fixtures all throughout. Golden chandeliers were hanging all around, the crystals hanging from them looking like sparkling diamonds. The tables and chairs were even made to look like gold as well. Beautiful paintings of cherubs and other contemporary paintings hung. Even the floor was made of a cream and gold marble. Making the entire space look like a grand ballroom from the palace of Versailles.

"It's so beautiful," I muse.

I can see Micah smiling at my reaction from the corner of my eye.

"French cuisine," I stated.

Not even needing to ask the question.

"Yeah. How'd you know? I thought you'd never been here before," he asks curiously.

"I haven't. I could tell it's French from the decor. It's magnificent."

Plus the name gave it away honestly, but the decor certainly solidifies it. He chuckles lightly. "Smart girl. Wait till you try the food," he muses.

The more I look at this beautiful place and it's patrons the more I feel like I'm dressed in a potato sack. This isn't just some "nice" place as Micah had described it. This is THE place. The place where all of San Francisco's rich and famous come to, the elite. Micah's phone begins to ring.

He pulls it out of his pocket, looking at the caller he says to me, "I've got to take this. It's work."

He turns around taking a few steps away to answer. From his tone, I can tell it's all business. Suddenly a man dressed in a tailored suit approaches me.

"Name on the reservation," he asks with a prudent tone, eying me up and down as he does. Clearly wondering if I had confused this place for a Olive Garden or a Red Lobster. This wasn't the place you just walked into from the street. This was a place you made reservations to months in advance; the place where Sunday's best attire was still considered semi casual. I begin to become nervous. Micah hadn't made a reservation. Would they let us in? How embarrassing if they didn't.

"Name," he says sharply; growing impatient.

"Um-" before I can stammer anymore Micah walks up.

"She's with me," he says, his tone is cold.

Until I found you

His eyes narrowing at the man.

"Mr. Eason, I apologize."

The man's attitude changes immediately from prudent to friendly.

"Welcome sir! Welcome madam. Right this way please," he says leading us into the dining room.

Micah takes my hand in his as we follow. My cheeks begin to heat as onlookers begin gawking at my and Micah's casual attire. Micah doesn't look the slightest bit unnerved by all the staring.

"A view," Micah states flatly as the man was about to seat us in the middle of the room.

"Yes of course, Mr. Eason. Right this way please, sir."

He seats us at a table sitting in front of a floor to ceiling length window with a beautiful view of the city. It's almost sunset. This spot also had more space between each table giving us more privacy.

"Well what do you think so far," Micah asks, already smiling.

My eyes widen.

"I think that when you said this place was nice, that was a bit of an understatement. This is the nicest place I've ever seen! The decor is phenomenal. It's like King Midas himself decorated it," I say jokingly. "I think even Marie Antoinette would approve," I add laughing lightly.

He chuckles.

"Get ready. The food is fantastic here," he says.

"I really wish we would have come another time though," I say looking around.

"Why," he asks furrowing his brows.

"Because, we're so completely underdressed. I mean have you looked around at everyone else? I look like I'm wearing a potato sack compared to them."

He begins to laugh lightly, "You shouldn't worry about that. At all. You'd be sexy as hell even if you did wear a potato sack," he says eying me as he licks his lips.

I smile. "Wait, how did that guy know you? Do you come here a lot," I ask, curiously.

Micah gives me a look that makes me feel as though I'm not in on a secret of his. He smirks. "Remember when I said I know the owner of the restaurant? You're looking at one of them." My eyes widened a bit in response. He smirks.

"Wow. You own a restaurant! That's amazing," I say; impressed and happy for him.

That has always been a dream of mine. He chuckles.

"Thanks. I'm not a hands on owner though. In fact, I'm not involved with it at all. Other than to reap from the profits."

"How is that?" Suddenly it dawns on me "Investor," Micah and I say in unison.

I shake my head knowingly.

"You must be really good at what you do," I say.

"Actually I am," he says smiling.

It's not an arrogant smile like I thought it would be. More of that he's proud of his accomplishments, as am I for Him. Suddenly I feel the vibration from my phone ringing. I pull it out of my bag and notice I have 3 missed calls from Jean. A lump rising in my throat.

Until I found you

"Is everything ok," Micah asks.

Before I can reply, a tall, middle aged man walks over slapping Micah's back gleefully. "Eason! I haven't seen you in ages. How've you been?"

"Reggie. It's been awhile. Good to see you," he says formally.

I'm assuming Reggie is a business associate of his. His friend looks over towards me, giving me a friendly smile. Micah introduces us then.

"Reggie, this is my girlfriend Leyna. Leyna, this is Reggie. A pal of mine."

I offer my hand and he takes it smiling.

"It's a pleasure to meet you, Leyna," he says.

He and Micah then begin chatting back and forth.

A moment later, my phone rings in my hands. It's Jean yet again. Ok, something definitely must be going on. I excuse myself from the table as they continue to talk. I use this as an opportunity to head to the restroom to call Jean back. Once I'm in the restroom I dial my mother back. It rings and rings. I begin to become agitated, almost ending the call when she finally answers.

"What," she asks sharply.

I'm a bit confused at her crudeness. Isn't she the one that's been calling me? This is Jean. So why am I surprised really?

"You called," I ask just as sharply.

"Yes. Over and over. But apparently you don't have the ability to answer."

I roll my eyes, "I've been busy," I say, trying to lower my voice as someone enters the restroom.

"Busy? So busy you can't answer my fucking calls or texts," she snides.

"Do you not remember our last conversation? It didn't end well," I retort. "What is this all about Jean," I ask her, already losing patience with this conversation.

I'm ready to get whatever this is over with.

"Jean."

She repeats laughing, actually laughing.

"Boy have I pissed you off. I remember there was a time you only reserved that name for me when you were the angriest at me growing up."

She says it like it's a memory she had of a neighborhood kid instead of her only daughter.

"Yeah, well that's a lot lately," I say flatly.

I can hear her laugh a little non laugh.

Getting impatient with where this conversation is going I say, "I'm in the middle of something right now. What is it that you need?"

Money probably.

"I need you to come by tomorrow," she says.

Her voice took on a strange tone.

"I can't. I'll be busy," I tell her.

"Well could I come there then? It's important I talk to you."

Whatever it is, she's desperate.

"No. I told you before, I'm not giving you my address. Last thing I need you to do is barge in high or drunk into my house with one of your sleazy boyfriends. If you want to talk to me in person, I'll have to come by Friday morning. What is this about anyway? Why can't you just talk to me about whatever this is over the phone now," I ask, becoming more frustrated with her by the second.

Why must she be so fucking dramatic and cryptic?

"Friday works. I'll be at Jackie's," she says, completely ignoring the last of what I said.

"Fine see you then," I say before hanging up.

Forty-one

I see the reflection of myself in the mirror as I slip my phone into my back pocket. My cheeks are flared, a tale-tell sign that I'm flustered. I begin to take in deep breaths calming myself before I go back to Micah. I don't want him knowing Jean got to me. There's no need in letting her upset me anyway. Just then a tall, slender woman with a red cocktail dress comes from around the bathroom stalls. She's ogling me over. Taking me in as if I were an obstacle she was preparing to conquer. I stare back at her waiting for her to notice I've caught her staring at me. Our eyes meet and she sneers at me. What is this bitches problem?

"Can I help you?" I ask rudely.

She places one of her hands on her hips.

"So this"- she motions with her other hand up and down towards me. "is the new toy?"

She smiles at me smugly.

"I suppose Micah likes to try them in all shapes and sizes," she snickers.

My heart drops. She wasn't what I pictured at all. I pictured a leggy blonde with fake lips and tits that carried a Prada bag with a teacup Chihuahua inside of it. She was the complete opposite of what my mind had envisioned her to look like. She was taller than me, had six inches on me easily. She was slender like a fucking Victoria secret model and was dark complected. She looked exotic, like she was middle eastern. Beautiful.

"You're Nadia," I state simply.

"I see you've heard of me," she smiles smugly, flipping her long dark hair behind her shoulder. "Let's get something very clear," she says, stalking forward towards me in her short dress and stilettos. "This little thing between you and Micah, it isn't going to last much longer. He'll grow tired of you. He'll become bored with you and soon he'll drop you faster than you can scarf down an entire box of bonbons."

Fat jokes. Really? I give this bitch my best shit eating grin and step towards her until I'm inches from her face.

"Is that what happened to you? He got bored with you? And for the record, Micah loves my curves. The way he grabs my hips as he thrusts into me or the way he smacks my fat ass… I suppose I have the boxes of bonbons to thank for that," I say slowly, smiling at her.

She wasn't expecting me to clap back at her. This much was certain. Her jaw drops momentarily before she collects herself. She must have assumed after the second body shaming insult that I'd run out of here crying like a middle schooler. She was wrong.

She pulls her lip back over her teeth as if she's growling at me.

"You know what you little skank, it wasn't too long ago that those hands of his were all over my body too. In fact,-" She gives me a look of deep satisfaction. "it wasn't too long ago that he fucked me at his house."

My heart instantly falls out of my body. She's lying! She's lying! My inner voice yells.

"Liar," I say, trying to compose myself.

I can feel the tears beginning to pull at my eyes. She notices it too. Triumph taking over her smug features.

"Oh but I'm not," she says smoothly, crossing her arms over her chest, "In fact, it was the very night after your first little date. Later that night he called me over and fucked my brains out on the couch. He must not have wanted you after all," she says smiling sinisterly.

I want to grab her by the throat and slam her head against the wall repeatedly until the hurt in me is no longer there. But what's the point? No amount of violence is going to change the fact that I'm a total dumbass. He promised to be different and I believed him. I. Believed. Him. How many times was I going to let myself feel this before I learned my lesson for good? How many times was I going to set myself up for heartache? Why did I allow my walls to come down so easily with him? Why did I allow them to come down at all? Knowing that I would regret it. I stupidly fell for someone I shouldn't have. Expecting a happily ever after somehow. There isn't one. At least not for me. Never was. This is proof of that.

Until I found you

Why I thought this would be different, why I thought *he* would be different just proves how truly foolish I am. And the most unbelievably heartbreaking part in all of this is coming to the realization that I am in love with Micah, even though I wish I wasn't. The pain I feel in my heart is utter torture. I just want to turn it all off. I don't want to feel any of it, anything at all. Feeling nothing is better than feeling this. Feeling love is to have hope. Hope that life will be kind to you for once. Knowing damn good well it won't. I'm not sure what the fuck to do with myself. She's still staring at me.

"Aww is the chubby little ginger heartbroken now? At least you have those boxes of bonbons to keep you company at night," she goes in for the kill.

I could punch her. Slap her. Drag her by the hair of the head. I could do so many things. And yet, I simply turn around and walk straight out of the restaurant without Micah noticing. I keep walking in no certain path down the street, wrapping my arms around myself as I do so. As if I'm literally holding myself together so I don't fall apart. Suddenly my phone begins to ring in my back pocket. I don't have to look at it to know who it is. It's him. I turn my phone off and decide to keep walking. It's dark when I finally come to a stop at a park.

I sit down on a bench, pulling my legs to my chest. Wrapping my arms around them as I begin to tremble with flowing tears. I bury my face into my knees and let it all out; all the hurt, all the disappointment. I'm not sure how much time has passed when I'm finally done crying. For the time being anyway. It could have been ten minutes or two hours. I pull my phone from my pocket and turn it back on.

    The light from my phone blinds me momentarily. Suddenly it begins to ring. Micah. I almost threw my phone into the bushes seeing his name and the picture we took today flash across the screen. Instead I decline it and call another number instead.

Forty-two

"Jared is at the hospital working his shift and I'm with Jo. We can leave now and come get you. It'll take us an hour to get there. I hate you being in the city after dark by yourself Leyna!" Maggie's worried voice pierces through the phone.

"Ugh what a fucking jerk! I could kill him. Jo doesn't know anything about it yet. I haven't had the chance to tell him. I'll ask him what he knows about it," Maggie says.

"No," I say stopping her. "Don't. I don't want this shit messing anything up between you and Jo. Besides, Jo is going to be put in between a rock and a hard spot if you involve him in this. Micah is his best friend. You are his girlfriend. I'm not going to allow you and Jo to be involved. I'll figure out a ride back home," I say.

I was in such disbelief and heartache that I walked right out of the restaurant without even going back to our table long enough to grab my purse. I don't really know how I'm going to get back home. I could call Rachel or Tony. I'm sure they'd help me.

"True. But you're my best friend. And if you won't let me and Jo come get you, then I'm sending in a reinforcement of my own," she says stubbornly.

"Who," I ask.

Twenty minutes later, Connor pulls up to pick me up. It was by sheer luck that he was working late at the law firm tonight. If I weren't so desperate, I wouldn't have allowed Maggie to call him. I get in, mortified already.

"Thank you. You didn't have to do this," I say staring out ahead.

Refusing to make eye contact with him. Once he pulled up, I got a glance at his bruised face. The evidence of his and Micah's brutal fight in front of my house.

"Actually I did. Maggie would have killed me otherwise. Plus, it isn't safe for you to be out here at night by yourself," he says looking at me from the corner of his eye as he drives.

Knowing Maggie, she told him as little as possible and made him swear not to ask me questions.

Connor being Connor breaks the awkward silence by saying, "Ok I have to know… what happened? The truth this time," he adds.

His voice taking on a stern tone towards the end. I take a deep breath knowing that I owe him an explanation. I turn my body towards him, allowing myself to look at his bruised face. I instantly feel guilt looking at him, seeing the damage Micah did to him.

"I'm so sorry," I say finally, gesturing towards his face.

Connor rolls his eyes, "He hit like a bitch," he says.

UNTIL I
found you

From the swelling of Connor's left jaw I'd have to disagree. As I'm looking over his face I see how handsome he is. It's only been two years since I've seen him last. But in those two years, his looks changed from a young adult to a man. His jaw was more chiseled than before. His dark brown eyes looked wiser somehow. His black hair cut in a professional manner. Giving off the law student turned Lawyer vibes.

"So are you going to tell me what the hell happened," he asks, trying to be patient with me. "Long story short, I trusted someone that didn't deserve it. And, in doing so I proved myself correct about something and I'm heartbroken by it," I say trying to fight back the tears threatening to spill.

He ponders this for a moment.

"He lied to you then," he asks.

"Yes."

Lied. Broke my heart. Cheated? I mean technically we weren't official then. But why does it feel like he did? Why does it feel like this?

I expect Connor to ask what he lied about but instead he says, "I'm not surprised. Eason isn't the most stand up guy I've ever met."

I look at him.

"Why do you say that? How do you two know each other?"

Connor looks over to me then, "he hasn't told you?"

I shake my head.

"Interesting. I figured he'd jump at the opportunity to give his side of the story to you."

I'm growing impatient.

"Which is?"

"Micah and I went to high school together. He was the biggest asshole on campus. Always showing off. Always had a different girl on his arm. He was your stereotypical self absorbed jock that bullied almost everyone. He even had the nice car that daddy bought him to match. All of that didn't bother me half as much as what did to me."

My heart drops. This can't be a good story. I have to know.

"What did he do," I ask, my voice barely above a whisper. "Let's just say he used girls as a sport. Every conquest a notch in his belt. A prize. My girlfriend at the time being one of them." My jaw drops.

"He never cared about her. Never had any intentions of being with her. Just wanted to make a point to me."

I swallow the lump in my throat.

"Which was?" I ask, almost afraid of his answer.

"That he could take whatever he wanted. And no one could do a damn thing about it."

I look away from Connor. My hand instinctively goes to my heart. I can't believe what Connor is telling me. That doesn't sound like my Micah at all. My Micah would never do those things. Connor breaks me from my thoughts, "I can only imagine how you feel right now hearing this. You need to know he's not a nice guy, Leyna. Whatever you think you know about him is all a façade. Trust me on that."

Suddenly I become angry.

"You don't know him like I do! People change. You knew him in high school. Tell me one

Until I found you

person you know of that hasn't changed since then? We were all a bunch of teenage assholes. Some more than others, granted. But that doesn't mean he's like that now!"

Connor looks at me with a flat expression on his face, "then why are you in the car with me?" Tears pull at my eyes.

"If he's a changed man and he's so different from the guy I knew him to be then why are you in my car crying?"

I look away from him and wipe the tears from my eyes.

"That's what I thought," I hear him mumble lowly to himself.

A few minutes pass by in silence before Connor looks over to me. Clearly testing his limits.

"I do have to ask you something. And I need you to tell me the truth ok," he asks, gauging my response.

I nod. Suddenly I'm nervous of his question.

"Has he ever-" he pauses a moment. "does he hit you," he asks, his fists tightening around the steering wheel as he does.

My eyes widen in horror.

"No," I shout. "No. He's never hurt me."

Not like that at least.

"Ok. That's all I wanted to know," he says.

His fists, visibly relaxing from the wheel.

"Why did you ask that?"

He shrugs his shoulders, "Eason was always fighting in school. And clearly he's a violent person," he says pointing to his face.

I look away from him. Awkward silence ensues again.

Moments later he breaks the silence by saying, "If it's any consolation, you look lovely tonight."

I snort indifference. I don't feel lovely. Far from it. He begins to laugh. I look over at him. "Sorry. I don't mean to laugh but you looked disgusted by my compliment and you snorted a little. I can't help but laugh at you right now," he says trying to fight the urge to laugh again. "Still such a sour patch kid."

He muses to himself, smiling. Suddenly I'm reminded of the nickname Connor gave me a short while after we met. It was at Maggie's birthday party our senior year in high school. She had transferred halfway through her junior year. It was hell for her I'm sure. But we instantly became friends her first week at school and have been best friends ever since.

"Why did you even call me that to begin with? I never got the full story on that. I just assumed it was because I was chubby back then," I say.

He looks over to me taken aback.

"Wait, you think I called you that, making fun of you," he asks looking at me instead of the road.

"Well what other reason was there" I ask curiously.

He shakes his head, "Leyna, you've got it all wrong. I didn't call you that to make fun of you. Jesus is that what you've thought all this time?"

I nod.

"Well you were wrong. I called you that because of the slogan behind it. First they're sour, then they're sweet?... get it?"

UNTIL I found you

He looks at me with a grin. Suddenly it all comes together like a puzzle piece. I begin to laugh. He joins me.

"Awww no! Why'd you bring that up," I laugh as I cover my face with my hands.

Memories of Maggie, Connor and myself at Maggie's birthday party come into play. It was a pool party at the Donahue's house. Connor was in his sophomore year in college. Maggie and I were in our senior year of high school. Her parents invited the entire class over for the grand celebration. A few of the jocks thought it would be funny to throw me into the pool. They even though I couldn't swim. It was at the very least, general knowledge that I was terrified of the water. So when they picked me up to throw me in, I immediately went into a panic attack screaming for them to put me down. Connor ran over forcing them to put me down. Once they did they all started laughing at me.

The leader began teasing me trying to embarrass me further. I shoved him with all of my force and got on my tiptoes to tell him a thing or two about himself. I gave him a taste of his own medicine in the form of the most epic roast that school had ever seen. His own teammates began snickering at him. All but one. His cheeks turned red and he walked off. At first I was overjoyed at the fact that I just bullied a bully. Until his only loyal teammate came up to me and informed me that he had been picked on and slapped around by his father at home. Once I got the mental picture in my head, my previous words began drowning me in guilt. I ran to find him in his car about to leave when I begged him to let me apologize. I remember crying to him from my guilt.

After talking, we found out he and I had a lot in common when it came to our home life. We started the day as enemies and ended it as friends. "

I've never seen someone look so remorseful in my life," Connor begins to laugh.

"Maggie told me you even did the guys homework the rest of the school year."

I laugh. "I felt very bad, ok?"

Connor smiles looking at me.

"You've always been a sweetheart. Well, when you weren't biting someone's head off."

He laughs.

"Ok enough about me. Let's talk about you! What have you been up to these two years you went M.I.A? Huh," I drag out the last word.

He smiles before going into telling me about his last two years of law school and what that was like. I'm vaguely listening as I turn my phone back on. Instantly I regretted it. I have 18 missed calls, six voicemails, and 12 text messages. All from Micah. Holy shit. I have two missed calls from Maggie as well.

"Everything ok," Connor asked worriedly.

My face must say it all. Before I can reply Connor's phone begins to ring.

"Hey Maggie. What's up," Connor says over the Bluetooth connect.

"Hand the phone to Leyna," she demands.

"You're on speaker mags" Connor says, giving her an eye roll. Maggie wastes no time, "Leyna, Micah is going insane about you! Especially not knowing where you are. He called Jo asking where you were. Jo didn't know what in the hell was going on. I told Micah that you were safe and heading back home. I don't think he's going to just leave it at that. Plus, he has your car keys and wallet and stuff you need to get back from him anyway."

I groan.

Maggie continues, "I'm on the way home now. If he's there when I get there I'll tell him to leave and to give you some space."

Connor looks angry.

"Just call the police Maggie," he shouts, clearly becoming pissed.

"No," we both say at the same time.

"Micah is a hothead but he's not dangerous," I say, defending him.

Why do I keep doing that?

Connor points to his face, "Clearly not," but says nothing else.

We pull up ten minutes later and see Maggie unlocking the front door. Connor surveys the area like he's searching for a hooded figure in the shadows. I roll my eyes.

"Thank you for the ride. And I'm sorry you got dragged into this yet again." I say looking down. He surprises me by lifting my chin up with his fingers. I instinctively jerk back from his touch. He acts like my reaction didn't offend him.

"First, your welcome. Anytime I can help I will. Second, I wasn't dragged into anything. Well not the first time anyway. I involved myself that time. So I guess the tally is tied," he says, giving me a small smile. "Maybe we can hangout one weekend without it resulting in physical injury or chivalrous acts of rescue," he jokes.

I rock back on my heels.

"Don't think my boyfri-" I stop myself.

A pain jolts through me.

He steps closer to me, "Boyfriend or not you're allowed friends."

"That's true. But why do you want to be friends with me all of a sudden," I ask.

He nods. "Why wouldn't I want to be friends with you? What? We can't be friends because we're the opposite sex," he asks, lifting a playful brow.

"Not exactly what I meant. But it does complicate things when your friend's boyfriend punches you in the face," I say.

He laughs lightly, rubbing the back of his neck.

"That may be. But I don't see why we couldn't be friends. Maggie being my cousin. You being her roommate and best friend. Odds are we'll see each other from time to time. Might as well cultivate a friendship. And I'm a damn good one to have," he says smiling.

I give him an awkward wave before I say, "Thanks again for the ride."

"No problem," he says, giving me a small smile.

"I owe you one," I call over my shoulder as I turn towards the driveway.

"Later, sour patch kid," He calls before getting in his car.

I spin around and flip him off before I go inside and shut the door.

Forty-three

I'm mentally and physically exhausted by the time I take a shower and climb into bed. My phone had eventually died from all the unanswered calls and unread text messages from him. Maggie lays on her bed, rolling over to face me.

"Spill it. Every damn detail," she says simply.

I take a deep breath and start from the beginning. It's almost 2am by the time Maggie and I tell each other everything that happened to us today. Maggie's day went a million times better than mine. For that I was grateful.

"Leyna, this might make you angry with me. But hear me out... ok?"

I nod at her.

"I'm in no way saying Micah is totally innocent in this. But, I would talk to him and get the full side of the story before I would abruptly end things between you two. And I'm only saying this because I could hear the pain and utter fucking panic in his voice at not knowing where you were tonight.

He may not have told you yet, and he may not have even realized it until tonight….but he loves you, Leyna. That much I'm certain of."

My heart breaks all over again. Tonight is when I admitted it myself too, the true depths of my feelings for him. Imagining Micah in pain doesn't help that heartbreak either. Maggie's words have me wondering. Does he love me? Does it even matter if he does? If what Nadia said was true? If what Connor said was true? Was that the type of person Micah truly was? More importantly, is that who he still is?

"I'm not saying that bitch was lying completely, but she wasn't telling the complete truth either," Maggie adds.

"What do you mean," I ask furrowing my brows.

"Do I believe Micah and her had sex before? Absol-fucking-lutely. Do I believe that's still a current thing? Absol-fucking-lutely not. I found out tonight that Nadia is actually Jo's first cousin. So Jo knows her better than anyone. But he also knows Micah better than anyone too. I asked Jo about it and he told me that they were in fact, a frequent hook up at one point. But since he's met you, that's stopped. He's never seen Micah like this, so caught up in someone. He's also never seen Nadia so furious and put out before either. Do you know what that tells me?"

She looks at me as if she's giving me all of life's answers. I smile half heartedly at my best friend.

"What does that tell you?"

"It tells me that Micah fell out of interest with her, and fell in love with you."

Her words sink in slowly. Marinating on my heart.

"It's just a lot to take in Maggie," I tell her, draping my arm over my eyes and head.

"Plus Connor told me some things about Micah when they were in high school. I just don't know what to think," I say looking over at her.

Maggie sits up arching her brow at me.

"High school? Leyna, people change from then. You can't judge someone for what they've done years ago."

"I know Maggie. I won't judge him for that. I need to know if he has changed. Is the Micah I know now, my Micah, truly different from the person I was described tonight?"

I stare up at the ceiling in deep thought.

"Only way you'll find out is if you talk to him, Leyna. You owe him and yourself that much."

I nod at her.

"I will."

She smiles at me half heartedly.

"Good. Well, I'm exhausted. Goodnight," she says flipping over on her side.

I flip the lamp off and lay back willing my mind to shut off so that I may actually be able to sleep tonight.

A moment later I say, "Hey Maggie? Thank you by the way. You know I love you, right?"

She says sleepily, "I know. I know, I'm the bomb. Love you more."

I chuckle at her before I turn over and attempt to fall asleep.

Strong arms wrap around my waist pulling me closer to a warm bare chest. I nuzzled my face into it, immediately recognizing his scent. Micah. I hum to myself as his fingers play in my hair. I look up at him to find his beautiful blue eyes staring into mine.

"Miss me yet?"

My eyes fly open and my hand instinctively flies out to the empty space on my bed. I fist the sheets in my hand. I realize that it was only a dream, tears begin to silently flow down my face as I cry myself back to sleep. When the morning comes, I'm awoken by a tall figure standing over me.

"Jesus," I say in surprise.

Grabbing my chest as my heart beats like a drum. Jared chuckles.

"Sorry."

He smiles.

"Here, drink this," he says as he hands me a cup of coffee as he sits on the edge of my bed. "Thanks. I need caffeine this morning," I say drinking it.

The warmth feels good to my throat.

"Yeah me too, but it's decaf. Sleeping booty over there can't read apparently. I don't know why I sent her grocery shopping."

Jared says gawking at a passed out Maggie as she lays on her stomach snoring. Her thong is in full view for the world to see. I shake my head at both of my best friends.

"You're cranky," I note.

"Sorry. I haven't had my caffeine fix in two days because dildo baggins over there don't know how to read apparently. I'm just annoyed. Plus, you

Until I found you

and I are having boy troubles. Work was shitty last night. It's just... much," he says rubbing his temples.

My brow shoots up. "Boy troubles? You talked to Maggie already? And what happened between you and Jamie," I ask.

"He twirls his head around to me and says, "I didn't talk to Maggie."

Jared turns to yell in her direction.

"She's currently in the land of the dead if you haven't heard."

Maggie's snoring falters a bit before she resumes again. This time louder.

"Ugh, hand me a pillow I'll just smother her," he says.

I cover my mouth with my hand to keep from laughing. I love cranky Jer. I get up taking his hands in mine, pulling him up off the bed.

"How about this? How about we solve our need for caffeine and boy talk by going to D&D's? Huh? Sounds like a plan?" I ask, giving him a hopeful smile.

"Anything to get me away from the chainsaw gladiator over there," he says towards Maggie as he throws her stuffed bunny at her ass.

She doesn't even stir. After I've dressed in my yoga pants and my favorite comfy shirt, I slip my vans on and throw my hair into a messy bun at the top of my head. As we walk out the door, Jer hands me my purse.

"Oh thanks."

Then reality hits me.

"My purse! How? Where do you-"

Jared cuts me off.

"He pulled up at the same time I did. I was just getting home from work while he was heading to work I suppose. Anyway he handed it to me."

I look at Jared waiting for him to go into further details but he doesn't.

"Did he say anything about last night?"

"Nope. Just handed me your stuff. He said your clothes were still at his house and he would drop them off later."

"Oh," I say.

My face and heart are falling.

"Mmm hmmm what's that about? I knew something was going on. Neither of you had to say it. I can tell by the behavior. I already know you stormed out. It explains why he has your things. What did he do? Do I need to beat a mother fucker? Because if I do, I'm going to need my caffeine fix first."

I laugh, "No, no. That won't be necessary."

"Can you drive? I'm out of it until I have my coffee."

I nod and we get into my car. A few minutes later we arrived at our favorite coffee stop, Dunkin Donuts. This place was special to me and Jared. It's where our friendship blossomed. Our fall semester in college had just started, Jared and I would come here at the same time, every single day. We were strangers to begin with. It was merely coincidental but soon it just became a given we'd see each other there. We sat at the same booth every morning hanging out before we went off to our classes. Soon Maggie was joining in. And ever since then we just became the three amigos. I smile at him as I watch him take in his first

UNTIL I found you

sip of hot caffeinated coffee. His eyes roll dramatically in the back of his head.

"Better than sex," he whispers as we sit down at our famous booth.

His statement instantly brings Micah to my mind and the way he would make love to me. There's not a cup of coffee in the world that could trump that.

"Remind me to just buy a bag of this shit before we leave," Jared says, breaking me from my thoughts.

"Will do. Now spill," I say encouraging him.

He finishes his bite of donut before taking in an exaggerated breath.

"We did the deed and now he's acting distant. What's worse is he's in the closet. He has an aunt that knows. But, the rest of his family doesn't. I'm not sure if he's just not ready to tell them yet or he isn't even fully sure himself. Whatever the situation is, it's stressful and confusing."

He says pushing his locks back with his hands. That's how I knew when Jared was stressed or upset about something. He always brushed his hair back.

"Oh no Jer," I say sympathetically. "Have you tried-"

Jared cuts me off, "Talking to him? Yes I have, but he won't pick up the phone. I blew the bitch up last night and haven't gotten a word back. So I'm backing off and we'll see what happens. I just want to know where we stand. It's the closure I want, really. Like if it's done just say it. Let me move on, ya know?"

He says becoming worked up again. Suddenly I feel the urge to call Micah back. I'm doing the same thing to him that Jaime is doing to Jared. It's not fair. I know I don't want to call things quits with Micah. Far from it. The very thought makes me feel sick to my stomach, but I need answers too. I make my resolve to call him when I get back home. I take Jared's hand in mine.

"It'll be ok. Give him some time to process and think. Once he realizes what an amazing man he has in front of him he's bound to call you. Just give him time to think about it."

Jared nods deep in thought. Seeing him so anxious, I decided to humor him.

"Hey Jer."

"Yeah?"

He looks up at me.

"You donut even know how much I love you," I say, holding up a donut and giving him my goofiest smile.

It does the trick. He snickers and shakes his head smiling widely at me.

"Fucking dork," he says laughing now.

"But you love me anyway," I say.

"I donut protest that fact."

"Oh good one!" I cheer giving him a high five as we both laugh.

UNTIL I
found you

Forty-four

"What are we doing for Maggie's birthday next weekend," Jared asks as we're pulling up to a red light.

I know he's in a better mood now since he's had his coffee. He actually called Maggie by her name instead of insulting her. I fight a chuckle.

"I'm thinking Aztecs? Invite the gang. And Jo," Jared ponders.

"Yeah. But we did that last year, remember," I say.

"Shit. I forgot. We'll figure it out," Jared says.

"What about Dave and Buster," he asks laughing.

"She's banned from those," I say laughing along with Jared.

Jared's laughter comes to a halt.

"Holy shit! That lady is about to get run over," he says clamping his hands over his mouth in horror.

I look up to see a woman walking head on into traffic, more like stumbling into traffic. Cars zip around her, blaring their horns as they do so. Others come to a screeching halt in front of her, nearly causing a pile up on one side of the intersection. I take a double glance at the lady. "Jean," I scream as I jump out of my car, running towards her.

Car horns blaring. Jean is about to step in the way of an oncoming transit bus.

"Jean move," I scream as I fight my legs to run faster.

"Leyna," I hear Jared yell after me.

"Mom," I reach Jean just in time as I grab her back right before she walks out in front of the bus.

Both of us land hard on the pavement.

"What are you doing? Get up," I shout at her as I try to pull her to her feet.

"Just leave me," she slurs.

We're still in the way of traffic, still in danger. Jared reaches us then. He lifts her up and we walk towards my car.

"Put her in the back," I instruct Jared as I open the door.

He lays her down immediately assessing her.

"Just let me go," she mumbles, tears falling down her face.

"We have to get out of traffic. Pull down that road," Jared orders.

I do as I'm told and get us out of all the commotion. Once I pull over safely, I run around the other side of my car and look Jean over as Jared does the same.

"Jean? Jean can you hear me," Jared asks her as he flashes the light on his phone into her pupils.

She squints and starts slurring profanities.

UNTIL I
found you

"I think She's ok," we say at the same time.

She reeks of cheap liquor and cigarettes.

"Definitely messed up on something. I don't think she's showing signs of an overdose. But we need to bring her to the hospital as a precaution," Jared states.

I brush the hair away from her face looking her over. There's bruises still on her face from her assault. Fresh hickeys on her neck. Bile rises in my throat at the thought that someone could have touched her while she was in this state, and there's something that catches my attention on her arms. Other than the healing bruises left there...

"Leyna-" Jared starts.

"I know," I say.

Trying everything in me not to break down and cry right there on the side of the road. Track marks. My mother is high on something other than pills and weed. Something she swore to Lyle and me she'd never do. But she's a beautiful liar, my mother.

"Let's just get her home," I say, shutting the car door.

"What about the hospital," Jared asks.

"She'll live," I say coldly.

"Let me drive. Ok," Jared asks softly.

I nod before getting into the passenger seat. We pull up to Jean's house, and right away I can tell something's off. I haven't been here in over six months but the property looks completely different. The yard is mowed, there's flowers planted by the windows and there's a child's swing set by the oak tree. I notice a name plate hung above the doorway.

It reads "The Pounds' family." Right away I know what's happened. It all makes sense now. The past few times I've dropped her off, it's been at someone else's house. My mother was evicted. She's homeless. I look in the back seat and I'm disgusted by what I see. I'm not only seeing the woman that single handedly made my and Lyle's life a living hell, not only am I seeing just a neglectful alcoholic, pill popping mother, I see a junkie. A worthless junkie that's chosen to throw her life in the gutter instead of being there for her only remaining child.

"What do you want to do," Jared asks me, breaking me from my thoughts. "

We're taking her to the hospital. After that? She's on her own," I said as resolve set in my heart and mind.

After we've admitted Jean into the hospital, I call the officer assigned to her case and explain everything that just happened. I'm informed that she failed to appear to her court hearing and now has a warrant out for her arrest. That is what she wanted to tell me. Since I'm the one that bailed her out, I'm being held financially responsible, up to five thousand dollars. Normal people would be losing their minds right now. Normal people would be outraged. Me? I just found out my mother broke the one and only promise she ever made to me and my brother. The only thing we ever begged of her.

My mother is a junkie, a drug addict. No longer classified as "just an alcoholic." No longer classified as "addicted to alcohol and pills". No, My mother is a drug addict that ran out on her only surviving child. You'd think I'd be crumbling. I'm not. I'm numb. Jared is standing behind me rubbing my shoulders up and down, comforting me the best he can. Sometime later, the nurse asks if I want to

UNTIL I
found you

see Jean. I think about just walking away, not bothering to even see her again. She's got what's coming to her. What I'm about to say, as I walk in, I see her crying. This should weaken my resolve on what I'm about to do, but it doesn't.

"Leyna-" she starts.

"Don't," I say coldly to her. "Don't you fucking dare," I point my finger towards her. "Heroin?" She almost looks ashamed. What an act.

"How could you? How. Could. You," I choke.

"I was in pain," she cries.

"Oh that's rich! You were in pain? Did it ever occur to you that you aren't the only one suffering?" I shout, angry tears begin to pull in my eyes.

"You don't know what it's like to lose a son," she shouts through her sobs. "

You don't get to use that card! You were never there for Lyle. You were never there for me. You were never there for either of us! We needed you and you weren't there. You were never there! You were off drunk and whoring around all the time with one of your countless boyfriends. Did you know Lyle had to save me from one of them when I was 12?"

Her eyes widened in horror.

"While you were out drinking he came in and grabbed me. Forced me onto the couch. I called out for you! Begged for you to help me. I needed my mom..." I say through my sobs.

She shuts her eyes as if doing so will make all of this go away.

"If it weren't for Lyle, I would have been raped that night, because you sure as hell weren't there to save me. Where were you? Huh? Where were you when that happened? Better yet, where were you when Lyle died Jean? Where were you when your son died?"

She begins sobbing.

"You don't think I live with guilt every damn day of my life over that? I live with that! I miss him every single second that goes by," she shouts holding her chest.

"You miss him? You beat on him until he got big enough to stop taking that shit from you! You miss him? I miss my brother! I miss the only family I ever had," I say viciously, wiping tears from my eyes.

"I'm your mama," she says sobbing. "I know I've fucked up but we still have each other. We're still a family," she says. "Please Leyna just help me get through this and I promise-"

"NO," I yell. "No more empty promises. No more lies. No more disappointment. You skipped bail and now you have a warrant out for your arrest. The police are here and as soon as you're cleared by the doctor you're going to jail. This will be the last time I ever see you again."

She begins shaking. Literally shaking.

"Leyna please don't do this! Help me please. I'm begging you!"

She stands up from the hospital bed walking over to me. I put my hands out in front of me blocking her from coming closer. Memories of me being a little girl flying my hands out in front of me to keep her from beating me when she was drunk, fly through my mind.

"Get away from me," I yell at her.

Until I found you

"You can't do this to me! I'm sick, Leyna," Jean cries grabbing on to my arms.

A nurse comes in, "what the hell is going on in here? I'm calling security!"

Just then Jared runs in the room, "No don't! We're leaving. Leyna, baby let's go," he says pulling my arm.

Memories of Lyle grabbing Jean off of me during her drunken rages come flashing through as Jean refuses to let go of me.

"Leyna please," she begs.

"Let go of me" I say and panic.

Pushing her off of me as she falls to the ground. The nurse is helping her up when Jared puts his arms around my waist practically running me out of the hospital. Once we're out in the parking lot he puts me in the passenger seat and hurriedly drives off. I rest my head against the window as I process what just happened. No tears flow. I feel numb. Jared keeps looking over at me as he drives us home. We're nearly there when Jared pulls over and hurriedly reaches over to open the passenger door. Without another moment passing, I begin to vomit out onto the pavement. He rubs my back soothingly as I do so.

After a few minutes I asked him, "how did you know?"

I didn't even know myself that I was about to puke.

"Your coloring. Plus I know you well enough to know your nerves get the best of you," he says quietly.

He is still rubbing my back. He doesn't ask me if I'm ok. He knows I'm not. Instead he drives us home. As we were walking through the door Maggie greeted us cheeringly.

"I think I figured out what I want to do on my birthday day," singing the last part in a high octave.

Jared must not have had the chance to inform her what happened yet. She catches the expressions on mine and Jared's faces. Her expression suddenly matches ours.

"What's going on," she asks slowly, worry etched in her face.

I point to Jared as I sit on the couch laying my head in my hands. Jared begins telling Maggie everything that happened.

"Oh My God, Leyna. I'm so sorry. Look, everything will be ok. Ok? We've got you! It'll all work out. I promise," she says as she walks over to me on the couch, pulling me in for a hug.

Jared follows suit, sitting on the other side of me. Making me the middle of the sandwich. I almost begin to cry but for some reason the tears just won't come.

"We're here for you baby. We're here for you," Jared says soothingly as he rubs my hair. Maggie pats my back. They hold me like this for a while.

"You guys are the only family I have left," I say more as a statement than anything.

"We're all you need," Maggie says.

"We may be a dysfunctional family, but we're a family nonetheless," Jared adds.

After a while I get up and decide to take a shower and brush my teeth, hoping that will make me feel better. I sit on the shower floor for a long

UNTIL I found you

time. My knees pulled to my chest, my arms wrapped around them. I sit there until the water turns cold. After getting out and getting dressed I lay on my bed. I stared at my phone, at mine and Micah's pictures. I decided I might as well be brave and read Micah's texts and listen to his voicemails from yesterday. I glanced through all of the texts and listened to all of his voice messages. They're mostly all begging me to answer the phone, to let him explain, to please at least let him know I was ok. He even threatened to send the police out looking for me to make sure I was ok. I actually almost laugh at that thought. Some were even angry, demanding me to speak to him. But every one spoke to me the same. Whether they were angry, pleading or threatening, I could see how upset and worried he was for me. He cared.

Maggie's words play through my mind.

"He loves you, Leyna."

I look back at our pictures and before I know what I'm doing I'm walking out the front door and starting my car.

Forty-five

This doesn't make any sense to me either. So I wouldn't expect it to make sense to anyone else. Especially him. I pull up in his driveway before I know it. My mind may not know what it's doing, but my heart does. It led me here to him. Knowing he'll be back from work any minute, I walk around to the backyard waiting for him. I sit in front of the Lilies, the green grass is a thick carpet beneath me. I'm looking out across the river taking in the peaceful view. It's almost sunset. The last rays of sun are hitting the tops of the water. I listen as the wind blows through the trees. The wind chimes hanging above the lilies, plays.

    I close my eyes and enjoy the serenity. I don't hear him walking towards me but the wind blows his delicious scent to me right before I feel his presence near me. He's sitting next to me now. Like mine, he pulls his legs up to his chest and his arms lay atop his knees. We both just stare out on the horizon. Just him being near me, I can feel myself relax already.

UNTIL I found you

He turns his head to look at me then. I do the same to him. He looks sad, almost defeated looking. He's wearing all black; black pants, black belt, black button up dress shirt. His outfit matching his grim mood.

We just stare at each other. His eyes have dark circles under them, evidence of lack of sleep. Suddenly his brows pull together and a pained look marks his face as he slowly lifts his hand to my face, wiping tears away from my cheeks. I hadn't even realized I started crying.

"Baby, please don't cry. I can't bear it," he says in a low, shaky voice.

Remorse and regret evident in his tone. Tears begin to pull in his eyes.

"Please, let me hold you," he asks, extending his arms.

I climb in his lap then, wrapping my arms around his neck pulling him into an embrace. His arms wrap tightly around me as he holds me close to his heart. Holding me as if I'll disappear from him should he let me go. The way he's burying his face into my neck, the way I'm holding him close to my chest, We needed each other. We're home in each other's arms.

"I'm sorry," we both say in unison.

I squeeze him a little tighter in response. He begins to pepper soft kisses to my neck where his face is buried. The combination of his warm breath and facial hair on my neck as he kisses me sends goosebumps over my body. I run my hands through his hair then as his hand moves up to the back of my neck. Grasping it, he tilts my head back giving him better access. He begins gently kissing up my neck as he works his way towards my jaw. He sits up some, pulling me to straddle him. My legs on either side of him. I melt as he holds me this way. With one of his large hands wrapped around the back of my neck, he takes the other and snakes it around my back pulling me closer to him. I cup his face with my hands as I bring his lips to mine. His mouth meets mine like a magnet as our tongues dance along each other. Instinctively, I begin to rock into him and he moans before bucking his hips into me. Feeling his hard flesh beneath me a whimper escapes from my lips and it breaks us both. We need each other, body and soul. I begin to unbutton his shirt as he pulls mine up and over my head. His mouth finds my breasts as he sucks and licks my nipples. Growing impatient I rip the buttons off his shirt as I slide it down his arms. I admired his strong, chiseled chest. I grab his belt and hurriedly undo it's clasps along with the button and zipper on his pants. He kicks his pants off along with his shoes as he grabs me around by my waist and flips us over, hovering over me.

    Grabbing my pants and panties as he pulls them down my legs. I grab his large, hard length palming it in my hand. He moans as he pushes my thighs apart, dipping his head down he presses his hot, skillful tongue on my clit. I arch my back at the incredible feeling and look down at him in between my legs as I run my hands through his hair before tugging on it. He moans in response, sending vibrations through me.

    I whimper his name from the pleasure he's bringing me. He looks up at me then as he licks his lips. He spreads my thighs further apart then before spitting on my pussy. The act caused me to quiver in

Until I found you

anticipation. He positions himself between my legs before he pushes the tip of his large cock in me. Going in a quarter of the way before pulling out and pushing back in only a little, slowly stretching me to fit him.

I'm about to beg for more of him when he grabs the side of my hip and thrusts into me all at once in a slow, deep movement. A few tears fall from my eyes at the incredible feeling. I'm home now. I stretch around him then taking all of him. He moans before his mouth crashes down onto mine, his kisses are wet and uncalculated, lost in his passion for me. He runs his other hand through my hair, gently tugging as he rocks his hips into me. I glide my foot up his leg until I press my heel into his ass cheek, encouraging him to go faster into me.

He obliges before wrapping his arm around my lower back and flipping us over to where I'm on top of him. The feeling catches my breath at first. He's so full and deep in me like this. He lays back on the ground. His hands on either side of my hips as he guides me to ride him for the first time. I lean back swirling my hips as I rock onto him, the feeling is incredible. I moan as his hands palm my large breasts.

He looks down to where our bodies meet then and growls before rubbing my clit in tight circles as I ride him. My head falls back. I can feel the pressure building. My mouth falls open into a perfect "o" shape as I stare into his eyes. He removes his hand from my clit as he sits up and wraps both of his arms around my back. Pulling me closer to him, our chest touching each other as he begins licking my neck and jaw. Biting on the sensitive flesh just below my ear. He begins to suck there. The sting dulls as he licks the pain away. He pushes his tongue into my mouth as he thrusts harder.

I feel myself coming to the edge. My head falls back as I moan his name and squeeze around him. He furrows his brows and bites his lower lip watching me coming so close to my release. Suddenly he flips us over. Pinning me beneath him as he thrusts into me harder.

"Cum for me baby. I need to feel you."

He growls. My orgasm rips through me, then wave after euphoric wave. My mouth falls open and I cry out. Micah places his mouth on mine and swallows my moans greedily. I begin to squeeze around him, he buries his face into my neck pinning me completely down beneath him as he thrusts into me relentlessly.

"I can't- I can't stop," he moans into me.

Biting on my collarbone as he does. I push the small of his back into me further and he joins me in ecstasy. I feel him as he spills into me. I hold him close to me as our ragged breaths synchronize together. Our mouths find each other once more. Our kisses are slow, sensual and full of deeper meaning. The way we're holding one another, the way we're kissing each other says the things we haven't yet spoken to each other. Like magnets, our souls collide. And like a raging fire, our Love grows stronger.

Forty-six

We're silent as we're getting dressed. Micah zips his pants and puts his dress shirt on not bothering to button it. That's when I realized I ripped the buttons off his shirt.

"I can fix it," I offer.

He looks at me quizzically.

"I'm not worried about the shirt. I'm worried about us. Talk to me," he says standing over me. I'm pulling my shirt over my head when I say to him.

"I have so many questions."

"I'll answer all of them, just don't leave," he says taking my hand in his.

"Is it true? Did you have sex with Nadia recently?"

I hold my breath.

"Yes, but not since we've been together I swear it."

Pain takes over again.

"When," I ask, not looking at him this time.

"That first night you came over. After we got into that argument about Jared. I thought you were never going to talk to me again. I thought-"

I cut him off, "Why?"

He looks confused, "why what?"

"Why did you do it?"

He lets out a long breath through his nose. "After I dropped you off, I honestly thought you never wanted to see me again. I felt like I had nothing else to lose when Nadia called me later that night. I found myself imagining it was you I was with. I know that sounds sick and you probably think I'm a fucked person. But, it's the truth. I never thought you'd show up at my door the next night. The way you barged in demanding an explanation from me for why I stood you up. I never expected it. When you did it gave me hope Leyna."

"Hope for what?"

He takes the side of my face in his large hand, "That you felt it too. This connection with me. That I got under your skin the same way you got under mine. I've never felt this before. I never thought I would. I've gone through countless women in my life and not one of them has ever come close, not even a fraction to making me feel the way you do. None of them were you Leyna."

Tears sting my eyes. I do feel it. He's been under my skin since the first moment I saw him. No other guy has ever come close to Micah.

"I know you talked to her at the restaurant. What did she say to you," he asks, bending his knees to where his eyes are level with mine.

Tears brim over and fall down my face at the memory of it.

UNTIL I found you

"Basically she insulted me and told me that I was just a toy for you to amuse yourself with and that eventually you would get bored with me. Oh, and the fact that you two have sex," I said, my voice breaks at the end.

His nostrils flare and he looks at me sternly.

"Had. As in past tense. I would never touch her, or hell any woman as long as you're mine," he says taking both sides of my face in his hands. "I need you to believe that Leyna. I would never hurt you. Especially in that way."

I look into his eyes and see the desperation behind them.

"No more lies," I say to him.

"I'm not lying to you," he says defensively.

I push him away.

"You withheld the truth! That is also lying!"

"I thought I'd never see you again! We weren't even together then. I'm not using that as an excuse but fuck sake what else do you want me to do to convince you I would have never touched her had I known what I know now?"

He's standing in front of me. His arms outstretched in frustration.

"You act like I fucked her yesterday. She is nothing to me! Never was anything to me other than pussy, so get that through your head!"

Anger boils within me. By the expression on his face, he knows he went too far.

I shove him, "fuck you," I turn and walk towards my car.

His arms wrap around my waist stopping me, "Stop. Hear me out," he says turning me to face him.

"What? What," I practically yell, wailing my arms around.

I know I must look crazy but he's making me that way.

"Calm down," he says sternly at me; which only further pisses me off.

"Calm down? Do you know what kind of fucking day I've had? Scratch that. What the past 24 hours have been like for me?"

He nods.

"Yeah, hell. It's been hell for me too. You left without so much as a word to me. Do you know how utterly fucking panicked I was? I didn't know what to think. I didn't know if you had passed out in the restroom or if someone had taken you. Only to find out what happened when Nadia walked over gloating to me that she just met "my new pet." The bitch sat there and let me sweat it before finally letting me in on you leaving. You left and didn't even have your bag with you. No way of getting home. Not even bothering to answer my calls or texts to let me know you were safe. I drove around searching the streets for you myself for over two hours. You didn't even let me explain! You never gave me that option. You just took what a bitter stranger had to say about me and ran with it."

He's angry with me.

"She told me you slept together! What else was I supposed to believe, Micah?"

He explodes.

"Me! You're supposed to believe me! You're supposed to trust me enough to ask me instead of believing a complete stranger," he shouts at me.

I take a step back at his outburst.

UNTIL I found you

"Trusting people has never gotten me anywhere in life," I shout back at him as tears brim over. Every time I put my trust in someone it always slaps me in the face. The events of today with my own mother proving that fact.

"What is it going to take with you," he asks exasperated. "What else am I going to have to do or say to prove to you I'm here, that I'm not going anywhere? That I-."

He pauses.

"God you're so fucking difficult you know that," he almost growls.

"Then why not walk away," I say, challenging him. "Since I'm so fucking difficult, why not leave?"

"Because I-" he shouts but stops himself.

After a moment of containing himself he nods his head.

"Yeah you'd like that wouldn't you? To prove a fucked up point to yourself. God, it kills you to have someone actually try to be there for you doesn't it? To care about you, to have someone that wants to get close to you. You'd rather believe lies about someone than to believe what your own heart already knows about them."

I begin to cry harder. He's right but I can't hear it. I walk towards my car then.

"So what then? You're leaving? You're walking away from us? The going gets tough and Leyna decides to bail."

He's following me.

"Why did you even come here then? huh? Was this your version of goodbye? Come here, make love to me and then leave?"

I open my car door to get in when he slams it shut. Pinning me against the car with his hands on either side of me.

"You are terrified. I get that. This is your worst fear. Trusting someone with your fragile heart. I know it's been broken more times than should be allowed in a lifetime. I know you've been hurt. I can see it in you as clear as I'm looking at you right now. You think there's nothing left of you to give. You think there's nothing that can heal what's been done to you. But I can love you past your pain. I can't change what happened. But I can love you through all the pain you've endured if you'll just let me," he says, his voice breaks at the end.

He looks into my eyes pleading with me. Tears stream down my face as I say,

"I'm broken, Micah. I've been broken for so long that's all I know how to be. You don't want this," I begin sobbing. "You don't want me. I can't be fixed. There's no point in loving someone so broken-"

He silences me by grabbing my face in his hands and kisses me feverishly. As though his life depended on it. I mold into him as he kisses me this way. My heart breaks and mends back together simultaneously.

He pulls away, staring into my eyes as he says, "I want you, Leyna. Hell, I need you, I need you in my life because you are the only good, pure thing that's ever been in it. I've lived feeling as though I'm missing something from myself, always feeling this anger in my chest like wildfire. I thought it would consume me until there was nothing left of me. And then, you came into my life. You calm the raging storm within me. You bring me so much happiness. You bring me peace. You're broken. I'm broken. But together, we make a whole. You are the missing piece of me Leyna."

His words unravel me as I begin to sob into him. He wraps his arms around me tightly as he nuzzles his face into my neck, soothingly shushing me. I feel his warm tears fall onto my neck as he holds me close.

Forty-seven

We're walking up to the front door hand-in-hand when he stops us hesitantly.

"I need to warn you it's messy in there. I have a cleaning service scheduled to come in tomorrow."

I nod my head.

"How bad can it be," I asked as he opens the door and we step foot inside.

I look around at the disheveled mess scattered across the floor. My jaw drops at the havoc. There's broken glass and debris everywhere. The table that was set beside the front door is now flipped over all the way by the staircase. I step over shards of a broken lamp. Books, glass sculptures and other decor are scattered across the living room floor. The tv that was hanging above the fireplace is now broken against the wall near the kitchen. The farthest kitchen wall has a stain of some kind of liquid running down it.

That's when I notice the broken whiskey bottle laying in pieces on the kitchen floor. I look over at the wall by the front door and notice a hole in the drywall from where Micah punched it with his fist. My hand clamps over my mouth in shock at the amount of damage.

"I told you it was messy," he says sheepishly as he rubs the back of his neck with his hand.

"I thought you meant not picking up after yourself."

I look around me.

"But Micah-" he cuts me off.

"I know," he says ashamed.

I look over to him trying to understand how he can get so angry that he turns violent at times. "There's no excuse. I was just so angry. So- so beside myself. I had a million thoughts and emotions running through me at once. I held them together until I found out fucking Connor was the one that took you home. I just kept picturing him taking you back to his house, touching you all over your body."

His hands are in fists at his sides recounting his thoughts. I walk over to him. Glass crunching beneath my feet. I take his hands in mine. He looks down at me. His expression, grim.

"First of all, I would never let another man touch me. Second, nothing happened. He picked me up and drove me home," I say.

"He didn't try anything on you? Or say anything to you," he asks, looking into my eyes.

"No. He didn't try anything. But, he did mention how you two knew each other."

Micah tenses.

"What did he tell you?"

I look down at our hands as I say quietly,

"You weren't the nicest person back then, that you viewed and treated girls like a game. Including his girlfriend, that he was in love with at the time. You bullied people a lot and that you were violent."

I look around at our surroundings. Connor got that part right at least. I can feel him staring at me.

A long moment of silence ensues before he says "it's true."

I look up at him, shocked at his confession. I expected him to downplay it or even go as far as to flat out deny it but he doesn't.

"You have to understand, I wasn't a good person back then. I had a lot of built up, unresolved anger within me and truthfully, I still do I guess. I took it out on nearly everyone I met, so yeah I was a bully. I felt empty, completely void then, so I tried burying my sorrows into every girl that pranced my way. Soon, only fighting and pussy could distract me from the storm raging in me. Nothing ever calmed me. I was an arrogant asshole back then. I put on the front that I had everything I ever wanted. Deep down nothing in my life brought me happiness. I started self medicating with alcohol my junior year in high school. Nearly got my ass expelled a few times because of it. If it wasn't for my father writing a generous donation check those times, I would have. I was a miserable son of a bitch back then and I wanted everyone around me to feel the hell I was feeling. So yeah I slept with Connor's girl strictly for kicks. It brought me an ounce of pleasure to know that he felt miserable. I know that's fucked up, believe me I do. It's the truth. It made me feel less... alone, to know that someone felt even a fraction of what I did. I made bad choices because of my drinking. Choices that I wish I could go back and

Until I found you

change. Things I'm not proud of. It wasn't until my early college years that I vowed to someone that I would quit drinking and that I would get my shit together to become a better person. Even then nothing filled the emptiness inside of me. No matter how many women I would bury myself in, nothing made me feel whole. Nothing calmed me. I felt like the world kept turning and I was stuck never moving forward. Nothing made me feel alive. Nothing made me feel complete. Until I found you."

He's looking into my eyes as he touches the side of my face with his warm hand.

"You've changed me Leyna. You've awoken feelings in me I thought I wasn't capable of having. You bring out the best in me. I thought I knew who I was. I thought I knew what I wanted in life and where my life was going but then you came into it and changed all of that. You were what I was longing for. You were what I needed."

My breath hitches as I process everything he's just said. I look into the eyes of the man in front of me and I know in my heart he's a different person from the angry, toxic boy from before. He has changed. Standing in front of me is the man I could have only prayed to have as mine. The man that has brought me more happiness and love in just this short amount of time than I've felt in my 21 years of life. Never have I felt this kind of passion in my life. Something I never thought I would experience.

Before him, I was merely the shell of the woman I am now standing in front of him. I was like dying embers, barely hanging on to the spark inside of me. That was until he came into my life and ignited the raging fire within me. He awakened me too. He stokes every part of me. He makes me angry, livid even, but this man makes me feel alive. He makes me feel beautiful and desirable. Wanted. He claims I've changed him for the better, but he has changed me too. I felt I was too broken to be loved. I thought having a person like him would never be in the cards for me. I thought I didn't deserve him. I believed he couldn't possibly love a broken creature like me.

Even though he hasn't said it in words yet, I know this man loves me. Without a shadow of a doubt, I know that I love this man. I love him more than my own life. He claims that I'm his missing piece, that I was what was missing in his life. Truth be told, he's mine. He's my missing piece. He's the other half of my heart.

His beautiful blue eyes nervously search my face. "Say something," he says, barely above a whisper.

I step on my tippy toes as I bring his face to mine. He wraps his arms around me tightly as I place my lips on his. One of his hands goes into my hair deepening our sweet, tender kiss. The way he's holding me, the way he's kissing me, I know no matter what we may go through in life, no matter what obstacles life may throw at us, I want to go through it and battle it with him. No matter what turmoil I may face, he is my solace. He is my safe haven. He is my home. He touches his forehead to mine as he looks down at my lips, smiling. His arms still wrapped around me.

"You're everything to me," I breathe to him.

He cups my face as he starts planting soft kisses to both my cheeks, my nose and finally my

until i found you

forehead before saying, "And you are my everything."

Forty-eight

It took us over an hour to clean up the mess- no havoc, Micah wrecked. He tried stopping me at first, insisting on the maid service he hired to clean it up. I couldn't wait that long. I picked up the broom and started cleaning it myself. Knowing he wasn't going to win this one, he started picking up the bigger shards of glass off the floor.

Once everything was swept up twice over, I made him go back over everything with the vacuum cleaner while I cleaned the whiskey off the kitchen wall. Micah double bagged the broken glass and took the trash out. I'm putting the vacuum cleaner up in the hall closet when I notice an old box sitting on top of the highest shelf with a photo album laying on top of it. I go to grab it but it's out of my reach even on my tippy toes. Dammit, I hate being short. I try jumping to grab it but that's futile. "What are you doing?"

I hear Micah behind me. I jump a little from being caught as I turn around to face him. He's leaned up against the wall with his arms folded across his chest. His sexy six pack is on full display through

UNTIL I
found you

his unbuttoned dress shirt. He's so hot. I bite down on my lip as he gives me an amused look.

I give him a guilty smile and say, "I saw the photo album on top of the box and was being nosey. Apparently there's a height requirement for that."

He has an unreadable expression on his face before he chuckles and walks over grabbing the photo album off the top of the box before handing it to me. I open it and see baby pictures of Micah. I sit down on the floor crossing my legs as I flip through all the pictures.

"Awe! You were so adorable!"

He chuckles at me before sitting down next to me and pulling me to sit in between his legs, my back to his front. He wraps his arms around my waist bringing me closer to him. I flip the pages and see a picture of his mom. She's in a yellow dress, her long ash blonde hair is wind blown as she's holding a baby Micah in her arms, smiling down at him adoringly. You can tell even through this picture, her son was her whole world.

"She loved you so much," I said, thinking out loud.

He tightens his grip around me as he kisses my shoulder. I flip through the rest of the album finding his father Keith in only three of them. This is bitter proof that his father was always absent in his life. The cutest picture of all was the one of him naked, he looked to be around 2 years old. From the looks of it, he was running away from Lillian when she snapped the picture.

"Oh God, not that one," Micah groans, laying his head back against the wall.

"You have the cutest butt on the planet."

I giggle. He looks down at me fighting a smile.

"You think my butt's cute?"

I roll my eyes at him before looking back down at the photo album.

"It is pretty cute," I say, fighting a laugh.

"Just cute," he asks as he tickles my side.

I laugh, wiggling around him.

He begins to tickle me harder before I say, "ok, ok! It's the sexiest ass I've ever seen!"

He throws his head back laughing when he hits the back of it on the wall. He rubs it still laughing.

"Ha! Pay back," I say as I go in for the kill.

I flip around straddling him as I begin tickling his ribs. He laughs harder than I've ever seen him as he kicks his feet and tries grabbing my arms to stop me.

"Oh, you asked for it," He says through his booming laughter as he tackles me to the floor pinning my arms above my head as he blows raspberries into my neck.

I lose it and go into a fit of snorts and ridiculous giggles. Micah nearly collapses on top of me from his laughter at my snorting. He lets go of my arms and rolls over onto his back. Holding his sides as tears fall from the corners of his eyes. Watching him like this it's hard to believe that mere hours ago we went from impending doom, to having makeup sex in the back yard, to fighting again, to expressing our deep feelings for each other and now we're playfully wrestling and tickling each other on the floor. This is us. Messy and passionate, but more importantly we're absolutely crazy for each other.

I'm grinning like an idiot at him when he looks over at me smiling.

"Come here, baby," he says, pulling me to lay on top of him.

I lay my chin on his chest as he tucks my hair behind my ear. He reaches my face, teasingly brushing his lips to mine before giving me playful quick repetitive pecks to my lips. We laugh at each other gleefully before he looks at me smiling.

"You're mine," he says, running his hand through my hair.

"I'm yours," I smile.

I hand him back the photo album as he puts it back on top of the box before placing it on the shelf.

"What's in that," I ask curiously.

"Nothing much. Just some paperwork," he says shutting the closet door.

"Are you hungry," he asks.

Actually, I'm starving. I haven't really eaten anything since yesterday. I nod. He takes my hand in his leading us up the stairs to his bedroom.

"Delivery or dine in? Either way I'm changing clothes," he says as he lets his ripped dress shirt fall to the floor. I stare at his muscular toned back and watch as he unzips his pants. His hard muscles flex as he bends down, pulling them down his legs until he's in only his boxers. He really does have the sexiest ass I've ever seen. He turns around and catches me staring. "Enjoying the view?"

"It's my own strip tease," I say biting my lip as I imagine him putting on an actual strip tease for me.

He smirks, grabbing a pair of jeans and a black t-shirt before putting them on. Even wearing the most casual of clothes, Micah still looks like a Greek God. I look over on his night stand and see my bag. I walk over and grab it, looking for something to wear when I notice my favorite perfume is missing. I dig deeper in the bag but it's not there. Micah catches me searching for it and looks at me sheepishly before opening his drawer and handing it to me.

I give him a quizzical look before he says, "I thought you were leaving me so I had to have something of you to remind me. I sprayed some on my pillow just to get me through the night." My heart breaks and soars simultaneously. I close the gap between us, wrapping my arms around his waist as I pull him into me.

My head on his chest, "I'll never leave you Micah," I say into his chest.

He gathers my face in his hands gently forcing me to look up at him.

"You swear?"

I raise up on my tippy toes, "I swear, baby."

A huge smile spreads across his face at my words.

"Baby," he muses before kissing my forehead sweetly.

I rummage through my bag and find my black ruffled trim shorts and pair it with the white fitted top Maggie had gotten me a while back. Once I'm dressed, I ogle at my own chest in the mirror. This top definitely brings out the size of my breasts. The material clings to my waist in a flattering way, showing off my hourglass figure. The shorts fit snug

UNTIL I found you

against my hips. A little too snug for my liking. Not that they're too small, but I normally wear my bottoms a size up so it doesn't cling to my ass like this.

As I look in the mirror, I see I have a panty line in my shorts. I huff, taking my shorts and panties off before pulling my shorts back on. Apparently I'm going commando tonight. I slip on my heeled ankle boots and sigh. I'm walking down the stairs when Micah sees me from the hallway.

"Holy shit," he says, eyeing my chest before staring at my ass.

I begin to blush.

"Should I change," I ask.

He reaches me, "I'm not sure. On one hand, what you're wearing is clinging to every sinful curve you have making my dick throb even now as I look at you. And on the other hand, if I so much as catch a mother fucker looking at you I'm going to jail tonight."

I shake my head amusingly at him before smacking him playfully on the butt. We decided on Mario's Italian restaurant for dinner.

Once we are seated in a booth Micah says, "I suppose tonight will be my makeup date with you. Since I was a complete asshat and didn't bother showing up here last time."

He smirks.

"Don't remind me. I was super pissed at you that night."

He chuckles at the memory.

"Indeed you were. I've never seen a wilder, more beautiful woman in my life then when you came barging in my house tearing me a new one," he muses. "I remember wanting to throw you against the wall and take you right there. You wore those same heels the night we met. Those are by far my favorite shoes on you. Call me sentimental or maybe it's just the way you look wearing heels but fuck does my dick throb when I see you in them."

I swallow at his words. My throat is already becoming dry.

"Is that right," I ask quietly as I rake my foot slowly up his leg under the table.

He licks his lips and shuffles in his seat some before grabbing my calf and giving it a squeeze. "Unless you want me to fuck your brains out in the bathroom stall, I'd watch yourself," he says in a husky voice.

My breath hitches and my lips part. He licks his lips noticing my reaction. I can feel my cheeks turning rosy. He squeezes my calf a little more under the table as he bites down on his bottom lip. I can feel pressure in between my legs as I squirm in my chair. He tightens his grip on my leg as he starts massaging higher up. I swallow.

"Are you wet," he asks with hooded eyes.

"Mm hmm."

He licks his lips again.

"Are your panties soaked?"

I smile mischievously, "I'm not wearing any."

His eyes go wide before he swallows, "Fucking hell baby you're killing me."

He shifts in his seat. Just then the waiter comes up taking our drink order, breaking the sexual teasing game we were playing, for the moment anyway. I pull my leg away from Micah and he reluctantly lets go of me. He seemed agitated at the waiter when he took a little too long listing the specials for the evening. I had to cover my mouth to hide my smirk at Micah's expression.

He looked like the waiter pissed in his Cheerios. After he walked away, I finally let a small laugh escape. Micah rolled his eyes and exhaled a deep frustrated breath through his nose before looking over at me.

Saying in a low, husky voice, "Best believe you're getting it when we get home."

I bite my lip in anticipation knowing what's coming and I can't wait.

Forty-nine

Once we've finished eating and Micah pays the bill, we're walking towards his corvette hand in hand when a voice calls my name from behind me. I turn around and see that it's my mother's friend Jackie.

"Where's your mom? I've been trying to reach her for days."

Micah looks between me and the man, his arm going protectively around my waist at his side. "She's in jail and probably won't be out for a few months. I'm not sure how long honestly," I say.

I don't miss the way Micah is suddenly staring at me but I don't acknowledge it.

"What happened," Jackie asks.

"She skipped out on bail. It's a long story," I say looking up at Micah on the last part.

He nods his head once at me before kissing me on top of my head.

"I'm sure it is. Listen since she won't be back for a while, I have her stuff in my garage. Would you come by sometime this week and pick it up?"

"Sure. I can come by tomorrow?"

Until I found you

"That'll work. See you then kid," he says as he heads in the restaurant.

I look up at Micah who's already peering down at me.

"Told you the last 24 hours have been hell," I say, laying my head on his chest.

"Want to talk about it," he offers, opening the car door for me.

"Not right now. Maybe later?"

He smiles, "whenever you're ready, babe."

He takes my hand in his as he pulls out of the parking lot. I stare out at the city lights as they pass us by trying desperately to push any thought of my mother to the back of my mind. It's not working. Micah turns the radio up then. The Weeknd's "The Hills" begins playing throughout the car. I look over to him and he gives me a small smile.

"I figured you could use a distraction."

I smile back at him.

"Thanks. I definitely need one."

He looks over to me, taking his hand out of mine only to place it on my thigh as he rubs slowly up and then over between my legs. My heart quickens and my mouth becomes dry as he rubs the thin material over my clit.

"How about this," he asks seductively.

I arch my back in response. I look over at him as we come to a red light. He removes his hand from in between my legs and begins dipping his fingers into the waistband of my shorts. I spread my legs and moan as his fingers began rubbing small circles on my clit. He hisses as I reach my hand over and rub the hard bulge in his pants. His fingers rub in faster circles on my clit as I unbutton his jeans and zipper and begin stroking him. Pumping his large, hard cock in my hand.

"Fuck," he whispers as he lays his head back on the headrest.

Closing his eyes momentarily before the light turns green. He takes off driving erratically as we bring each other closer to the edge. I buck my hips into his hand as he slips one finger inside of me. Giving me slow, deep pumps. I bite my lip as I whimper his name. He looks over to me.

"Oh, fuck this," Micah says turning into a nearly empty parking garage then.

He goes up to the second floor and parks into the darkest spot, furthest away from any car. Once he puts it in park he lets his seat back all the way before pulling his jeans and boxers down his legs. He then grabs my shorts pulling them down my legs in a haste before lifting me up by my waist and lowering me onto him. We both moan as his large cock buries deeply into me. I cry out at the incredible full feeling.

"You're so wet for me, baby," he muses as he places both hands on my ass, squeezing handfuls while guiding me to rock and bounce onto him. He removes his hands from me then, only to remove my shirt and bra. He wraps one hand into my hair fisting it. With the other, he palms my breast in his hand before attaching his hot mouth to my nipple sucking harshly as he does. The stinging intensifies. Making me rock harder into him.

"Fuck," he hisses before removing his hand from my breast to wrap it around my throat claiming me.

Until I found you

I moan as his fingers press into my neck. I love when he does this. With his other hand, he places it on my ass before palming and slapping it. Sweat begins to pull at him, enveloping the car in his delicious scent. His brows are pulled together, his lips are parted, glistening from licking my breast.

"Who's pussy is this," he asks and growls.

Bucking his hips into me as he does.

"Yours, Micah," I moan.

"You're mine. No one else's. You only belong to me," he says between hot puffs. "Say it," he commands.

"I'm only yours," I say panting as I push my throat further into his hand.

He squeezes his hand around my throat with a bit more pressure and it's all it takes. I come over the edge and my orgam rips through me as I cum and squeeze around him. Crying his name out as I do.

"Fuck, baby," he hisses as he bucks into me with a few faster thrusts before spilling himself into me.

He buried his face into my neck as he does. We're a panting hot mess. Both drenching in sweat from our shared euphoria, I lay my head on his chest trying to steady my breathing. His chest is rising and falling rapidly, matching my own. He wraps his arms around me, his face still buried in my neck. He begins kissing and licking the salt from my neck. I bring my mouth to his tasting him. He wraps his hands through my hair as we kiss. The tinted windows of the car fogged. Shielding us from any wandering eyes. He reaches over and gets my shirt pulling it over my head as I stick my arms through it.

My hair clings to my back, grabbing it in his hands, Micah pulls it out of my shirt as I slip it on. He trails his fingers lightly on the tops of my thighs before kissing my lips softly. I cup his face in my hands as our foreheads touch.

We stay like this for a moment, enjoying the feeling of being wrapped in each other's arms. I'm the one that breaks away as I lift off of him. The sudden emptiness stinging slightly. We're both wet from the evidence of our orgasms.

We're pulling our pants up when he looks over at me and says with a shy smile, "you need to get on birth control baby. It seems I can't keep my hands off of you."

I smile back at him.

"It seems you can't. I'll call tomorrow to make an appointment."

He seems satisfied with my answer as he drives out of the parking garage, his hand wrapped tightly in mine. I text Maggie and Jared to let them know where I've been and that I'm ok. We're pulling into Micah's driveway when I get a text back from Jared.

"It seems today ended better than it began for the both of us. Jamie called me back. I'm with him now. Probably won't be home tonight. Love you be safe."

I smile, feeling incredibly relieved that things worked out for Jared. I look over to Micah and suddenly I feel so abundantly happy. A feeling that has been a stranger to me until recently. I reach over planting a kiss to Micah's cheek.

He smiles at me sweetly, "what was that for?"

UNTIL I found you

I shrug, "Just because."

We're walking up the steps to his front door when I say to him, "I need to get going soon."

He looks over at me confused. "Why are you leaving? What's wrong?"

"Nothing's wrong. You have work early in the morning. Plus, I have to dog sit Charlie tomorrow remember? And I need to run a few errands tomorrow too before I go."

"So? That doesn't mean you can't stay here with me." I'm about to give in when he says, "You already have some clothes and a toothbrush here. You can leave in the morning. Just stay," he says cupping my face with the side of his hand.

I nod my head and he smiles kissing my lips as he unlocks the door.

"I figured you'd be tired of me by now," I say jokingly.

He turns to me, "On the contrary. I find myself wishing you were here with me when you're not around." I smile and he leads us up the stairs to his bathroom.

He surprises me by drawing us a hot bath instead of taking a shower. I pull my hair up into a messy bun atop my head before stripping my clothes and stepping into the hot water with Micah, laying my back against his chest. His arms wrap around me as he begins peppering kisses across my shoulder. I lay my head back into his chest and revel in the blissful state I'm in. I've never been so relaxed in my life than in this moment with him. Micah is bathing my chest with a cloth while he hums a familiar melody into my ear sweetly. I smile.

"What song is that?"

I can feel him smile as he kisses just below my ear.

"I started listening to that artist you love so much. Sleeping At Last, his song Atlas:Two makes me think of us. It's become my song to you," he says nuzzling his face into my neck. That precious song is his song to me? The lyrics and knowing he feels that about me, tears of happiness begin to brim my eyes. He never fails to make me feel so completely wanted and loved, even during the difficult times. We may fight, we may become so ridiculously angry at one another but in the end I know we love each other. I feel the abundance of love this man has for me. I never thought I would feel this, this kind of devotion from someone. To feel this kind of earth moving love, no matter what life may throw our way I know I can face it head on. Micah is my solace. My safe haven. I am his. His heart is my home. He notices my tears then, pulling his head back to examine me.

"Baby?"

Worry clear on his face. He turns me toward him wiping my tears away with his thumb as he asks,

"Baby why are you crying? Did I- did I say something wrong?"

Worry spreads across his features.

"No, you did nothing wrong."

I pause.

"You do everything right Micah. I feel so incredibly happy. Something I never thought I would feel. Not on this level at least."

He lifts me to straddle his legs as he wraps one hand around my back pulling me closer to him while his other hand cups my face.

He looks at me intently.

UNTIL I found you

"Listen to me, I can't promise you hearts and flowers all the time. I can't even promise you that bad times won't come often. I'm going to screw up. I'm going to piss you off. I can tell you that I will love you through any obstacle that comes our way."

He holds his breath for a moment, searching my face as he slowly exhales.

His face contorts from a look of worry to complete resolve as he brings his face closer to mine and says "I love you."

My heart quickens and my breathing hitches.

Still staring into my eyes he says, "I've never said that to anyone before. I've never loved anyone before. Until you. I love you, Leyna."

I wrap my hands in his hair as I connect our mouths. The kiss is deep and slow as his tongue swirls with mine. His arms wrap around my back tighter pulling me skin to skin with him. With one hand in his hair, I use the other to stroke the side of his face lightly as I kiss him. When I open my eyes slightly during our kiss I see that he is watching me with every embrace we share. I pull my face away looking at him as I trace his lips with my fingers.

"I love you, Micah."

He sucks in a sharp breath and removes my hand from his lips.

"Don't say it unless you mean it. I don't want you to feel pressured or-" I silence him by placing a finger over his lips.

"I mean this with every fiber of my heart…I love you Micah Eason." I say to him slowly as he places his forehead against mine.

He stares into my eyes and lets out a shaky breath before cupping my face in his hands and kisses me tenderly.

"I love you so much."

He breathes.

UNTIL I found you

Fifty

By the time we finish bathing and I lay my head on Micah's chest I'm already half asleep. He has one arm around my back while the other plays in my hair, further coaxing my drowsy state.

In a sleepy voice he says, "Good night, my angel. I love you."

I tilt my face up and peck his soft lips as I say, "Sweet dreams baby. I love you."

He smiles and pulls me closer into him, nuzzling his face into me as we fall asleep wrapped in each other's arms.

When I wake up, I'm alone in the bed. I call out Micah's name with no answer. I look at the clock as it reads 9:26am. He's left for work already. I rub my eyes groggily as I sit up in the bed. Looking over on the nightstand next to me, I notice a note and a red rose laying next to it. I smile, picking the rose up and bringing it to my face smelling it's fragrance before reading his note.

You looked too beautiful to wake. I'll see you tonight baby. I love you.

Suddenly giddy, I crawl out of bed and get dressed for the day ahead. I'm about to exit the bathroom when I see our dirty laundry and the towels laying on the bathroom tile from the night before. I decide to do a load of laundry and load the dishwasher before heading out. By the time I'm finished and on the road to run my errands before having to go to Mr. Edgar's, it's already past lunch. I pull into Jackie's then to collect Jean's belongings. I'm not really sure what to do with them. I suppose I'll have to rent a small storage unit until I know what to do with all of it. Jackie meets me at his garage door.

"Hey kid. Thanks for coming."

I nod awkwardly.

"No problem. I may have to make two trips though depending on how much stuff she has."

He lifts the garage door then.

"I don't think you'll need to. It's not much. Mainly clothes and paperwork shit by the looks of it."

He hands me a full black garbage bag containing her clothes and shoes and two boxes. One containing her makeup and toiletries. The other box marked "personal" filled with pictures and paperwork of sorts. He helps me load them into my trunk before waving me off. As I'm driving I can't help but think about my mother. The fact that she's in jail. How long will she be there? As a first time offender, I hope the judge goes easy on her. I wonder if being in jail would sober her up? I think about the fact that her whole life is summed up in a hefty bag and two boxes.

UNTIL I found you

Before I allow myself to sink into a depression over it, I turn the volume up on my car stereo letting the music drown out my thoughts. I'm at the red light turning into the mall when my text tone goes off. I look down to see it's Micah.

"Hey baby. How's your day? Can't stop thinking about you. It was hell leaving you this morning. Thought about calling in just to stay with you. I love you."

I smile like an idiot at my screen and reply, "Awe there you go again sending butterflies through my belly. My day is ok just missing you too baby. How's yours? I love you. P.S. The rose was beautiful."

I'm walking into the mall when my cell phone begins to ring in my purse. Pulling it out, I don't miss the way my face falls slightly when it's not Micah calling me. It's Tony.

"Hey Leyna. I was wondering if you'd made a decision about coming back or not. We really need a manager. Like soon. So if you don't take the job I'll have to hire someone over the weekend to do it. And I'd much rather hire you than a stranger. You already know the ropes and all."

I pause for a moment before answering. Micah will be pissed but I need my job.

"Yes absolutely. I can start Monday?"

"Tomorrow would have been better but I can make it to Monday. See you then."

"Bye Tony."

After being in Macy's for almost two hours trying on clothes, I spent over $300 dollars on some cuter, more flattering outfits. I smile knowing Maggie will be proud that I actually bought clothes in my size instead of buying them two sizes too big for once. Micah has made me feel so confident lately, so beautiful. I smile widely just thinking about him. I walk into a lingerie boutique, feeling completely out of my element. I've only ever been in here with Maggie when she was buying herself lingerie but I've never been a customer myself. I'm looking around at all of the selection they have when an associate walks up to me.

"Hi, my name is Amber. Can I assist you with anything or are we just looking," she asks with a friendly smile.

"I'm looking to get a few sets today. I was looking at this actually." I say, pointing to a sexy navy blue sheer lace teddy.

"Great choice! Do you know your measurements?"

I shake my head and she pulls out a pink measuring tape. "Well let's get you sized then." Sitting my Macy's bags down, I awkwardly raise my arms above my head as she measures my chest. She escorts me to a fitting room and hands me three lingerie sets and four bras to try on. I try a cream colored corset and garter on first and stare incredulously back at the person in the mirror. Surprisingly, I love how I look in it. Micah is going to ravage me when he sees me in this. I instantly feel pressure between my legs imagining it. I swallow hard and begin trying on the other pieces. I try a black set and love the contrast of my hair with it. Next is the sexy navy blue sheer lace teddy andI love it almost as much as I loved the cream colored corset with the garter. By the time I've tried on everything I decide to go with the navy blue teddy and the cream

UNTIL I
found you

colored corset along with three new sexy bra and panty sets. The associate talked me into getting the panties in the cheeky style instead of my regular hipster style. They weren't fully a thong, so it was an easy transition. They were incredibly sexy looking, nonetheless. After leaving the lingerie boutique, I'll be needing to work soon. Just from today's shopping alone I've wiped out over a quarter of my bank account. But Micah's expression of seeing me in these will have made it all worth it.

It's around 6pm when I pull up in my driveway. I'm struggling to unlock the front door with all of the shopping bags in my hands when the door opens from the inside. The lingerie bags drop, causing all of the sexy pieces to fall out. That's when I notice Connor standing in the door. My eyes go wide as I look between him and my lacey lingerie at his feet. We drop down at the same time. I begin picking it all up, shoving them back in the bag as quickly as possible. He picks my black lace panties and red bra up before handing it back to me. I take it from him, surely waiting to die any minute from embarrassment. I expect him to move out of my way or even leave but instead he stands there blocking my entrance with his hands in his pockets, a wry smile on his face.

"What?" I ask defensively.

He looks me up and down before returning his eyes to my face. I squirm uncomfortably.

"Nice choices from what I saw."

He laughs. I shove past him.

"Hey I'm kidding. I mean not really but don't be mad."

"I'm not mad, Connor. I'm mortified," I huff.

He walks closer to me leaning against the wall.

"Oh come on sour patch, don't be embarrassed. So what if I saw your panties?"

I look over at his devilish grin.

"What are you even doing here? Where's Maggie?"

"Ouch. It's nice to see you too. I was in the neighborhood and decided to drop by. Maggie is in the bathroom getting ready."

I place my hands on my hips, looking at him suspiciously.

"You were in the neighborhood?"

He chuckles, "I did move back here you know. I'm only 10 minutes from here actually."

I nod awkwardly.

"Well it was great seeing you. But I've got to head out. Tell Maggie I'll be back later for my overnight bag," I say walking in my room laying the shopping bags on my bed.

"Head out? I thought you just got here," he asks confused.

"I did. But I have to dog sit and I'm late for it so I'll see you later," I say waving at him as I walk out the door.

I let out an exasperated breath as I walked across the street to Mr. Edgar's. That's when I finally notice Connor's car parked a little ways down the street. Using the key under the grill I let myself in. Charlie instantly hopped up on me as I walked in.

"Hey boy! Did you miss me," I ask as I give him ear scratches.

UNTIL I found you

He begins to lick my chin and whine. I unlock the back patio door and step outside with Charlie, letting him run his energy out. I pick up his frisbee and toss it letting him catch it. After a while of us playing we head back inside.

Fifty-one

A little while later my phone begins to ring. It's Micah FaceTiming me. I answer it, smiling from ear to ear when I see his beautiful face on my screen.

"Hey baby," we both say at the same time.

I chuckle lightly at our unison.

"I've missed you today," I say shyly.

He smiles, "I've missed you too baby. Today was a headache," he says rubbing the bridge of his nose before pushing his hair back away from his face.

I frown, "Uh oh. What happened?"

He goes into telling me about his day. It was one of those, if it could go wrong it did, kind of days. It began with one of his staff accidentally spilling their hot coffee on Micah's white dress shirt this morning. By lunch, he and his father had already gotten into a heated discussion about one of their accounts. And by the end of the day, he fired his secretary. Apparently she screwed up and somehow scheduled him for meetings with 3 different clients at the same time, causing the rest of his schedule for that day to be royally screwed up.

Until I found you

"I'm sorry babe. It sounds like you definitely had a rough day. At least it's the weekend right?" I offer with a smile.

"Honestly it worked out for the best."

"What do you mean," I ask.

"You're coming to work with me Monday," he says it like it's a sure thing.

It's like he's already worked it out in his head. He must see hesitation on my face.

"If you'd rather another position, there's some available on my floor. Obviously you being my secretary is the position I'd like you to fill."

He is laying on the couch, his muscular arm tucked behind his head. I want to reach through the phone and lick it. I'm getting distracted.

"About Monday.." I trail off.

"What about it?" He narrows his brows in confusion.

Here we go... "Tony called me today."

His face already contorting into a look of agitation.

" I start back Monday," I say nonchalantly.

"We already discussed this. You're not going back there Leyna. That place is a shit show and I won't allow you in an unsafe environment," he says with finality.

I take in a deep breath, controlling my temper. The last thing I want to do is fight with him. We're both just so stubborn.

"Micah, I need the job. My mother skipped bail and now I have over five thousand dollars I have to pay because of it. Not to mention my student loans and monthly bills."

He studies my answer for a moment before saying, "Don't worry ok? I'll pay the bail money and anything else you need me to. You don't need to go back to that piss hole."

My eyes widen, "Um, no you're not! You're not spending money on me!"

He gives me a bored expression, "Leyna, I'm in the position to help you. So let me. It's not that big of a deal."

"It is to me," I say.

"Fine. Earn it then, but come work for me. The pay is higher plus it comes with benefits. And there are no drunken assholes staring at my girlfriends tits and ass all day," he says that last part under his breath but I catch it.

I look at him.

"Say I did accept? There has to be conditions."

"Name your terms Miss Blake," he says smiling from ear to ear.

He knows he's already won.

I fight a smile as I say, "You have to treat me like everyone else. Meaning no favoritism. And no special treatment. While we're punched in, I'm your employee not your girlfriend. Got it?" He bites his lower lip seductively, "So that means I can't bend you over my desk and take you?"

Pressure instantly forms between my legs at the thought. I shake my head. Not trusting my voice to sound resolute.

"Hmm. So that also means I can't have you for lunch everyday," he replies and licks his lips.

I swallow as my mouth becomes dry, "No," I squeak.

UNTIL I found you

He has me and he knows it. He removes his arm from the back of his head. Teasingly lifting his shirt up so that I see his rock hard abs and toned stomach.

"That's too bad. I like eating sweets at lunch hour."

My lips part. I can feel the blood pulling to my cheeks and to other areas. My cheeks heat. "Am I bothering you baby," he asks seductively.

"I'm definitely bothered right now," I say barely above a whisper.

"Me too," he says, moving the phone down.

Giving me a perfect view of his massive erection in his hand. If cartoon hearts could be busting through my eyes and chest right now they would be. I almost have to pick my jaw off the floor at his vulgar move. Micah is so comfortable and confident when it comes to sex. His bold moves and filthy words never cease to amaze me. Or do things to me.

"I wish I was there. I would have slid my dick into that beautiful mouth of yours just now. Open wide and inviting for me."

I can tell from his chest moving that he's stroking himself. The pressure in between my legs aching. I'm nervous. I've never done anything like this before.

"Relax baby. Don't overthink it. Just feel," he says in a soothing voice.

Seemingly reading my mind. I lay back on the guest bed and spread my legs as I slip my fingers into the waistband of my pants.

"Good baby. Are you touching yourself," he asks with hooded eyes.

I nod and he licks his lips.

"Picture it's me. I'm swirling my tongue on your delicious clit in faster, wider circles."

I close my eyes and bite my lip. I look back at the screen and see that his expression matches mine.

"Show me my pussy, baby. I want to see how wet you are for me."

I nearly cum from his words alone. I remove my hand from myself and pull my pants and panties down my legs. Pointing the phone to my core.

"Fuck," he hisses. "Prop the phone at the headboard of the bed and position yourself in front of it. Your head near the end of the bed. Legs apart."

I do as I'm commanded, eagerly.

Once I'm in position he instructs me further, "Spread your legs wider, baby. Show me my beautiful pussy."

I open my legs wider and make contact with my clit again. I whimper as he points the screen down showing me as he fucks himself with his hand. The erotic novel of what we're doing sends me over the edge as I cum already. I cry out riding my wave. Him seeing me in my euphoric state causes him to come undone. He pumps his cock twice and I watch him spill onto his hand. I lay back on the bed panting.

After a moment of catching my breath, I sit up and grab the phone. Micah is drinking a bottle of water replenishing himself.

"Miss me," I ask jokingly.

He chuckles.

"Couldn't you tell?"

Until I Found You

I grab my panties and pants sliding them up my legs. Ignoring the wet, messy feeling between them.

"Fuck, I've never cumed that hard over the phone before. Maybe it's your lack of experience that turns me on, or the fact that I love you but damn if that wasn't intense," he says wiggling his brows and wiping sweat away from his forehead.

I should feel flattered but my insecurities pick up on several key points in his statement. Like the fact he's had video sex with other women before or the fact that I'm inexperienced.

My face must speak my mind.

"What did I say?"

Worry clear on his face.

"So you've had video sex before?"

He gives me an apologetic look, "I told you before, I've had my fair share of women. But, it was all before you baby. Just ancient history."

It's not so ancient to me. In fact, one being fairly recently. Nadia's face comes to my mind along with violent thoughts about her.

"Hey," he says sweetly.

"Look at me, baby. They're just part of my past. You are my future," he says reassuringly.

I smile at him then.

"I love you," I say to him.

Charlie comes jumping on the bed with me suddenly.

"I love you, baby," he says. Just then Charlie barks before growling. Micah chuckles.

"I love you too Charlie."

Charlie begins to bark and growl more. The fur on his neck and back sticking straight up. Charlie backs into me snarling this time.

"Leyna, what's wrong," I hear Micah ask me.

His face and tone are full of alarm.

"I don't know."

My voice is lost in between Charlie's furious barks and growls and Micah shouting for me to lock the door and hide under the bed. Suddenly, I see a large hooded figure staring at me with a masked face from the dark hallway. Ice runs in my veins. I blink but the nightmare that's happening doesn't end. I have seconds to react, but terror takes over me and I'm afraid I won't be able to move. The man takes a step towards me and I let out a blood curdling scream.

Fifty-two

I jump off the bed, quickly running over to twist the lock into place before attempting to slam the door shut. That's when I feel the man push against me with the door. Charlie is snapping at the gap between the door and the frame. I'm using every ounce of strength within me to fight, to keep this intruder from barging in here with me. I hear Micah screaming my name from the phone. The complete terror and desperation in his voice pushing me to fight harder. The man then uses all of his strength to bust in. The force of it throwing me hard onto the floor. I scoot backwards in a desperate attempt to get away.

"Micah," I scream out in terror as the man steps towards me. I hear Micah yell my name as the man grabs me by my shirt ripping it as he lifts me off the floor. I begin kicking and scratching at him in all of my desperation to get away. Just then Charlie jumps and grabs the man by his arm shaking it in his teeth like a rag doll. The intruder yells in a foreign language as I hear Charlie's sharp teeth rip into his flesh. The man drops his hold on me and steps back into the hallway, trying to shake Charlie off his arm with all of his strength.

Charlie has his pit bull grip on the man. I get up and run over grabbing a lamp as I throw it, hitting the man. I grab one of Mr. Edgars bowling trophies off the shelf and clobber the intruder's head with it. I get one good hit in before he knocks me back with brute force throwing me back into the room from the hallway. I hurry off the floor and shut the locked door behind me, sobbing. Charlie is still out there. There's nothing I can do. I'm defenseless. I hear beating and banging before I hear a sharp yelp from Charlie before the man runs down the hall. I crawl over to the bed and grab my phone, only to realize it died on me. Panicked, I crawl over to the closet and get inside as I begin to tremble. I cover my mouth as tears stream down my face.

A fucked up sense of Deja vu washing over me as I'm hiding inside a closet from violence yet again. The irony is not lost on me. Deafening silence ensues. That is until a while later I hear heavy footsteps run into the house only to slow down then speed up as it gets closer to me. I begin shaking beyond control then. He's come back. I scoot myself as far back as I can.

My back hits the wall. There's nowhere else to hide, nowhere else to run. Panic sets in. Choking sounds escape my lips. Just then the closet door flies open and I scream. I begin kicking my legs and feet at the man. Suddenly strong arms grab me up.

"Leyna! It's me baby! It's me," Micah yells pulling me to his chest tight before pulling away to look me over. I begin sobbing into him as my entire body shakes. I hear a clank on the floor next to me.

UNTIL I
found you

Looking down I see it's his handgun. He wraps me in his arms before pulling away, scanning me over. He notices my ripped shirt and busted lip then.

"Did he hurt you? Did he touch you?"

His voice breaks on the last question. Tears of murderous rage falling from his eyes. I can't speak from sobbing so hard.

"Baby answer me," he growls.

I shake my head. He kisses my forehead hard before grabbing his gun and lifting me off the floor. Cradling me in his arms as he walks us out.

"Char-Charlie?" I ask through my sobs.

That's when I see Charlie laying at the end of the hall barely moving when I call his name. I begin to sob harder. Micah shushes me soothingly as he walks us across the street over to my house. He walks us inside, gently sitting me on the couch. My heart is racing out of my chest now. Beating so hard I'm afraid it'll explode. Everything is spinning.

"Baby," Micah asks.

Suddenly I feel like I can't breathe. I begin to gasp.

"Leyna?"

Panic and terror takes over me. I feel like I'm being pulled underwater by a weight. I grab his wrist tightly in one hand, my other hand flying to my chest. I go to breathe but I'm choking on air. My eyes go wide then and I fall onto the floor gasping for air. He catches my head before it hits.

"Baby," he shouts.

Just then sirens blare in the distance.

"Baby, hang on ok?"

Just then I see Jared running up the stairs shirtless. His shoes are on the wrong feet. He runs to my side quickly analyzing me.

"What's happening? Why is she breathing like that," Micah shouts petrified.

"She's hyperventilating. She's having a panic attack," Jared says with forced calmness to his voice. "Leyna, look at me. Keep your eyes on me, baby girl. Focus on my voice. I need you to calm down or you're going to pass out."

"Breathe baby," Micah begs.

"Squeeze Micah's fingers. I need you to respond ok," Jared says looks me over again. "Leyna this is important, answer me does one or both of your arms hurt?"

I'm trying to answer him but no words form.

"Leyna I have to know this come on now! Squeeze if they both hurt."

Micah looks over at him, "Why does that matter?"

"She could be having a heart attack. She has a heart murmur," Jared says.

Micah's eyes go wide before looking back at me. The paramedics walk in and Jared starts speaking medical terminologies to them. Jared takes the hand Micah isn't holding of mine. "You're going to be just fine baby, ok? Just focus on breathing. Keep looking at Micah," he says looking between me and my vitals that the paramedics are taking.

One of the medics proceeds to put an oxygen mask over my face. I look at Micah and wish I could take the pained expression away from his beautiful face.

UNTIL I
found you

"Good job Leyna keep it up. Keep steadying your breathing," Jared coaches.

Micah never takes his eyes from mine as the paramedics work on me. Maggie comes running in then, frantically asking if I'm ok. Jared assures her everything is fine but she's at my side in an instant.

"Ma'am, you're going to have to step back and give us room," the paramedics say.

Jared stands then walking Maggie and himself closer to the hallway. Micah grips my hand tighter in his, refusing to leave my side. Eventually they stabilize my breathing along with my blood pressure and heart rate. They were cleaning my various cuts and scratches on my arms and face when one of the paramedics asked me if I wanted to go to the hospital to be checked out. I declined. Micah threatened to throw me over his shoulder regardless if I was kicking or screaming, I was going to the hospital to make sure everything was fine. Knowing I've already lost this battle, I agreed to go.

Micah held my hand the entire time we were there and as I suspected I have a hard head. No concussion and no broken bones. After having an EKG test done, my heart checked out fine as well. Micah looked so incredibly relieved when he found out I was ok.

"God and luck was on your side, Miss Blake," the doctor said as he exited the room.

That may be, but a dog named Charlie was my hero as well.

I begin to cry into Micah's chest, "It'll all be ok baby. You're safe. I won't let anyone hurt you ever again. I promise you that."

He holds me tighter in his arms before placing his lips on my temple.

"Charlie is dead because of me," I cry.

Micah takes my face gently in his hands and says, "Charlie is fine. The police found him beaten up pretty badly. Jared and Maggie took him to the veterinarian and they've given him a full prognosis."

Tears of relief fall from my cheeks as Micah wipes them away. A little while later the police arrived to take my statement and ask me some questions and I give them all the information I know. It's nearly 4am by the time the police leave and the emergency room doctor discharged me.

Fifty-three

Micah hasn't spoken to me since we left the hospital. I glance over at him and see that he's staring straight ahead, his brows are pulled together and his fists are tightened around the steering wheel. I place my hand on his forearm.

"Hey," I say in a soothing voice.

He turns to look at me. His face is set in a deep frown.

"I could have lost you tonight. Do you understand that?"

I remove one of his hands from the wheel, taking it into my own.

"But you didn't. So let's move on."

He lets out a long deep breath through his nose.

"I'm calling and having a security system installed at your house Monday," he says.

"No you're not. That's not necessary-"

"Don't argue with me," he all but shouts.

I instinctively pull my hand away from his and stare out the window as we pull into his long driveway.

"Look, I'm sorry. I just- I don't know what I would do if something happened to you," he says looking over at me with a pained expression as he parks the Corvette.

"Well I'm fine," I say as I step out of the car.

"No, you're not fine, Leyna. You have a hole in your heart. When exactly were you going to tell me that?"

He's following behind me.

"It's not that big of a deal Micah. People are born with them all the time."

He catches my wrist in his hand turning me around to face him.

"You want to talk about withholding the truth, that it's a lie. Well you lied to me about this, Leyna. Why didn't you tell me you have a heart condition?"

He's becoming angrier. I pull my hand away from him.

"Because, it's not that big of a deal! Many people have murmurs and many people live long, mostly healthy lives with it."

"Not that big of a deal," he shouts bewildered.

"I'm not arguing with you," I say as I turn around and walk up the steps.

"Oh that's rich! Tear me a new asshole every other day over the shit I do but when Leyna is in the wrong, oh no, we're not going to talk about it. No you don't get off that easily sweetheart," he says walking up the steps to me, temper fuming.

"I'm in the wrong for not wanting people to treat me like I'm some fragile little thing? To tell me I

UNTIL I
found you

can't do the same things that everyone else does? So you mean to tell me if I would have told you, you wouldn't have started treating me differently," I raise my brows at him.

He opens his mouth about to say something before shutting it again. His nostrils flare slightly as he takes deep, frustrated breaths through his nose containing his anger. I stare at him, softening my eyes. I place my hand on his face, lightly rubbing his cheek. My touch instantly calmed him.

"I'm going to be ok baby," I say to him in my most comforting voice.

He takes my hand from his face and places it on his chest right over his heart, his hand on top of mine. I can feel his heart beating under my touch.

"My heart belongs to you. It beats for you. Just as your heart belongs to me. Please keep it beating for me," he says staring down at me intensely.

I take his free hand and place it over my heart.

"I promise you Micah, I'm going to be ok," I say to him before he wraps his arm around my back bringing me closer to him as he kisses my forehead and opens the door leading us upstairs.

He opens his drawers and takes out one of his white t-shirts, walking over to me with it. He watches me as I begin pulling my pants and panties down my legs before removing my bra and ripped shirt off. He stares at my naked body in a way he's never done before. Like it's the first or last time he's seeing it. Taking in every detail of me. He lightly brushes his fingers over my jaw and across my lips.

"You are so beautiful," he breathes before kissing my lips tenderly.

He bumps noses with me softly before instructing me to raise my arms up as he pulls his shirt over my head. I slip on the panties he's brought me from my bag before climbing into bed. After stripping to only his boxers he lays in bed next to me wrapping his arms around my waist and laying his head on my chest. Our legs intertwined. I begin to play in his hair as he nuzzles the side of his face into my chest more.

"What are you doing," I ask smiling.

"Listening to the most precious sound in the world."

I smile as I kiss his hair and begin grazing my nails up his bare back, humming our song to him. He looks up at me and smiles. The smile doesn't reach his eyes. I grasp his face between my hands and push his cheeks together causing his lips to pucker out.

"Stop worrying," I say to him as I give him a playful kiss.

I let go of his face and he looks at me with a serious expression.

"I can't. I can't lose you," he says his voice clipping at the end.

"You won't lose me baby. What happened was terrifying but I'm ok. I'm safe. The officer said there have been reported burglaries in the area recently. I was just at the wrong place at the wrong time. It could have happened to anyone."

"It didn't just happen to anyone. It happened to you. I swear to God you're a magnet for catastrophe."

UNTIL I found you

He rubs the bridge of his nose in frustration. I choose to ignore that statement and instead go with something else.

"When we wake up, it'll be a new day. I don't want to talk about it anymore. I don't want to dwell on it. Which means no security system. All it will do is remind me everyday what happened. I just want to move on from it. Please?"

He analyzes my face for a moment before reluctantly nodding his head in agreement before kissing me goodnight. I'm sleeping peacefully for a while until I roll over and feel Micah's side of the bed empty. I groggily open my eyes and call out for him seeing the bedroom door is open. Getting no reply, I climb out of bed and walk downstairs calling out for him. I hear whispering coming from the kitchen as I get closer. It's dark and my eyes aren't fully adjusted as I strain to see. I glance around the room seeing nothing.

I turn around and suddenly strong hands are around my throat lifting me into the air before slamming me down into the floor. The hands are tightening around my neck. That's when I see it's the man. He's come back. I try to scream for Micah but there's no air. I try to fight the intruder off but it's no use. He's staring at me with his cold black eyes. I fling my eyes open and jump. My heart is pounding in my chest. Micah's arms are still wrapped around my waist and his head on my shoulder. He wakes then.

"Baby? Are you ok," he asks groggily.

I look around realizing it was just a bad dream.

"Yeah, I'm fine. Go back to sleep," I say as I wrap my arms around his back anchoring myself to him as I steady my heartbeat.

Micah is already back asleep in moments and it takes me until the sun rises to finally drift back to unconsciousness.

Until I found you

Fifty-four

The following day went by smoothly. Micah wouldn't let me far from his sight however, asking me every five minutes if I was ok. Whenever I'd give him a glare, he insisted that it wasn't about my murmur but the fact that I was taking yesterday's events so well. He was afraid I was in shock because I wasn't a jumpy, paranoid mess.

"Do you not remember me freaking the fuck out and the ambulance coming," I had asked, raising my brow at him.

He gave me an impassive look before saying, "That's not something I can easily forget. You're just taking this so well. Too well."

"You don't have to put on a brave face in front of me you know," he says taking my hand in his. "For the 50th time since we woke up, I'M FINE. But if you ask me that again, you will be the one that's not fine. Got it?"

He chuckles and shakes his head.

"Have you talked to Jo? Is Maggie ok? She says she's fine when I talk to her but I know she's freaked out over what happened."

"That's because she's normal," he jabs before continuing, "Yeah I talked to him. She's ok. Just anxious."

Jared was too. He was almost as bad as Micah, checking on me. Texting me 20 times throughout the night and day to see if I was alright. I sit there thinking what I could do to remove all of the anxiety from everyone when it hits me.

"I have a fun idea if you're up to it?"

He looks over at me smiling. "What's that?"

"What if we invited them over to swim, maybe cookout and have a bonfire? I think that's what we all need. Some fun."

He looks at me with a wicked grin.

"Not the type of fun I thought you were referring to. I'll certainly take it if it means I get to see you in that bikini again, baby," he says walking over to me then wiggling his brows.

"You are such a sex addict!" I tease smacking his bare chest.

"Only with you my love. I can't get enough of you. Look how sexy and beautiful my girl is," he says wrapping his hands around my ass and squeezes playfully.

I giggle.

"Later Cassanova," I say slapping him on the butt.

He chuckles.

"Call Jo," I say, already dialing Jared as I head into the kitchen.

"Yes dear," he says sarcastically.

An hour later Jared, Maggie and Jo arrive with beer and wine coolers in tow. The boys are in the backyard drinking beers and firing up the grill

UNTIL I found you

while Maggie and I are in the kitchen preparing the food. Maggie calls herself cooking. She's not the most experienced cook around but I appreciate her attempt at helping.

"Hey Mags, Jo is looking for you."

Jared walks over to me as Maggie goes out the back door.

"He's not looking for her. I smelled something burning and knew I needed to rescue you. We actually want to eat this right?"

I give him a look and fight a smile.

"You're so mean," I say to him.

Soon after the food is ready. Everyone is outside eating while I'm wiping down the counters and loading the dishwasher when Micah comes in. He takes my hand,

"Baby enough cleaning. We'll do that later. Come outside and eat. This isn't considered having fun and fun was your idea today."

"I will. I promise I just need to start the dishwasher."

He grumbles before bending down and slinging me over his shoulder like a caveman. I shriek in surprise and he laughs.

"Put me down," I demand through my giggles.

He carries me down the back patio stairs this way as everyone begins to laugh. "

That's it Micah, show her who's boss," Jared cheers clapping.

"About time you got your ass down here," Maggie adds.

Both already tipsy from the beers and wine coolers.

"Swim anyone," Micah asks as he suddenly starts running with me to the docks.

"Don't you dare," I yell through my laughs, kicking at him as he runs off the end of the dock and jumps into the water with us.

When we bob up, Micah still has his arms around me holding me above water.

"You are so dead," I yell at him splashing.

He laughs and lets me go as he begins splashing back. Suddenly Jo jumps into the water creating a cannonball effect.

"Come on Maggie, get in," he yells for her.

She's laying out on a beach towel tanning.

"Maybe later," she calls out in a bored tone.

"Get your ass in here," I yell at her.

Jared winks at us and pours a little of his wine cooler on her. Maggie shrieks and comes up swinging at him. We laugh as we watch Jared pick her up and attempt to throw her into the water with us. Except, she's hanging onto him like a spider monkey so they both fall in. We spent the remaining hours of sunlight swimming and watching the boys do tricks and stunts from the rope swing and off the dock. I loved seeing Micah so playful and carefree and how hot he looked doing flips.

I smiled; feeling incredibly lucky that he is mine as I watched him. Later Jared was the referee in a game of chicken between Micah, Jo, Maggie and Myself. Micah and I won. We ended the day all laid around by the bonfire listening to music. I'm sitting in Micah's lap as Mr. Blue Sky starts playing on his speaker. Jared starts singing along to it drunkenly bobbing his head dramatically to the tune as he sings. We all snicker at him but he's too drunk to notice.

UNTIL I found you

Maggie's ass is just as intoxicated as she joins in on the improv karaoke hour. She makes Jo sing along with her.

All three started bobbing their heads and shaking their shoulders to the music. Micah pulled me closer to him as he laughed into my back at the trio. I laughed before finally joining in. Micah peered up at me with a huge grin before shrugging his shoulders.

"Oh why not?"

All five of us sounded like an off key glee club. After getting a drunken Jared and Maggie into Jo's car we wave them off and head inside to take a shower.

Micah is washing my hair when he says, "I forgot to mention it to you earlier but I'll be leaving Monday to go to Chicago. Keith and I are expanding the company and I'm considering setting up a branch there. I'll be back Thursday morning."

"That's exciting! I'm happy for you babe. I'll miss you though," I admit shyly.

He kisses my forehead.

"I'll miss you too baby. We can FaceTime while I'm gone."

I chuckle.

"I'll be fine. You go handle your business. I'll be here when you get back."

He smiles before kissing my lips. Once we're dressed, Micah puts the new Batman movie on as we cuddle on the couch together. I'm between his legs, my head laying on his chest, his arm is wrapped around my back while his other hand plays in my hair. The feeling is incredibly relaxing. My eyes become heavier the more he does it and soon I drift to sleep. A little while later I wake in a haze as he lifts me off the couch and cradles me to his chest as he climbs up the stairs with us. He gently lays me on the bed next to him, pulling me closer to him. I fall back asleep listening to the thrumming of his heart.

Until I found you

Fifty-five

When I wake the following morning, I open my eyes and find that he's propped on his elbow watching me with a warm smile across his face. I cover my face with the sheet playfully, peering my eyes back out before hiding under the covers again. He chuckles at my game of peek-a-boo as he pulls the sheet over his face joining me under the covers. We're smiling at each other youthfully.

"Good morning baby. Are we playing hide and seek today," he says in his sexy morning voice that I love.

I giggle as I remove the covers from us.

"I look terrible when I first wake up," I say covering my face with my hands.

"That is a blatant lie. You're beautiful all times of the day," he says removing my hands from my face. "Even when you snore," he adds laughing.

"I do not snore," I replied defensively.

"You most certainly did! It was adorable. You've never done that before. You must only do that when you're exhausted," he says grinning.

"How embarrassing," I say, covering my face with the sheet again.

He chuckles, removing the sheet as he brings my face closer to his.

"I wouldn't trade your loud snores for anything," he says, giving me playful quick pecks to my lips.

Once I get dressed for the day, I go into the kitchen and cook us a Sunday brunch. Micah looks at his plate of steak, eggs and breakfast potatoes.

"This looks delicious, baby. I'm going to have to wifey you up," he says teasingly as he digs in. I smile and ignore the sudden flutter of my heart. I know he was only kidding but I'm not sure marriage is something I want. Besides Maggie's parents, I don't know one couple that hasn't been divorced or that is happily married. Marriage changes everything. It makes both people overly comfortable with the other. You get so used to the idea that that person belongs to you that you stop fighting to make them yours all together.

"Baby?"

Micah breaks me from my thoughts. I smile at him.

"Sorry, I was lost in thought. Maggie's birthday is coming up Thursday and I was thinking what Jared and I were going to do for her."

"So is Jo. I'm sure they'll plan something together," he says frowning.

I arch my brow at his expression.

Micah sees and explains, "Jo and Nadia are cousins but they were raised like siblings. So they're close. Meaning every year she's always there and with

Maggie sharing the same birthday with him, I'm not sure how that group event is supposed to work."

I click my tongue to the roof of my mouth, "Ah."

"Yeah," he says knowingly.

We sit there in silence for a moment before I say, "Well sounds like she's going to feel like the odd ball out that night because we're going. There's no way that we can't show up to our best friend's birthdays because of one person. So we're going."

He looks at me doubtful.

"Are you sure? I mean last time you crossed paths it didn't end well," he says becoming bitter. I take his hand in mine.

"Yes, I'm sure. She can't get under my skin anymore."

He doesn't look convinced.

"If all else fails I'll just throat punch her. That'll shut the bitch up."

He laughs nearly choking on his food. Once we're done eating, I'm cleaning the kitchen while Micah is in his office preparing for his business trip tomorrow when my phone starts to ring. Looking at it I see it's a local number.

"Hello?"

"Hey Leyna, it's Connor."

My lips part in surprise.

"Um, hi. Wait how did you get my number?"

"Maggie gave it to me that night I picked you up. I just heard what happened and I was worried about you. I wanted to call and check on you. See if there was anything I could do?" Silence ensues. I wasn't expecting this at all.

"Leyna," Connor asks.

"Um, yeah. Sorry, yeah I'm fine," I stammer. "I'm a little surprised you called me. Confused even. You've never called me before," I admit.

"Leyna, I told you we were friends now. Friends call and check on each other," he says smoothly.

"Yes," I say slowly. "But, I also have a boyfriend that punched you in the face the last time he saw you and if he knew that you were calling me right now he'd likely do it again."

I hear him let out a sarcastic huff.

"I'm not scared of Eason. Unlike you, I don't allow him to control what I do."

My temper flares.

"He doesn't control me," I practically seethe.

I can almost hear the cocky smirk in his tone when Connor says, "I don't know. It sounds to me like he does if he dictates who you can and can't be friends with."

"Fuck off, Connor."

He laughs.

"Easy Sour patch, I'm only kidding. I mean not really but don't get mad about it. I honestly was worried about you," his voice takes on a genuine tone at the end.

"Well, I'm fine. I appreciate you checking on me but I have to go," I say.

"Let me guess he's around you so you can't talk to me?"

I'm becoming pissed.

"That has nothing to do with it! I'm just busy."

"Too busy to talk to a friend," he asks with humor.

"Sure am. Thanks for calling, goodbye Connor," I say in a sarcastic friendly tone before hanging up on him.

I huff a frustrated breath through my lips as I read Connor's text: "See you for Maggie's birthday, sour patch. Hopefully you'll be sweet instead of sour this time. You're going to get permanent frown lines if you keep this up."

I roll my eyes. He thinks he's so cute.

"Uh oh who pissed you off?" Micah asks, startling me.

I hadn't even realized he walked downstairs. I consider not telling him that Connor called me to keep us from arguing about it but I'm a terrible liar and odds are he'd find out anyway. "Connor," I say flatly.

His amused expression quickly morphs into a look of annoyance.

"What about Connor?"

"He called me and-"

"Why does he have your number? And why was he fucking calling you," Micah interrupts me, his brows are already pulled together in frustration.

My temper flares at his demanding questions but I rein it in. I don't want to fight with him, especially over Connor.

"Well if you wouldn't interrupt me you'd find these things out wouldn't you? He got my number from Maggie that night he picked me up and he called to check on me because he heard what happened."

Micah is pissed now.

"Called to check on you? Since when did you and Connor become such best friends?"

I'm becoming angry, making it harder to contain my temper.

"We're not best friends. But even if we were, what's the big deal? Do you not trust me," I ask with defiance.

His chest is rising and falling with a more calculated pace now. He's pissed but I can tell by the way he's looking at me he's trying to control his anger.

"Of course I trust you. It's him I don't trust! He has no business calling you!" he spits angrily.

I gently place my palm to the side of his face, calming him.

"There's no reason for you to be jealous," I say in a soothing voice.

He sneers.

"Jealous of him? He has nothing that I want. He does want something that's mine and that's you! So no, I'm not jealous of fucking Connor. I'm territorial of what's mine," he says standing over me, looking at me in a way that builds pressure in between my legs.

I bite my lip as he licks his own.

"You don't own me you know. I'm not your property," I say to him with no conviction in my voice as he steps closer to me.

"You're not some property to me but you do belong to me just as I belong to you. No other man will ever have you. Only me. You're mine and I'm yours," he says in a low voice.

"Is that so," I ask seductively.

He nods as he stares at my curves, his chest rising and falling at a quicker pace as he looks my body over before meeting my eyes.

Until I found you

"Show me," I say.

He wastes no time, lifting me up by my ass as my legs wrap around his waist. Our lips collide and his delicious tongue invades my mouth. My hands go into his hair, tugging as he moans into me. He strides over to the kitchen table, laying my back on it as he pulls both my shorts and panties off in a quick motion before spreading my legs apart. I'm aching for him now. I arch my back and head as his hot tongue presses flat against me and begins working fast circles on my clit. He reaches his fingers to my lips then. I open my mouth and begin to swirl my tongue around them, sucking on them. His eyes are a vibrant blue as he watches me.

He pulls them away then and inserts them into me, pumping at a torturously slow pace as he sucks on my clit. The combination of his tongue and fingers eliciting euphoric cries from me. He stops abruptly then, "Not yet baby."

He pulls my shirt up and over my head. His hands and mouth finds my breasts as he begins to squeeze and suck on them. Whimpers escape my lips as he sucks and bites his way up my neck before grabbing me by my waist and flips me over onto my stomach. My heart is pounding in my chest, my hunger for him raging like wildfire. He pulls his grey sweat pants down his ankles then and wraps my long hair around his hand.

Using it to force my head back he wraps his other hand around my throat and hisses into my ear, "I'm about to show you who your heart and your pussy belongs to," and slams into me.

I scream out in pleasure as his large cock pounds into me relentlessly. He lets go of my throat and grabs onto my hip anchoring me to the table. My hair still wrapped around his hand he tugs on it with slightly more pressure causing me to look over my shoulder at him.

"Fuck, baby, you're so tight and wet for me," he hisses through clenched teeth.

I bite my lip as he thrusts into me from behind. He moves his hand from my hip to my breast palming it as he thrusts faster and deeper into me. His large cock is painful but it's an amazingly good kind of pain. I squint my eyes shut as I moan and cry out from the pleasure, coming closer to the edge. He lays his chest onto my back as he rams into me.

"No other man will ever have you, Leyna. Not your heart, not your body. You're mine, only mine. You belong to me," he growls into my neck as he kisses and sucks on it.

This, in combination with his words and the way he's claiming me, sends me over the edge.

"I only want you," I practically cry as I come undone.

My orgasm rips through me as I cum and squeeze around him.

"Oh fuck, baby," he seethes as he buries his face into my neck and spills into me.

We're both a panting mess as we ride out our euphoric highs together, still holding me he begins lazily kissing up my shoulder.

"You are everything to me Leyna," he breathes.

"You are my everything," I say to him.

Fifty-six

"Ok, last one, you've got to go," I say between kissing him.

We've been parked in my driveway for a while now.

He chuckles, "One more."

"You said that five kisses ago," I say giggling.

"Is it my fault that your lips are like velvet? I can't get enough. I'm going to miss these soft, big lips and the beautiful girl attached to them," he says kissing me.

Suddenly I become a little sad thinking of him leaving, even if it is for four days.

"Be safe traveling ok? Text me when you can. I know you'll be busy."

He's holding my face in his hands.

"I'll text you as soon as I touch down and I'll FaceTime you every night baby."

I smile at him.

"Ok. Now go. You have an early flight and you haven't even packed yet," I remind him.

He chuckles, "I love you," he says kissing my lips softly for the final time.

"I love you," I say to him before grabbing my bags and waving him goodbye.

The next four days are going to be lonely without him. We both have become so completely attached to one another. Part of me worries that we're already so inseparable but I push that thought to the back of my mind as I walk through the front door. I'm greeted by Jared and a guy shorter than him with brown curly hair and hazel eyes standing next to him.

"Just in time, dinner is almost ready. Leyna this is Jamie, Jamie this is Leyna."

He waves between us.

"Hi Jamie, it's nice to finally meet you," I say smiling.

"Likewise. I've heard great things about you," he says smiling back at me.

"Something smells delicious," I hear Maggie say from our room.

"It's because I cooked it," Jared calls back to her.

I walk into mine and Maggie's room to greet her then.

"Well hello there. Still hung over," I ask her as I flop onto my bed with my bags.

"Ugh the worst. I'm never drinking again," she says rubbing her temples, "Well except for this weekend for mine and Jo's birthday."

I shake my head amusingly at her.

"Speaking of which, I actually wanted to talk to you about my birthday," she says in a serious tone.

"Uh oh. What's wrong?"

Until I Found You

"Nothing's wrong per say. I'm just in a predicament. Besides you and Jared, I want Connor there too now that he's back and Jo will have Micah there obviously but he also wants Nadia there too since she's like his sister. But with Connor not getting along with Micah and you not getting along with Nadia, plus her being Micah's ex-fling, I'm not sure what to do. Jo and I really wanted to share our birthdays together this year and have all of our loved ones there celebrating with us but I'm worried that can't happen. I feel so caught in the middle. I don't want you feeling uncomfortable with Nadia there and I don't want Micah starting his shit with Connor but Micah is Jo's best friend so it would be weird for him not to come and you're my best friend so I want you there but I don't know if you feel comfortable even coming now. Ugh, it's all just too much," she says holding her face in her hands.

I sit beside her on her bed and move her hands away from her face.

"Maggie I love you, but you seriously need to stop over stressing! It's your birthday for God sake. You shouldn't be so stressed over your own birthday. We are all grown adults. Surely we can all be in the same room without chaos erupting."

Even as I'm saying it, I find that seriously doubtful. Maggie looks at me with skepticism.

"Are you sure?"

"Yes, totally. I want you and Jo to enjoy yourselves ok? Don't worry. Let's just have fun."

She smiles at me then.

"Ok I'll let him know. Oh also, We've rented a private party suite at Club Odyssey for Saturday night. It's got a stripper pole and it's own mini bar and everything so you know it's going to be a blast," she says excitedly.

I laugh at her dramatics.

"Sounds fun."

"Alright guys and gals it's time to eat," we hear Jared saying from the kitchen.

After we've all eaten, we sit in the living room laughing hysterically as we play Cards Against Humanity. Maggie and I come to find that Jamie is definitely one of us, he fits right in with our dysfunctional little family.

"Shoot babe, my phone is about to die," Jamie says to Jared, "Do either of you have an android charger possibly," Jamie asks between Maggie and I.

"Sorry we're Apple people around here," Maggie teases.

Jean's box of stuff comes to mind.

"Actually I think I have one in my car. Let me go look."

I'm opening the trunk of my car when Mr. Edgar walks over.

"Leyna, I'm sorry I'm just now getting to come by and check on you. How are you dear?"

I hug him.

"I'm fine. How's Charlie?"

"He's doing great. He gets to come home tomorrow. Listen, I can't begin to tell you how sorry I am for what happened," he says looking sad.

I can't stand to see a elderly person looking sad;that and the ASPCA commercials with the starving animals and their big sad eyes. Ugh instant depression.

Until I found you

"No, no! Don't apologize! It could have happened to anyone. Really it's no big deal. I'm so glad Charlie is ok and that you were safe. How did the tournament go? Did you kick the other team's butts?" I ask cheerfully, hoping the change of topic lightens the grim expression on his face. It works.

"Shoot child, We won by a landslide," he smiles proudly.

"That's great! I knew you would. I hate to cut our conversation short but I was actually running out here real quick to grab something for a friend. You and Charlie come by for a visit soon." He smiles; "We'll do that. You have a nice night dear."

I wave at him before grabbing Jean's crap out of the back of my car and walk inside with it. I hand Jamie the charger and decide to store the two boxes and the bag of Jean's clothes into our garage for the time being. I had walked a few steps away before curiosity got the better of me and ended up taking the box containing the paperwork and pictures to my bedroom. I sat down on my bed and began going through it's contents. First with the stacks of unorganized paperwork, most of it being either rental agreements from various apartments over the years or old contracts for loans. I grab an old binder from my book bag inside the closet and decide to organize this clutter of paper the best that I can. Once it's all tucked into the binder neatly I start looking through the collection of photographs. A bittersweet smile spreads across my face at seeing pictures of me and Lyle. Words fall flat when it comes to describing how much I miss my brother. I feel his absence every single day. Five years later and my heart still hurts as if I just lost him yesterday.

Rose Kennedy's quote comes to mind when I think of Lyle, "It has been said that time heals all wounds. I do not agree. The wounds remain. In time, the mind, protecting its sanity, covers them with scar tissue and the pain lessens but it's never gone."

Thinking of my brother, I often wonder what our lives would have been like if he had taken a different route home that day. I wonder if he and Claire would have been married by now? How many nieces and nephews they would have given me? Who they would have favored more, Lyle or their mother?

Would Micah and my brother have gotten along? What would they have bonded over? I imagine my brother giving me away at my wedding. I imagine our kids running around laughing and playing together, being the inseparable best friends to one another like we were. Except none of that will ever happen. I'll never get to see Lyle be the amazing man he was growing to be. I'll never create new memories with him and his family. I'll never get to see all of the amazing things he would have accomplished in his life. All of those possibilities are gone with him.

He was the only family I ever truly had. Losing him, I lost a part of myself the day he died. Unwanted tears brim my eyes and stream down my face as I wipe them away. Maggie walks in then.

"Leyna? What's wrong," she asks, walking to my side.

I hand her the picture of Lyle and I on the beach. Claire had taken it and it was one of the last pictures we took before he died. She looks at it with

Until I found you

a sad expression before handing it back to me. I wipe my tears away as she gives me a hug.

"It can't rain all the time you know. Eventually the sun has to shine through."

She offers me a comforting smile. I smile half heartedly at her and grab my photo album from the shelf above my bed. I begin to put all of the pictures from the box in the sleeves of the album. I'm nearly at the bottom of the box when I notice a busted picture frame. Taking it out I examine it carefully.

"What is it," Maggie asks.

It's a picture of my mother laying in the hospital bed cradling me in her arms. Two year old Lyle is sitting beside me smiling. Careful of the glass, I remove the picture from the frame to show it to Maggie when I notice a second picture behind it. Like in the first, it's a picture of my mother laying in the hospital bed except now a teenage boy with red hair is sitting next to her, holding me in his arms. I stare at the boy and realize I'm looking at a picture of my father.

Fifty-seven

I stare at the picture as every emotion sweeps over me at once. This is my father. It has to be. It's the same red hair, the same colored eyes, the same nose. The resemblance was too much of a coincidence for it not to be. Jean told me she didn't know who my father was, that he was just some teenage waste of space. From this picture that was a lie. There was never a name under the father on my birth certificate but this picture proves I had one. One that cared enough about his newborn daughter to visit her at the hospital but what happened after this picture?

Was it all too much for him? Did the reality of being a young father hit him? Did he not want me? Or did Jean keep him away? Suddenly I have more questions about my father than I ever did before.

"Leyna," Maggie's tone is full of alarm.

Without saying a word, I pass her the photo.

"I think I just found a picture of my father," I say barely above a whisper.

"Leyna, how do you know that's your father? It could be anyone," she says.

UNTIL I found you

"Because, I look just like the man in the picture, Maggie. That's not a coincidence."

"I mean the resemblance is definitely there but how do you know that's not Lyle's father," she asks.

" I've seen Lyle's father before and this isn't him." I say taking the picture from her and holding it up, "This has to be my father," I say looking at the man holding me; "There's only one way to find out, I have to talk to Jean."

"Leyna, I don't know if that's such a good idea. Honestly I don't think she would even tell you the truth."

"I know. But there's no other way."

She looks at me with pity, "Maybe there is. Try consulting with a private investigator. See if they could find out something from this picture," she says hopefully. I nod. "

It's worth a try I suppose."

"It's better than going to Jean. She wouldn't tell you out of spite anyway," she says.

I huff in frustration knowing she's right.

"Put this away for now and shove all of it to the back of your mind. Because you're about to come in here and help me embarrass Jared by telling stories to Jamie about him," she says, taking my hand and leading us to the living room.

After forcing myself to be sociable for a while longer I end up going to bed or rather lay curled into a ball trying desperately to shut my mind off. After tossing and turning half the night my mind and body finally lose the battle and I succumb to a deep sleep.

My first day back at work went unexpectedly. Instead of the manager's position I was promised, I was hired back as a waitress. Chelsea somehow weaseled her way out of the kitchen and back to her manager position. To say I was utterly annoyed by that fact would be an understatement and it doesn't help that I started my period this morning. Although I had to admit I was relieved that Micah was away on a business trip for it. I'm shutting the water off in the shower when Micah facetimes me. I wrap a towel around me before answering.

"Hi baby."

He greets me with a wide smile. I grin at him.

"Hey babe. How was your day?"

"It was ok. A bit aggravating. My flight was delayed by four hours. That's why I always leave a day early. How was your day, pretty girl?"

I contemplate telling him about the picture I found of my father but decide that's something I'd rather talk to him about in person.

"At least you plan ahead in case stuff like this happens right? My day was ok, aggravating as well," I say.

"What happened?"

"I started back work today. I was supposed to start as the manager but Chelsea somehow gained her position back."

He furrows his brows.

"I thought we talked about you not going back. I don't like the idea of you being there, Leyna," he says flatly.

The last thing I want to do is argue with him. I know he means well and this is just him being

Until I found you

protective over me but his stubbornness over the issue pisses me off.

I take a deep breath and say, "I know that but I have to have a job, Micah."

"Well then it's settled, come to work with me. The pay is higher, you'll have benefits and you can actually work in a safe environment. Please just consider it," he says.

I grumble.

"Fine, I'll think about it. It still stands, no special treatment and no favoritism."

He smirks as he replies, "You have my word Ms. Blake."

I put the phone down long enough to put a tampon in and pull my baggy shirt over my head. "Where'd you go? All I see is the ceiling," he says.

"I was putting my clothes on."

"That's the part I wanted to see," he teases.

I pick the phone back up.

"You're such a horn dog."

"Have you seen how unbelievably sexy my girlfriend is," he asks, smiling at me.

I roll my eyes at him playfully. Suddenly I begin to cramp. I open the medicine cabinet and take two Tylenol. He notices.

"Why are you taking Tylenol? Did you get hurt today?"

I feel my cheeks blush red. Before I can come up with a lie he asks, "What did you start your period or something?"

My eyes widen slightly in response. He notices.

"That's it isn't it?"

He hides a smile as he asks. I'm officially mortified.

"Baby it's ok. It's not that big of a bloody deal," he says.

"Oh my God, don't. Just don't," I say covering my face.

He chuckles.

"You're so cute when you're embarrassed."

"Well I must be very fucking adorable right now."

"Yes you are," he smiles at me, "But there's no reason to be embarrassed baby."

I grab my panties and shorts before putting them on.

"So did Jo tell you the plans for Saturday," I ask, changing the subject.

"Yeah, Club Odyssey. I promised him I'd be cool as long as Connor stayed the fuck away from you and he kept Nadia the hell away from us."

I sigh as I lay on my bed.

"Everyone needs to keep their heads cool for Maggie and Jo's sake and by everyone I mean you," I clarify.

He places his hand on his chest dramatically.

"I'm offended. Are you insinuating I'm a hot head madam?"

I laugh. "Oh I'm not insinuating it, I'm saying it."

He laughs along.

"You're not wrong there. But so do you, I think you're underestimating your feisty temper baby," he says with amusement.

I fight a smile, "We're not talking about me."

"Oh no," he smiles crookedly.

"Nope!"

"Well that's not fair," he responds.

"Yeah well neither is life," I retort.

He laughs.

"Miss me yet?"

"Yes. I could barely sleep without you laying next to me," I admit shyly.

"Me too baby."

Just then I hear a knock coming from his door. He answers it. I see that it's room service. "Babe I'm going to let you go so you can eat, ok? Goodnight, I love you."

"Alright baby. Sweet dreams, I love you. I'll text you tomorrow."

I blow him a kiss before hanging up. I end up tossing and turning for half the night before finally drifting to sleep.

Fifty-eight

The following days go by at a slow pace. Tuesday was pretty much the same as Monday. Chelsea was a bitch as usual and two of the waitresses didn't even bother to show up to work, leaving me to work both their sections and to close that night. Wednesday was a little better than the day before. I got off work early that day to make my appointment to start birth control. I decided on the depo shot knowing I'd forget to take a pill everyday anyway. Plus it was a bonus to learn I would have shorter, lighter periods every month. The standard procedure pregnancy test they required beforehand was a bit nerve racking though. Micah and I have been so careless recently.

  I was extremely relieved when the doctor said it was negative and that the shot would begin to work immediately. Micah was just as relieved as I was. Thursday finally gets here and I find myself excited. Today Micah flies home from Chicago. I'm clocking out of my work shift when he begins FaceTiming me.

UNTIL I
found you

"Hey, baby. Have you landed yet," I ask smiling from ear to ear.

His face falls at my expression and I see he's still at the hotel.

"That's what I'm calling you about, baby. I won't be coming home until tomorrow. It's taking a little longer than I thought to negotiate some terms on this damned contract," he says, frustrated with the situation.

Putting on my best fake smile I say, "It's fine babe."

"I'll be home tomorrow night. I'll make it up to you, we can go on a date," he says.

"Actually I have plans with Maggie and Jared. It's her birthday today but she couldn't get off so we're going tomorrow night to have dinner and see a movie. I'll see if it's an open invite though? I'm sure they wouldn't mind," I offer.

"It's fine baby. Tell her happy birthday for me."

I smile, "I will. I miss you."

"I miss you more baby. I'll call you tonight."

He smiles. My heart flutters.

"Bye, handsome."

"Bye, beautiful."

He winks at me before hanging up. Once I get home Jared is busy in the kitchen baking Maggie's favorite cake, three layer red velvet with buttercream frosting.

"Oh my God it smells amazing Jer," I say as I inhale the delicious sweet aroma. "She's going to love it!" I add.

"Bitch better," he teases.

"What time are you going to Micah's?"

"He's not coming home until tomorrow." I frown.

"Aww, you miss him. I love seeing new couples in the honeymoon stage. It's adorable," he says smoothing the icing on the cake. "Will he make it home in time to go with us tomorrow night," he asks.

"Do you think Maggie would mind? It's usually just us three."

"She invited Jo. I invited Jamie. We already assumed you would invite your boo thing to come. It'll be a cute triple date."

"I'll mention it to him. What time are we going to the movie?"

"She ordered tickets to the 7:15 showing," Jared says as he puts the candles on the cake. Just then Maggie walks in from work.

"Surprise," Jared and I yell at her as we show her the cake.

She laughs.

"Oh my gosh, I totally wasn't expecting to come home to a delicious red velvet cake," she says sarcastically.

"With buttercream frosting for my boochie," Jared adds.

"Happy birthday, beautiful," I say as I give her a long rectangular box with mine and Jared's name on it.

We went in together and bought her a sterling silver bracelet with blue sapphires on it. Sapphire's are Maggie's favorite. She opens the box and immediately tears up.

"You guys! It's beautiful! Thank you," she says putting it on and pulling us in for a group hug.

UNTIL I
found you

We're all sitting on the couch binge watching The Vampire Diaries when Jared says through chewing his popcorn, "Ugh, Damon is so yummy."

"Yeah but Stefan is a whole ass meal. Like look at that jawline though," Maggie says with a mouth full of chips.

I laugh at them ogling over fictional characters. One of the characters named Matt has striking blue eyes that remind me of Micah's. Ugh, I miss him. The doorbell rings then, answering it I see it's Jo with a bouquet of flowers.

Smiling I yell, "Maggie, it's for you."

She comes around the corner then and starts skipping towards Jo when she sees him. A huge smile on her face, she hops up and wraps her legs around his waist.

"Surprise," he says kissing her.

"You told me you had to work late."

"I know I wanted to surprise you. Happy birthday baby girl," he says walking in still holding Maggie as she wishes him a happy birthday too.

I smile and shake my head at them as I shut the door. Jo is so good to her. I'm so happy Maggie finally has a good man in her life. After she goes into our room to retrieve Jo's gifts, she hands me her bouquet of flowers to put them in a vase. I'm filling the vase with water when I hear Maggie scream in excitement. I jump at the sound and hurriedly walk in the living room to see what the commotion is about.

"Are you serious," she asks, jumping in his arms again hugging him tightly.

"I know how much you idolize him," he laughs.

"What's going on?" I ask, giggling at Maggie's reaction.

"He got me front row tickets to see Adam Levine in concert! And a backstage pass for a meet and greet!"

UNTIL I found you

Fifty-nine

A little while later Jamie came over. He and Jared went out to dinner after Maggie ended up leaving and going to Jo's to spend the night. Using the time alone I go to my room and grab my laptop searching for private investigators. This was nagging at me. I had to find out the truth about my father. I had to know why he's been absent from my life this whole time. Did he not want me? Or did Jean keep him away? This was going to eat at me until I found out the truth one way or another. I'm on my laptop for a while when my phone begins to ring. I see it's Connor FaceTiming me. I declined it at first but he just keeps calling. Finally I answer it. "What," I ask flatly.

"Hey sour patch," he smirks.

"Quit calling me that! And what do you want," I huff.

"And you wonder why I call you that? I need advice on what to get Maggie for her gift. What does she like?"

"She likes jewelry. She's obsessed with Heath Ledger and Adam Levine. Her favorite color is ballerina pink and her favorite perfume is Joy by Dior."

He looks confused.

"Ok but what do I get her?"

I laugh.

"Just get her a gift card to Sephora. You can't go wrong with that."

"Sounds like a plan. How was your day," he asks.

"It was ok. How was yours?"

"Eh, it was ok. Won my case in court today. An innocent man was set free," he smiled proudly.

"Wow Connor, that's amazing! I'm so happy for you."

"Thanks," he smiles shyly. "How are you?"

"I'm fine. Why?"

"Oh I don't know, it's not like you didn't experience an attempted burglary or anything."

I grimace.

"I'd rather not dwell on that."

"Fair enough. So let's talk about something else then," he says laying across his couch.

"Like what?"

"I don't know. Anything. Like what is the true meaning of life? Does bigfoot really exist? Why is Trix cereal just for kids? What exactly is a hotdog made of? That shit can't be real meat."

I laugh and a small snort escapes.

"Did you seriously just snort?"

I cover my face as he begins to laugh so hard he's wheezing. Which in turn makes me laugh even harder. Five minutes later and we're still laughing at each other. I wipe tears from my eyes.

"Oh my God, I can't. You sound like an asthmatic when you laugh," I say, still giggling.

"Those with glass houses shouldn't throw stones," he says adding a mock snort at the end.

Until I found you

I playfully flip him off and he smiles.

"What are you doing Sunday," he asks.

"I'll probably be at Micah's. Why?"

"I thought we could hangout sometime. As friends," he clarifies.

"I'm not sure how that would work out," I say to him.

"Why? Because I'm irresistibly charming? Good looking? A great catch?"

He teases.

"No," I say, dragging out the word. "It's because I don't think Micah would like that too much." He rolls his eyes.

"So he doesn't control you?"

My mood shifts from playful to pissed.

"No," I say.

"Well which is it? Either he doesn't control you and you can be friends with whoever you want or you can only be friends with people he approves of," he asks, raising his brow at me.

"First of all, I'm not on the stand, so quit questioning me. Second, he doesn't control me! You two hate each other so why would he want me hanging out with someone that hates him?"

By the look on Connor's face he knows he's pushed too far. "I wasn't trying to upset you. And I don't hate Eason. I just don't like the guy. I don't trust him and truthfully I don't think he's good enough for you. I'm saying that only to be honest with you. You don't know him like I do. Just be careful," he warns.

"How about not being so honest then? He's not the same person he was when you knew him.

The person he is now, that is who I know. Who he was before is irrelevant to me. People change."

"Yeah, and what if he hasn't?"

We stare each other down for a moment before I say with forced calmness, "Either way it's really none of your business."

His jaw clenches slightly.

"You're right, it's only my business when I pick you up on the side of the street after you've been crying over the guy. My apologies. Just don't come crying to me when he shows you his true colors."

My temper flares.

"Trust me I won't," I say with venom before hanging up on him.

I growl in frustration, becoming angrier by the second. The fucking nerve of him. Connor has always been outspoken but this goes beyond that. I get a text from him then.

"I'm sorry I shouldn't have taken it that far. I'm just trying to look out for you. That's what friends do right?"

I stare at the text and wonder if I can really be friends with him. I know it's going to cause problems with Micah and I'm not willing to risk what I have with him over a friendship with Connor. I delete Connor's number from my phone, resolved in my decision.

Instead of laying here fuming over it all, I decide to be productive and hang up my new wardrobe in the closet. I'm hanging the last item on the rack deciding what I should wear Saturday night when I see the emerald green spaghetti strap dress Maggie got me for my birthday last year. I take it off

UNTIL I
found you

the rack and try it on for the first time. I zip the back as far up as my arm will reach and walk in front of the mirror to see. My eyes widen at my own reflection. The dress is short, really short. Something I wouldn't normally even attempt but the dress is stunningly sexy. It clings to my hips and thighs in a sinful way. The material hugs my curves in the best possible way, showing off my hourglass figure. The cleavage of my breasts showing from the v neck of the dress. I turn around and see that the style of this dress and the way it hugs me, makes my butt look even bubblier. I laugh and bite my lip thinking about seeing Micah's reaction when he sees me in this.

He's made me feel so confident in myself, so beautiful. His love for me and how he treats me, is what's done that. I smile and silently thank whoever is listening for bringing him into my life. Thinking of him I begin to miss him terribly, more so than I already have this week. I'm taking my dress off when, as if he's read my mind or knew I was missing him, Micah begins FaceTiming me. I hurriedly throw my shirt back on before answering.

"Hey sexy," I say and greet him with a smile.

"Hello my love," he smiles widely at me, his dimples showing, "Fuck, I miss you."

I giggle.

"I miss you too, baby. I was just thinking of you."

His smile grows and he licks his lips.

"Oh yeah? I was thinking of you too beautiful. I had an idea actually," he starts with a playful smirk. "Before my trip got extended an extra day, I had plans to take you out on a date. But then I thought to myself, why should we allow distance to stop that? I mean why not go on a date right now?"

I giggle, "How do we do that?"

He's grinning from ear to ear. Suddenly the doorbell rings.

"You should answer that," he says smirking.

I arch my brow at him playfully as I run to answer the door. It's a Grubhub woman holding a takeout bag from my favorite restaurant.

"Oh my God are you serious," I laugh giddily as I take the bag.

He laughs along, "That's not all, one of your favorite movies comes on in 10 minutes on HBO. I thought we could eat and watch it together."

I'm smiling like an idiot at him. I can't believe how lucky I am to have such a thoughtful, wonderful man like him.

"I love you," I say simply. "I love you, baby. I just wanted to make it up to you somehow."

"You definitely did. No one has ever done something like this for me. Thank you," I say getting emotional.

We stayed on FaceTime as we ate and watched The Peanut Butter Falcon together. We laughed and talked for hours afterward, being playful and flirty with each other. It was nearly 3am by the time Micah and I said goodnight to each other after the amazing virtual date he planned for me. I had a warm smile on my face as I drifted to sleep thinking of him.

Sixty

I'm awoken from a deep sleep by my phone ringing, I groggily reach for it and see that Maggie is calling me.

"Good morning bitch! We're getting mani and pedi's today! We're also shopping for something sexy to wear tomorrow night, so get up and get dressed. I'll be pulling in to pick you up in 10 minutes. Chop! Chop," she instructs before hanging up.

I roll my eyes and crawl out of bed. After finishing my morning ritual of getting ready and discovering that my period finally ended in time for Micah's arrival home, I'm slipping my vans on when Maggie pulls up and honks her car horn for me. It's been a while since just me and her have had a day together.

"We've so needed this. Pedi's are the best," Maggie says with her eyes closed as she enjoys soaking her feet.

"Mmm hmm," I replied, enjoying the combination of the hot water and my back getting rubbed from the message chair I'm sitting in.

"What color are you getting," she asks.

"I think I'm going with this one," I say pointing to a maroon polish.

"Oooh pretty! That'll look great with your skin tone. Micah will love it," she says.

I smile at the mention of him.

"I've missed him," I say.

"You know what you should do? Go over there dressed in your lingerie and just completely blow his mind! A naughty welcome home gift," she giggles.

"I was already planning that," I admit, my cheeks blushing.

"Look at you being a total vixen now," she teases.

I laugh and roll my eyes at her.

I received a text from Micah then, "Good morning beautiful. Sorry I didn't have the chance to call you. I was running late. I can't wait to see you later today, baby."

I grin as I read his text.

"Let me guess, Micah?"

Maggie smirks. I nod.

"See what time he'll be back. We have that movie tonight, he can meet us there. I already bought his ticket."

I text him, "It's ok, baby. I can't wait to see you either! What time will you make it in? Maggie got movie tickets for all of us to see the 7:15 showing."

He texts back a frown emoji, "I don't think my flight will touch down in time babe. I'm sorry."

UNTIL I
found you

I relay Maggie his message before replying, "It's ok. I'll come over afterwards when you get home, sound good?"

He texts back, "Can't wait baby."

After our nails and toes are done we head over to Macy's. "

What are you planning on wearing tomorrow night," Maggie asks looking through some short dresses on a rack.

"I was thinking of whipping out that dress you got me for my birthday."

She looks up smiling, "Yes! It's about time you finally wear it. That color will look amazing on you! You'll look like a total hottie. You need to get some cute heels to match though."

While Maggie is in the changing room trying on some dresses, I walk over to the shoe section. I come across a pair of sexy black open toe platform stilettos, grabbing my size, I try them on. Once I secure the ankle straps, I stand up in them. I feel like a giraffe in these beauties. They make me half a foot taller and I look incredibly sexy in them.

"Damn girl," Maggie says from behind me.

"Yes, definitely need to get these!"

She gives me a thumbs up. I laugh before attempting to walk in them. I definitely feel like a giraffe in them, a newborn giraffe. I'm wobbling some in between steps.

Maggie chuckles, "It will take some practice but you've got this! Just relax and don't worry about falling in them or you will. Walk with confidence! The world is your runway," she says dramatically.

I giggle at her.

"How do you like the extra height?"

Maggie smirks at me. I decide to amuse her.

"I have such a better vantage point now, like there's an entire world up here I didn't even know about."

She laughs then. We're going to check out when I decide to stop in the men's section and buy Micah a new black button up dress shirt since I ripped the buttons off his old one. I bite my lower lip as the memory of it plays out in my head. After having Micah's shirt gift wrapped we head back home to get ready for tonight. After shaving and showering, I'm drying off when my text tone goes off. I immediately recognized the number as Connor's.

"I wanted to apologize to you again. I know I stepped over the line. I was just concerned. Hopefully you will accept my apology."

I think about replying but decide against it.

I'm blow drying my hair when Jared walks in. "I think we're taking separate cars tonight. Maggie is staying with Jo again and Jamie is staying here with me. You can ride with us," he offers.

"It's ok. I'm staying with Micah tonight too so I was just going to take my car anyway," I say staring between my curling iron and straightener deciding which I want to go with.

"Ok have fun, be safe. Go with the curling iron," he says before disappearing down the hallway.

After curling my hair and putting it in a half up half down bun, I apply some makeup. I go into my room to pack an overnight bag when I get a text from Micah.

"I should be home by nine, baby. I can't wait to hold you. I've missed you so much."

UNTIL I found you

Butterflies swarm my belly. I smile excitedly knowing in just a few short hours I'll be in his arms. In addition to some of my new outfits, I also pack my new bra and panties along with my cream colored lace corset and garter. I can't wait for Micah to see me in this, just imagining his reaction I begin to feel pressure in between my legs. I throw my toiletries along with my makeup and curling iron into my bag before zipping it up. I dress in my new high waisted skinny jeans and my black long sleeve fitted crop top. I put on my black high heeled ankle boots and look in the mirror at my curves I've come to accept and love about myself.

I wouldn't have worn this kind of outfit before but Micah has made me open my eyes to see myself, to accept and love all the perfect imperfections of myself. He gives me so much confidence with how he treats me and how he loves me. Just then Maggie walks in.

"Holy shit, Leyna," she says as her eyes go wide.

"What is it," Jared asks, walking up behind her.

His mouth gapes open at my appearance. I begin to blush and second guess my choice of outfit.

"Should I change? Does it look bad," I ask looking back into the mirror.

I wasn't dressed immodest. The top covered my breasts completely. The only thing showing was two inches of my bare waist.

"No," They both say in unison.

"You look so hot." Maggie says proudly.

I giggle. Jared walks over hugging me and kissing me on top of the head.

"What was that for," I ask smiling.

"I'm having a proud moment right now. My baby is all grown up," he teases.

I place my overnight bag, green dress and my new black heels into my car before we head out to eat. We're walking through the restaurant when the hostess asks how many to seat.

I say "Five." as Maggie says "Six."
I look at her confused.

"Micah said he wouldn't make it in time, remember," I say.

"I know. I had an extra ticket so I called Connor."

"You what," I ask.

Just then Connor comes walking in still dressed in his dress shirt and pants from work. His eyes widen some as he takes in my curves. His eyes rake over my body, lingering on my hips and breasts before settling on my lips, he meets my eyes then and we both look quickly away from each other. Well this is about to get hella awkward. The hostess seats us at a table for six. Maggie sits next to Jo, Jamie across from Jared which leaves me sitting right next to Connor. Yep, hella awkward.

Sixty-one

The respective couples are chatting away with one another leaving me and Connor to just sit there awkwardly in silence. Jared tried involving me in his conversation as much as possible before Jamie started venting to him about a lazy employee at his job. After that I was on my own. Maggie was oblivious to the fact Connor and I weren't on friendly terms at the moment. She's chatting away with Jo about something when Connor speaks to me then, "You look great," he says quietly as he gives me a small smile.

"Thank you." I say before looking away from him.

"I'm sorry about last night," he says, still looking at me.

"I saw your text," I say looking at the table.

"So you're going to stay mad at me forever then," he asks, arching his brow.

I look at him, "I'm not mad at you."

"Then what then? You're ignoring me for the fun of it," he asks, amused.

"I'm not ignoring you."

He smirks, "Ok then, let's talk. How was your day?"

I let out a frustrated breath, "It was fine Connor."

He smiles, "Quit frowning sour patch, your face is going to get stuck like that."

"Then quit bothering me," I counter.

He chuckles, "So I'm bothering you now? Why exactly is that?"

Before I can answer he adds smugly, "Is it because I get under your skin?"

I glare at him and I'm about to fire back something when the waiter comes by getting our orders.

"I'll take that as a yes," Connor smirks.

I step on his foot under the table with my heel.

"Ow!" Everyone looks at him then.

"Sorry. Bumped my knee under the table," He lies.

Now I'm the one smirking. He looks over to me shaking his head amusingly as he says quietly, "for someone so small you sure are feisty."

I fight a smile as I say, "Haven't you heard? Dynamite comes in small packages."

He laughs then. Shortly after our food arrives, I'm taking the fork out of my napkin when it falls onto the floor. Instinctively I go to grab it when Connor does the same, our foreheads colliding. "Ow!" We both say as we begin to rub our heads.

Until I found you

"Jesus you're lethal tonight," he says jokingly as I laugh.

"Sorry," I say grimacing as he smiles at me.

After we're done eating, it's time to go to the movie. Maggie ended up choosing the new Ryan Reynolds comedy. Connor passes me a bag of popcorn but I decline it, still full from the meal. A little ways into the movie and everyone is laughing. Connor begins to wheeze he's laughing so hard which in turn makes me laugh harder and snorting quickly ensues. I'm not sure if people are laughing at the movie or at mine and Connor's ridiculous laughter. By the time the credits roll we're both wiping tears from our eyes.

"I don't know what was funnier, the movie or you snorting," Connor says through his laughter.

I playfully smack him on the arm, "Shut up wheezy! Where's your inhaler when you need it," I retort.

Just then my phone buzzes, looking at it I see Micah has texted me that he's made it home now. I smile giddily knowing I'm only 20 minutes away from him.

"I had a blast guys. I'll see you tomorrow," I say as everyone waves their goodbyes to me as I'm walking to my car. I text Micah that I'm on the way.

"Leyna," Connor calls after me.

I turn around to see he's walking towards me.

"Yes?" I ask him with my brow arched.

He looks at me thoughtfully for a moment before saying, "Nothing. I thought you dropped something but you didn't."

He clearly decided against whatever it was he was about to say.

"Ok then." I say awkwardly. "I'll see you tomorrow Connor," I add before getting in my car and driving off.

A little while later I pull up in Micah's driveway and suddenly become so eager to be in his arms. My heart soars out of my chest when I see him step outside his front door to greet me. He's smiling bigger than I've ever seen as he holds his arms out wide for me to run into them. I leap into his strong arms then and they wrap tightly around me as he twirls me around. His face nuzzling into my neck. God I've missed him so much. He smells heavenly.

"There's my angel," he says skimming his lips up my neck before placing them on my mouth. My legs wrap around his waist as he lifts me higher onto him. My hands cupping the back of his neck as he kisses me. He walks us inside then still holding me.

"I missed you so much, baby," I say to him.

He gives me a playful pout as he says, "I've missed you more, my baby."

I giggle at him as I squish his face in between my hands causing his lips to pucker out even more. As I'm kissing him, he shuts the front door with his foot before walking us over to the couch sitting on it as I straddle him. He wraps his arms around my back pulling me flush to him as he sweetly kisses me across my jawline. His nose bumps into mine before he places his forehead against me in the sweetest gesture. We just stare at each other for a moment, smiling and enjoy being wrapped in each other's arms. These past five days have felt like an eternity without him.

Until I found you

"I love you so much," he says to me quietly, like a prayer.

One of my hands begins to play in his hair, while the other is gently stroking the side of his face as I say, "I love you more."

He licks his lips and smiles sweetly at me.

"Not possible," he says as he rubs light circles on my back.

He looks down my body as I straddle his lap before looking back up to my face, taking in my eyes and lips.

"You're so beautiful, baby."

He breathes. I lean in closer to him, barely brushing my lips with his before pulling back slightly and skimming my tongue lightly across his lips, teasing him. His lips instantly part, his tongue peaking through as it glides across mine. He pulls back then, taking my bottom lip between his teeth before tugging and grazing it with the tip of his tongue. I moan and he removes one hand from around my back, moving it to the side of my neck. He releases my bottom lip from his teeth then before he attaches his mouth to my jaw. Kissing and nibbling as he works his way down my neck. Pressure builds between my legs as I feel him growing hard through his jeans. He licks up my neck before attaching his mouth to mine once more, pulling my hair as he does. Goosebumps rise on my skin at the incredible feeling and a soft moan escapes me.

He swallows it as his tongue laps around mine. I begin rocking my hips against him and he growls as he cups my ass with the hand that isn't on my neck. Before I know it we're groping one another and having a heavy make out session. I remove my hands from the sides of his face before grabbing the hem of his black shirt and pulling it over his head, throwing it on the floor. I bite my lip as I stare at his beautifully chiseled chest. His abs are hard and tight as I run my hands over his six pack. God he's so hot and all mine. He glides his fingers over the exposed bare skin of my waist before grabbing the hem of my top and pulling it over my head. His eyes widen when he sees my new red bra.

"Fuck, when did you get this," he asks as he runs his hands on the undersides of my breasts. "I did some shopping. Do you like it," I ask.

"Do I like it? You tell me, baby," he says as he presses his large erection into me.

I gasp lightly and begin to rub myself against him.

He moans, "Period or not if you don't stop I'm going to flip you over and take you here and now."

I bite my lip and smile, "My period ended this morning."

UNTIL I
found you

Sixty-two

He wraps his arms up under my ass as he lifts us off the couch then.

"What are you doing," I ask giggling.

"I'm about to bury myself into you and show you just how much I've missed you baby," he says kissing my neck.

We're at the staircase as I say, "Wait a minute."

He stops, pulling back to look at me.

"What's wrong," he asks worried.

I slide off of him.

"Nothing is wrong. I bought something for you and wanted to give it to you."

He arches his brow curiously as I walk over grabbing my bag before taking his hand in mine and leading us to his room. I have him sitting on the bed waiting patiently as I put on the cream colored lace corset and garter. I take a look in the mirror at myself and can't wait to see his reaction to it.

"Baby, the suspense is killing me. What are you doing in there?"

I giggle at him before saying, "close your eyes and don't open them until I say."

"Fucking hell woman, you're killing me right now."

I open the door to see he's covering his eyes with his large hands. I bite my lower lip and smile at the sight of him this way. I grab his gift wrapped shirt and climb behind him on the bed. I place my arms over his shoulders and hand him the gift box.

"Ok open your eyes but don't turn around. There's two gifts for you," I say to him as I peck kisses onto his neck.

He removes his hands from his face then and looks down at the box in his lap.

"Baby, you didn't have to get me anything. You're all I need," he says kissing my hand.

I kiss the shell of his ear and whisper, "Just open it."

He chuckles, "Yes ma'am."

I watch as he unboxes the black button up dress shirt.

"I felt bad about destroying your other one so I got you a new one."

He laughs.

"Baby, you can rip the buttons off my shirt anytime," he teases. "Thank you, Angel," he adds as he kisses my wrist.

"And now for your other gift, without peeking walk towards the bathroom and stop. Don't turn around until I tell you," I instruct.

He licks his lips as he walks a few steps away before stopping. I climb off the bed and stand in front of it before pulling my hair down and letting

UNTIL I found you

my long waves fall past my shoulders. "Turn around," I say quietly.

He turns around and his lips part. His chest rising and falling at a faster pace, his eyes wild as he greedily takes in my body. The sexy lace of the corset is hugging my curves, accentuating my hourglass figure. He looks at me with hungry eyes as he licks his lips and walks over to me grabbing either side of my waist in his large hands.

"You are the most beautiful woman I've ever seen," he says slowly, as he takes in my every curve before staring at my full lips. "You're so beautiful it hurts."

He breathes as he looks into my eyes. I blush and smile shyly.

"I know you've probably seen other girls look better in-"

He cuts me off, "Don't," he says sternly, taking my face gently in his hands forcing me to look up at him. "Don't you dare question your beauty, Leyna. No other woman has ever or will ever be as beautiful to me as you are."

He looks into my eyes before scanning over my body.

"Instead of trying to convince you this in words, I'm going to show you. I'm going to worship every part of you until you believe it," he says scooping me up in his arms then before laying me down on top of the bed.

My heart begins to race as he hovers over me and collects my wrists in his hands, pinning them on the mattress above my head. He begins kissing me passionately before he lowers his face to the base of my throat. Trailing hot, wet kisses down my neck towards my breasts. He gathers both my wrists in one of his large hands while the other slides down my arm before he pushes down the material covering my breast, attaching his hot mouth to it.

My hips buck off the bed as his tongue sucks and flicks over my hard nipple. He presses his large erection into me as he does the same to my other breast, this time lightly grazing his teeth over me. I moan and try rubbing myself against him desperately needing the friction. "Settle down baby," he coos. "I haven't even started yet," he adds as he pushes the lace up and swirls his hot tongue just below my navel.

Both of my wrists in his hand, he lowers my arms down, pinning my wrists just above my head.

"Keep them here. Don't move them," he commands as he moves his large hands down my breasts palming them in his hands before sliding them down my waist. He leans down, grabbing my hips as he begins lightly trailing kisses atop my thighs. His facial hair and warm breath sends goosebumps over me. I fist the sheets in my hands as he begins kissing and licking the inner parts of my thighs. Teasingly nibbling the sensitive flesh as he gets closer and closer to my sex. He blows on my wetness then and my hips instinctively buck off the bed, pushing myself into his face.

My hands fly into his hair then, eager for his tongue to be on me. He grabs my wrists and pins me back onto the bed smiling seductively.

"Not yet baby," he whispers in my ear before tugging on my earlobe with his teeth.

He grabs my leg up under my calf and begins unhooking the stocking from my garter straps. He slowly pulls it down my leg while his other hand is wrapped around the back of my thigh. Once he pulls the stocking completely off he begins kissing my ankle and up my leg, licking and sucking as he does. By the time he does the same to my other leg I'm aching for him at this point. I reach down and rub his large erection through his jeans. He hisses.

"Fuck," he whispers.

"That's the idea," I say as I unbutton his jeans and pull them down his legs hastily.

I grab his large cock in my hand giving him a few pumps.

He kicks off his jeans before hoovering over me as he says, "I'm not fucking you this time. I'm going to go slow, baby. I want you to feel how much I love you. How much I crave your sinful body."

He took my wrists in his hands once more before spreading my legs far apart with his knees. He's kissing me as he pushes the tip of himself into me before pulling out and pushing back in only half way. Each time my hips buck up to get more of him inside of me before he pulls out. He does this teasing motion for a while before my toes start to curl into the mattress. I can't take this cat and mouse game anymore. He still has my wrists pinned beneath his hands adding to the frenzy of wanting him so badly.

"Baby, please. I need you," I say into him.

He pushes into me fully then and we both let out moans at the fullness of him being inside of me. I'm home now. He buries his face into my neck as he thrusts deeply, his hips rolling into mine. He lets go of my wrists then and places one of his hands onto the back of my neck grabbing a fistful of my hair while his other wraps up under my lower back, grabbing my hip and squeezing as he thrusts into me at a slow, deep calculated pace. I can tell by looking into his eyes it's taking everything in him to stay like this. For so long he fucked without any feelings for anyone, it was all just a distraction. It was a way to escape his own pain and now this man is making passionate love to me.

The way he's holding me, the way he's looking into my eyes as he makes sweet love to me, I know without a shadow of a doubt I'm it for him and he's it for me. No one else could ever come close to him. No one else could ever have my heart besides him. He is my everything and I am everything to him. Other girls have had his body but none have ever had his heart or his soul. He belongs to me the way I belong to him. None have ever calmed the storm raging within him, none were able to bring him peace. None of the countless women from before has ever had the privilege of hearing him declare his love for them.

I am the only woman he's ever loved and he is the only man I will ever love. He's looking deep into my eyes as he moves inside of me.

"I love you, Leyna. I love you so much," he says placing his lips on mine.

Tears roll down my temples, "I love you. I love you so much, Micah," I say as I gently stroke the side of his face.

He presses his forehead to mine as he increases his pace. I close my eyes and moan at the ecstasy of him filling me completely. He places his mouth over mine then, swallowing my moans greedily as he thrusts into me. His fists tighten in my

Until I found you

hair as his large cock hits my g-spot and I lose it. I cry out, my head and toes dig into the mattress as I cum harder than I have before my orgasm rips through me in pure euphoria. I squeeze around him.

He moans loudly, "Fuck, baby," as he spills into me before collapsing on top of me.

His large body pinning me completely down beneath him. His hand is still wrapped in my hair as he pants into my neck, his hot mouth on my skin causes goosebumps to form as I'm riding out my blissful state. We're both heaving heavily, our breaths ragged. I begin rubbing his head and gently stroking his hair as our breaths even out.

Sixty-three

We lay there in each other's arms as Micah plays with the ends of my hair. I'm rubbing light circles on his back when he begins kissing my forehead.

"You're incredible, you know that," he says suddenly.

I peer up at him, "Why do you say that?"

"Because you are. I've never in my life had someone like you before. You are the best thing that has ever happened to me. I don't know what in the fuck I've done to deserve you but I'm beyond grateful for it," he says pushing my hair away from my face.

"I love you, Micah," I say smiling as I stroke his face.

He takes my hand bringing it to his lips as he begins kissing my palm.

"I love you. You're everything to me," he says never taking his beautiful blue eyes away from mine.

Until I found you

I lean up and bump noses with him playfully, "And you are my everything," I say as he grins widely.

A little while later we're in the shower together, I'm washing his back with the loofah when I ask him, "How was your trip? Did you end up finding a property you liked for your expansion in Chicago?"

He shrugs, "Terms couldn't be met. So I'll expand somewhere else," he says sounding bored as he turns around taking the loofah from me.

"Where do you have in mind," I ask.

"Not sure. Anything interesting happened while I was away?"

He changes the subject. I wonder if Maggie hadn't told Jo about my father and Jo mentioned it to Micah somehow. Why else would he ask that?

"Well actually that you mention it," I begin.

His eyes flash a look of worry before he quickly regains himself.

"I picked up Jean's personal belongings and was going through them when I found a hidden picture behind a frame of a man holding me. I think it's my father."

His eyes widened in surprise. He definitely didn't see that coming but then what could he possibly have meant otherwise?

"Your father? Have you asked Jean about it?"

I shake my head.

"Not yet. I considered hiring a private investigator but I really don't have anything to go on except the picture. There's not a name listed under the father section of my birth certificate. As much as

I want to avoid it, I don't think I have much of a choice but to talk to her."

"Do you think she'd even tell you?"

I shake my head feeling hopeless.

"Let me see what I can do. I can't promise you anything but I will try."

I look up at him.

"What do you mean?"

He smooths my frown lines away, "Don't worry baby. Leave it to me ok?"

Suddenly his phone rings in the bedroom.

"I have to get that," he says as he steps out and wraps a towel around his waist before answering the phone.

"Yeah, hold on," he says stepping out of earshot.

I find that odd but ignore my suspicions. After rinsing my hair, I step out and dry off. I grab one of Micah's shirts out of his drawers and put it on as I hear him raise his voice to whoever he's on the phone with. I quickly slip a pair of panties on and walk into the hallway. I hear him speaking from his office.

"I told you this was a bad fucking call and now your arrogance has once again-" a man's voice cuts him off. I can hear the other person yelling but can't make out what they're saying. "Well it's a little too late for that isn't it, Keith," Micah seethes at his father before hanging up. A moment later, it sounds as if he's thrown something hard against the wall and I hear glass breaking. I run into the room as I see Micah punch a hole through the wall angrily. His chest is heaving, his brows furrowed and his hands clenched into tight fists of fury at his sides. My eyes

UNTIL I found you

glance down at the broken glass scattered on the floor and to the hole in the wall. He looks over at me then, his eyes flashing several emotions as they meet mine. Anger, relief, sadness. I see the storm raging behind his eyes. I walk over to him then, careful of the glass. He breathes harsh breaths through his nose, his chest rising and falling rapidly. He's looking down at me with furrowed brows and a clenched jaw as I step on my tiptoes to gently stroke the side of his face, willing him to calm down. I can see the war battling within himself. He doesn't want to be like this anymore but he doesn't know how to bring himself out of the dark storm he's in.

I've become his beacon of light to pull him out of that darkness within himself. I place my hand over his heart as I begin rubbing light circles onto his cheek with the other, never taking my eyes away from his. He visibly begins to calm down as I touch him and look into his eyes, his chest begins to rise and fall at a steadier pace.

"That's it baby, breathe. Calm your mind. Come back to me, let the anger go and come back to me," I say in a soothing tone.

His eyes stare deep into me before he cups either side of my face as he places his forehead against mine.

"I'm sorry," he breathes before nuzzling his face into my neck.

I wrap my arms around him, anchoring him to me as I begin soothingly shushing him. I hold him like this for a few minutes, gently stroking his hair as he nuzzles his face further into my neck. He kisses up my neck before skimming his nose across my jaw lightly, planting his lips softly on mine before picking me up by the backs of my legs and carries me to bed. His lips never leave mine as he lays us on the mattress and envelopes us in the comforter. After a while of us kissing, Micah begins playing with the ends of my hair as he holds me against his chest. I drift to sleep holding him close to me.

The next morning when I open my eyes, I find Micah's side of the bed empty. I call out for him but don't get a reply. That's when I hear Micah's music playing from downstairs. I follow the rock music to his gym room and find him working out in only his grey sweatpants. I lean against the door frame and practically drool as I watch him grab the suspended bar above him and lift his whole body into the air with only one arm and touch his chest to the bar before lowering himself to the ground slowly. He repeats this several times before he walks over to the weights then. His skin is glistening from the sweat and his sinful v line is showing from his pants hanging dangerously low on his hips.

I admire his tattoos and defined muscles. He looks like pure sex and he's all mine. He bends over then adding weights to the bar as I stare at his phenomenal ass. I'm biting my lip at him when he turns around, his eyes meeting mine.

"I've got the hottest fucking boyfriend in the world," I say to him.

He smiles widely as he walks over to me.

"Is that right," he asks playfully as he places his lips on mine.

"Mm Hmm," I say through kissing him.

He chuckles, "Well as it happens I have the most beautiful girlfriend in the world. Her sexy curves and big lips alone make me hard," he says, grabbing fistfuls of my ass and pulling my bottom lip between his teeth before letting go.

I playfully smack him on the ass then.

"Hungry," I ask.

"Starving," he says wiggling his brows as he looks me over.

"Come on Casanova, you need to eat," I say as I take his hand in mine leading us to the kitchen.

We're sitting at the table eating our breakfast when curiosity gets the best of me about last night's phone call.

"So what happened last night with your dad? It sounded serious."

He looks up at me, his expression unreadable for a moment.

"It was nothing," he says looking back down at his plate.

"It didn't sound like nothing. You were screaming at him and throwing stuff-"

He cuts me off, "It's nothing to concern yourself with," he says curtly, sipping his coffee.

I'm taken aback by his cold response and watch as he refuses to make eye contact with me. "Really," I ask.

He looks up at me then, his expression hard.

"In case you haven't got the hint, I'd rather not talk about it. So just drop it, Leyna," he says harshly.

I'm floored by him momentarily before I nod and stand from the table then.

"Don't forget to clean the shit you broke last night because I'm not doing it anymore," I call over my shoulder as I walk up the stairs.

"Leyna," he calls out but I ignore him as I walk into his room and grab clothes out of my bag to change into. I already have my jeans on and I'm hooking my bra on when he walks in.

"Look I'm sorry you had to see me like that last night," he says.

I pull my shirt over my head and ignore him as I place my stuff into the bag and zip it up. "Where are you going," he asks, looking between me and the bag as I put my shoes on.

"It's nothing to concern yourself with," I repeat his words back to him as I walk past him.

He grabs me around my waist stopping me.

"Don't go. I'm sorry, ok? It scares me that one day you'll see just how fucked up I really am and you'll leave me. I'm not proud of the person I once was and when I become so completely angry like that it reminds me of the person I was before. The fucked up person that didn't feel anything other than his own misery and loss. I've fought like hell to change over the years and now I'm trying even more to be a better man for you, because you deserve that. You fill the void in my soul. You came into my life and have brought me so much happiness, so much love. Something I never thought I would feel, something I never thought I deserved to feel after everything I've done. In truth, I don't deserve you. You're way too good for me I know that but you're all I want. You are what I need. You're it for me. That's why I can't bear the thought of losing you," he says as his eyes brim with tears.

I drop my bag and grab his face in my hands, looking into his eyes I say, "You won't lose me if you don't push me away. Remember what you told me?

You're broken, I'm broken but together we make a whole. Everyone has a past and everyone has scars but that's just what they are, scars. Baby, I won't judge you for who or what you were in your past. That's irrelevant to me. Who you are now, what you do now, that is all that matters to me."

He looks at me with sadness, "What if the things I've done before still haunt me?"

I stroke his face lightly as I say, "Then we'll face them on. Together. I'm here with you. I'm not going anywhere."

He wraps his arms tightly around me then, pulling me into a hug before he takes my face in his hands.

Fighting his tears back, he says to me, "You're everything to me, everything. You're my best friend, my better half."

My heart breaks and mends back together again at his precious words to me. Happy tears begin to fall down my face as he wipes them away with his thumbs and kisses me tenderly on my lips.

Sixty-four

I'm in the bathroom curling my hair for tonight when my phone begins to ring.

"Hello," I answer.

"Leyna," a familiar voice asks.

"Yes. Who's this," I ask, guarded.

"It's Claire. I wasn't sure if you'd still have the same number," she says relieved.

My lips part in surprise.

"Yeah it was just easier for Jean to remember I guess. How are you," I ask, confused that she's calling me.

"I'm good. I know this is so random and I apologize for it but I needed to call you. I've been thinking about what you said, about coming home and seeing Lyle. It's been a long time. Call it pregnancy hormones or guilt, but it's been eating at me since I've seen you and I think I'll feel better if I come see him. I was wondering if you'd come with me?"

I'm completely taken aback by all of this.

"Yes, absolutely just say when," I practically stammer.

Until I found you

"I know it's short notice but I'm coming into town tomorrow to see my parents. Could we possibly meet at the cemetery around two," she asks.

"Yes that'll be perfect," I say before hanging up.

I stand there in shock for a moment.

"Baby who was that," Micah asks, stepping out of the shower.

"It was Claire. She just called me out of the blue wanting to meet at the cemetery tomorrow to visit Lyle."

He wraps a towel around his waist then and walks over to me.

"Do you want me to come with you," he offers sweetly.

I nod and stand on my tippy toes to kiss his lips.

"Now get ready, sexy. Maggie will cut us both if we're late," I say, playfully smacking him on the ass.

He chuckles before walking over to the double sink and begins trimming his facial hair and brushing his teeth while I curl my hair to perfection. After he's finished, he leaves me in the bathroom to get dressed. I do my eyes in a beautiful soft smokey eye palette and color my large lips with a dark red lipstick. I look at my reflection in the mirror, I look glamorous, beautiful. I spray myself with my favorite perfume before walking in the bedroom and stepping into my short emerald green dress. Looking in the mirror, I see that I have a bad panty line with the way this dress clings to my ass. I huff in frustration and pull my panties off before placing them back into my bag. Guess I'm going commando tonight. Luckily for me, the bottom of the dress hugs my thighs tightly. I'm buckling the ankle straps on my platform stilettos when Micah walks in.

"Holy fuck," he says in a low, husky voice.

I look up at him and he looks divinely sexy. He's dressed in charcoal grey dress pants with black dress shoes, and a shiny black belt. He's wearing the new black button up dress shirt that I got him, the first few buttons at the top are undone showing off his yummy neck and Adam's apple. He looks like pure sex and suddenly I want him to throw me over his knee and spank me.

I bite my bottom lip and stalk towards him slowly. He licks his lips at me and places his hand over his growing erection as he stares my body down. His eyes trail from my breasts to my curvy hips and down my legs, stopping at my stilettos before he looks back up to my face. He closes the gap between us then and grabs my hourglass waist in his hands.

"It's taking everything in me not to throw you on that bed and fuck you senseless right now," he says with hooded eyes.

My breath hitches and I swallow, my mouth becoming dry. I squeeze my legs together to relieve some of the pressure forming between them. He notices my reaction and releases me, stepping away.

"We should go or we won't leave this house tonight," he says, taking my hand and leading us to the stairs. I stop when we reach them, looking between the stairs and my high heels wondering if I can make it down without twisting my ankle. Micah sees the hesitation on my face then. I go to remove my shoes when he smiles wickedly at me before dipping down and throwing me over his shoulder, his hands wrap securely around my bottom. I shriek excitedly at him and he laughs before palming and squeezing my ass.

"I must say baby, I'm loving the view. It's phenomenal," he says before playfully biting my ass cheek through my dress as he walks us down the stairs.

I laugh at him.

"You should see my view," I say as I pinch his ass.

Once we pull up, Micah hands the keys of his Corvette to the valet boy before putting his arm around my waist and walking us into the club. We walk upstairs to the V.I.P. section and make our way to the private party suite Maggie and Jo rented for the night. They along with Jared and Jamie are all seated at the mini bar with drinks in their hands. I study the layout of the room as we walk in. The front wall is made of mirrored glass with a long brass stripper pole sitting on a raised platform in front of it. To the side sits the stocked mini bar with bar stools and towards the back wall sits two long golden velvet couches. Looking up I see the ceiling even has its own strobe lights.

"Ok, this place is sick," I say to Maggie as we walk over to them.

"Told you! I can't wait to get on the pole later," she yells excitedly as she pours herself another shot.

I giggle seeing she's already tipsy and the night hasn't even begun yet.

"You're so in for it tonight just so you know," I lean over and say to Jo.

He smiles and shakes his head amusingly, "Yeah, Jared's already warned me about Mildred." I begin to laugh at the mention of Maggie's drunken alter ego.

Micah raises his brow, "Do I even want to know?"

"When Maggie gets drunk her inner wild party girl comes out in full swing," I explain.

"Like the bitch will climb on top of bar tops and shit. Don't even get me started on her level of liquid courage," Jared adds sipping his drink.

"Yeah, she can get pretty wild," I say grimacing to Micah.

He chuckles.

"This should be fun."

After a while, everyone is taking multiple shots except for Micah who's drinking a beer.

Jamie notices my bottled water then.

"Under age or designated driver?"

"Neither. I just don't drink," I explain kindly.

He cocks his brow at me and goes to say something when Jared leans over whispering something in his ear. Jamie nods his head then and smiles at me knowingly. Cardi B's Bodak Yellow starts playing and everyone dances along except for Micah. I begin to sway my hips to the beat of the music and see from the corner of my eye Micah watching me. He looks so sexy with the way he's slouched on the bar stool, his legs apart, the top of his shirt is unbuttoned and his hair is pushed back away from his forehead.

God, he's so hot and all mine. His eyes take in every curve of me, licking his lips at me as he does. I call him over to me with my finger as I begin swaying slower. He reaches me, wrapping his hands around my waist pulling me close into him, my back to his front. I reach my arm behind me and place it on the back of his neck as I teasingly push my ass against his cock.

He growls into my ear and attaches his hot mouth to my neck sucking lightly. I bite my lip and begin grinding into him at a quicker pace, feeling him growing harder beneath me.

I lean my head back onto him as he whispers, "If you don't behave yourself, I'm taking you to the stalls, bending you over and fucking your brains out."

His hands tightening around my waist as a whimper escapes my lips at the thought. I squeeze my legs together to relieve the pressure building between them. I turn around then, pulling him close to me so no one sees and begin to palm his erection through his pants. His jaw clenches and he looks at me with hungry, hooded eyes as he grabs my wrist stopping me. "Fucking hell, baby, you're killing me."

Just then Maggie comes over taking my wrist and pulling me towards the pole.

"Come dance with me," she demands.

I look over at Micah who's sitting on the couch with his leg crossed over his lap. I smile wickedly at him and he shakes his head amusingly at me before licking his lips. Jo sits beside him and they drink a beer watching Maggie and I as she attempts to climb the pole. Jared spits his drink out when she falls landing hard on her ass. We all begin to laugh at her. She giggles and flips us off playfully as she dares us to do it.

I go sit on Micah's lap as we all laugh watching Jo climb half way up before falling back down. After Jamie, Jared comes the closest to reaching the top before he, Jamie and
Maggie dared me to go next. I shake my head and decline.

"Oh come on, Leyna, don't be such a party pooper," she yells.

"Get it bitch," Jamie shouts drunkenly.

"I can't," I say to them.

"Come on baby, show me what you got," Micah wiggles his eyebrows at me.

He wouldn't be encouraging me to do this if he knew I wasn't wearing any panties. I raise my brow at him and he smiles, nodding towards the pole at me. I step up to the platform then and wrap my hands around the pole as I begin to twirl myself around it. Everyone begins cheering playfully at me as I press my back against the pole before shimmying my shoulders as I slide down it slowly, kicking my calf out quickly before standing back up and swirling my hips as my hands wrap around the pole once more. Micah has a wide grin on his face as I flip my hair over my shoulder and wrap the back of my leg around the pole as I begin to carousel around it before stopping dead in my tracks when I see Connor standing in the doorway, staring at me in a way that instantly makes me blush.

Sixty-five

Everyone follows my gaze to Connor then.

"You made it," Maggie says as she walks over to hug him.

Connor's lips are parted as his eyes drift up and down my body. He meets my eyes then and instead of looking away he holds my gaze intently.

"Yeah, sorry I'm late. Traffic was at a stand still," he says to Maggie, never breaking eye contact with me.

I quickly look away then as I step off the platform and walk over to Micah who already has his arms outstretched, pulling me into his lap. His lips form a tense line as he looks over at Connor with primal eyes. I place my hand on the side of his face willing him to look at me. His beautiful blue eyes meet mine then and I give him an encouraging smile before placing my lips softly on his. He places his hand to the side of my face as he kisses me deeper.

"Eason," Connor says, interrupting us as he sits on the couch across from us then.

"Donahue," Micah says flatly before pulling me closer into him, his hand going protectively around my waist.

"You look incredibly stunning tonight, Leyna. Wow," Connor says, smiling at me.

"Thank you." I say, giving him a timid smile.

I can feel Micah tensing under me before he moves his hand from my waist to the side of my ass, palming it for Connor to see as he stares at him harshly. I look over at Jared who gives me a wry smile and shakes his head amusingly.

"Party's here!" a woman's voice yells.

I look over to see it's Nadia. She's wearing a short silver sequined dress with a diamond choker on, her long black hair is in a sleek high up ponytail. Admittedly she looks amazing. Connor barely looks her over once before looking back at me and smiling. She strides over to Jo then hugging him. She looks over towards us, seeing me on Micah's lap and the way his hand is spread possessively over my ass, she glares at us before rolling her eyes.

"Ignore her," Micah whispers in my ear.

"Planned on it," I say.

Maggie and Jared introduce themselves to her and she completely ignores them as she asks Jo to fix her a drink.

I watch as Jared gives her a dramatic once over before walking over to me and saying, "I'm getting basic bitch vibes."

Micah and I snicker at him.

Maggie walks over to me, "Come with me; I need to pee," she whines.

I can see she's already intoxicated and needs help getting down the stairs.

Until I found you

After escorting her to the ladies room, she says washing her hands, "I don't like that bitch. I tried being friendly to her just now and she's going to snub me and Jared that way? Fuck her! I swear if she comes at any of us sideways I'm going to slap her. Like I'll tear her hair out. Play me," she slurs.

I giggle at her, already seeing "Mildred" has come out to play.

"Come on slugger, let's go have some fun," I say taking her arm as we walk out of the restroom.

Jo is walking towards the men's room when he stops and asks, "Is she good?"

I nod my head at him.

"I'm good, I'm fine," she slurs as she waves him off.

I notice Jared and Jamie dancing in the middle of the club and smile seeing how happy Jared looks.

"Ooh let's go dance! Fuck those stairs," she says grabbing my wrist and leading us towards the boys.

I glance around me as she pulls us onto the dance floor and see Connor leaned up against the bar looking bored out of his mind as a pretty blonde is practically throwing herself at him but he doesn't seem the least bit interested in her. He makes eye contact with me then and begins talking to the girl. I turn towards Jared as he grabs my hand and spins me.

"Dance with me boochie," he shouts over the music.

I giggle seeing how drunk he is.

Maggie and Jamie are dancing with each other as I say to Jared over the loud music, "I'm going to grab Micah, I'll be right back."

I see Jo making his way to Maggie on the dance floor as I make my way up the stairs. I'm coming through the doorway when I see Nadia standing in front of Micah. His brows are set in a deep furrow as she speaks.

"You can try to convince yourself all you want but I know you, Micah. This little thing with her, it's not going to last. She'll be the one to leave in the end once she sees how dark you can get," she says, tossing her clutch onto the mini bar next to him as she stalks closer to him. "You don't know a fucking thing about her or me. You only saw what I wanted you to see. She sees me. All of me, who I truly am so keep your fucking mouth shut about her," he seethes.

"Oh I see you, I see the fear behind your eyes. What, afraid it won't last? She seems like the type that would run to her mommy scared at the sight of danger whereas I get off on it. You remember those times don't you?"

She taunts him as she grabs his cock in her hand. He quickly grabs her wrist and shoves it away roughly before pointing a finger in her face. He begins shouting profanities at her before he looks over and sees me striding over to them. He walks towards me then and I shove past him as I go to lunge at her. He grabs me around my waist stopping me as I swing at her. She steps back quickly, barely missing my fist.

Until I found you

"If you ever fucking touch him again I swear to God I'll rip your cock sucking throat out," I threaten her as I attempt to shove Micah off of me with all of my strength but he tightens his arms around my waist.

"Baby, stop," he pleads with me.

"Bitch, I already have! I've had his body many times over and will have it again before it's through," she sneers.

"The fuck you will," he growls at her.

I kick my feet at her before saying, "Well guess what? That makes two of us except I have something of his you'll never have and that's his heart! He loves me. Mind, body and soul. You? You're nothing to him. He was just using you as a whore like every other guy in the city has," I spit angrily at her.

She stalks towards me then and I lunge my arms at her as Micah swings us around but not before I make contact with her face. She stammers back, holding her jaw in her hand momentarily before she runs over and tries to punch me but Micah turns quickly then to take the force of her punch to the side of his mouth. She hit him, she fucking hit him. Suddenly, all I see is red and I lose it.

I begin twisting and thrashing in his arms violently as she swings at me again, Micah blocks her with his forearm giving me just enough time to pull out of his grip. I quickly swing and punch her in the mouth as she grabs a hold of my hair. We fall to the ground, her on top of me. She begins slapping at me and pulling my hair until I grab her ponytail using it to bring her face down to me as I begin punching her repeatedly. Micah tries desperately to pull her off of me but I'm the one not letting go of her.

I punch her over and over again in the face as Jo runs in and immediately helps Micah lift Nadia off of me.

"Get this crazy bitch off of me," she screams attempting to hold my arms back.

That's when the boys notice I'm hanging onto her like a spider monkey with a pitbull grip. "Baby, let go," Micah shouts at me, pulling me around my waist as Jo tries walking backwards with Nadia but ends up pulling me along with her.

The boys are essentially playing tug of war with Nadia and I.

"Stop, dammit," Jo shouts at Nadia as she swings at me, her fist connecting with my mouth.

I yank my arm out of her wrist then and punch her in the nose before swinging again and colliding my fist with her mouth as she screams.

"Leyna, stop," Micah yells as he finally rips me off of her but not before I kick her.

He swings us around once more before he pins me against the wall with his body as Jo drags Nadia out of the room.

"Let me at that fat bitch," she yells at him.

"I'm right here bitch, I'm right here," I call after her as Micah restrains me.

His hands pinning my wrists to the wall while his body is pushed up against mine. Angry tears begin to run down my cheeks as I growl from rage. He lets go of my wrists but still has my body pinned beneath his.

"Baby, stop. Calm down," he says taking my face in his hands as he looks me over and wipes my tears away with his thumbs, "Are you hurt," he asks, checking me over for any visible cuts or injuries.

Other than throbbing knuckles, scratch marks on my arms and the inside of my bottom lip being cut from my tooth, I came out unscathed. The same can't be said for Nadia. Her nose was pouring blood and so was her busted lip as Jo was dragging her out.

"I fucking hate her, Micah," I cry angrily as he comforts me.

Connor comes hastily into the room then.

"Leyna, are you ok? What happened," he asks me as tears fall down my face.

"This doesn't concern you, so fuck off," Micah spits angrily at him.

Connor's jaw clenches and he straightens his shoulders defensively.

"If it involves her getting hurt then yes, it is my concern."

Micah's eyes take on a primal look. "What the fuck did you just say?"

He seethes as he moves towards Connor. I grab a hold of his arms then.

"I didn't stutter. She knows I care about her. Who are you to say who she's friends with?"

He challenges.

"Connor, don't," I warn him.

I can feel Micah's muscles tensing under my touch and see the dark look in his eyes. "Friends," Micah sneers at him. "You don't want to be friends with her, you want to fuck her! I see the way you look at her. You'll never have her! You'll never even get close enough to try." Micah growls standing in front of him now, his fists clenched ready to strike. I get between them then.

"Connor, please just go," I plead as he and Micah stare each other down. "I'm telling you, you need to leave. Please."

I beg, knowing that if he doesn't leave now he and Micah will end up getting into a bloody brawl of their own. He looks at me then and sees the desperation in my eyes, without another word he reluctantly turns around and slams the door shut behind him as he leaves. I turn around and wrap my hands around Micah's large arm laying my forehead against it, relieved they didn't fight. I already feel bad that I ruined Jo's night. I force myself to shove that thought and my guilty conscience away for now. Micah looks down at me with angry eyes.

"That mother fucker can not stay away from you."

He hisses. He's becoming angrier by the second, I can see the storm raging behind them. "He'll never have you. No other man will. You're only mine."

I look deeply into his beautiful blue eyes as I say, "I don't want anyone but you. I'm yours, Micah."

He exhales a shaky breath as I touch the side of his face then, trying my best to calm and reassure him.

"Focus on me, baby. Shut everything else out ok," I say, bringing his hand to my lips and kissing his fingers softly.

He watches me with hooded eyes as his chest rises and falls. He licks his lips as he slides his thumb over my mouth slowly, I take the pad of his

UNTIL I
found you

thumb in between my teeth and gently bite down as I look into his eyes, batting my long lashes in full effect. He sucks in a harsh breath before grabbing my face in his hands and begins kissing me feverishly, his tongue lapping over mine. My hands go into his hair then as I begin to tug. He growls into me and pushes me against the wall once more, wrapping one of his hands into my hair while the other one squeezes my ass. I wrap my calf around one of his legs and he dips his fingers under my dress to touch me when he realizes I'm not wearing any underwear.

He pulls away looking at me with wild eyes, "You're not wearing any panties?"

I shake my head slowly and bite down on my lip as his fingers slide through my wetness as he inserts them inside of me, giving me a few pumps before drawing his fingers out.

"You're so wet for me baby." He says in a husky voice.

Sixty-six

He pulls my dress up above my hips as he bends down, guiding one of my legs over his shoulder.

"What are you doing," I ask panting.

He cups my ass with one of his hands while the other is wrapped around the leg that's on his shoulder.

"Eating your pussy," he says before attaching his mouth to my clit and swirling his tongue around it, my mouth falling wide open as I moan.

I lean my head against the wall as I cover my mouth with one hand while the other is tugging his hair. His hot tongue is working fast, tight circles on me. He moves his hand from my ass and begins to knead my breast in his palm, gently pinching my nipples between his fingers adding to the pleasure his mouth is already creating.

"So fucking sweet," he says into me, sending vibrations throughout me.

I look at the closed door worried that someone will walk in but the way Micah has me against this wall right now, I honestly don't care. He looks so sexy in between my legs.

I begin to crave him inside of me as I buck my hips at him panting, "Fuck me. I want you to fuck me."

He pulls his mouth away from me and looks up at me with wild, hungry eyes. He quickly stands up then as I impatiently undo his belt and pull his pants down his legs as his massive erection comes into view. He lifts me up into the air before slowly lowering me onto his huge, hard cock. We both moan as I stretch around him. One of his arms is wrapped up under my ass while his other hand has a fistful of my hair, tugging on it. My legs are wrapped around his waist as he pushes further into me, filing me completely. He begins bouncing me onto him as he thrusts into me, causing me to cry out from the pleasure.

"Fuck, baby, your little pussy feels amazing on my cock."

He growls into my neck. I whimper at his filthy words and wrap my hand into the back of his hair as he bites down on my collarbone. I tighten my hold around him as he moves both hands under me, grabbing fistfuls of my ass as he increases his pace. He is slamming into me at this point, the pain of it feeling heavenly in the most sinful way. I close my eyes and revel in how he is ravaging me against this wall right now. We're both panting and moaning when I hear a whimper then and open my eyes. Looking at the door, I see Nadia standing there, her mouth is open in horror as tears begin pulling in her eyes. From the look on her face she didn't think we'd still be in here.

I look over at the mini bar and see her clutch she left before looking back at her and smiling victoriously. Her finding us against the wall like this with my legs wrapped around Micah as he's burying himself into me is more rewarding than any fight I could ever get into with her. From the expression in her tear filled eyes, she seriously thought she would have him again. She thought I was only a play thing Micah was distracting himself with but now she sees that I'm the love of his life. She thought I would be so easily scared away, that I wouldn't fight for him. Boy was she wrong.

She's frozen in place, horrified at what she's seeing. Micah is oblivious to her presence as he thrusts into me relentlessly. The look on her face as she watches Micah fucking me against the wall in combination with his large cock hitting my g-spot, I cum harder than I've ever cummed before. My orgasm rips through me like a tsunami as I cry out in ecstasy. Micah places his large hand over my mouth to muffle my sounds.

"Fuck baby, I love you," he growls into me.

Tears fall from Nadia's face as she runs out of the room then. I smile victoriously under his hand, riding out my euphoric high as I squeeze around him. He grunts loudly as he spills into me then and I attach my mouth to his, swallowing his moans. He keeps us pressed against the wall for a moment longer as he catches his breath. He's still inside of me as he begins licking up my neck before kissing me just below my ear. I'm a panting mess as he lifts me up before slowly pulling out of me. I whimper at the loss of fullness as he sits me on my feet, steadying me.

Until I found you

After Micah zips his pants up and pulls my dress down, he walks us over on the couch to catch our breaths. He pulls me to lay on his chest, looking down at me he begins to laugh hard.

"What," I ask giggling at him.

"I told you you were a firecracker," he says through his laughter.

I begin laughing into his chest as I recall him calling me that after we first met.

"Seriously, I've never in my life seen a girl fight that savage before. My baby is a little badass," he says smiling amusingly at me as he pushes the hair away from my face.

I frown as my guilty conscience comes back to the surface then. "What's wrong? Did I hurt you," he asks, lifting my chin so I'm meeting his worried eyes.

"No you didn't hurt me. I just feel bad about ruining Jo's night. Do you think he hates me now?"

Micah chuckles, "No baby. He doesn't hate you. He knows how much of a shit starter she is." "I still want to apologize to him though, Maggie too even though I'm pretty sure she won't even remember anything that happened tonight."

He wraps his arms around me then.

"That's too bad because this was a hell of a night," he says kissing my lips.

A while later everyone made their way back up to the room, after talking with Jo he assured me that he wasn't mad at me at all, if anything it gave him something to laugh about for years to come. Once the night ended and we said our goodbyes to everyone I was exhausted and my feet were killing me.

Once we got back to Micah's I began hobbling towards the front steps when he chuckled before scooping me up in his arms and carrying me to the bathroom to take a shower. After undressing himself, Micah unzips my dress for me and I let it fall to the ground from my shoulders. I stand there naked with only my stilettos on as he looks my body up and down before he touches my face and breathes.

"You are so beautiful my love."

I smile sweetly at him as I place my lips on his, kissing him slowly. He bends down and starts removing my shoes from my feet, trailing his fingers lightly up my calf as he begins kissing the tops of my thighs as he works his way up to my belly, swirling his hot tongue just under my navel. I bite down on my lower lip as he makes his way to my breasts, palming the undersides he begins kissing them. Trailing hot, wet kisses slowly up my neck and jaw before finally attaching his mouth to mine.

My hands reach into his hair as his arm snakes around my lower back pulling me closer to him. He walks us backwards towards the shower as he turns the hot water on. Our kisses are slow and teasing as we step into the water. I practically melt into him as the hot water hits my back while he holds me tightly in his arms. He moves his lips from mine and begins trailing soft kisses across my cheeks, my nose and into my temples before kissing my forehead.

I look up at him and smile, "I love you so much baby."

He smiles widely and bumps noses with me "I love you more baby."

UNTIL I found you

"Na uh," I tease.

He chuckles grabbing the shampoo bottle and begins washing my hair, massaging my scalp as he does. I hum in relaxation. After cleaning ourselves we step out of the shower and get dressed for bed. We're standing at the double sinks brushing our teeth when I see Micah smiling at me.

"What?"

I arch my brow at him. He chuckles.

"You have your own area over there now," he says pointing to my makeup bag, perfume and other toiletries. "I love it," He adds, smiling.

We're laying in bed wrapped in each other's arms, as Micah plays in my hair.

I'm halfway asleep when he asks, "So Monday are you coming to work with me?"

I look up at him groggily and nod as I smile at him. I hadn't had the chance to tell him about my decision yet but after the way things have been going at the restaurant I'd be a fool not to. He smiles excitedly at me before kissing me on my lips and pulling me into his chest as we drift to sleep.

Sixty-seven

When I open my eyes the next morning I see Micah is already looking over at me smiling. I smile back at him as he moves a strand of hair from my face.

"Good morning, baby," I say to him as I reach over and kiss his lips.

"Good afternoon, my love," he replies.

Panicked, I look over at the clock afraid that I'm late to meet Claire when I see it reads only a few minutes past noon. I let out a relieved breath.

"You scared me," I say, playfully hitting his bare chest. "I thought I was running hella late."

I pout my lips at him. He chuckles and takes my face in his hands kissing my lips softly.

"I'm anxious about today." I admit.

He gives me an encouraging smile.

"I know it's going to be difficult but we'll get through it together, baby."

Once I've finished cooking and we've eaten, I begin to clean the kitchen. Going over the counters twice, doing anything I can to keep my mind busy to not think about how much this is going to hurt today. The last time Claire and I were there together was the day we buried Lyle. She was sobbing so hard it took both her parents to console her. I remember looking over at Jean and wishing she would comfort me that way but instead she was sitting there drunk and silent as they lowered her son into the ground. I came back later that night once they covered him up and began sobbing uncontrollably fisting the dirt my brother was buried under. Begging him to come back, wishing that this was all just a terrible nightmare that I would wake up from. I cried myself to sleep that night, laying next to his grave. When I woke up I had a blanket drifted over me and there was a bouquet of flowers laying over where his headstone would be.

Suddenly Micah's phone begins to ring pulling me from my memories.

"It's work," he says before answering it and walking out to the patio.

Looking around I see I have nothing else to clean, nothing else to keep my mind busy until the scattered mess Micah left in his office comes to mind. Grateful for the distraction, I go to the hall closet and grab the vacuum cleaner and the broom when it knocks into the box and photo album from the shelf, causing them to fall to the ground. The contents spill out from the box and I shove it all back in before placing it and the photo album back onto the shelf, pushing it further back this time. I tote the large vacuum up the stairs and clean Micah's office. I've just

finished when he walks in.

"Baby, I was going to clean this. You didn't have to."

"I know. It's just helping me not think about things."

I give him a sad smile before walking into the bedroom and getting dressed. Micah held my hand tightly in his as we drove to the cemetery. Once we pull up I see we're early, Claire isn't here yet. I step out of the car and take Micah's hand in mine as we walk through the gate. He looks over to me giving me a sad smile.

"This is where my mom is buried too," he says.

I wrap my arms around his waist pulling him close to me as I comfort him. We walked over to his mother's headstone then. I peer up at Micah who's looking grimly at where his mother is laid to rest.

"15 years later and not a day goes by that I don't miss her. Out of two parents the universe decided to take the only one that ever loved me."

Tears brim my eyes as he says this. It breaks my heart knowing he feels like Keith doesn't love him. I know what this feels like. It's unnatural and heartbreaking for a child to question whether or not their parent loves them. I hug him close to me as a tear falls from his face. "Baby, I'm so sorry," I say to him as I rub his back soothingly.

He hugs me tighter as he wipes his tears away.

"I love you so much," I say to him, knowing he needs to be reminded that he is loved.

He looks at me as he leans down planting a soft kiss to my lips as he says, "I love you."

We stand there holding each other in silence for a while before walking over to Lyle's grave. Letting go of Micah's hand, I walk over to my brother's headstone rubbing my fingers over his name etched in the marble.

Until I found you

"Lucas," Micah asks, confused by us having different last names.

"Different dads," I remind him.

Just then I hear a car door shutting and see Claire making her way up to us, she pulls me into a warm embrace. Her hugging me this way I begin to cry. Her and I are all that's left of Lyle. He only lives now in our memories.

"I know," she whispers knowingly as she lays her head on my shoulder and begins to sob into me. We're holding onto each other as I look over to Micah who has silent tears coming down his face. I know it breaks his heart to see my cry like this.

He wipes his face and says, "I'm going to give you two some privacy," before walking towards the car.

Being heartbroken over his mom and seeing me and Claire crying like this must have been too much for him. We pull away from our hug and take each other's hand as we stand in front of Lyle's headstone. We reminisce over the memories we shared with him, laughing as we recall all the good times we had with him.

"He was such an adrenaline junkie," I say thinking back to the way he'd do a backflip off a 20 foot cliff into the water or how alive he would feel when he'd race his car on the streets.

"The worst," she laughs, wiping tears from her eyes. "Remember the time he pulled the fire alarm in school for a prank?"

We both begin to laugh.

"He was crazy," I say shaking my head at the memory.

We stand there for a while before thunder strikes above us as it begins to sprinkle. I give her a final hug goodbye before I climb into the car with Micah. He looks so sad as I take his hand in mine. My heart breaks for him, I know what he's feeling right now, it's terrible. It's pouring down rain as we run up the stairs and into the house. I look over at Micah as he pulls his jacket off and notice that he's avoiding eye contact with me.

"Baby?" I ask him.

"I think you need to go. I'm not feeling well." he says in a flat tone looking at the wall behind me.

"What do you mean? What's wrong?"

"I just need you to go, Leyna," he says, his tone clipped as he refuses to look at me.

"What did I do to you," I ask hurt.

He looks over at me then anger in his eyes.

"You didn't do anything to me, I just need you to fucking go." He shouts at the end.

I take a step back like he's struck me. My heart aches in my chest at his cold demeanor towards me. Fighting tears, I grab my purse and keys before running out the door and into the rain.

Sixty-eight

I slam my car door shut and begin to cry into the steering wheel. Micah has never been so cold or heartless to me before. I get he's hurting, hell I'm hurting but that's no reason to push me away. How many times has he seen me broken? How many times has he helped me through my heartache? He's been there for me through every ugly thing. No matter how much I've pushed him away he's always there for me and whether he likes it or not I'm going to be there for him. Determined, I walk up the steps and back into the house. I hear a commotion coming from the hallway then.

"God Dammit!" I hear him yell before I run in and see him throwing the box from the closet at the wall, the contents spilling out on the floor as he repeatedly punches the wall in a rage.

I cover my mouth with my hands in horror seeing him like this.

"Micah," I plead through my tears.

He looks over at me then with wide eyes like he's seen a ghost. His chest is heaving like I've never seen before.

"Get out! Get the fuck out," he screams at me.

"Why are you doing this?"

I walk towards him when I step on a piece of paper with a picture on it, I glance down at it and my heart falls completely out of my chest.

"Baby no," Micah wails as I pick the old news clipping up.

My entire universe comes crashing down as I see a picture of Lyle wearing his football jersey with the headline "Local teenager dies in car crash." Micah walks over to me, panicked as he grabs my wrists in his hands.

"Baby, baby please listen to me, Ok? Let me explain."

But how can he explain this? He's had this news clipping this entire time, way before we ever met. Looking at the picture of Lyle in his Jersey, the number 33 on it, I look up at Micah then and grab his shirt lifting it to see the tattoo of a cross he has with the numbers 33 inked below it. My heart shatters into oblivion.

Micah's words from before play back in my mind, "These tattoos are to remind me of the people I've lost."

"I'm not proud of the things I've done before."

"What if my past still haunts me?"

My mouth falls open in horror as realization hits me.

"They said that he lost control of his car, that it was an accident but that's not what happened at all was it? You caused his crash."

I choke through my sobs.

UNTIL I
found you

Tears are streaming down his face as he says, "I tried saving him."

I gasp for air.

He holds my wrists tighter as he says, "It was a stupid race. He lost control and flipped. Leyna I tried everything to save him, you have to believe me."

He pleads.

"Believe you," I scream through my tears then.

Look where that's gotten me. I shove him back.

"I trusted you."

I sob.

"Baby, stop." he begs, tears pouring from his eyes.

"I trusted you. I trusted you." I say shoving him. "I trusted you," I scream, as I begin hitting his chest repeatedly before he wraps his arms around me and I begin thrashing in his grip.

"Let go of me," I scream, fighting his hold on me.

"Baby stop, please!"

He cries as he pulls me closer into him.

"I hate you! I hate you," I scream as I scratch him in the face.

He lets go of me to restrain my hands when I punch him in the mouth. He looks at me completely shattered as tears stream down his face. He hits the floor with his knees sobbing as I run out the door and down the stairs, speeding out of his driveway in my car. I'm sobbing uncontrollably as I drive through the rain. There are no words to describe the amount of earth shattering betrayal or the complete fucking heartbreak that I feel presently. It feels as though someone has brutally gashed me open and has ripped my heart from my chest.

    I begin screaming as though I'm being tortured. That's what this feels like after all. The only man that's ever fought his way into my heart, the only man that has ever wanted to love me through my pain and tragedies, the only man that I will ever love in my life is the same man that is killing me now. I feel as though I should die from the agony my heart is feeling as I begin to sob harder. My phone begins to ring glancing at it, I see it's Micah calling me.

    The picture on my screen of him kissing me with his eyes closed only adds to the heartbreak. I quickly look away from it but not before the car ahead of me stops abruptly. I swerve onto the other side of the road to keep from hitting it when I collide with the railing and jerk the wheel. I begin to hydroplane on the pavement when an oncoming car hits my side, flipping me over multiple times before my car finally lands on its top. I hear a car horn blaring as I begin to come to. I'm laying on my car's roof and there's glass everywhere. I cough and a stabbing pain slams into my lungs. I gasp from the pain, unable to breathe. I take in quick, shallow breaths finding myself unable to breathe regularly. I feel something wet and sticky coming from my mouth wiping it, I see it's blood. Looking down at my fingers I see that they're blue. I call out for help but the car horn blaring muffles my pleas. I manage to climb backwards out of my car as the rain pours onto my face making me gasp even more for air. I lay onto the pavement as I look out at the beautiful forest in front of me. Suddenly it stops raining and

UNTIL I
found you

the sun comes out. It's silent. The sound of the car horn blaring is gone. There's no sound, no movement. Just calmness. My pain vanishes.

I begin to close my eyes when a hand touches my face. It's warm and brings a feeling of peace and love with it. I open my eyes and see my brother in front of me.

"Hey, shortcake."

He says smiling down at me.

"Lyle," I ask, crying. "Is it really you?"

He lays next to me then.

"I've missed you so much," I say, taking his hand in mine.

It's just as warm and comforting as I remember.

"I've missed you too," he says smiling.

"I'm dying aren't I," I ask him.

"That's up to you."

"I'm ready," I say with resolve.

He chuckles, "No you're not. Not anywhere close."

"I want to be with you," I cry.

"And one day you will but it's not your time yet, kiddo."

"I don't think I can do this anymore. I'm not strong like you are," I say.

"You are all of me and more," he says squeezing my hand. "Leyna, you've always been the strong one, the one that fights through hell in search of your own heaven. Keep fighting. You were so close you know."

"What do you mean," I ask him.

Suddenly the brightness begins to dull and I can faintly hear the car horn blaring again. "What's happening," I ask, panicked.

"It'll all be ok, I promise," he says, giving me a comforting smile.

"Lyle please don't go."

I sob grabbing his hand tighter.

"Leyna before I go, you need to know something. It wasn't his fault, it was mine. Forgive him." "I don't want to," I say sobbing.

"Yes, you do. Forgive him and then help him forgive himself. You two are each other's solace. You're made for each other, that's why I brought you two together you know. Its fate, Leyna." He smiles.

"Even if I do diss his choice in cars," he adds teasingly. "Forgive him."

He begins to fade.

"Lyle!" I call out crawling to him then.

"I love you kid. Don't mess this up," he says before he disappears.

Suddenly the brightness fades and the warmth is gone. It's replaced by pain, both physical and emotional. I collapse to my side then, the ground is wet beneath me, warm from the crimson pool coming from me. I close my eyes just as I hear Micah screaming my name, terror reigning within it.

"Leyna!"

He reaches me, pulling me into his arms as he begins to cry "No, no, no. This isn't happening. This isn't happening," he says, panicked. "No! Baby, baby open your eyes. Look at me. Open your eyes Leyna!"

UNTIL I found you

He shouts as he takes my face in his hands shaking me.

"Please, please don't take her from me!"

He pleads to the universe before he nuzzles his face into my neck and sobs.

"I'm so sorry I failed you just please, please come back to me, baby."

I want nothing more than to come back to him, to go back to the way we were before this, before demons of the past came and dragged us both to hell. I hear the sound of sirens approaching as I fade into darkness.

Epilogue

Micah
5 years earlier

They're all blurring together. At this rate I don't even bother remembering their names. Jenny or Jessica, whatever the hell her name is, is saying something as I'm zipping my pants up. I tuned her out immediately once she started talking.

"How was that," she asks, wiping her swollen lips with her finger as she stands up from her knees before laying across her bed. Truthfully I've had a better mouth around my cock before but you can't win them all. I ignored her as I put my jacket on.

"Where are you going," she asks, clearly disappointed.

Like all the rest, she assumed we would cuddle in bed afterwards and talk about our dreams and aspirations. Maybe even go steady and live happily ever after and all that shit. And like all the other girls before her, she was wrong. I wasn't boyfriend material. I was strictly a good fuck. I never

UNTIL I found you

attached myself to a woman emotionally. It's not that I didn't want to, but none of them ever came close to making me feel something. They were merely just a distraction from the anger and void I felt within me.

"Micah, did you hear me," the girl asks.

"Yeah I heard you. I'm leaving, what does it look like?"

"Seriously Micah?"

She's pissed. From the amount of times I made this girl cum just now, she shouldn't be pissed at anything.

"Seriously," I say as I walk out the door.

"Fucking asshole," I hear her yell.

I smile to myself as I get into my car and light a cigarette. I turn the ignition and a sting spreads across my busted knuckles from the recent fight I got into. You really can't call it a fight, the guy never got a punch on me.

Just then Jo calls me, "Hey bro, my mom wants to know if you're coming over for Thanksgiving?"

"Don't I every year, dumbass," I ask sarcastically.

If it wasn't for Jo's family I would be spending every holiday alone the past few years. Keith hasn't spent a holiday with me since my mom died. The first few years after she died I would spend the holidays alone in that big house with an unfamiliar Nanny. I never kept the same one for more than a few months at a time. Eventually I would break the bitch mentally until she quit.

Being a young kid I thought if I kept it up my dad would have no choice but to come home and take care of me himself. Needless to say that never happened. I began fighting in school then discovering that it released the anger I had built up inside of me. In a fucked up way, it made me feel better to know someone else was in pain. It made me feel less alone.

When I was 15, I discovered through the last Nanny I had that burying myself in a woman would make me feel less alone too. That was the first time I felt alive since my mom died. Call it the thrill of fucking a 36-year-old woman for the first time or that I'm a fucked up person but soon only pussy and punches could distract me from the storm I had raging within me but nothing ever calmed me. Nothing ever filled the void. Jo chuckles, breaking me from my thoughts.

"Dude, you're such a dick," he says before hanging up.

Thinking of my fucked up childhood and my neglectful father, I grab the whiskey bottle from under the passenger seat and begin to drink from it. The warm liquid burning my mouth and throat as I guzzle it down. When pussy and punches don't do the trick, this shit sure does. I'm driving when my friend, Byron, calls me to inform me there's a street race happening nearby and that I need to get in on it.

I pull up soon after and look at the three assholes I'm racing against, sizing them up. This won't be much of a race, the only car worth a fuck is the Nissan 350 Z that's nismo tuned. Even then it has nothing on my Shelby GT 500. I smile cockily knowing I've already won this. Easy money. Byron pulls a coin out for lane choice.

"Lucas, call it," he says as he flips the coin.

Until I found you

"Heads."

Byron looks at the coin, "It's tails. Which side, Eason?"

Byron asks looking at me.

"I'll take the right lane," I say staring the other guy down.

"You got this Lyle."

Byron laughs as he pats the guys back. He knows I'm about to smoke his ass. We pull up to the line and rev our engines readying ourselves. Byron raises a white shirt in the air before dropping it, signaling the start of the race. I can hear the guy's turbo whining as he excellerates from the starting line when suddenly he breaks traction and smoke comes from his tires as he darts from left to right. I see him coming into my lane and jerk my wheel to avoid him hitting me. As I slam on my brakes, I watch in horror as the guy loses control of his car, he starts spinning in a 360 before smashing into the rail causing his car to flip several times before landing on its roof in the middle of the road.

Oh my God.

I hurriedly jump out of my car and run over to the guy, unbuckling him as I quickly drag him out of his car. Knowing the turbo oil line in his car will ignite it into flames any minute. I drag him into the grass as everyone else gets in their cars and speeds away. I look him over then and know he's in trouble, there's blood coming from his mouth and he's gasping for air. He knows it too.

"Lay. Lane," I hear him choke as he looks around him in a panic.

I pull out my phone and dial 911.

"Send an ambulance to Arthur's canal. There's been a bad wreck. Please hurry," I say before hanging up.

"I can't leave her. I can't leave her," the guy manages to say through his gasps. "Then don't leave her. Stay with her man. Helps on the way," I say as I watch tears fall from his eyes at the realization that he's leaving someone he loves behind.

"Lane," he manages to say as I watch the life leave out of his body then.

No, no!

I quickly plug his nose and blow air into him, "Come on man stay with me. Don't leave her! Don't leave her," I beg him as I perform CPR.

Minutes later I know it's too late, he's gone. I stare at his open eyes and see the panic and regret behind them. The sight causes bile to rise in my throat. I hear the sirens coming then, panicked, I run to my car and speed away before the cops can get there.

After pulling my car into the garage, I get out and begin slamming my fists into the hood repeatedly leaving dents in it. After throwing and breaking everything my hands came in touch with, I collapsed on the floor sobbing uncontrollably. I tried everything to save him but I failed her. Whoever she is, I failed her because he'll never come home to her again.

As the days go by, my guilty conscience leads me to find out everything I can about the guy. Lyle Lucas was only a year younger than me. He was set to graduate that spring and even had a football scholarship. He was voted most likely to succeed by his peers and always volunteered at community

UNTIL I
found you

events. Unlike me, he was a good person. I watched his funeral from afar, I saw how many people cared about him. I saw the amount of pain these people were in and for once someone else's pain didn't make me feel any better.

Even though he wasn't my brother or my friend, I found myself grieving him as well. With a whiskey bottle in my hand, I came back later that night after they buried him to place flowers on his grave and to tell him how completely sorry I was that I couldn't save him. As I'm walking up to his grave I see a red headed girl laid beside it sobbing into her arms. I freeze. This is her, this is the girl he was so scared to leave behind. Her entire body is shaking from how hard she's sobbing. I can tell she loved him a lot with how much she's hurting.

I contributed to her pain. I sit down behind the tree only a few feet away from her so she can't see me and listen as she cries for hours. The sound of her pitiful cries breaks what's left of my heart as I begin silently crying along with her. I fight every instinct within me to walk over to her and pull her into my arms, to comfort her the best way I can but I know better. If she knew who I was, if she knew what happened she wouldn't want me anywhere near her.

"This isn't real. This isn't real. It can't be," I hear her chanting to herself through her broken sobs.

I bite down on my lip and close my eyes as tears fall from my face. I wish more than anything that this wasn't real, that I could go back in time and change what happened but I can't. A while later her cries finally stop. I peek over the tree at her then and see she's laying next to his grave, not moving. Worried, I walk over to her and see she's cried herself to sleep next to him.

    I can't see her face from her hands covering it but I hear how steady her breathing is. My heart breaks all over again seeing her like this. I walk to the trunk of my car then and grab the blanket I keep in there, gently draping it over her as I sit next to her, watching her for a while as she sleeps. I look between her and the whiskey bottle in my hand and can't help but think if I had someone in my life like her, if I had someone that showed me that much love and that much devotion, I wouldn't be the fucked up person I am.

    I don't deserve a person like her, I don't deserve that kind of love. I'm a broken piece of shit and instead of trying to heal from my past I've allowed it to turn me into a selfish, cold asshole who drinks and fights and fucks his sorrows away. Resolve washes over me then and I make a silent promise to not only myself, but this stranger that I will change, that I will do better.

    For her, for me. I leave the flowers next to her and toss the whiskey bottle into the woods before getting in my car, determined that one day I will be the kind of man that deserves to be loved.

End of book one.

Until I found you

Acknowledgments

Warning! This may get a little lengthy, but hey it's my damn book and I'm going to thank every single person involved for making it happen! Without the love, encouragement and support of my family, dear friends and amazing team, this book would not have been made. With that being said, I'd like to shout out these amazing people now…

MY FAMILY. (My life)

To my loving parents, Glen and Christy Allen, thank you for always supporting me and encouraging me. Mama, I may not have come from your belly but you've never made me feel less than that. Thank you for loving me like you do. Thank you for loving a broken child that wasn't biologically yours and loving her enough to make her feel like she was healing. Daddy, thank you for teaching me to always find humor in everything. Thank you for all the late nights of us watching movies and laughing at each other. Thank you for all the times you'd bust up in my room and would jam out to whatever song you were obsessed with at the time. I definitely got my shenanigans from you. You two mean the world to me. I love you mama and daddy so much!

To my beautiful, strong, sassy, Aunt Boo who is a second mama to me, Laura Morgan, thank you for always supporting me, encouraging me and pushing me to be a better version of myself in life. Thank you for guiding my moral compass at times and for always holding me accountable. Thank you for your wisdom and relentless love. You've always been such a huge portion of my heart. I'm a miniature you after all. You've always been my best friend. You have no idea how much you mean to me woman. Thank you for loving me like a daughter. You truly are such an incredible blessing to me and my babies! We love you so much "Mawmaw Boo"!

To the most beautiful and pure soul I know, my grandmother, Nadean Allen. Where do I even begin with such an incredible woman like you? I would not be the person I am today without your limitless love and many fervent prayers. You have taught me that love and faith in God can get me through anything at all. I used to believe miracles only existed in forms of fiction or rare occurrences but you have shown me that every single day is a miracle. You truly are my earthly Guardian Angel. Thank you for being such an incredible blessing to our entire family! I love you so much Nanee!

To my amazing brother, Josh, even though we are nine years apart you've always been more like my twin than my younger brother. Thank you for being my "Lyle" when I needed it the most. No matter what you and I have faced in life you've always kept me going. I'm so proud of the man you have become. I love you so much!

To my other amazing siblings, Danielle, Lyssa and Bryson, you guys inspire me everyday. You bring so much light and happiness into my life. I wouldn't know what I would do without you. I love you so guys so incredibly much!

To the father of my beautiful children, Justin, thank you for your part in giving me such precious babies! We went on a journey together to be able to have them. A journey that will always be so dear to my heart. They love you so much daddy!

To my beautiful children, Shianne and Bentley, you are mama's entire universe. You two have completely mended and healed my heart since the moment I held you. You are the greatest joy I have ever felt. I have it all when I have you! Thank you for

UNTIL I
found you

bringing me an abundance of love and happiness. Thank you for saving my life. I love you, my babies more than words could ever explain. I'm so proud, honored and blessed to be your mama! You are a dream come true to me! You two are and will always continue to be my greatest accomplishment! I love you forever my babies!

MY FRIENDS. (My extended family really)

To my best friend/soul sister, Holly Senn, thank you from the bottom of my heart for always being there for me, for never allowing me to give up on myself and for always encouraging me to pursue my dreams. You are there through all the ugly and hurt that I go through. God knew I needed you. I couldn't ask for a better best friend. Also, thank you for reading 20 different versions of this fucker over and over again. Without you, I wouldn't have done this period. You and your precious family are such a blessing to me. I love you so much, beautiful!

To my best friend/kindred spirit Dot Dickens, thank you for always being such a beautiful soul! Thank you for laughing with me through my many shenanigans. Thank you for always encouraging me and letting me know that I'm not alone. I feel your genuine love and kindness and it's such a beautiful thing to experience. I'm in awe of you, Dottie! You and your precious family are a blessing to me. I still can not believe a dork like me gets to hangout with such a cool babe like you! You are truly a gift. I love you so much, beautiful!

To my amazing friend/kindred spirit, Vanessa R (A.K.A Wattpad author V.Rose), thank you for your loving support and encouragement! Thank you for gifting me with your friendship. That is the most precious gift out of all that you've given me. Thank you for always cheering me on. You are such a blessing to me and everyone that is fortunate enough to have you in their lives. You truly are such an incredible woman! Thank you for being such a precious, selfless soul. I look up to you so much and I can't wait for the world to fall in love with your story as I have! I will "ALWAYS" love you, beautiful boss babe!

To my amazing, beautiful friend, Tiffany Yawn, thank you for always supporting me and encouraging me. You are the real deal. Thank you for always hyping me up and for being the best, most honest critic. You are such an incredible person! So loving and beautiful and strong and fearless. Like you are the whole damn package, I can't even! You are such a blessing to me. I love you beautiful!

To my beautiful best friend, Leah McGinnis, thank you for always being my cheerleader and for telling me I've got this when I didn't think I did. Thank you for putting up with my hyper shenanigans and for not hanging up on me when I FaceTimed you. I always start the conversation with either showing you my most hideous face or doing a random celebrity impersonation. Thank you for always being there. You're such a blessing in my and my babies lives. We love you so much!

To my beautiful, amazingly creative friend, H.L. Swan. Not only do I consider you my mentor, but I am blessed enough to call you my friend. Thank you for your friendship, for your guidance and being such a kind, loving soul. I'll always be your fan girl! So proud of you for following your dreams of being an author! (You guys seriously have to check her out!) Love ya girl!

MY TEAM. (The best)

Book cover- To Jessica Scott at Uniquely Tailored, thank you for making my vision become a beautiful reality! You captured what I had in my head and brought it to life. You're simply an amazing girl!

Until I found you

MY READERS. (A portion of my heart)

I love you guys! Thank you so incredibly much for reading my debut novel and for allowing me to make my dreams become a reality! You guys are amazing! Thank you for letting this novel and myself become a part of your lives. I do not take any of you beautiful souls for granted. I hope this book has touched each of you in some way whether you found it emotionally gripping or emotionally relatable. And if it's the latter, just know that no matter what you may be going through currently or what you have experienced in the past, you are not alone. Somebody, somewhere out there has, is or will feel what you're feeling. We are all beautifully broken souls and it's ok to be broken for a little while as long as each of us mend back together again in the end. I hope that this book and its characters stay with you. I love each of you so much and can not wait to hear from you guys! Find me on all the socials. Can't wait to hear from you!

With all of my love, Kuristien Elizabeth

Printed in Great Britain
by Amazon